LAST OF THE TWENTY

The Setting of the Board

Michael Yeaton

©2014 Michael Yeaton
All rights reserved.

ISBN: 0692332359
ISBN 13: 9780692332351
Library of Congress Control Number: 2014920610
Mike Yeaton Publishing, Conway, NH

For Tasha.

Special thanks to Natalie Chambers Richoux for your editing and advice, J.K. Woodward for your terrific artwork, and all my friends and family for your encouragement.

1780:

The plan was simple enough. Get his pursuer up past the tree line; then ambush him.

When he looked back at the events of the last couple months, he still had a hard time imagining this is how it would turn out. The forced alliance he found himself in was strange enough, but the fact that this person, if you could call him that, was stronger than himself was what really scared him. For the first time in his life, he was faced with someone he couldn't physically defeat, but he was faster; and he hoped smarter. So he ran. The small trail he was following up the mountainside was narrow. Branches slapped at his face and arms and tore his shirt. The nighttime dew soaked through his clothes as he pushed through the thickets; he didn't notice. Up ahead, he knew help was waiting and it was his job to lure his pursuer into the trap.

He paused for a moment to get his bearings; he couldn't be that far from the tree line. How far has he been running? Five miles, ten? It didn't matter, as long as the man chasing him was still far enough behind to be safe but close enough not to lose him in the thick forest. He stopped for a moment and hid behind a large tree on the side of the trail. Listening closely for the sounds of approaching footsteps, or even the minute snapping of twigs and crunching leaves, he thought about how this all began. He reflected on the people waiting for him just beyond the tree line and the misunderstandings that started the foolish rivalry with them. Mistakes on both sides had drawn the attention of the monster they now had to destroy.

Slowly he risked moving closer to the path, the rough bark of the tree caught a frayed piece of his shirt and started to tear a strip off. Wincing at the sound he stopped and carefully pulled the fabric off the tree. He got lucky. The only sounds in the forest were leaves rustling in the breeze and an occasional hoot from an owl or some other animal making their nighttime rounds. Then he heard soft footsteps running through trees and brittle pine spills and getting closer. Knowing he should run before the man got too close for him to get away he risked another peek around the tree. A shadowy figure appeared around a bend in the path and slowed down to a jog just below his hiding spot next to the trail, then stopped. The figure bent down and looked carefully at the ground, then slowly looked up and held still, listening for any sounds. Knowing he was risking being caught by letting the figure get this close he watched and wondered how the man could see so well in the dark, or even how the man knew what to look for while tracking him.

He knew who the shadowy figure was and where he came from, a man from the towns far south of here who shouldn't know a thing about the country or forests. The man had fled Connecticut when the British burned his town, probably hoping to avoid the war. When the man arrived, he was new to this part of the country and to the way of life required to live here. The man had to hire help to so much as plant a seed in the ground, and he had certainly never been seen stepping into the woods. Yet here he was, tracking someone who had spent years living in the woods hunting and the fields farming, honing his own skills to avoid detection, blending into what was the way of life for most people who lived in the forests and farmlands of New England.

Watching the shadowy figure look around he snapped out of his daze and remembered he was too close for comfort. He could hear the man breathing deeply and could almost make out his features in the dark, not good. To run with his pursuer so close would almost certainly lead to getting caught before he could get to the tree line. The man stood up and started slowly walking towards his hiding spot as if he knew exactly where he was watching from behind the tree, and for a moment it looked as if the chase was over. Twenty feet, fifteen, the man moved with such purpose that he felt for sure he was spotted. He gripped the tree harder and felt his fingernails dig into the bark as he silently cursed himself for his mistake. Then a stroke of luck!

For a few agonizing moments the only sound was the wind blowing gently through the trees and the slow approaching footsteps of the figure; then suddenly an animal took off running just beside the trail above them. The man quickly looked to the sound and at that moment he took his chance to get away. It was only half a second before the man's head swung back to see him running away but it was half a second enough.

Running as fast as he ever had, ducking branches and jumping rocks and roots, hoping against hope he was putting enough distance between himself and his pursuer to get him into the open, into the trap.

Suddenly there it was, the trees around him were starting to thin and he could see it, the break in the tree line! A feeling of relief washed over him as he realized he was going to make it. The sounds of his pursuer were still behind him and getting closer, but not close enough to catch him. All he needed was just a few more seconds and he would be...

All thoughts were cut off instantly when a white hot pain erupted in his leg sending him crashing to the ground. The world around him became nothing but a blurred and spinning mess of dirt and rocks until he came to a sudden stop, crashing into one of the last large trees just a few yards before the sky opened up to stars. Wincing with pain he looked down to see an arrow sticking through his leg, the shaft was some sort of metal and warm to the touch when he grabbed it. Giving the shaft a painful tug he tried to pull it out of his leg but the arrow-head held it in place. It had shot right into the bone and lodged in place. Cursing he tried to force himself onto his good leg when the sudden impact of another arrow slammed through his shoulder, pinning him painfully to the tree.

A second later the man was standing over him as calmly as a man who was out for a Sunday afternoon stroll. With only the light from the moon and stars as help he couldn't make out the man's features clearly, only the shape of him as he leaned in and the slight gleam off his teeth as he smiled at him pinned helplessly to the tree. Then the man's hand clamped around his neck, cold and impossibly strong. The man lifted him off the ground, the arrow in his shoulder sending more pain through his body as it held firm in the tree and he was pulled along its shaft.

"What... are...?"

His words were cut off by a searing pain in his chest. Using all the strength he had left he managed to look down enough to see the gleam off a long blade as it sunk into his chest and through his heart. The world around him started to fade and all he knew at that moment was darkness and pain. The last thing he saw before the world faded away forever was the blade being pulled out so fast it seemed to vanish from his chest and disappear in the dark; then two bright yellow spots of light appearing in the center of the man's eyes just before the quick flash of metal as his blade swung down for the final time.

Then silence.

ONE

Present Day: Freedom, New Hampshire

It's funny what people will notice about someone else; that first thing they see that forces a second glance, then a third. For some people it's the eyes, maybe the way they move or the sound of their voice, or maybe something a bit more carnal. For Alex Woodard it had always been the color of her hair. Bright red, almost on fire. He watched her from his table at the small diner as she seemed to bounce from place to place, taking breakfast orders, refilling coffees, and charming everyone she served with her never ending supply of smiles and small talk. She was slim and athletic, and very pretty with bright green eyes that Alex swore shone with their own light.

Most of the guys that walked in for breakfast tried endlessly to get a date with her or even just her number, always without success. Her name was Nadia Roberts and she was one of the first people Alex had met when he moved to the small town of Freedom, New Hampshire several years back. From that first day on they had been best friends, spending every summer together chasing frogs or fishing off the shores of the small lake they both lived on. As far as Alex was concerned though, she was the first person besides his brother Mark that he had ever truly met.

When Alex was five he lost his parents to a horrible car accident. They had been driving home after his first kindergarten open house when his father lost control of the family car. The police never found a reason for the accident, the road was straight and dry, the weather clear. The car unexpectedly went out of control and swerved off the road and into an empty parking lot rolling over twice before coming to a rest. Both his parents died instantly with broken necks, Alex himself was nearly killed. He spent almost an entire month in a coma before waking up, a medical miracle. The ordeal left his brain injured and it wasn't until he was almost six before he was able to start remembering anything, all the years prior being no more than a blank space in his mind. The doctors counted it as yet another miracle when he was able to regain movement in his limbs and after months of physical therapy he was sent to live with his older brother Mark in the small state of New Hampshire.

Although those first few years were still a bit fuzzy to Alex he could still remember the first time he saw her skipping along the shore of their little lake. At a distance she looked like nothing more than a little red-headed pixie, hopping alongside the water and stopping every few feet to suddenly pounce on the ground like a two legged cat. After moving in with his brother it was a few weeks before Mark let Alex outside by himself, so he spent his time on the porch watching her play by the lake and wondering what she was always trying to pounce on.

A few times he would wave at her when she was close enough to see him and she would always wave back but would never venture close enough for Alex to talk to her. Finally Alex was allowed outside to play alongside the lake by himself. He spent the morning walking the shoreline slowly, ducking quickly behind a bush or tree whenever she would turn in his direction. He wasn't quick enough once and she spotted him from the corner of her eye. A smile spread across her face and she came running up to him excitedly with something cupped in her hands. When he looked up at her nervously she simply smiled down at him like she had known him her entire life and was simply playing a game of hide and seek.

"Look what I gots from the water!" she laughed

Sticking her dirty hands out in front of Alex's face with a sly grin and a giggle she opened them up to reveal a small frog sitting in the middle of her palm. It sat just long enough for Alex to get a look before jumping out of her hands and into the water. Alex would always remember the way she laughed when it hopped away and the way she looked at him from between the muddied red curls of her hair.

"Well, help me catch him again dummy!" she yelled laughing

Still acting a little shy Alex stood up from his hiding place and watched as she giggled and jumped back down at the frog splashing him with mud and water. No little boy wants a girl to show him up, so Alex jumped into the mud after her. They spent the rest of that afternoon catching frogs and running away from the occasional snake while laughing and getting dirty. Neither had to say much to the other and found they made quite the frog hunting team. Before the day was done then had made a cage out of sticks shoved into the sand and had it filled with the tiny creatures. When the sun started sinking below the horizon and turning the sky a red as bright as her hair a woman's voice called Nadia's name from across the little cove.

"I gotta go home, what's your name?" she asked with a childish huff of frustration.

"Alex." he replied.

"I'm Nadia," she looked at him and giggled, then looking him up and down she put both fists on her mud soaked hips and gave him a scolding look, "You're all dirty so no hugs!" Before Alex could say anything she leaned in and gave him a quick kiss on the cheek, laughing at him when his face turned red. "See ya tomorrow!" she said with a laugh.

Without another word she turned and bounded away still giggling, leaving Alex to pull the sticks out of the mud and let the frogs out. They spent the rest of that summer together playing on the shore and catching frogs, sharing secrets and swimming in the lake. Looking back it was the first time Alex could remember being happy.

"Alex... earth to Alex," startled, he looked up from his plate to see Nadia smiling down at him. "Thought I lost ya. Not hungry today?" She asked. He looked down at his nearly untouched plate of food. The egg yolks had hardened up and the plate had cooled off, even his coffee was cold.

"Nah, food was terrible." He said with a grin.

She looked down at the plate and made a pouty face, "and I had that made up special for you too!" She bent down and leaned on the table in front of him and gave him the same scold that he got every time she pretended to be serious. "And you'd better give me a damn good tip for that little remark..." She could only keep a straight face for a few seconds before laughing and standing up, "What you up to today besides wasting the restaurant's food?"

"Not sure yet, thinking about heading down to the pit and getting some shots in with Mark before too many people figure out winters over and crowd the place, you want to come?"

"You know I would if I could." She said while she wrote out Alex's bill. "Ethan's taking me hiking up to the cabin where we met, it's our one year today."

"Oh how wonderful..." he said sourly.

Ethan Thompson, her jerk of a boyfriend had been nothing but a pain for Alex from day one. Nadia often hiked up the many mountains scattered around to clear her head and take pictures of the scenery, usually avoiding the really crowded trails. But that day she wanted to get some pictures of the old cabin on the ever popular Liberty Trail on Mt. Chocorua before the tourists and day hikers overran it for the summer. It was a tiny cabin on the edge of the tree line held down with huge chains to keep from blowing off. During the summer months it was usually crowded with both locals and tourists and hard to get a decent picture of without someone getting in the way of the shot. Winter the year before had lingered on and left deep drifts of late season snow on the trails keeping a lot of the tourists away to look for easier places to explore. With hope that the cabin would be empty due to the lingering cold and pockets of snow, Nadia had borrowed her mother's camera and trudged her way up to the cabin through the snow and spring mud. When she finally made it to the cabin she found that she wasn't the only one taking advantage of the blissful quiet and hiker free scenery; there was smoke coming out of the little chimney. She took several pictures before the cold wind started to make her shiver. The sight of the smoke coming from the chimney was too tempting and she decided a little time in front of the cabin's wood stove would serve her well. When she stepped inside she found Ethan stoking a small fire in the old woodstove. They sat talking for the rest of the morning and into the afternoon while she sipped hot chocolate and as they say: the rest is history.

Ethan was new to town at the time so Nadia took it upon herself to show him around and the more time they spent together the more she started to like him. Less than a week later they were dating. Alex had the disadvantage of being both Nadia's best friend and a guy so Ethan took an immediate dislike to him and did everything he could to keep him away from Nadia. The few times Alex did manage to come around, Ethan took it upon himself to make Alex's life as difficult as possible.

Just to make life even better for Alex, Ethan never seemed to be without his friends Wes and Dillon Roberts. The two brothers were more than happy to knock the wind out of Alex with a quick punch to the gut or slam his head into the lockers as they walked by just to stay on Ethan's good side. The year before, the twins were held mostly in check by their older brother Daniel, who was the one person they listened to above Ethan. Unfortunately for Alex, Daniel graduated and soon after got a job with New Hampshire Fish and Game where he was transferred three hours north to Pittsburg, leaving Alex to fend for himself.

"Are his two lapdogs going to be joining you on your little hike?" he asked bitterly.

She gave Alex another scowl, this time without a hint of humor in her eyes, "Be nice" she said flatly. "Really, I wish you all would learn to just ignore each other. I know he doesn't like you but I'm getting tired of being put in the middle with you two acting like dogs trying to rip each other's heads off."

Alex bit his tongue. He knew Nadia would break things off with Ethan if she ever found out how much he actually went through, but a combination of pride and guilt about his own feelings kept Alex from saying anything to her.

"Speaking of dogs..." Alex said glancing out the window. He cut himself off when the door opened and Ethan walked in.

Blonde haired and dark eyed, Ethan stood just a hair under six foot six and had the build of someone who spent way too much time in the weight room. He looked from Alex sitting at the table, to Nadia standing over him, and back to Alex. Their eyes met for just a second and Alex could imagine what Ethan would have wanted to do to him right there in the middle of the restaurant. Nadia turned and smiled at Ethan, then ran over and tried to reach up to give him a kiss on the cheek. Ethan jerked his head back before she was able to and gave her a half smile.

"You know I don't like that," he said, Nadia looked crestfallen for a moment then looked up at him sheepishly and smiled.

"Had to try," she said with a wink.

She walked back to Alex's table and tossed the bill down beside his plate, then turned to Ethan and mouthed the word "behave" before heading to the back end of the restaurant. "Be right back, going to go clean up and clock out" she called to Ethan over her shoulder.

Watching Nadia walk off Ethan sat down next to Alex; his dark eyes burning holes in Alex's. He picked a cold piece of bacon off of Alex's plate and shoved it in his mouth. "I don't know what the hell you think you're doing here," he said spitting small pieces of bacon onto the table, "I told you I don't want to see you sniffing around here. The only reason I'm being so nice is because of how much she likes you, otherwise I think I'd have to make sure you wouldn't be *able* to sniff around."

Alex looked back at Ethan, he felt blood rushing to his face but forced himself not to show how angry he was getting. "It's a free country," he said, "I've been coming here long before you moved here, and I've been friends with her a lot longer than that."

Ethan smiled and shook his head with a sigh, then picked up Alex's cup and spit the bacon into the coffee. "You should really eat more," he said, "girls like guys with a little more to them than twig boys like you. Probably why you've been nothing but girlfriends with them your whole life." Ethan's eyes seemed to get even darker as he leaned in close to make sure only Alex could hear him. "Go and find someone else to be girlfriends with for a while and leave Nadia alone till I'm done with her." Smiling darkly he leaned over and whispered in Alex's ear, "Don't worry though, once I get what I want from her I'll be gone, and you can have the scraps." And with that Ethan patted Alex on the cheek, giving him a little slap as he leaned back into his own chair.

Alex's face burned hotter than ever, his hands balled up into fists and started shaking under the table. Ethan leaned against the table and smiled, "what?" he asked quietly, "something you want to say?"

"What are you doing?" Nadia asked as she walked back up to the table.

Ethan looked smiling, "eh, just talking. I figure its senior year so we should at least *try* to get along with him before we all move on." He got up and patted Alex's shoulder, "right buddy?"

Too angry to say anything, Alex sat there looking down at his plate. If Nadia hadn't been there he may have been tempted to throw his ruined coffee right in Ethan's face, even knowing if he did that he'd pay for it later, but still Alex couldn't help thinking it'd be worth it.

"Ready babe?" Ethan asked.

Nadia nodded, "Just have to stop at home and grab my jacket." As she reached out to take Ethan's hand he quickly pulled it away and shoved it into the pocket of his windbreaker pretending he didn't see her reach for it. Nadia looked crestfallen; the hurt in her eyes obvious to Alex, but either Ethan didn't see it or just plain ignored it. With a small sigh Nadia looked down to Alex with a weak smile.

"See you later sweetie" she said giving his shoulder a squeeze.

As they started out the door Ethan swung his arm over the table and knocked Alex's coffee over onto his lap. Alex jumped back and nearly fell out of his chair, "what the hell!?" he yelled. The cold coffee and pieces of the chewed up bacon that landed in his crotch ran in streams down his legs, yet another reminder of why Alex hated Ethan.

Nadia shot Ethan an angry look and hit him in the shoulder. For a second Alex hoped that she would tell him off and cancel their date out of anger but Alex had no such luck.

"I told you to behave!" she looked down at Alex. "I'll help clean you up." she offered.

Shaking with anger Alex shook his head trying not to look her in the eye. "Don't worry about it," he said. She opened her mouth to say something but Alex waved her off with one hand while he used a napkin to mop up the coffee on his lap. At least it had been cold instead of steaming. "Go on, I'll see you later, it was an accident anyways," he mumbled.

Nadia glanced at Ethan standing next to the door trying not to laugh, she shook her head and sighed. "I seriously doubt that," she said.

After a moment she turned and walked towards the door, before walking out she looked back at Alex a final time and mouthed the word "sorry" before pushing Ethan towards the door. Ethan grinned at Alex as Nadia shot him another angry look and walked past. While she walked by Ethan held his hand in the air over her backside and pretended to squeeze it, grinning at Alex. Once she was out the door he gave Alex the finger and walked out laughing to himself.

Why do girls always go for the jerks? Alex thought ignoring the looks on the faces of the other customers. Face still bright red and hands shaking, he threw some money down on the table and walked out the door without so much as a glance for anybody else.

TWO

Sarah and Jason Stowe were both avid hikers and campers who led what they considered a boring office life selling insurance out of Boston, Mass. To break up the monotony of city life and endless phone time they spent as much time hiking and camping in the White Mountains of New Hampshire as possible. They had both grown up at or near what is known as the lakes region and loved going back together. Sarah thought of herself as an amateur wildlife photographer whenever they were in the woods and loved to show off her work on their small apartment walls and at the office. Jason didn't have much interest in animals or pictures, but he loved to spend time away from the city and head back to his old stomping grounds, and the fact that he could spend that time with Sarah made it even sweeter.

After close to seven years together and four years of marriage, he still got the same jitters when he looked at her as he did the day they met. Try as he might, Jason did his best when they were out to help her spot wildlife and took it on the chin whenever she got mad at him for being too loud and scaring off some deer or fox that she had spotted. She had already punched him in the arm twice today for stepping too heavily in the remaining snow and scaring off a pair of snowshoe hares she was trying to sneak up on.

He was about a hundred feet in front of her when he came over a small ridge in the trail and spotted a monstrous moose at the edge of a small pond in a clearing just off the trail. Quickly ducking down and trying to keep from making too much noise he gestured excitedly at Sarah. She was too caught up in trying to get a shot of a small yellow bird perched on a pine tree to notice.

"Psst! Psst!" He whispered, trying to get her attention before the moose took off.

She didn't hear him; she was crawling on her knees through a light snow drift trying to creep closer to the bird. Jason could see his whispers were having no luck, so he picked up a small rock and threw it underhand towards her without success. Still too busy with her bird to notice his attempts, he crawled as slowly as he could manage in his excitement trying to get closer to her. Every crack of a twig or crunch of snow made him cringe and freeze in place. *I must look like an idiot*, he thought to himself, glad Sarah was too busy taking pictures to realize how much of a fool her husband was being as he half walked half crawled through the mud and snow. After a painfully long minute or two he was close enough to toss a rock and gain her attention without spooking the moose, at least he hoped.

Picking up another rock he gave it a toss, this time sending it bouncing off the tree her bird was perched on. With a frightened squeak it took off over her head earning him a sharp look. She began to scold him when he cut her off with a finger over his mouth, franticly gesturing for her to follow him. Looking confused and slightly annoyed she started to stand up to follow but he held his hands out and motioned for her to stay down and come quietly. With a shrug she slung the camera over her backpack and followed him on all fours, all the while mouthing questions. Ignoring her, Jason crept back to the ridge and peeked over; the moose was still quietly grazing in knee deep water. *Good*, he thought, *this should make up for all the other animals I've scared off today.*

"What is it?" she whispered harshly when she had crawled up beside him.

He grinned at her and pointed over the ridge, "Told you I'd make it up to you." He gloated, doing his best to keep his voice down. Her look of annoyance faded quickly when she poked her head over the ridge. Jason couldn't help but grin when he saw her eyes widen and mouth drop open.

"Oh wow, he even still has his antlers! I've never seen them keep them this long!" she leaned over and gave him a quick kiss on the cheek, "yea, I guess you did good honey."

He crawled backwards to get out of her way and pulled himself up to a sitting position where he could watch her work, all the while smiling to himself while she fumbled with her camera bag to put a longer lens on her camera. *She's cute when she's excited,* he thought to himself. She looked back over her shoulder and gave a quiet giggle before crawling on her stomach to get a better shot. He felt butterflies at that giggle; knowing how happy this made her and loving every minute of watching her do it, even if he did screw up every now and then.

The moose continued its lazy grazing while she quietly snapped pictures. They had hiked these trails several times over the last year or two but this was the first moose either of them had seen. Jason could almost feel her excitement building as she took more pictures and crawled closer to the animal, not even noticing the patches of cold mud and snow soaking her clothes while she shimmied along the ground.

Doing his best to stay low and quiet he up crawled beside her, carefully avoiding the worst of the mud puddles and trying to keep at least some of his belly off the wet ground. *She's more of a man in the woods than I am,* he thought bitterly but couldn't help snickering at himself. She turned and shot him a look when he got a little too loud for her liking. He mouthed a silent apology and slowly pulled himself off to the side and sat up against a tree to watch. No need to scare the moose off and mess this up for her, she looked like she was having the time of her life.

Still watching the moose Jason settled himself on the driest patch of ground he could find next to his tree. He knew she was going to be here as long as the moose was so he thought he may as well get comfortable. *That thing is huge; I'd think it was a horse if it didn't have those horns sticking out of its head.* He thought as he reached back to break off a small branch that was digging into his back. It took no notice of the couple that sat watching it just up the hill, content with its eating and the fact that it was the biggest thing in these woods.

He had just pulled his water bottle out of his pack when he heard the sounds of something big running through the woods somewhere off to his right. He turned to find the source of the sound but the trees and brush were too thick to get a clear view. Shrugging he turned back to the moose and saw a flash of brown move between the trees just behind the animal. Suddenly the moose didn't seem so calm; it swung its head back and forth and made huffing and snorting noises at the woods. Jason put his bottle down and watched as the moose took a few nervous steps towards the bank, its snorting noises getting louder and more frantic.

Sarah didn't notice the change in the animal's behavior, instead fumbling with the back of the camera and not looking at the scene in front of her. She did turn her head enough to notice Jason looking at her out of the corner of her eye; she flashed him a quick smile. Still looking at Sarah Jason heard the sounds of snapping twigs and the crunch of snow behind him, then he saw Sarah's eyes go wide. The look of fear that spread over her face made his heart leap into his throat. She motioned franticly for him to be quiet and get down and he could see all the color draining from her face. His heart started beating faster; he had never seen her react like this before. As slowly as he could manage he sunk to his belly and pushed himself under the lowest branches of the tree. The sounds behind him grew, moving slowly through light snow and letting out a deep rumbling that made Jason's bowls threaten to let go. Forcing himself to turn his head to the noise he had to choke down a scream at the sight of the creature that came into view.

A huge grey wolf, bigger than any dog he had ever seen, was standing at the edge of the trees, its eyes locked on the moose and baring a set of huge white teeth. The deep growls coming from its throat made Jason feel like his bones were vibrating; the look of predatory hunger on its face would give Jason nightmares. It slowly walked out of the trees and edged closer to the moose, its head lowered but its eyes remained locked on its target, its body ready to pounce at any second. Jason could feel his heart threatening to beat out of his chest, he had never seen anything that put more fear into him than the monster slowly stalking past. The beast looked like it could swallow his head whole, or at the very least rip it off without any effort on its part. The moose instantly spun and lowered its head to face the wolf, snorting and stomping its feet and all the while slowly moving backwards towards the other tree line.

Jason could hear the blood pounding in his ears as he watched the two animals face off. He turned to see Sarah with a look of total shock and disbelief. She still had the camera pointing at the animals but wasn't taking any pictures. Like Jason she was focusing too much on the slow standoff between the two animals to bother with anything else. The wolf's growls got deeper and more ferocious as it closed in on the moose and Jason kept waiting for the moose to turn and run but either fear or the need to stand its ground kept the animal from fleeing.

The tension of the standoff was instantly broken when a burst of dark brown fur and white teeth erupted from the trees behind the moose. Another wolf as big as the first launched itself into the air and bit into one of the moose's back legs. Jason felt his stomach lurch when he heard the animal's leg snap and saw a chunk of bone poke through the fur. In a panicked frenzy the moose let out a cry of pain and swung its head on the new attacker, desperately trying to knock the wolf to the ground and off its broken leg. The first wolf lunged forward the moment the moose's head turned and sank its teeth deep into the back of the moose's huge neck. The grey wolf pulled the larger animal down almost effortlessly and began to shake its head back and forth while still clinging to its prey. Jason's stomach took another turn as the moose's neck started to tear off its shoulders, with one final agonized cry its head and neck was torn off the body and thrown off to the side. The huge animal's remaining legs buckled and it dropped into the shallow water at the edge of the pond while its two killers let out howls that made Jason's teeth rattle.

Jason put his hand over his mouth in a desperate attempt to keep his lunch from coming back up. He had never seen so much blood in all his life, the edge of the water had turned a dark crimson almost instantly as the moose's huge heart pumped for the last time, then the forest turned eerily silent. That's when things got really strange.

Watching the two wolves Jason swore he saw them look at each other and nod. Wolves don't nod do they? *Click.* There was a sudden sinking feeling in his chest when he heard Sarah's camera go off. He looked at her in horror as she held the camera up and continued snapping pictures. The second the sound of the camera went off both of the wolves heads snapped around and looked up the hill. A mixture of con-fusion and terror filled Jason when the grey wolf actually looked at the dark brown wolf and motioned its head in Sarah's direction. To Jason's horror the other wolf nodded its head and started walking in her direc-tion, head down and teeth barred. Fear and disbelief held Jason to the ground for the first few seconds until blind instinct finally swept over him and he jumped to his feet. In a few quick strides he was standing over Sarah and pulling at the back of her jacket.

"Get up and run!" he screamed while he dragged her off the ground with every bit of strength he could manage.

There was another moment of panic as she resisted; he knew she was feeling the same fear and disbelief that had momentarily paralyzed him, but in her daze she kept trying to take more pictures of the scene. Jason gave her another pull, ready to reach down and slap her if he needed to when she suddenly snapped out of her daze and jumped to her feet. With her camera clutched tightly in hand they both turned and ran down the path. Still looking somewhat dazed she tried to pick up her pack on the run but Jason held firmly onto her jacket and pulled her along.

"Leave it!" he screamed, all he wanted to do was get out of there before they turned out like the moose.

The brown wolf broke into a run and Jason knew there was no way they could outrun it. His only hope was that they could put enough distance between themselves and the two wolves that they would stop chasing the smaller prey and go back to their original meal. Rounding a corner on the trail the grey wolf suddenly appeared on Jason's left and took a snap at him, the end if its cold wet nose brushed the side of his arm and he let out a yell. Suddenly the path broke to the right cutting the wolf off with thick brush, Jason heard it snap at them in frustration as it crashed into the bushes.

Neither bothered to look back as they ran as fast as they could down the mountain, both barely keeping their footing on the mud and leaves covering the path. The brown wolf crashed out of the trees behind them and slid in the mud, angrily snapping its jaws and barking until it slid into a large tree and let out a loud yip as it fell on its side. It was back on its feet almost instantly as the couple rounded another bend in the trail, snarling it leaped over the path and into the woods, cutting them off when the path turned sharply to the right. Sarah screamed as the brown wolf lunged out of the trees and snapped at the hand holding the camera, missing it by inches.

Suddenly Jason's feet gave way as he slipped on a patch of snow, instinctively grabbing hold of Sarah's jacket and forcing them both to the ground. They fell into an icy patch of mud and rolled off the path out of control down a steep ridge. Jason didn't have time to realize Sarah had landed on top of him when he felt a bright flash of pain as his head smashed into a rock at the bottom. He felt the side of his head turn warm as blood poured out from a gash the rock had opened in his scalp and when he opened his eyes all he could see were white spots floating in front of him. The pressure on his back eased momentarily as Sarah tried to stand up but he was suddenly forced down again when she screamed and fell down grabbing her ankle, her face twisted in pain.

Deep rumbling growls came from either side of them as Jason looked up in horror to see the grey wolf approaching on their right and the brown wolf on their left, cutting off any hope they may have had of escape. Their teeth looked like daggers and sent cold shivers up his spine. They came slowly; barking and snapping at the air between deep growls that made Jason's whole body vibrate. Sarah had slid off his back and was crying and shaking in fear beside him, her face covered in mud and tears. The mixed expression of terror and pain on her face would haunt Jason's dreams for a long time; that is if they survived this. Suddenly her eyes widened as the animals moved in for the kill. Jason tried with everything he had to put himself between her and the wolves but his strength finally left him as the world around him started to darken. Then the grey wolf was in front of his face growling, its teeth less than an inch from his nose. He felt its warm breath on his face just as the world went dark. The last thing he heard before he passed out was Sarah's terrified scream.

THREE

When Alex got back home, he went straight to his room and slammed the door. Stripping off his coffee stained clothes he threw them in a pile at the foot of his bed, then trying to get hold of himself he stood for a moment looking at his reflection in the mirror. His face was still red and his hands were visibly shaking with rage. Alex closed his eyes and took a few deep breaths attempting to relax but all he could hear over the pumping of his own heart was Ethan's voice taunting him. All he could see in his mind's eye was Ethan's hand in the air pretending to grope Nadia. Rage boiled up stronger than ever, no matter how hard Alex tried he couldn't get his mind off Ethan and his own humiliation. The anger felt like electricity running through his body, threatening to explode if he didn't so something to release it. Alex screamed at himself in the mirror, then without thinking he kicked the corner of his bed as hard as he could. Sharp pain instantly ran up his leg and he fell onto the floor grabbing at his foot. When he looked down there was an ugly red mark covering three of his toes that were already starting to swell and bruise. "Great" he scoffed. Getting up tenderly he limped to his dresser and threw on new clothes.

His foot was already throbbing, sending more pain up his leg with every step while he limped into the small living room where he and Mark kept their rifle cabinet. Alex considered skipping his plans to meet Mark at the sand pit but shrugged the idea away; he needed to do something to get his mind off Ethan and Nadia. If there was ever a way to get his mind off this morning, shooting some bottles in the sand pit with Mark would be it. Shooting was one of the few activities that Alex was genuinely good at and just about the only thing both Alex and Mark loved to do together. Alex didn't have much in common with Mark, but he was a much better shot. When he took aim Alex was always able to forget everything around him and just concentrate on what he was doing, it was like he knew where the bullet would hit before he pulled the trigger. Nothing in the world felt more natural. Mark was always trying to get him to enter local and even state shooting competitions, but Alex wasn't the type to enjoy the spotlight. Showing up his big brother in private was enough for him.

Before he could make it to the living room, a note on the kitchen counter caught his eye. It was rare for Alex to pass by a note Mark left for him, but being ticked off is one of those small things that can ruin anybody's concentration.

Why are you even reading this? If you don't hurry your ass up and get down here I may just decide to shoot off all your ammo! I need the practice more than you anyways you little jerk!
-Your big bro!

Alex smiled to himself and dropped the note. Except for Nadia, and despite the fact that they had nothing in common, Mark was the only other person in the world he really got along well with. He had a few friends at school but he barely spoke to them outside of his classes, they were really more like acquaintances. Although Alex never really felt comfortable around anyone besides Mark and Nadia he never put much thought into it. In small New England towns the simple fact more often than not was if you weren't born there, you're an outsider no matter how long you've lived there. Finally smiling to himself a little Alex paused long enough to pick up his car keys before limping out the door in a slightly better mood.

Alex turned onto the small dirt road that led down to the sandpit and was disappointed to see a line of cars parked bumper to bumper stretched out almost all the way down to the entrance. Alex clenched his jaw dreading the walk. Limping along a dirt road when your foot felt like it was full of nails would be irritating enough, but having to limp down an unmaintained hill covered in large rocks and foot deep trenches makes it even worse. Alex felt his foot swell a little more with every painful step and was starting to wonder if he broke his toes when he kicked his bed. Every rock and branch he stepped on sent shots of pain up his leg. He just hoped the limp wouldn't be too noticeable so he wouldn't have to explain to Mark why he got mad and kicked his bed while wearing nothing but his boxers.

The sound of guns going off was deafening, there must have been at least thirty or so people in different groups shooting at the same time. Alex stood for a few moments searching the crowd until he finally picked Mark out at the back of the pit. He was leaning on the dropped tailgate of his truck with his usual blue cloud of cigar smoke floating around his head. He was built much heavier than Alex and stood a full head taller, he had a constant five 'o clock shadow covering a heavy jaw and crooked smile. All in all he was almost the polar opposite of Alex; one would never think they were brothers just by looking. He worked the graveyard shift at a local company that made wood flooring out of pine, so the most time they got to spend together was in the afternoons, usually here shooting whatever targets they could pick out of the sand.

Alex shook his head at the smoke cloud above Mark's head; he didn't like to see his brother smoking but knew he wasn't going to change any time soon, so instead he settled for making comments here and there to tease Mark. Alex took a deep breath anticipating another painful walk and tried his best not to look like he was limping. While he slowly made his way across the pit trying to look normal Mark saw him coming and met him with a questioning look.

"I wish you'd stop smoking those things," Alex said, trying to keep the subject off his limp.

Mark took the cigar out of his mouth and tapped an ash onto the ground, then scrutinized Alex with a crooked smile. "Looks to me like I'm still taking better care of myself than you boy, what the hell'd you do to your foot?"

Alex didn't say anything for a moment, trying to think of something to tell Mark that wouldn't involve him losing his temper and kicking his bed barefoot. Mark was a pretty easy guy to live with and treated Alex more like his kid brother than a father, a fact Alex was always thankful about. Unlike Alex however, Mark was even tempered and had an almost annoying habit of thinking things through for what seemed like days on end before he did anything. One of the things that Mark didn't like and always called Alex out on was what he called "doin' idiot things without thinking."

"Got a little mad and kicked my bed barefoot," Alex finally mumbled while looking at the ground.

Mark put the cigar back in his mouth and started loading his rifle, "Feel pretty stupid I bet. Look pretty stupid too, waddling down here like an old granny." He said out of one side of his mouth.

Alex felt his face get hot again; he envied Mark's even temper and tried his best to be like him in that regard. Unfortunately though, Alex failed at that more times than not and ended up embarrassing himself with stunts like this. Hopefully it wouldn't result in spending the summer in a cast just because Ethan got to him; that would really give Mark something to go on about.

When Mark finished loading he put his rifle on the tailgate and took the cigar back out of his mouth, he tried to shoot Alex a stern look but started laughing instead. "Bet you won't do that again, will ya? Why'd the hell you get so bent up in the first place?" he asked.

"Ethan." He said simply. "Hate the way he is with Nadia and hate how she can't see it."

Mark rolled his eyes and picked his rifle back up, looked down at the rifle to double check the safety, "way of the world buddy, way of the world." He said as he sat on the tailgate and laid the rifle across his lap. "Just don't you go startin' anything stupid about it, now get your little girl's gun out and let's get to shootin', I already got stuff setup down there and you're lucky I haven't shot it all already."

Now it was Alex's turn to roll his eyes, "you couldn't hit the broad side of a barn, and don't be jealous when you have to reload and I'm still taking all your targets out before you can get going again."

Alex pulled his gun out of its case and began loading it, a lever action .22. Mark always poked fun at the little rifle, instead opting for his much more powerful hunting calibers, but even he had to admit his younger brother was a much better shot with the little gun than he would ever be. Alex stuffed plugs in his ears and waited till Mark was on his feet with his gun ready and signaled him to shoot first. He watched as Mark shot at the row of bottles he had setup down range. The first five shots were a miss, with nothing but large puffs of sand flying behind the bottles; finally he was able to hit one on his last shot. *The deer are the safest things in the woods,* Alex thought laughing to himself.

"Got one!" He slapped Alex on the back, "alright have at it."

Alex shot Mark a half smile and took aim, hitting the next eight bottles back to back while working his gun so fast Mark couldn't get his gun loaded in time to get another shot off before all the bottles were blown apart.

"Your turn," He said with a grin, slapping Mark on the back.

Mark looked at the bottles shattered on the ground, then back to Alex taking another puff off his cigar while he shook his head grinning.

"Little punk," He said.

They spent the rest of that afternoon shooting whatever junk they found lying around the pit. At one point, a group of Mark's co-workers showed up and joined in, none of them could shoot half as well as Alex but they were all better than Mark, and before long they had joined Alex in taunting Mark's lack of shooting skills. When the shadows had grown long across the pit everyone packed up, Mark's co-workers heading out first after a few final taunts. When it was just the two of them Mark gave Alex a ride back up the hill, sparing him a long and painful walk. His limp had only gotten worse throughout the day and his foot felt more swollen than ever. Although Mark didn't say anything about it Alex knew he wasn't missing the pained look on his face whenever he moved. After they loaded the guns up into Alex's car Mark finally voiced his concern.

"I can drive ya home if you need me too, I'm not due at work for another hour and I'm sure nobody'll try to steal that rust bucket of yours," he offered, gesturing at Alex's car.

Alex hit his hurt foot on the ground a few times, choking down the pain as best he could while managing to keep himself from wincing at the pain shooting up his leg every time it hit. He didn't like people worrying over him, especially Mark. "I'll be fine," he insisted, "I'll take some pain pills when I get home and put it up, I'm sure it'll be better by the morning."

Mark kept looking at him with obvious concern and Alex knew he wasn't buying it. When Mark looked at the clock on his phone Alex almost sighed with relief. "You sure?" Mark asked, "I got time, besides, I don't need you tripping at home and getting my gun all scratched up." He tried to look stern, but couldn't keep the small smile off his face.

Alex shook his head and hit Mark in the arm, "I'm sure, get your ass to work before you blame me for getting fired."

For a moment Alex thought he'd insist on driving him home anyways, but finally Mark just shook his head and got into his truck. Alex rolled his eyes as Mark pulled out yet another cigar and clipped the end off.

"Don't look at me like that; I need it after getting my ass kicked shooting all day, so keep your mouth shut." Mark grinned one last time as he blew a puff of smoke Alex's way. "Take care of that foot boy; otherwise I may have to break the other one to teach you a lesson." He joked laughing before driving off.

Alex stood and watched Mark leave. When his truck was out of sight he lifted his foot off the ground with a moan and hopped slowly to his car. His boot felt like a clamp being pressed around his foot, and he was worried that he may have really broken it. The drive home was miserable to say the least; no matter how gingerly he stepped on the gas he wanted to yell out. He even tried to use just the heel of his foot but it didn't help, every time he lifted his foot he would hit his toes sending more pain up his leg. Alex felt his frustration build with the pain and almost drove off the road twice.

When he finally made it home he decided to leave the guns in the car till he could get some pain killers into his system, walking was bad enough without carrying anything to add to it. Limping inside he hopped on one foot to the sink and pulled some medicine from the drawer. He counted out three of the strongest pills he could find and threw them in his mouth without water. Hopping over to the fridge he grabbed a bottle of water and downed it in a few large gulps on his way into the living room before plopping down on the couch. Alex slowly untied his boot and carefully took it off, peeling back his sock and wincing with every movement.

His foot had indeed swollen and had turned an ugly shade of black and purple. Alex tried to move his toes but the pain was too much and caused him to cry out. Frustrated, he wiped tears out of his eyes and sat back looking out the window at the lake. The sky was just beginning to turn pink and Alex could hear the first loons of the season calling out, breaking the late afternoon silence. A movement at the beach across the cove caught his eye and he could see a figure with red hair walk up to the water and sit down on the sand, it was Nadia. Alex considered calling her on her phone till he saw her pick up a rock and skip it over the water. She only did that when she was upset and went there to think things over. Knowing she would be there for a while he decided to go talk to her. Fighting back more tears Alex winced as he tenderly slipped his foot back into his boot, tying it as loosely as he could. The pain pills were starting to work but every movement still made him want to shout out. What was one more walk for the day? He was sure he couldn't hurt it anymore. Hopping on one foot, he went out the door and down to the little path that led to the lake.

FOUR

"Wake up, oh god please wake up....!"

The words seemed to be coming from the end of a long tunnel while Jason fought to regain consciousness. As he began to open his eyes a hand slapped Jason across the face and he felt himself being shaken. Slowly he forced open his eyes, his head was a throbbing ball of pain where he had hit the rock and his right eyelid was partially stuck closed with dried blood. His clothes were soaked through and he was shivering uncontrollably. Like him Sarah was also covered with mud, her blonde hair hung limp around her face in thick dark clumps, but when Jason was finally able to focus on her the look of relief he saw on her face made her the most beautiful person he had ever seen. Before he could ask what happened she grabbed him with both arms and hugged him so fiercely that his head smacked into her shoulder making his gashed forehead flare up in another bust of pain. He didn't care.

"Oh thank god," she whispered, "thank you, thank you, thank you..."

She held him tighter and started crying, her whole body shaking with every sob. Jason let her hold him a few moments before gently pulling her arms off and sitting up. His muscles were stiff and his back was killing him, every movement required more effort than he would have liked, but at least he was alive. Still crying Sarah threw her head into his shoulder and hugged him again. He held her like that for a few minutes, letting her get it all out before pushing her away once more and gently picking her chin up with his hand, forcing her to look him in the eyes.

"Are you alright?" he asked.

She looked at him and nodded; her breathing finally starting to slow down. When Jason saw Sarah shivering as badly as he was he looked up at the sky, it would start to get dark soon and Jason knew the temperature would drop with the sun. If they didn't get off the mountain and back to the car before then things would get very bad for them.

"Yea I'm alright, I think I sprained my ankle when we fell but that's all." she said, "I was afraid you weren't going to wake up, you hit your head pretty bad."

"What happened to the dogs?" he asked, "I thought they were going to rip us to pieces."

"They weren't dogs; they were wolves, big ones too. I've never heard of them in NH, and I've certainly never heard of them acting that way. Jason, they weren't normal."

"I could have guessed that," Jason said with a groan, "what happened after I got knocked out? What made them leave?"

She stared at the ground and just shook her head. Her shivering was getting worse and her teeth were starting to chatter. Jason knew they really needed to get moving but he had to know what happened.

"Sarah, what happened when I passed out?"

"I don't really know," she said, "I remember I was afraid that you were going to get your face chewed off, then you passed out and it just, well, it ignored you and came to me. It's like they weren't trying to hurt either of us, they just walked up to me and, and..."

She broke off and started crying again. But now the sky was starting to turn from dark blue to orange and red and Jason could feel the air getting colder; even in the spring New England could be bitter cold at night and dangerous. He stood up slowly. His head was still throbbing badly but he knew the pain of that wasn't nearly as dangerous as hypothermia. He helped pull Sarah to her feet gently, trying to help her keep weight off her hurt ankle. She leaned against him with her ankle off the ground and together they started making their way down the trail. It was going to be slow going but at least they weren't that far from the road. They made their way carefully down the path, after a short distance Sarah's breathing had slowed down and her crying had stopped.

"...not normal..." she whispered.

"What did you say honey?" he asked, looking down at her as she tried not to step down on her hurt ankle.

"They weren't normal; they shouldn't have acted like that, they're animals."

He looked down at her with a sideways glance and caught her eye. Sarah looked up at him and stopped moving, turning his shoulders so they were facing each other. Jason could feel her fingers digging into his shoulders; she had a look on her face like she had just realized something important but wasn't sure if anyone would believe her or even cared.

"What do you mean just animals? What did they do?"

"When you passed out and they came to me, they didn't try to attack me or bite me or anything. Jason, one of them pulled the camera out of my hand. They took my camera and ran away with it.

FIVE

Doing his best to hide the pain, Alex slowly walked along the shore toward Nadia. She was lost in thought and didn't notice him approaching till he was standing next to her.

"Mind if I sit here too?" Alex asked.

She jumped in surprise when Alex spoke, then looked up at him with a small smile and patted the sand next to her. Alex winced as he accidently put weight on his hurt foot then again when he dropped down next to her a little harder than he intended. Alex worried that she would say something about his wincing and was relieved when she didn't; she was too deep in thought and too busy watching her rocks skip across the water. Relieved, Alex sat in silence for a moment, watching the sky turn to a deeper shade of red that matched the color of her hair.

"Sorry about Ethan today" she said breaking the silence, "I gave him hell for it later if it makes you feel any better."

Alex shrugged, "I'm used to it, he's always hated me. I don't think that's ever gonna change. Besides, big guys like him seem to love going after smaller guys like me."

Nadia didn't look at him, just stared at the sky and shook her head, "No, he's not like that, he's just jealous of you" she admitted. "I guess he thinks you're in love with me or something." She looked sideways at him and winked, then finally relaxed a little and sat back, letting out a long breath.

Alex didn't respond. The simple fact was that he was in love with her, always had been. His feelings for her had started that very first summer they spent together. He had never told her how he felt about her fearing it would drive her away. As time went on he became more and more afraid to tell her, and hated himself for being such a coward. Now it was his biggest regret, and it was only made worse by the torture of watching her with someone else; someone that not only didn't care for her the way she deserved, but also kept her away from him.

"Alex what's wrong with me?" Nadia asked; frustration obvious in her voice.

Alex broke away from his thoughts and looked at her in the fading light. He desperately wanted to hold her, to tell her how perfect she was and that Ethan didn't deserve her. He wanted to somehow make everything the way it should be, to make her as happy as she deserved and leave no doubt in her mind of just how special she was.

"Nothing's wrong with you, you're perfect." Alex whispered softly.

Nadia smiled at him again and hit him in the arm. "I'm being serious you jerk, am I ugly or not girlfriend material or something?"

"What do you mean?" he asked. "Did something happen?"

She looked back at the sky and shrugged "I don't really know, I was with Ethan up at the cabin and... Oh sorry, I'm sure you don't want to hear this."

As soon as she had said Ethan's name Alex had rolled his eyes and the hurt look on Nadia's face when he did sent a wave of guilt through him. Sure he didn't like Ethan in the least, but Nadia was his friend and he wanted to be there for her regardless. "Sorry go on, I promise I don't mind." He tried to reassure her with a grin but she had gone back to looking out at the lake.

"Alright," she still sounded annoyed, "just try to keep the remarks to a minimum."

Taking a deep breath she started again. "Anyways we were up at the cabin, and for once we got lucky and didn't have many people around. Everything was going good at first; we talked about this year almost being half over, classes, the senior dance, that kind of stuff. Then when I asked him if we would still be together after graduation he stopped talking and just stared off into the distance. I don't know why but he almost looked angry about something. I asked if he was ok and he said everything was fine, but he kind of snapped at me when he said it so I said things didn't sound fine and I got nervous and asked if he was planning on breaking up with me. He kind of laughed off the question and said he wasn't planning on it, but when I leaned in to try to kiss him he jumped back and I swear it looked like he was repulsed by me. I guess I looked hurt because he apologized for jumping back and said it was nothing, but I don't get it. We've been together a year and I can count on one hand the number of times we've kissed. It's like he never lets me kiss him and barely lets me touch him, hell I can barely get him to hold my hand. I mean I love spending time with him but it seems like talk is all he wants to do with me and.... I'm sorry I'll shut up now, TMI right?"

Even in the fading light Alex could see how red her face turned; she gave a nervous chuckle and turned away from him. As jealous as Alex was that Nadia was talking like this about Ethan and not him he had to admit he was a little relieved to hear that Ethan didn't seem to want much to do with her physically, but at the same time he was confused. Why was Ethan with her if he didn't want her that way? High school seems a little early for guys like Ethan to act like they just want to settle down and date a girl for the right reasons. Or was Alex wrong about Ethan, maybe he was really just a good guy acting like an ass towards Alex out of jealousy.

Starting to feel like an ass himself Alex watched Nadia as she skipped another rock across the water. As the stars started to appear in the blackening sky Alex could see moonlight reflecting off the tears forming in her eyes. He desperately wished he knew what to say to make her feel better. He wanted to tell her how he felt about her, tell her to dump Ethan and be with him, that he would never make her feel unwanted. But those thoughts were selfish, especially now that he was starting to have second thoughts about Ethan's character. Still the hurt he saw in her eyes hurt him. All he wanted to do was wipe the tears off her face, to touch her soft cheek the way Ethan wouldn't and hold her close. Mixed feelings of guilt and longing started to fill him up, unsure of what to do or say he moved in closer and lightly put his arm around her, feeling a jolt of electricity run through his body when she leaned against him and put her head on his shoulder.

"I'm not really the one to ask about relationships you know." Alex admitted, "And I don't want to sound selfish and say break up with him even though I wouldn't complain if you did..."

He felt her give a small laugh when he said that and Alex allowed himself a small smile. They sat together in silence looking out at the lake while the moon's reflection danced on the water's surface. Alex could feel the warmth of her body against his and pulled her in a little closer, wishing they could stay just like that for the rest of the night, hell, the rest of his life. He prayed that she couldn't hear his heart beating a thousand miles a minute and giving his feelings away but knew she probably did. Still she didn't pull away.

"How do you really feel about him? Physical frustrations aside?" Alex finally dared to ask.

She laughed against him once more and slipped her arm around his waist in a hug, Alex thought his heart was going to beat out of his chest.

"Honestly, I'm not sure." She said. "I really do like him, call it a schoolgirl crush I guess, and I don't want to just throw my senior year with him away..."

"But?" Alex urged quietly.

"But I can't go on feeling rejected like this all the time. I want to feel like he wants me, not just time with me. He's so sweet when we're just talking together but I want more than that. I need the kisses, the hugs. I need to feel like he *wants* me, you know?"

"So what are you going to do?" Alex asked nervously.

"I'm going to think it over I guess. I'm not going to break it off with him and waste the year we've been together until I've talked it over with him and figured out what he wants out of this and where it's going."

He held her a moment longer and felt her start to shiver. The night sky was full of stars and it was getting colder every moment, even with them sharing each other's warmth it was becoming more than uncomfortable. Reluctantly, Alex let go of her and they both started to get up, him a little slower. She was up on her feet before he could even get to his knees.

Trying to lighten the mood he looked up at her and grinned, "Or maybe he just likes other guys, he does spend a lot of time with his buddies."

She looked at him in shock for a second and broke into a laugh, pushing him back to the ground. "I told you to be nice; it's hard enough keeping you two from going at each other's throats without you talking like that." Still chuckling she held out her hand and helped him back up before brushing the sand off her own legs. "I'll just give it a while longer with him, who knows; maybe it'll work itself out. At least I hope it does"

Alex smiled at her as he brushed the sand off his hands, "you know I'll back you whatever you do, just can't promise I'll like it."

She leaned over and hugged him, giving a kiss on the cheek. Alex felt shivers run up his spine. "Thanks for listening to me; I hope it wasn't too awkward for you."

"Very, but I'll live." He stammered, hoping she couldn't see how red his face was.

Alex watched her walk away until she disappeared into the darkness of a small path that led to her house. When she was gone he looked up at the moon and wished he could turn back the clock enough to be holding her again, to feel her lean her head on his shoulder as he held her. The regret of not telling her how he felt about her years ago hit him like a hammer as he realized just how much he had been holding back all these years, how much he had been suppressing in fear of scaring her away. Now he stood facing the reality that his inaction may have lost her anyways.

The first step he took made Alex realize that the pills that had worked a little before were starting to wear off. Every step made his foot cry out in agony as he made his way along the shoreline. By now he was certain he had done more damage to his foot than he first thought, and staying on it all day long certainly hadn't helped it. Cursing to himself with every step he slowly made his way up the small path that led home.

"Great..." he mumbled, "I'm going to probably go through the whole spring with my foot in a..."

All thoughts were instantly cut off by a blinding pain that filled his head. The pain seemed to grow out of the center of his brain and spread like an exploding bomb. Alex didn't hear himself screaming in agony and barely felt his knees give out as he went sprawling down the hill. The pain increased beyond anything he had ever felt before and the world around him became white, even with his eyes clamped shut it seemed like he was staring into the sun. For one blissful moment it seemed as if the pain was lessening, he tried to get to his knees when the light and pain behind his eyes came back twofold and he fell to the ground once more in bitter agony. He knew he was screaming, but for the second time he couldn't hear himself, couldn't feel the mud soaking into his clothes or the rocks digging into his back and sides as he rolled on the cold ground. The world was nothing but light and pain for what felt like an eternity. Then everything went dark.

SIX

Sitting behind his desk at the Conway Police Department Officer Raymond Steward let out an exasperated sigh and dropped his head into his hands. He was now an hour late getting off his shift and from the sound of things he didn't think his luck was going to change. A young couple had come into the station a few hours before to file a report about an incident that had happened in the woods; both had new bandages and looked pretty tired and beat up. Thinking it would be a quick report since there was no real crime involved; Raymond had volunteered to take the report down before he left for the night. Now here he was, nearly three hours later trying to calm the young woman down enough to get her out of his office and to the correct people. This was out of his jurisdiction.

"Ma'am I'm going to need you to calm down..." Raymond started to say for the hundredth time.

"BUT I'M NOT CRAZY!!!" she yelled, cutting him off also for the hundredth time.

Letting out yet another sigh, Raymond leaned back in his chair and rubbed his temples. Why didn't he take all those promotions he had been offered throughout the years? If he had he wouldn't be sitting here listening to a hysterical woman go on about an unbelievable animal attack that should be reported to the Fish and Game offices anyways. We deal with people; he had tried to tell her. He was really going to need an aspirin after this, or a stiff drink. Raymond took a deep breath in preparation for a speech that would probably earn him another screaming fit.

"Ma'am, once again I am not trying to say you're crazy. I am not trying to say that your story is false. All I'm trying to make you understand is that this is out of my jurisdiction. There was no crime involved, so there can be no investigation. Wild animal attacks are the responsibility of the NH Fish and Game department, not the Conway Police Department. Now I can give you the number to NH Fish and Game, you can e-mail them or go directly to their offices. But ma'am I'm going to be honest with you, your story is going to be a tough sell."

He looked over to her husband but once again he was no help. The bandage covering half his forehead had been getting redder as the shocked and wounded man sat there, making Raymond nervous. She needs to be taking him to the hospital, not trying to fill out a crazy report, he thought.

"And why is it going to be a tough sell? We got attacked by wolves in a state park and they need to be removed or shot!" She yelled with tears filling her eyes.

"Because, according to your story, two wolves, a species that does not live in NH by the way, killed a full grown moose by tearing its head clean off its body; Ma'am, I do not believe even a bear can do that. That's not even the hard part, you reported that not only did the wolves spot you taking pictures of them during this, but that they chased you down and took your camera. Now, you have to understand that I cannot officially file a report on wolves stealing a camera, and I would suggest if you have insurance on it that you file it as lost in the woods after an accident. What I can do is give you the number to the N.H. Fish and Game offices, and strongly suggest you get your husband up to the hospital to get his head looked over and a proper bandage on your ankle." Raymond talked very slowly and deliberately, trying to will the young woman to calm down and see reason.

He held out the card with the information on it and almost sighed with relief when she snatched it out of his hand and nodded. Her husband got up and helped her out of the chair, shooting Raymond an apologetic look when she had her head turned. She stuffed the card into her jacket pocket and allowed him to help her to the door. Raymond had a funny feeling she was restraining herself from coming back in the office and yelling again. As he escorted her out he stopped one last time and turned to Raymond.

"Thanks for your time anyways, it's been a strange day for us and I hope we didn't waste too much of your time."

Before Raymond could respond they were out the door. He looked down at the report and shook his head. No way in hell was he going to turn this one in. He picked it up and crumpled it into a ball before dropping it into the trash can. Wolves stealing cameras, that was definitely a first.

"I know what I saw Jason..." Raymond heard her groan from the hall.

Raymond shook his head and sat back waiting for them to leave. *They don't pay me enough for this,* he thought.

SEVEN

Voices, so many voices. All yelling, all angry, were they arguing? They all sounded like they were at the end of a tunnel, Alex tried but he couldn't make out what they were saying or how many of them there were. He sensed he was in the middle of a crowd, he could see figures standing everywhere, surrounding him. Something was different about them, something Alex couldn't put his finger on. Beyond the mass of figures Alex could scarcely make out the sky, as blood red and distorted as it was; it was like he was looking at a water painting through tears. He could feel a slight breeze, and dry hot air. Alex looked past the figures and saw mountains surrounding the group, or were they hills? Where was he? Most importantly, why did he feel like he had been here before? Alex felt certain that he was part of the reason all these figures stood shouting at each other, a big part. Suddenly, one voice rang out above the rest and everyone went silent. Alex could feel the tension in the air, though he had no idea what was happening. Then the voice started to speak...

The scene faded away into a black haze and Alex began feeling a sensation of vertigo as everything changed. The distortion was replaced by a third person perspective, like he was floating in the air. Alex saw himself, years younger and standing in a very familiar place, Nadia's kitchen. He remembered this all too well. Nadia had been too sick to come to school and Alex had been told he couldn't go see her until she was better. Alex remembered getting the idea of sneaking a can of chicken noodle soup out of his house to take to her because that's what made people better. He was afraid her mother didn't have any if Nadia was still sick after almost a week. Alex had waited for Mark to fall asleep on the couch before quietly sneaking out and down the little path along the lake that led to her house.

Nadia's mother, Margret, answered the door. Alex recognized the ragged look on her face as she smiled down at the little boy holding up the unopened can of soup. She let him in, telling Alex to stay in the kitchen, Nadia was too sick and she didn't want Alex catching whatever she had. Alex watched the scene unfold beneath him, unable to speak or move.

He watched himself standing in the doorway to Nadia's room while Margret stepped into Nadia's room and sat down on her bed. The dream was as clear as the day it happened, and from his perspective Alex could hear Margret telling Nadia that Alex had come to see her. Alex could remember how scared he had been back then when she didn't respond to her mother's words, he could see the worried look on his younger self's face as he waited for his friend to say something. Margret put her hand on Nadia's forehead and then to her own mouth, wide eyed and looking very worried. She took a thermometer off the small table next to the bed as Alex kept peeking around the doorway to watch. When she finally took the thermometer out of Nadia's mouth she looked down at it and started to cry. Margret quickly sprang to her feet and ran past Alex to the phone in the kitchen, quickly punching in three numbers with a shaking hand.

In the dream Alex stopped listening to what she was saying; he could only watch his younger self turn nervously to Nadia's mom and then peek back around the doorway to the girl on the bed. He watched his younger self walk into the room and recognized the pale look on Nadia's face and her shallow breathing. She didn't look up at him when he held her hand or respond to any of his pleas to wake up.

Alex remembered all this; the sound of Margret was crying on the phone and yelling for someone to get there, the feeling of helplessness he felt as something bad he was too young to understand was happening to his best friend. He watched himself look back out the door to see her mother still crying on the phone then down to the sick little girl on the bed.

"Please get better," Alex watched himself whisper with a small and shaky voice. The three words rang like thunder in his head as the younger version of himself spoke. Then he bent down and kissed her on the cheek. Even from his vantage from above Alex could still feel her hot skin on his lips and feel her tiny hand in his own. As soon as the boy's lips touched Nadia there was a flash of brilliant light Alex didn't remember from that day all those years ago. Nadia's whole body shuddered as she suddenly squeezed down on his hand. As Alex watched from above the color returned to her face, suddenly she took a deep breath like someone coming out of the water after holding their breath too long. She slowly opened her eyes and looked up at Alex's younger self and smiled.

"Hi," she said with a whisper. Alex saw his younger self jump as Margret came rushing back into the room and the vertigo once again returned as the scene faded away.

Alex woke at the bottom of the path with nothing but the sound of spring crickets and an occasional loon call to greet him. The pain in his head was quickly fading, as was the memory of the dream he had been having. His right arm felt like it had been plunged in ice and was partially numb. Alex sat up and found himself sprawled out at the bottom of the path by the edge of the lake. He pulled his arm out of the water wondering how long had he been there. What had happened? He could see the moon over his head so at least it was still night time; though he had no idea what time. He stood up and stretched the stiffness out of his limbs. He was cold and soaking wet, the mud caked onto his clothes made them feel heavy. Shivering, he turned and slowly walked back up the hill still wondering what had happened. The last thing he remembered was walking along the lake, then a sudden pain before blacking out for God only knew how long. Had he been dreaming? If he had, it had faded away as quickly as the pain that had sent him rolling down the hill.

He made home and stepped inside. Mark still wasn't home so he knew it couldn't be much past midnight. Alex kicked off his boots at the door and walked to his bedroom. When he flipped on the light his eyes involuntarily shut at the sudden brightness. Still shivering from the cold mud he stripped off his clothes on the way to his small bathroom and looked at himself in the mirror. He looked terrible, his eyes looked sunken and his face was pale. Mud was caked and drying to the side of his face. He had never felt so tired in his life.

Shivering and cold, Alex turned the water in his shower on as hot as he could stand it, then stepped in and let the cold drain from his limbs. He didn't want to think about what had happened just yet, he was too tired and wanted sleep.

He stepped out of the shower and dried off. He was physically drained and his eyes were half closed as he threw on some boxers and stumbled to his bed, almost falling over into it. He would have fallen asleep at once had a thought not suddenly occurred to him; he had *walked* here. No pain. No limp.

The entire day had been a miserable battle through pain every time he took a step or moved, yet he had walked up to the house and into his bedroom without so much as a groan. Shaking with a slight fear, he sat up and flipped the light back on again. He was almost afraid to look down. Had he somehow killed the nerves in his leg? Had he done more damage than he thought? Pain like that doesn't just go away, yet the pain in his foot was gone. As Alex looked down he felt the blood leave his face and a cold sweat break out across his forehead. The ugly swelling and bruise that had been there just hours before was gone. His foot was completely healed.

EIGHT

D aniel sat down on a log next to the small pond and pulled out a bottle of water. It had been a long day already, an unusual heat wave had brought the temperature up near the 90's and the woods felt sticky and humid. He didn't mind being back in his home town, in fact he had volunteered for the job when he heard about the fuss a young couple had made about a wolf attack. He had called up his boss and offered to help out for a few weeks, search along the trails and hills and report anything he found that may prove the story true or false. Relaxing along the pond, he turned to take advantage of one of the few light breezes that gave temporary relief to the steam bath the day had become. His clothes were weighed down with sweat, tempting him to take them off and jump in the pond, but the bugs would eat him alive and he was irritated enough for one day.

He took his cell phone out of his pack and looked at the time: 1:00, he needed to check in. Flipping it open with a practiced flick of his wrist he hit the speed dial to the local Fish and Game offices, taking another long swallow of water before it stopped ringing.

"Hey Dan, how's it going out there in the woods? Find anything yet?" An overly cheery voice asked.

"Not a thing Linda. I've been up and down every trail I can think of. No sign of a moose, footprints, fur, anything. I did manage to find their packs, no camera though. I guess you can call them up to come get them. What are you so cheery about over there?" he asked.

"Air conditioning and iced coffee! Dave wants to know how much longer you'll be out there today, says we've spent enough time chasing wild geese and wants you to make out a final report."

Daniel sighed, iced coffee sounded really good right about then. Still, he had to finish up out here first. "Give me another hour out here and I'll be on my way back, and have a coffee ready for me will ya?" Daniel jested.

Linda laughed. Daniel wished she would transfer up his way. They could use someone that didn't sound bored all the time, and the fact that she was cute was a bonus. "No promises, but I'll see what I can do." She said, sounding flirty.

Daniel hung up the phone and looked over at the moose carcass feeling his irritation return. There was still a lot of moose left to drag off and bury. Not to mention the bugs and smell were driving him insane. Why did there have to be a heat wave now and not after he had cleaned this mess up?

Movement caught his attention. Daniel looked into the tree line he made out a dark brown shape coming towards him, a grey shape not far behind. The two wolves walked into the clearing and approached Daniel, heads hanging down.

"The next time you two idiots decide to come out here and play, clean up your own mess," he yelled, "Now where is it?"

Daniel held out his hand, the grey wolf slowly came to him and dropped a camera into his hand. He held the camera up and shook his head at it. Never, in the entire history of the pack had anyone been this careless. Hunting was permitted, even encouraged; the problems came when they didn't check to make sure they were alone, and worse, when they hunted this close to a well-used path. He turned to the pond and threw the camera as far into the water as he could. *At least they took the camera,* he thought. Not only did it take away any real proof the couple might have had, but it made the story so unbelievable that he wouldn't have to worry about a real investigation.

The two wolves were lying on the ground with their heads in their paws looking up at him. *Stupid pups,* he thought. They got lucky this time. Daniel didn't know how much longer he was going to be able to stick around to keep them out of trouble. He knew he should have waited to apply to Fish and Game till he had had a chance to teach these two how to live without getting seen. He stood for awhile thinking, *if I could buy myself at least another week or two I might be able to teach these two enough common sense to keep from getting themselves discovered or killed,* he thought. Looking over at what was left of the moose he got an idea.

"One of you start dragging what's left over to the hole I dug in the woods, I need the other one of you to get one of the antlers and bring it to me. Make sure you put some teeth marks on it too, it's no good to me if you don't."

The grey wolf trotted to the remains and started chewing on one of the antlers while the brown wolf began dragging pieces of the carcass into the woods. Daniel watched for a few minutes. Satisfied that they were doing what they were told, he bent down by the pond.

Daniel pulled his pack closer, swatting at a cloud of black flies as he fumbled with the latch. He then took out a small book and flipped through to the tracking chapters. Picking up a small rock and a stick, he set to work in the mud, checking the book every now and then for comparison. When he was satisfied with the impression he had made, he pulled out a small bag of dry plaster and a cup he kept for mixing. He heard a yelping from the side and looked over; the brown wolf had stepped too close to an early ground hornet nest and was franticly running around to escape the swarm. Daniel laughed to himself, *serves him right for all this trouble,* he thought. Turning back to his project, he mixed the plaster in the cup and poured it into the impression in the mud. He stood up and stretched the stiffness from his back, then walked over to the grey wolf still chewing on the antler. The brown wolf had dragged what was left over to his hole and was sitting on the ground sneezing and pawing at the stings on its nose.

"That's good enough" he said, "now get out of here so I can finish up, and no games on the way back. You two idiots have made things hard enough on me already."

The grey wolf stood up and stretched its legs out, then nodded at Daniel and took off running into the woods with the brown wolf not far behind. Daniel took another gulp of his water and looked into the woods where the moose was about to be buried and sighed. *Idiots,* he thought to himself. It took him over an hour to bury the moose enough to stay covered for a few days. He knew animals would come dig it up but by then it shouldn't matter; he just needed it hidden from the path in case the couple came back looking for it.

The plaster had dried up by then. He picked that out of the mud and placed it into a plastic bag, then picked up the chewed antler and tied it to his pack. Finally, he was on his way out of the woods, the couple's small daypacks in his hands and his on his back. *They really owe me for this,* he thought.

NINE

A series of loud groans erupted in the classroom, snapping Alex out of his thoughts. He hadn't told anyone about his blackout a couple of nights back and didn't really want to. At first he had been terrified, thoughts that something was wrong with him or that he was going crazy filled his head every night until he fell off to a dreamless sleep. People don't just heal themselves of broken bones and ugly bruises. Then again, he could have thought he hurt himself worse than he actually had.

The possibility existed that maybe his mind was playing tricks on him again like it did when he was young and the doctors had feared brain damage after the accident. Alex just couldn't figure out why if that were true, it would have taken so long for something like this to happen. An injury might explain the voices he thought he dreamed when he woke up from the blackout, but why now after so many years had passed? Besides, he really didn't remember enough from after he woke to know if he had been dreaming or if he had just imagined everything.

The only thing he knew for sure at the moment was that he was scared. His biggest fear was that he could just be starting to see the early stages of some sort of illness from some lingering injury from the accident all those years ago. He had to try to figure out some way to get checked out quietly, without Mark knowing and having to worry about him all over again.

His thoughts were interrupted when a blue notebook was dropped on his desk. Alex looked up to see his history teacher, Mr. Ludolf smiling down at him. One of the few teachers Alex really liked, Ludolf was tall and thin nearly to the point of being a walking skeleton. He always seemed to be in a good mood and his smile and lightheartedness usually disarmed even the most stubborn students, including Alex himself.

"You may want to pay attention to this" he said, and moved on to hand out more notebooks to the rest of the class.

For the first time in days Alex's thoughts were taken off the blackout. He looked down at the empty blue notebook and sighed. Everyone that took Mr. Ludolf's senior history class knew what that notebook meant. Most students liked taking his classes, they were usually light on homework and tests and Ludolf seemed to know how to not only get all his students involved in class, but even interested in what he was teaching and the projects he assigned. This one was different, however, and everyone that took his class dreaded it. The tall man looked at the discouraged faces of his students and chuckled.

"That's right, it's time to talk about you're final. You'll have the rest of the year to research and write a ten, yes ten page report on whatever subject you're lucky enough to have drawn. Don't give me that look Lisa you have plenty of time," Mr. Ludolf said to a dark haired girl in the front of the room who gasped when he gave the length of the paper he wanted.

"The report will be worth one third of your total grade for the year. I'm sure you've all heard the complaints about how high my standards are, so I suggest you take this seriously and not wait until the final week to get started. You know how this works: you'll each draw one subject out of the box. No ideas about cheating either, no two are ever the same so don't get any ideas about using the reports you were foolish enough to buy off last year's class."

Several of the students slumped in their seats and groaned. Every year, there were kids who took his class that would sell their reports to anyone that would believe them when they said that their subject was standard and everybody got it. They told them not to worry, that Ludolf was handed so many reports that he would never know the difference as long as they changed a few things here and there. Every year a few were always stupid enough to buy them.

Ludolf walked to his desk, picked up a worn shoebox, and shook it a few times. The box was painted bright yellow and had a crude smiley face drawn on its sides. Going from student to student he took out a small piece of paper and dropped it on one desk after another, sometimes smiling to himself when the student looked at the paper and groaned.

"I expect the report to include both historical facts and your own interpretation of them as well as a detailed list of all sources used. I also want the contact information of any person you interview and quote for the report. If they don't want to give you that information don't bother using them. I *will* contact them." More groans from the class.

As he continued to pass out subjects, more groans and mumblings came from the students. As he passed by Alex's desk Ludolf dropped a small folded paper onto his notebook. Letting out another sigh Alex picked it up and unfolded it. Local history, families.

At least there would be plenty of places to look for that. All in all, Alex thought he may have gotten off lucky, now he just had to find a family willing to share. He felt a tap on his shoulder and turned around to look at the boy sitting behind him.

"What you get?" he asked

Alex held up his paper, "local history, families. What about you?"

"Damn you got an easy one! I'm stuck with the industrial revolution. Wanna trade?" he asked looking at Alex hopefully.

"No thanks, I think I'll stick with this one."

Looking disappointed, he turned around and asked the girl behind him what she got. Alex heard the boy to his right complain about losing forty bucks on a fake report and laughed to himself. Losing interest, Alex turned around and flipped through the blue notebook. Not really much in it except the format for the paper, an example of an outline, and a bundle of blank papers to jot notes down on.

"I'll need each one of you to write your names on the back of your subject and hand it in on your way out today, so make sure you write it down in your notebook. I won't tell you the subjects again, and I will grade you accordingly if you forget." Mr. Ludolf said, talking above the whispered conversations that had broken out throughout the classroom.

When the bell finally rang at the end of class everyone dropped their subjects on Mr. Ludolf's desk with more than a few complaints. The teacher simply shook his head and smiling, told them to get over it. When Alex dropped his paper in front of Ludolf, he was surprised to get a grin in return.

"So you're the lucky one huh?" he asked with a smile. Alex looked at him confused, but before he could ask any questions the teacher continued. "This is the only subject I hand out every year, and so far no one has been able to give me the report I was hoping for."

Curious, Alex looked down at the paper and back up to the teacher, "what do you mean?" he asked.

"All I will say about it is try to look around in more than just the usual places when you do your research," he said, "you may find a few families in this town's history a little more, shall we say, interesting than you may think." Giving a wink, Mr. Ludolf stood up from his desk and gathered up the scraps of paper. Before Alex could say anything else, Mr. Ludolf waved him out without another word.

TEN

"There's something out there, I just don't know what yet."

Daniel placed the chewed moose antler down on the table in the Fish and Game office. Then he took out the rough plaster cast he had made and placed it down beside it. One of the local officers picked up the antler and looked at it closely.

"Are you sure it wasn't a bear, or maybe rodents chewing on a shed?" The officer picked up the plaster cast and turned it over a few times in his hands, his brow wrinkling in concentration, "and are you sure what this is? It's not very clear, could be a young black bear."

"I'm pretty sure, that track looks more like a wolf track to me, I tried to find more tracks and looked all over the area but couldn't find any. And that doesn't look like any bear track I've ever seen. I have seen wolf tracks and that looks a lot closer to them. I think one may have migrated down here from Canada, but I'm not sure. I'd like to stick around if I can and try to find whatever made that, I know these woods like the back of my hand and I think I could be helpful."

"Well what about coyotes? We have plenty of them around here to chew up antlers," the officer retorted.

"The track's too big for that as far as I can tell. Look, I'd like to stick around and be sure. If wolves are back in NH I'd like to know, especially if they are around here."

The officer still didn't look convinced, but Daniel didn't care. All he cared about was getting permission to stick around for a little while until he could get a few things straightened out. He took the antler and cast back, giving the other officer a shrug.

"Look," he said, "I have family down here that spends a lot of time in those woods, not to mention tourists. I've grown up in them and know them better than most of the guys you have working for you. I'm not saying it is a wolf and I'm not saying it isn't. I just want to go back out there and setup some trail cams and look around some more, make sure there's nothing out there that may be dangerous. I'm sure they can handle things up north without a rookie anyways."

He was getting worried that he was going to be sent back up north anyways. It didn't look like he was convincing anyone here to keep a rookie around just for the possibility of a few wolves back in the woods; they could handle that themselves and Daniel knew it. Finally, he let out a sigh and shook his head, "do me a favor and have Linda give the two hikers a call, let them know we have their packs if they want to come get them and that there's nothing to worry about. At least think about letting me stick around for a bit to help, call it a personal favor if you want."

"Yeah, I'll think about it. I hope you're wrong though, it's only my second year here and I don't want to be chasing wolves around all summer, way too much red tape when it comes to relocating them. Want me to drop that stuff off for you?"

Daniel nodded and put them back down on the table. He wanted to change before he took off anyways. "Yeah thanks, I owe you one."

The officer nodded and picked the antler and cast off the table. "Don't worry about it, just try to make sure you're wrong and I'll be happy. We have enough work to do finding lost hikers."

ELEVEN

The final bell rang and the hallways filled with students making their way out the door for home or to sports. Making a beeline for the door, Alex wormed his way through the loud mass of students choking the hallways. He was almost out the door when he realized he had forgotten to grab his homework from his locker. Alex had almost made it to his locker when he spotted Nadia packing the last of her books into her bag. Working his way between a couple making out and a group of football players yelling about the upcoming games, he caught up to her just as she was turning to leave.

"Hey you doing any better?" he inquired.

She turned around and shrugged, doing her best to smile. "Yeah, I guess, I haven't been able to concentrate in class all day. I've been too busy wondering if it's going to work out between me and Ethan. I haven't really said anything to him, just that I needed the day and I'd call him later."

"You decide anything yet?" Alex wondered.

"Not really, I mean I don't want to break up with him but I don't want to feel unwanted either, know what I mean? I'll talk to him tonight, but I'm kinda thinking for now I'll give it until graduation, see how things work out. Do you think that's a good idea? I know it's not a very long time for anything to change with him but it's something. I'm not trying to put you in the middle or anything, I'd just really like to know what you think."

Even though Alex was hoping she'd decide to break it off with Ethan, he didn't say anything. He may not like Nadia dating Ethan, but even with how he felt about her he didn't feel right about trying to influence her either. "I think you should do what feels right to you, don't let me influence you because you already know what I think of him." Alex replied.

Nadia rolled her eyes at him, nodding her head. "I know, I know. I'll talk to him about it tonight. By the way, he kind of figured out that I talked to you last night, so tell me if he says anything about it alright? I told him you had nothing to do with this and to leave you alone but you know how he gets. Let me know if he says or does anything stupid before I get a chance to talk to him, ok?"

"I'll be fine, it's not like I'm going to go looking for him anyways. Let me know how it goes though alright? I'm sure things will work out when you talk to him." Alex assured her.

The hallways were empty now except for them. Nadia looked down at her phone and gasped, quickly scooping up her backpack. "Shoot I'm going to be late for work. Food orders are coming in today and I need to be there to make sure it's right. Boss is out of town this week and he put me in charge of getting things ready for the weekend. I'll talk to you tomorrow!" She hollered over her shoulder as she rushed off.

Alex watched her rush off before heading to his own locker. Homework packed away, Alex made his way out the building. He was one of the last people still walking around the halls and he could see the parking lot was about empty through the windows. *Good, at least I won't have to deal with Ethan today,* He thought.

Walking to his car Alex's thoughts returned again to what had happened to him after his talk with Nadia the other night. The more he thought about the fact that he had passed out after getting such a sudden and intense pain in his head, the more it terrified him. Throughout his early life he had spent a lot of time in and out of the hospital undergoing tests and scans on his brain. Although nothing had ever been found that would cause concern, Alex had always had a small fear in the back of his mind that they had missed something; he had taken quite the blow to the head the night his parents died.

Then there was the matter of his foot, a minor concern in the grand scheme of things but it still kept forcing its way into Alex's thoughts. When you grow up spending as much time as Alex had wandering hallways of hospitals and sitting in doctor's offices, you tend to overhear a lot of conversations. Usually involving other patients you don't know and their medical conditions. Sometimes the conversations moved onto medical miracles that doctors and nurses, who don't think anyone's listening, have seen. At least once or twice he had heard about wounds healed and conditions reversing that the doctors had no real hope for, but he had never heard of someone healing themselves to that degree, and that quickly. Alex tried to shake the thoughts out of his head, this was all too much and too confusing to think about.

He was just about to open his car door when a hand grabbed the back of his shirt, and before he could react he was spun around so fast he was afraid his neck would break. Alex tried to cry out when he felt a forearm push roughly into his throat as he was shoved against his car. Through watery eyes he looked up to see Ethan standing over him.

Pinned against his car, Alex looked into Ethan's dark eyes and could almost physically feel anger coming at him in waves. Where did he come from and how had he got to him without making a sound? Alex cursed himself for being so lost in his thoughts; he should have been paying attention until he was safe in his car. Suddenly, Alex saw two figures nearly as big as Ethan come running across the parking lot. It was Wes and Dillon, both looking ready for a fight and grinning.

"What did you say to her?" Ethan screamed in his face.

Alex grabbed at the sleeve on Ethan's jacket, trying desperately to pry his arm away from his throat, to force enough space to breathe. All Alex gained from his efforts was to be pushed harder against the car until his feet were dangling off the ground. Alex felt his face getting red as little black spots began forming in his eyes.

"What are you talking about?" he choked out.

"Your little chat with Nadia last night. I don't know what you said to her but she won't even talk to me, said she needed to think. So again, what the hell did you say to her?" Ethan barked.

Alex had seen Ethan mad before, but never like this. Alex looked beyond the three boys to the parking lot hoping someone would be there to break them up, they were alone. Alex knew he couldn't defend himself against just Ethan, but with Wes and Dillon here he knew it could get ugly. As much as he hated all three of them, he knew he had to give in. He had to say something to keep from getting beat up or even killed right then and there.

"I didn't say a damned thing to her" he choked out, trying to sound calm. "She was confused about something that happened between you two but didn't tell me what; all I did was listen to her, something you don't seem to... "Alex trailed off. He didn't realize what he was saying until it had started to come out. It was probably lucky for Alex that Ethan pushed harder against his throat and cut him off. *So much for calming him down,* Alex thought. The black spots were getting bigger as Alex felt himself getting light headed once more. Panic was starting to set in as it was becoming impossible to get even a little air.

"Watch what the hell you say or you'll be lucky to come out of this without a trip to the hospital! One little talk with you and she has to think? I'm not going to lose her, especially not to a little pissant like you! Maybe I should just make it so you can't talk to her again at all!" he growled.

Behind Ethan one of the two brothers started laughing; "Come on, let's just kick his ass and get outta here, I'm getting hungry!"

Ethan looked over his shoulder and gave a little grin; "I got other ways to deal with this" he said before turning back to Alex. Ethan moved close to Alex's face, looking him in the eyes. For a second or two Alex thought he was about to get his ass kicked, but then he felt some pressure leave his throat. Ethan's angry look melted away, and as he looked into his eyes Alex swore he could feel something, as if suddenly all he wanted to do was please Ethan, to do whatever he told him to do...

"I want you to leave her alone until after I'm done with her, let her make her own decisions. She needs me right now, a boyfriend, not a girlfriend like you. She needs you to leave her alone so she can be happy..."

Ethan spoke in a low, almost soothing voice. As he talked he moved closer to Alex, till they were almost nose to nose, his stare boring into Alex's eyes with the determination of a predator, never flinching, never letting go. Then, as Alex looked into Ethan's eyes, a small headache started to grow. Slowly the need he thought he felt to do what he was told melted away as the headache grew and for the first time Alex felt defiance and anger. It didn't matter to him that Ethan had two other boys to back him up, didn't matter that he would stand no chance if things broke out into a fight. Although Alex couldn't explain why later, he was starting to feel like Ethan was smaller than himself, and weaker. As Ethan continued to stare into his eyes the headache grew, and so did his anger.

"No" he said simply.

For half a second Ethan broke off his stare down with Alex looking shocked, and if Alex's mind wasn't playing tricks on him, a little afraid. Confusion filled Ethan's face, like he wasn't used to being told no and didn't know what to do. As Ethan once again broke his stare with Alex he looked back at the other two, as if he needed help. Alex took the moment to try to break out of Ethan's grip, but suddenly Ethan's eyes narrowed and he looked back to Alex, the pressure returning to his throat.

"What did you say?" Ethan spat in a voice so low it was almost a whisper. Behind him the other two boys had stopped smiling, shooting nervous looks between Ethan and Alex. Even with the pressure on his throat and the small headache that was forming, Alex felt a sense of satisfaction by their confused expressions.

Alex looked back to Ethan and met his stare. He was able to breathe again and felt strangely calm, even though he was angry at the same time. "I said no" he said quietly.

By then Ethan's arm was shaking with rage, his fist clenching harder by the second as he held Alex's shirt. Behind him Wes and Dillon were moving in closer, slowly at first as if they didn't know what to do. Ethan looked back at them and nodded, they started moving in with purpose. Alex closed his eyes and braced himself for the first blows when the sound of squealing tires tore through the parking lot. Alex felt Ethan's grip on his shirt lighten and was able to take in a deep breath.

"What do you three think you're doing?" A familiar voice screamed over the sound of a powerful engine.

A truck pulled up quickly beside them and Alex heard the brakes lock up as it came to a screeching halt. Both Wes and Dillon's faces went white as the truck's driver threw it in park and quickly jumped out, slamming the door shut behind him. Ethan let Alex drop to the ground as heavy footsteps ran up to the group. Alex looked up and immediately recognized Wes and Dillon's older brother, Daniel, as he grabbed both his younger brother's shoulders and shoved them roughly towards his truck. All three boys were big, but Daniel was bigger and he had no trouble getting them moving.

"You know what could happen if you start fighting!" He shouted at them as they threw their bags into the back of the truck. "Do you two idiots know how close you were?!"

Daniel turned on Ethan, grabbing his shirt and pulling him away from Alex with one hand. Alex thought he saw Ethan's feet leave the ground when Daniel pulled him away, but then again he may have just been seeing things, still it made him feel strangely good.

"And you, I know you know what could happen. Three on one! And you three especially! What the hell are you thinking?" Daniel demanded getting right into Ethan's face.

"He..." Ethan started

"I don't care!" Daniel screamed, "Get your stuff and get out of here... now!"

Alex could tell Ethan wanted to argue until he looked at Wes and Dillon in the truck, both slumped down. Finally he let out a sigh and picked his bag up off the ground. As he turned away, he gave a quick glance over his shoulder to Alex.

"I'll be seeing you around... remember what I said." The look on his face told Alex he wasn't kidding.

Daniel shook his head as he watched Ethan walk across the parking lot and disappear behind the school, then turned and looked at Alex. "You alright?" he asked, turning to Alex.

Alex fixed his shirt and looked up at Daniel, "yea, I'm fine" he said, trying his best not to sound shaken up. At least the headache had gone away.

Daniel looked down at him and let out an exasperated breath before picking up Alex's bag and handing it to him. "Try to be careful with them, or just avoid them completely if you can, ok? They don't know their own strength and I won't always be around to stop them, so keep your distance. I'll have a chat with those two later on, put the fear of god into them, they should be good for a while." He said, gesturing over to the truck. With a final nod Daniel turned and headed back to his truck, then looked back at Alex, "take it easy," he said.

Alex let out a huge sigh of relief when Daniel got into his truck and drove off; he had a funny feeling he had just narrowly avoided a very bad situation. As they drove off, Alex could see Daniel's head turning back and forth and his hand pointing at his two brothers, it wasn't hard to guess by the way he was moving that he was letting Wes and Dillon have it.

"Good" he mumbled to himself looking up at the sky. *Plenty of light left,* he thought, enough time to get some shooting in and get his mind off things. Feeling strangely calm, he got into his car and drove off.

TWELVE

"You can't seriously be thinking of going back up there."

Back in their small apartment in Boston, Sarah threw Jason an irritated glance; she had been in a bad mood all morning. He watched helplessly as she threw clothing and camping supplies into a large hiking pack, mumbling to herself. The night before the New Hampshire Fish and Game office had left a message on her phone to tell her that no evidence was found of possible wolves in the area and that no warnings would be issued throughout the state parks. Jason tried to tell her to just forget about it, that they can start going somewhere else to camp and hike. She responded by going out and buying another camera and camping gear, as well as ammunition for her father's rifle.

"How are you going to feel when somebody gets killed up there?" she snapped. "Those wolves are dangerous and need to be removed, and if it takes me shoving pictures of them down their throats to make them do something then that's what I'm gonna do" she quipped!

If that damned cop had just pretended to take her seriously she wouldn't be doing this, he thought to himself. Jason threw his hands up, walking out of the room, then thought better of it and turned to try and reason with her. "Well how am I going to feel if you get yourself killed? And is this really about you being worried about someone getting hurt, or are you just mad that nobody took you seriously, and now you have to prove them wrong?" He yelled.

For the first time that morning she hesitated, a mixture of hurt and shock spread across her face as she looked back at Jason. She knew what he said was true, but this was the first time he had ever talked to her like this. For a moment she considered putting everything away and not going, but her stubborn streak kicked in and she kept packing.

"Look," she said taking a deep breath, "You're probably right about me, but the fact of the matter is I know if I don't go up there and some hiker, or worse, some kid gets killed I'm not going to be able to forgive myself. Look, I have my dad's rifle, plus if anything goes wrong we'll have our cell phones if we have to call for help. I just really think this is something I have to do, but I can't and won't go up there without you. If you're determined not to go, if you really think it's too dangerous, I'll stay."

The pleading look in her eyes filled him with guilt. Sure, it was dangerous but they were caught by surprise last time, and this time they would at least be armed. He let out an exaggerated sigh and shook his head. He knew she was like this when he married her; in fact it was part of what made him fall for her. *No point in trying to change her now,* he thought.

"Just pictures right? You're not going to try to do anything silly like shooting them are you?"

She smiled up at him; she knew she won the argument. "Nope, I promise, just pictures. I'll set some bait up around trail cameras and not even leave the campsite. It'll be fun, like an adventure."

"What about work" he asked, already knowing what the answer would be.

"We have laptops, you know that" She was in a much better mood now, and Jason knew it was because she had gotten her way.

"Ok, let me cancel all of our meetings at the office for the next week. That's all you get though. One week then we're back here, proof or not, deal?"

"Deal" she said with a grin.

With a final sigh he left the room to start packing a few of his own things. *I have got to stop letting her talk me into this stuff,* he thought. If he had known this was going to be the last trip they ever took, he might have taken his own advice.

THIRTEEN

The house was quiet when he walked in. Mark must have been called in for another double. Throwing his backpack onto the floor he walked over to the kitchen table and sure enough there was a note for him. He picked up the note and quickly read it.

Went in to work a double. Suppers ready whenever you make it. New pain killers if you're still being a sissy about your foot. Try not to do anything else stupid and I'll see ya tomorrow.

-Me

Rolling his eyes Alex dropped the note back onto the table. It was only 4:30 but this time of year it got too dark to shoot around seven, so dinner could wait. Walking quickly he opened the gun case in the living room and grabbed his .22 and a brick of ammo. Packing it all quickly away in his case he stopped briefly to grab a bottle of water and head out the door.

Alex was relieved to find the sand pit empty for once; in fact he was able to drive all the way in. Carefully driving around piles of broken glass and old targets, he made his way to the back and parked about 50 or so yards from the end. Grabbing a few soda cans and beer bottles off the ground as he walked he lined them up on the steep bank and walked back to his car. He loaded up his gun quickly and stuck some ear plugs in. Working the lever almost as fast as he shot he destroyed all his targets in just a few seconds. Alex looked at the broken glass that used to be bottles and the shredded tin cans 50 yards away and sighed. He really needed to invest in some medal targets.

"Nice shooting" someone said from behind him.

Alex turned to see Nadia making her way across the pit, a rifle slung over her shoulder as well. "Thought I'd find you here," she said, "mind if I join you?"

He looked at her and grinned, then gestured to his ruined cans. "If you setup some more targets you can" he said.

Nadia rolled her eyes, handing Alex her rifle before heading over to setup for another round, "fine," she said, "but I get the first shots before you go and show me up."

While Nadia worked on setting up new targets Alex loaded their rifles. Nadia's was the same lever style gun he owned. He had bought it for her for Christmas a couple years before so she would stop stealing his every time she went shooting with him and Mark. Alex had just put the last few rounds into Nadia's rifle when she leaned against his car beside him. Alex handed the rifle over and stood up to shoot, but Nadia held her hand out to stop him and took a few steps forward herself.

"No, I told you I go first; I want something left standing down there before you knock everything down." She winked and sent a few rounds downrange, she was a pretty good shot, not nearly as good as Alex, but she could hold her own against any of the usual guys that shot in the pit.

"I'm sorry about Ethan" she said between shots, "I called him after school to talk and he told me what happened, said to tell you sorry..." The expression on Alex's face must have told Nadia exactly what he thought about Ethan's apology because she shot him a look of genuine annoyance.

"And don't look at me like that, I know he was just buttering up to me but at least he said it." Nadia exclaimed.

Alex watched her shoot off a few more shots before walking up beside her. "I wasn't even going to say anything about it. Dan came and gave them hell for me anyways. Now move over so I can show you how it's done." Alex gave Nadia a playful shove trying to lighten the mood.

She rolled her eyes again but did smile as she stepped aside. Alex winked at her playfully before firing off a series of quick shots, knocking down the remaining cans one after the other before reshooting all the cans Nadia had knocked over herself. Alex grinned back at her and laughed when she smiled and gave him the finger "Show off," she said, "by the way what did you say to Ethan today, he sounded weird when he mentioned you."

"What do you mean?" Alex inquired.

"I don't know, usually he sounds jealous or irritated when he mentions you, but I don't know, today he just sounded strange. It was almost like he was afraid of you or something."

Alex felt that small sense of pride pop up again but didn't want it to show too much. He'd rather not piss off Nadia again by acting smug about freaking her boyfriend out. It didn't matter how much of an ass Ethan could be, she still got defensive about him, even to Alex. Instead he just shook his head and shrugged. "I don't know, I really didn't say anything. I just didn't let them intimidate me this time. I don't think they were ready for that."

Nadia looked over her shoulder and laughed, "no I guess not."

"Well what about with you two, you said he called to talk?" Alex asked trying to get the subject off himself. He really didn't want to think about what happened earlier anyways. All he wanted to do was forget it happened and hope that Dan had talked his younger brothers out of coming back after him. He knew they didn't like the idea of someone standing up to them and they would be looking for a reason to go after him. Since Daniel was the only person Alex had ever seen them listen to he hoped that it would be enough to keep the brothers at bay, at least long enough for them to focus on someone else.

"We're fine for now I guess," Nadia grumbled, "I asked him again why he acted the way he did, but all he told me was that he had his reasons and he would explain them when he could. Said part of it was that he didn't want me to think he just wanted one thing. We decided to see how things went until at least this summer and talk about it again after graduation. He's not even sure he'll be around anyways." She didn't sound very happy when she said that last part, and even though Alex couldn't help but feel a small sense of joy at the thought of Ethan being gone he didn't show it. The look on her face hurt Alex more than the thought of Ethan leaving made him happy, and the last thing Alex wanted was to see Nadia hurting. He tried to think of something else to talk about and felt relief when Nadia beat him to it.

She shot off the rest of the rounds in her rifle and turned back to Alex. "I heard you got Ludolf's final, a couple of my friends got it last year and barely passed. What subject did he stick you with?"

"Local history, I have to find out about one family that's been around a while and write up the paper about them." Alex answered, "but he was strange about it though, he told me not to look in the usual places for research, said something along the lines of colorful family histories or something, what do you think he meant by that?"

Nadia shrugged, "no idea; probably has to do with affairs or something, plenty of those happening all the time, but I don't think they'll want you to write about them in a report." She laughed, "at least it sounds like you got a decent subject. Most people I knew that got it had boring ones." The sky had begun to darken about that time. Nadia took her phone out of her pocket and glanced at the time. "Well I'm late for dinner again. I just knew I'd find you here and wanted to say sorry for Ethan and make sure he didn't hit you or anything. He's really a sweet guy when you get to know him, just a little strange. I wish you two would at least try to get to know each other, I bet you'd get along better than you think."

Alex rolled his eyes at her, "yea, I'm sure we'd just be the best of friends." The sarcasm in his voice made Nadia sigh and shake her head.

"Boys are so stubborn." Nadia quipped. She slung her rifle over her shoulder and gave Alex a kiss on the cheek. He felt a kind of electricity run along his spine and his face turned red. Alex only hoped it was too dark for her to notice.

"See ya tomorrow," Nadia called over her shoulder as she walked back to her car.

Alex watched her drive off before packing everything up. For the life of him Alex would never understand why girls always assumed guys could just be friends.

Alex woke early the next morning to the smell of burnt eggs, bacon, and cigar smoke filling the house. The combination was both sickening and amusing at the same time. *He'll never learn to cook,* Alex thought to himself chuckling. After a quick shower, Alex went into the kitchen and found it empty, burned food still in pans on the stove. Alex loaded up a large plate of the burned eggs and a cup of coffee, looking through the living room window to the porch to see if Mark was sitting outside. Although Alex couldn't see him he could hear the clicking sounds of Mark's cigar cutter coming through the open sliding doors. Alex grabbed his plate and coffee and walked outside, plopping down on the chair next to him.

"Coffee's not good for ya" Mark said, a cigar still hanging out of his mouth, "How's the foot?"

Alex took a sip from his coffee and pointed at the cigar, "your cooking's not good for me either. And neither are those things for that matter. The foot's fine I guess, I didn't do as much to it as I thought."

Taking a bite of eggs Alex made a show of grimacing and pretending to choke. Mark ignored Alex's antics, just sat in his chair looking over the lake, a cup of coffee in one hand cigar cutter in the other.

"Why are you still up anyways? Usually you're dead to the world by now." Alex asked.

"I *am* dead to the world in case you didn't notice," Mark said with a laugh, "hell I just got home an hour ago, been a long night. I swear if they don't bring in more people I'm going to demand a raise or quit. These all-nighters are killing me."

Mark let a breath out and took a few sips from his coffee before chewing on his cigar and turning back to Alex, "you gonna survive if I ain't here to babysit you? These all-nighters might go on for a while."

Alex shot Mark a look over his plate, "I'm sure I'll manage. How long you think you'll be working doubles?" he asked.

Mark snorted, "The hell if I know. Work's so backed up they can't get caught up on orders and need to force extra hours down our throats, and to top it all off they don't have anyone to cover it except my sorry ass it seems." Mark glanced down at his watch and yawned, "I'd say you need to finish up and get your ass to school. You gonna need me to get supper ready for ya before I head out tonight? It'll be cold but I'm sure you can work a microwave."

"Don't worry about it. I'll get something I don't have to choke down when I'm out tonight," Alex said between bites, "I'll be spending a lot of time at the library getting a paper done, I'll just pick something up on the way home."

"Suits me, you bitch when I cook anyways."

"You burn everything."

"Get over it."

He stood up and stamped out what was left of his cigar and drained his coffee in one gulp, "well I'm head'n in so try to keep it quiet on your way out. And by the way try not to kick over any furniture when I'm not around, ok? I'd hate to have to kick your ass," Mark joked.

Alex gave mark the finger and made another show of grimacing while taking a bite of eggs; Mark just snorted and pushed Alex a little in his chair as he walked by. Choking down the rest of the eggs Alex followed Mark back into the house and threw his plate into the sink. Grabbing his backpack on the way out the door he stopped long enough to fill up a mug of coffee, he had a feeling he was going to need it. After school he'd head over to the library to get started on his report and try to figure out where to start looking for information on families and hope at least one of them would be willing to let him use them. *May as well start it now,* he thought, besides, with a small town like Conway, he really didn't think he was going to have much to work with anyways. Alex figured it was going to be all he could do to punch out ten pages worth of material. *This'll be one boring project,* he thought.

Alex had no idea just how wrong he was.

FOURTEEN

The day was hot and cloudless. Trevor Wilson, a college student who grew up in the area sat alone on top of Mt. Chocorua, looking out over countless hills and lakes that stretched on endlessly in front of him. The lakes were like blue mirrors surrounded by bright green hills, and the heat of the day was made bearable by a light breeze. Looking out across the familiar landscape Trevor wished he could stay up here for a week and forget his schoolwork and upcoming finals. He had taken a few days off of school to clear his head and get some rest in before his finals started, something he'd done every year to maintain his sanity. He had taken a few extra classes this semester so he could graduate early and not have to stick around New Hampshire for another summer, wanting to move on to bigger and better things.

At first, the extra workload had been no big deal, but as the year wore on his teachers piled on more and more assignments, until it was beyond his ability to keep up without a severe lack of sleep. The stress of all the extra work had built up steadily over the last few weeks, and he didn't want to go into his final tests burned out. So, here he sat, looking out at the view and enjoying the light breeze. It was the last day he planned on staying in the White Mountains, and he was enjoying the peace and quiet before he made the drive back to college.

Out of all the mountains he had hiked in the last few days, this one was by far the easiest, but it was also his favorite. He had taken countless overnight hikes up here with both the boy scouts and his friends when he was younger, and had stayed in a small cabin that stood alone at the edge of the tree line more times than he could count. Trevor could see the top of that cabin from his vantage point on top of the mountain, the sight of it bringing back memories of years past and tempting him to stay one last night before heading off to the rest of his life.

"What the hell, why not?" he wondered to himself.

He had enough food to last him another night, and there was a small wood stove in the cabin that he could light to stay warm. Besides, wasn't doing things spur of the moment one of the advantages of being a college student? He looked down at his watch; it was only a few hours from dusk. If he was going to stay he would need to gather up a little bit of wood for the stove or it was going to be a very cold night. Almost regretfully Trevor stood up and stretched the stiffness from his legs and back, taking one last look around at the view from his childhood before making his way down the rocky path to the cabin.

The temperature dropped with the sun as the sky filled with stars, but Trevor soon had a nice fire going in the wood stove and the little cabin was starting to get comfortable. Digging through his pack he pulled out a small tin bowl and water bottle. He filled the bowl and put it on the wood stove to boil, a pack of dried noodles and instant coffee waiting on the rough wooden bunk next to his pack. It was good to be back in this old cabin, it brought back a lot of memories he hadn't thought about for years.

Trevor dipped his finger in the water on the stove, it was just getting warm. Having a few minutes before it would boil he stepped outside and sat on the steps and looked up into the night sky. He was going to miss this, going to school in a large town he never saw many stars in the sky. He figured when he moved on and into some city he would see even less of them. All in all he was really glad he came on this little trip, you can't get this kind of quiet on a college campus. The best part was the fact that all this time in the woods alone had drained away the stress that seemed to choke him from the moment he got out of bed in the mornings till he dropped into bed at night. "Back to reality tomorrow" he told himself as he stood up and stretched the stiffness out of his limbs.

He stopped next to the door to pick up an armload of the firewood he had gathered up that afternoon when the sound of snapping branches caught his attention. The sound was coming from just inside the shadows of the trees and moving around slowly. He dropped the armload of branches and clicked his flashlight on, swinging it in large arcs between the trees, following the sound as it moved slowly through the trees. Moving the light slowly Trevor caught movement out of the corner of his eye and quickly focused the light at the spot, a pair of yellowish eyes reflected back at him for a split second and disappeared quickly into the brush. Trevor heard a few more branches brake as whatever it was took off running deeper into the woods. His heart racing, Trevor took a few timid steps towards the woods: the only sound besides the wind was that of his own footsteps crunching small rocks beneath his feet.

"Hello," he called out hoping nothing would answer.

Nothing answered, Trevor let out a breath he didn't know he was holding in, swinging the flashlight back and forth a few last times. Nothing else was out there as far as he could tell. *Must have been a deer or something,* he thought. He shrugged and went back inside, pausing long enough to pick up the load of wood before stepping back into the warmth of the cabin.

The water was boiling and ready to go. Trevor dropped the wood on top of the pile next to the stove, grabbing his cup and the packet of noodles off the bunk. He filled the cup with the water and a packet of the coffee and set it off to the side as he dropped the brick of hard noodles and flavoring into the remaining water. By now his stomach was letting off a steady series of rumbles and the smell of the noodles cooking did nothing to help matters. Forcing himself to wait, he picked up his coffee and sat down to relax.

"Oh that smells good..." a voice called out suddenly from the doorway.

Not expecting anyone else on the mountain tonight, Trevor jumped off the wooden bunk and spilled coffee all over the front of his clothes. He jumped up with a curse and turned to face a tall figure standing in the doorway of the cabin. The figure wore a hooded sweatshirt with the hood pulled over his head so that only a pale face was exposed.

Maybe it was a trick of the light, but the face under the hood looked wrong, blurred out and almost disfigured. Trevor rubbed his eyes and looked again, but the only feature on the man's face he could make out were his eyes, dark black, the color of charred wood. Even with the rest of the man's features blurred out, it was the eyes that sent shivers up Trevor's spine. Unhuman, full of malice. The man leaned against the doorway, his hand stuffed into the pocket of his sweatshirt, and even with features Trevor couldn't make out he knew the man was grinning broadly.

"Sorry you scared me half to death," Trevor said shakily, "I wasn't expecting anyone all the way up here after dark."

"Yes, people tend to avoid the trails at night this time of year, gets too cold and there are... animals... about," The shadowed figure said with a chuckle.

The sound of the figure's chuckle sent shivers up Trevor's spine, there was something very wrong with this man; he could feel it in the air. He wiped his eyes with the back of his hands again, but still the man's face remained a strange distorted blur. The two stood facing each other in an uncomfortable silence; Trevor was getting genuinely scared of the man standing in the doorway.

"Do you want to come in for some coffee? It's not very good, instant, but I have enough for a few more cups if you want to warm up." Trevor tried to keep his voice steady, the night plays tricks on people's minds, after all, and he didn't want to seem like a scared little kid in the woods in front of some stranger.

"Oh, no thank you. The cold doesn't bother me. I am, however, glad to have found you up here though. A real stroke of luck I'd say! My intention for the night was to simply prepare a little welcoming beacon for some friends I plan to bring into town. It's a very powerful place you know, this mountain, so much has happened here over the centuries... Anyways I was on my way to the summit when I happened to smell your little fire and notice the lights on. I was curious who could be up here this early in the spring so I decided to come and have a look. I'm in need of a little assistance, and since I find you so conveniently in my path tonight I'd like to ask if you could do me a little favor."

"A favor?" Trevor asked, the fear in his voice now becoming obvious. The bad feelings he had about this man were intensifying. Trevor still couldn't make out anything but his eyes and there was something in his voice that hinted of insanity.

"Oh it's nothing really. See I recently discovered a friend of mine is in town, and the way things are going for him it looks like he's going to have to leave soon. I don't want that. You see he came to help his family out a few weeks ago, but I'm afraid the job that brought him here is over. Now he's trying to start a little rumor about dangerous animals in these woods so that he would be required to stay and help out. Sadly I'm afraid he failed his attempt, not enough evidence you see. That's where you come in."

There was no doubt that the man was smiling as he spoke, Trevor heard joy in his voice and was able to almost make out the man's teeth through the distortion that masked his face. Trevor had no idea what the man was going on about, but he knew he had to get out of there, fast. Trying to not look terrified Trevor stepped over to his pack and picked it up slowly, not bothering to close it. Slipping the pack on Trevor grabbed his flashlight and took a step forward, leaving the small pot of noodles boiling over on the stove.

"Look, I don't know what this is about but I really don't want anything to do with it. You can have the cabin to yourself tonight if you want. I've got to get back down the trail and head out. I just remembered that I have class in the morning and it's a long drive," Trevor said taking a few cautious steps towards the doorway.

The man made no attempt to move out of the way as Trevor walked to the doorway; he simply stood in place watching Trevor approach, the smile never leaving his face. He waited until Trevor was a few feet in front of him before taking a step forward, blocking the way before Trevor could make it out the door. Trevor tried stepping to the man's right to slip out the door, but he shot out his arm and grabbed the opposite side of the doorway with his hand so that his arm was just above Trevor's chest.

"Oh I'm afraid you're not going anywhere..." he said quietly.

With blinding speed Trevor didn't think possible the man's hand clamped onto Trevor's jacket and threw him back across the cabin like

Trevor weighed no more than a doll. Trevor slammed hard into the back wall and landed on top of the stove, stars filled Trevor's eyes from the blow against the wall. Before he could pull himself up Trevor screamed out in pain and fear as his hands came down on the hot metal filling his body with more pain than he thought was possible. Trevor pulled his hands off the stove screaming when he felt a hand clamp around his throat and lift him off the ground, giving Trevor a strange sense of weightlessness as his feet dangled a few inches off the floor. Through tears and confusion he looked into the figure's eyes. They were dark, evil, and smiling.

"Tell me..." the man whispered into Trevor's ear, "have you bathed in blood?"

Trevor tried to cry out, tried to beg the man to put him down, but the pressure on his throat threatened to crush his windpipe and prevented him from making anything but wheezing gasps. The man leaned in close to his face and inhaled deeply. After a terrifying moment the man pulled back a little and looked deep into Trevor's eyes, his head tilted slightly.

"Pity for you, but you haven't, too bad really, you would have been so much more useful to me if you had."

The man carried Trevor by the throat into the darkness of the forest humming quietly as Trevor helplessly struggled with everything he had to try to break free of the man's grip. "Such a nice night," the man said to no one in particular as he carried Trevor into the shadows. The night was cold and clear, with just enough wind to muffle out the sound of Trevor's dying screams.

FIFTEEN

With a grunt of frustration, Alex closed the book he was reading and dropped it onto the table. Except for the families who had opened ski resorts and outlet malls, he was having a hard time finding anyone with enough printed about them to fill ten pages worth of material. Sure, a few guys painted Mount Washington, but come on, that's good for what, two, two and a half pages? And one achievement from one person does not make a family history.

Maybe Ludolf was right, he was going to have to look elsewhere if he wanted something better, but where? Alex picked up the few notes he could gather and put the books back on their shelves on the way to the front desk.

The librarian on duty was an older woman, short and slightly hunched over. She was probably the oldest person in the library and yet had more energy than most of the small children that swarmed into the kiddie section on storybook days. As Alex watched her going from person to person, he considered giving up for the day and coming back when it wasn't quite so busy. He couldn't help but feel a bit of that selfish irritation everyone gets when they think people aren't paying attention to their needs fast enough, but at the same time she was the only one working and she still had a look about her like there was nowhere else she wanted to be at that moment.

Just as Alex was ready to give up trying to get her attention and going home for the day she waved at him and mouthed that she would be right there. Alex put his backpack down and waited until the last person had checked out leaving him alone at the desk. She walked over to him and greeted Alex with a cheery smile, making him feel a little guilty about feeling irritated at his wait.

"What can I do for you deah," she asked in a thick New England accent.

Alex couldn't help but smile as he held up the few pages of notes he was able to gather in the last few days. "You don't happen to know if there are any more books on local town history, specifically families that lived in town. I have a pretty big report coming up and I don't think I have enough to go on." Alex handed her the sheet of paper on which he had listed all the books and family names he had managed to find so far. The list was short. She typed a few sentences into her computer and shook her head.

"I think that's all we have for books like that deah. Small town you know. You may try the old papahs. I think we have some in the computah, but it's too busy for me to go looking through them today." She said with an apologetic look before checking a schedule next to her computer. "If you come back tomorrow, I may have more time to look. I'm here by myself today and my minds not as sharp as it used to be." She looked up at him thoughtfully, "what about the other towns around? Do you need to stick with just Conway, or can you use those too?"

Alex hadn't thought of that and felt a small ray of hope; maybe he could pull this off after all, "I don't think so, as long as it can be considered local, I think it could work."

The small woman brightened up and looked at him with a smile, "I think I may have something that would be interest'n to ya, remind me when you come back and I'll print off a few of the old papahs. If I remembah right, there are a few stories you could try to start with. I'm afraid you'll have to try to find some actual people that'll tell you more though. Not much written in the old papahs about them, but I know some people will remembah. Lots of old families still livin' here you know; and you know how us old folks like to tell stories."

By now the line had built up, she gave a quick glance and nod to the first person waiting and held up her finger to tell him she'd be there in one minute, then looked at Alex and shrugged, still smiling. "I have to get back to work deah, but come back and I'll help ya get stahted. My name's Peggy, just ask for me. I'll be workin' downstairs tomorrow." She reached up and patted Alex on the cheek, "You remind me of my grandson," she said. Then, with her usual cheer she turned and walked back to the small line that had formed at the checkout.

Feeling somewhat hopeful, Alex left the library and headed down Main Street, his stomach steadily rumbling by then. He had done enough for the day, time to get some food.

One of Alex's favorite places to eat was a small pizza place across the street from the middle school, and the moment he stepped out of the library the smell caught his attention. Parking there was usually a pain and it wasn't a long walk from the library so he left his car in the parking lot and ran across the street to a back road that would take a block or so off his trip. The road was connected to a couple empty parking lots of a few small businesses and hit Main Street not far from the pizza place. As he made his way across the empty lots something large caught his eye near a drive up ATM building he was passing, it ducked away quickly at his approach and hid behind the wall on the far side. Curious, Alex walked over to the building.

"Hello," he called.

The sound of movement in the bushes behind the building was his only answer. Alex hiked his backpack up a little higher on his shoulder and slowly made his way to the other side of the small building. It wasn't until Alex had just about made it around the corner when a deep growling started, the vibrations seeming to shake his bones. Alex stopped in his tracks; the growling had to be coming from something big, very big. The vibrating in Alex's bones became more intense as the animal side started growling even louder.

Alex took a slow step back; suddenly the desire to see what was on the other side of the building left him. Alex's foot bumped into a bottle as he stepped back sending it clanking along the pavement a few feet, at the sound the animal's growling became aggravated and louder, rattling Alex's teeth. Alex stood still, terrified and anticipating an attack when the animal suddenly let out a thunderous snarl and bark off in the other direction. Alex let out a long breath and leaned against the building, nearly laughing with relief. Heart pounding in his chest, Alex slowly walked around the corner and looked around on the ground. The animal was gone but a track on the ground caught Alex's eye. Hands still shaking Alex bent down and examined the track. It looked like the track of a large dog, no real surprise there since he had heard it growling after all.

The problem was he had never seen dog tracks that big in his entire life.

By the time Alex walked into the pizza shop he had shook off the last of his jitters, feeling foolish for getting so worked up over a loose dog, no matter how big it may have been. He ordered some food and dropped his backpack on a small table in the corner and pulled out a few other assignments he needed to get out of the way while he waited for his pizza to be ready.

He was working on some math homework when his order was called, greasy pepperoni pizza with extra bacon, the perfect distraction to stressful days and homework. Alex chewed thoughtfully, half watching a couple of kids play arcade games while trying to come up with some way to find a cooperative family he could write a report on that would be even halfway interesting. Coming up with nothing, Alex shook it off and got back to his other assignments. Why worry about one class when he had five others to work on at the moment?

His pizza was half gone when the bell above the door rang and Daniel walked in. Alex didn't say anything, just looked down at his homework hoping that Daniel would get his dinner and take off without noticing him. The two kids playing games suddenly yelled out and Daniel turned around and saw him. He gave Alex a nod before turning to order his food. He was dressed in a dirty Fish and Game uniform and looked exhausted.

Alex could tell it must have been a long day for him in the woods; he was covered in what looked like a mixture of pine pitch and dirt and had mud almost completely covering his boots. Alex sighed when Daniel ordered his meal and walked over, sitting down next to Alex with a groan. Alex really didn't want the company, but at least it wasn't his younger brothers or Ethan; that would have ruined his day.

"How you doing?" Daniel asked.

"I'm good, trying to get caught up on some schoolwork, been kinda busy lately," Alex took another bite from his pizza, and pretended to get caught up in his reading again; Daniel didn't seem to notice and kept talking.

"So what was going on with you all the other day at school? I thought the deal was you all were going to ignore each other this year, I'm not around to stop these things anymore you know."

Alex shrugged. Before Ethan had moved into town and started dating Nadia, Alex didn't even know who Wes and Dillon were, or even Daniel for that matter. Then after Nadia met Ethan it wasn't long before everything had started up with him and the other boys. Ethan had taken an immediate dislike towards Alex and did everything he could to try to scare him away from being around Nadia. Nadia thankfully had nothing to do with that and even threatened to break if off with Ethan if he kept it up. For a few weeks after that things had been better, that is until Wes and Dillon decided to make it their job to make his life difficult, picking up where Ethan had left off. They just did it behind Nadia's back.

The three were always together at school, Wes and Dillon following at Ethan's heels. It was only when Ethan was off with Nadia at school or elsewhere that Wes and Dillon would start to gang up on Alex. Typical high school bullying stuff at first, they would shove Alex into lockers and walls as they walked past or knock his lunch onto his lap in the cafeteria, usually with a message from Ethan to leave Nadia alone. The more Alex refused the worse they got. They probably would have ended up fighting and beating him up had their brother Daniel not gotten involved.

Daniel didn't really care about how Ethan treated Nadia or the fact that Alex was her friend since childhood. All he cared about was the fact that his younger brothers were turning into bullies and seemed genuinely afraid of them fighting for some reason. He made it clear to them that he was not going to put up with it and stepped in whenever his brothers started in on Alex. He seemed to have a sixth sense on where they were and when they would show up, suddenly appearing before the two boys had a chance to start. Alex was sorry to see Daniel graduate and even sorrier when he was moved by Fish and Game. Things had slowly started to go back to the way they were since he had moved.

"Just a misunderstanding with me and Ethan, he thought I had said something to Nadia about breaking up with him I think."

Daniel shook his head and sighed, Alex could tell he was already sick of this same old fight again. "Still fighting over a girl huh? I didn't think you were after her, have you changed your mind?"

"No, we're still just friends."

"That's what I thought, why don't you just tell him that, or at least keep some distance till after you all graduate? I'd rather not see them acting like that, they don't need the attention, and you don't need to get hurt. I'm not trying to sound like I'm picking sides, just trying to tell you the truth. Last thing they all need is to do something stupid like ganging up on one person. They don't need that kind of attention..."

Alex laughed, "you sound more worried about them drawing attention than me getting beat up."

Daniel chuckled to himself, "sorry about that, I guess it's true. They are family after all and not very bright about certain things. And even though Ethan's not family, he's been good for them and vice versa. I still don't want to see anyone getting hurt though. I guess that's why I'm asking you not to aggravate them by getting emotional about some girl. I know she's your friend, and Ethan's no saint, but sometimes you need to keep a little distance and let someone decide things for themselves."

Alex was already tired of hearing this same speech; he had heard it more than once before and from more than just Daniel.

"So why are you in town anyways," Alex inquired, changing the subject. "I thought you were sent up north after you graduated?"

Daniel smiled a little, "I was, I'm still too new to decide where to be assigned. This is just a volunteer job for me. I know these woods better than the people working here now, just came down to help out till a mess is sorted out."

"With what? I didn't hear about anything going on?"

"Nothing really, just some hikers claiming to have seen wolves in the area. I don't put much faith in it and neither does the rest of the department, but they put up enough of a fuss to force us to look into it. I doubt I'll be around very long anyways, there haven't been wolves around here since long before I was born. Probably just some coyotes or a few stray dogs. I think the towns just worried about their summer tourism and a story like this may scare some people off. Economy's bad enough without losing money to imaginary wolves."

"Found anything to prove them wrong?"

"Nope, I hope I do soon though. I don't mind spending time in the woods, it is my job after all, but these treks up and down the mountains all day are starting to wear on everybody. I just want to get this put away and get back up to Pittsburg. I have enough to do up there as is. It is nice to come back and see the old stomping grounds though."

"Sir, your subs ready," a girl behind the counter called to Daniel. He stood up and stretched his back, it made several loud pops that made Alex cringe. "Just think about what I said, things will work out at the end. For now try to keep some distance and keep things calm, alright? Think of it as a favor to me for keeping them off your back all last year."

Alex nodded, in a way he was right. There was no real reason to start trouble where it didn't need to be started. Alex just couldn't shake the bad feelings he had about Ethan and Nadia. She was his best friend after all, and he couldn't help but want to watch out for her. Well, that and the fact that he was in love with her. "I'll try, but no promises," he said.

Daniel gave him a pat on the shoulder, "guess that's the best I can hope for. Let me know if I need to talk to them again though ok?"

"I will, get your food and get some sleep. You look like you need it."

Daniel laughed, "I do" he said.

Throwing some money down for his sub he gave Alex a last nod and headed out the door. At least one person in that family has a little sense in his head, Alex thought.

SIXTEEN

Voices were shouting all around him, angry cries overlapping each other, mixing together into a chaotic thunder. He tried to look around but saw only watery shapes and movements, figures closest to him seemed the clearest, yet they remained nothing but dark shapes against a blood red backdrop. One voice shouted out above the rest, a deep and ominous shout that sent shivers up his spine, immediately all other cries were silenced. He listened closely, trying to make out what was being said, but although the powerful voice shook the very ground he stood on, the words seemed like nothing more than broken whispers in his mind, completely unintelligible.

He knew he should speak, knew he should cry out against the thunderous speaker, but the words wouldn't come. He didn't know where he was or what was happening, the memories refusing to connect in his mind, yet he knew that he was somehow a major part of it, a key figure in this gathering. Why couldn't he remember? Why did everything around seem so strange, and yet so completely familiar at the same time?

He tried again to make out the figures surrounding him, but it was like trying to look through a thick, opaque liquid. Their movements seemed too fast, too distorted to focus on. Their features were nothing more than a dark haze against the red sky behind them, a red sky that looked so much like an image from a water painting, like a storm so calm and violent at the same time that it could only have come from an artist's mind. Were there mountains around him? Were there...

The powerful voice and surreal landscape faded away, replaced by an intense pain and bright light. There was a sensation of falling through time itself, of crossing vast distances in the blink of an eye. As the intense pain enveloped him, finally fading away as the red landscape melted away. The red sky gave way to a cloudy white and grey, the powerful voice that shook him like thunder was replaced by the distinct sound of a real thunderstorm in the distance.

Different voices began to multiply around him, many more than before and further away. Instead of angry they were excited, almost bloodthirsty. As the confusion of pain and change faded a new sense of belonging and purpose filled him. He felt like he should be doing something urgent, that he should stand before something terrible happened.

Looking around in the dreamlike fog of his surroundings he could see a huge building surrounding him, and could almost make out the shapes of tan four legged creatures, angry, hungry, and close. Though he couldn't see them clearly he knew they were trying to get to him, barely held back by thick chains. The sounds of the chains and roars of the beasts all seemed to be coming from the end of a long tunnel. He tried to stand but a sudden and sickening feeling of vertigo forced him back down.

The shouting grew louder, more ferocious. Amidst his confusion he somehow knew all the voices wanted something terrible from him, or to happen to him. There was sand under him, he could feel it now, real and imaginary at the same time, it felt wet, sticky. A dark figure emerged in front of him, filling the white and grey sky. Standing over him, too blurry to see clearly, it stood dark and menacing. The shouting became louder as the dark figure started to move...

The dark figure and shouting voices melted away as another painful flash of light and sensation of falling enveloped him. Suddenly everything around him became a sticky black. The white pain disappeared, replaced by a powerful sense of terror, a deeper fear than he even knew existed. Nothing could be seen around him but darkness, and fire. He could feel its heat burning his flesh, smell its rank smoke as it filled his lungs, choking him with the putrid smells of rotting eggs and charred, decaying flesh.

It wasn't moving right though, this nightmarish hellfire. Through the black and poisonous smoke he could see the flames flickering not up, but down, cascading to the ground like a fiery waterfall. The fire was moving towards him, like it had shape and purpose. The voices that had surrounded and shook him were gone. In their place hellish growls and angry snarls of hunger filled the air with rage, and hatred.

He tried to push himself up from the ground when something blazing hot and extremely heavy landed on his back and forced him down. He screamed out in pain as molten claws dug deep into his back, slicing through clothing and flesh like razor sharp blades. He could both feel and hear the fiery claws scrape against his bones, the taste of acid filling his mouth as a sudden urge to vomit erupted through him. The air filled with even more growling and snarls, coming closer, surrounding him. The vile smells were so intense they threatened to suffocate him.

This can't be real, this can't be... all thoughts were cut off when a pair of reddish yellow eyes lowered in front of his face and stared into his own, growling, snarling. He could feel its hatred, its rage. The creature was shaped like a massive and emaciated wolf, made of smoke and fire, its body covered in cascading flames and foul smoke instead of fur and flesh. Its eyes swirled like pools of molten stone; its teeth glowed like white hot metal in a mouth of fire and ash. The flames and smoke fell from its body, surrounding him in a thick and poisonous cloud the same way dry ice creates a falling fog when it hits water. Molten drops of saliva fell from its snout, sizzling and lighting tiny fires at the hellhound's feet.

He felt his terror rise as it faced him, barring its teeth and snapping inches from his face. He could feel its pure hatred for him, its desire for blood. The hellhound stood over him, relishing the moment before it made its kill. It let out a vicious growl, the hot and vile fumes of its breath burning his face as the jaws opened wide and lunged at his face. The world became a bright red, white hot blanket of pure pain...

Alex woke up on the floor of his room covered in a cold sweat. He opened his eyes slowly, trying to shake off the disorientation that filled him. Where was he? The last thing Alex remembered was driving home and walking into his room. Everything was still dreamlike; terror still ran through him like acid. His head was throbbing, and for a moment Alex was afraid the headache would come back with another bright flash of pain, but it mercifully faded quickly. His heart raced and his arms threatened to give out as he slowly pushed himself off the floor. Alex tried to hold onto the dreams that were quickly fading from memory. He wanted to make sense of them, needed to sort them out, somehow. But the images that had filled his head faded away as quickly as the pain, and he found it impossible to hold onto them.

Shaking, Alex pulled himself to his feet, quickly falling back to his knees as a wave of nausea threatened to empty his insides. Finally, after a few unsteady minutes, he was able to stand and stumble to the light switch. The room was silent except for the sound of crickets outside and the loon's eerie calls on the lake. A light breeze came in through the open window and helped to wake him.

What happened? Alex wondered in a daze as he stumbled to the bathroom and flipped on the light. Alex leaned against the sink and stared at himself in the mirror. His face was pale; his hair was plastered to his forehead. He stood while the shaking in his arms slowly subsided and his racing heart finally started to calm. He splashed cold water onto his face; grateful to see color returning as his heart slowed to normal.

What was happening? Did he have a tumor? Brain damage undetected till now, or was he going crazy? Alex turned the bathroom light off and walked back into his room, instantly feeling the cold sweat return and his heart start to race again.

"What the hell..."

His bedroom looked completely destroyed, like some huge animal had gone crazy and torn it apart. His bed was on its side against the wall, as if something had grabbed hold and flipped it over. His dresser was pushed over and flung against the far wall; a couple of drawers pulled out and cracked. His nightstand had been thrown and laid in pieces under his window. Standing back he looked at his entire room and changed his mind; it didn't look like an animal had torn it apart.

It looked more like a bomb had gone off in the middle of his room, centered on the very spot he had been laying.

SEVENTEEN

"Well, you got your wish."

Daniel stared at the man who had met him at the door of the Fish and Game offices with a questioning look. His sole purpose for coming back to the offices today was to turn in borrowed keys and equipment before making the three hour drive back up to his own management unit in Pittsburg. His attempts to convince the local district wildlife manager to let him stay had failed. There just wasn't enough evidence to support his theory of a potentially dangerous animal, or animals, in the area. Now here was one of the local officers meeting Daniel at the door with a grim look on his face.

"What are you talking about? I thought you said there wasn't enough evidence to let me stick around? I was here to turn in the keys," Daniel was genuinely confused, had something happened?

"Local hikers found what's left of a kid in the woods just off one of the main trails on Chocoura. It won't hit the papers till they notify his family and we'll be working with the police on the investigation. Kid was torn up pretty badly I'm told, said his throat was completely torn out. Scene's a mess, I'm told, so I hope you have a strong stomach. I'm on my way up there now and you're coming, I've already made the calls to your office. You're the only one I know of that's had any experience with wolves so it'll be a favor to me. At least that's what I told them in Pittsburg."

"What do they think did it?" Daniel asked, now he was really worried. This made no sense.

"That's what we're going to find out. I wish the snow had stuck around a bit longer, going to make tracking whatever did this a lot harder. Either way you better get ready for a lot of time in the woods." He walked off towards the parking lot punching numbers into his cell phone. Before he got into his truck he looked back at Daniel and yelled, "get your stuff ready and call me in an hour, I'll let you know where to meet us." Then he put the phone to his ear and shut the door behind him.

Daniel watched him drive away, his heart starting to race. There's only one thing in these woods that would be able to do that, except for maybe a rabid bear, but that would leave obvious signs...

"It can't be..." he muttered to himself, then went into the building to get his stuff ready to go.

EIGHTEEN

E verything looks normal."

Alex let out a sigh of relief. He had spent the night picking up the remains of his room trying to talk himself out of going back to the hospital. Mark had always told him to go straight there if anything, and he meant anything, strange happened. He hated going though, it wasn't just the fear that something may show up, it was also that he truly hated the doctor that had been in charge of his case as long as he could remember.

Dr. Eric Richardson was a short, balding man who always seemed to have a smirk on his face and a never ending supply of snide remarks. He treated every patient that came into his ER as children who knew nothing about their own symptoms, and felt it was his duty to inform them that not only were they overreacting, but that they had no right to be there in the first place. Alex often wondered how the man had continued to stay employed by the hospital when it was obvious he had the people skills of a rattlesnake. Even now he sat next to Alex typing into his laptop with a frown on his face, occasionally glancing over just long enough for Alex to catch him rolling his eyes or scoffing at him while shaking his head.

He closed his laptop and pulled up a seat in front to Alex. Alex could remember the endless weekly and monthly tests he had to go through growing up, and sincerely wished that the doctor sitting in front of him had retired or moved on to another hospital. Maybe if he had

Alex wouldn't have spent so much time talking himself out of getting checked out. Alex looked at the short man sitting in front of him and braced himself for the scolding he knew was coming. He had always had the impression that the good doctor didn't like him, and the way he was being looked at made Alex think that things had not changed in the years since he had last been here.

"You're sure nothing showed in the scans? I've never had headaches like this before, it feels like the inside of my head is trying to tear itself apart. I'm just worried that it may have something to do with the car crash, maybe it's something that just never showed till now, some kind of damage or something." To tell the truth, Alex was almost hoping it was a brain injury, at least then it would be something treatable and he would know he wasn't going crazy.

Dr. Richardson rolled his eyes again and sighed, Alex had a funny feeling that he was trying to keep himself from going on a long winded speech about just how wrong Alex was. *Must have too many people to see and not enough time to make me feel like an idiot,* Alex thought.

"Yes, I'm absolutely sure," The doctor grumbled irritably, "just like every test before. The scans today show nothing out of the ordinary. No brain swelling, no growths, no noticeable injuries. If there was anything to be seen I would be able to see it, but I can't so there's not. Now is there anything else going on or is it just the headaches?"

Alex was half tempted to tell him about the blackouts that came with every headache and the nightmares that came along with them, but the last thing he needed was his good friend the doctor having him sent away, or worse telling Mark that his little brother was crazy. Besides, he really didn't want to stick around for another series of tests with this man. And he honestly didn't remember any details of what he dreamed when he passed out, or even if he really had the nightmares at all, so why grasp at straws if he wasn't even sure in the first place.

"Nope, nothing else. What do you think could be causing the headaches then?"

"Stress," he said shortly, "I've already had your brother called at work, and he signed the release we faxed him and your all set to go. Please stop rushing in here for every little headache. If something serious happens, call 911, if not take two aspirin and get some sleep." He stood up with a groan and opened the door for Alex, the look on his face plainly said the conversation was over and it was time for Alex to leave.

"Well thanks for looking anyways, I'll let you know if something happens" Alex muttered. The shorter man looked at his closed laptop as Alex passed and muttered something about wasting his time, but Alex didn't catch it all and didn't really care anyways. He walked past the doctor in a hurry. The sooner he got out of here the better.

NINETEEN

"My God..." Daniel muttered to himself, looking at the gruesome scene before him.

He was standing next to the district wildlife manager, both doing what they could to stay out of the way of the police working the scene and trying to hold down their breakfast at the same time. The morning had quickly heated up and the area was buzzing with a mixture of swarms of insects and people, mostly police.

Daniel had seen a lot in his life, done a lot of hunting, seen the messy results of animals taking on large moving vehicles and even seen a crash or two on his own. This was something else entirely. The smell was unlike anything he had ever encountered, sickeningly sweet and rotten at the same time. The body was on the ground about thirty feet in front of him, or at least most of it was. He had been torn apart and scattered, the biggest piece left intact was his torso and head, the rest had been ripped off and scattered. Only half of the boy's face remained attached to the skull, the rest had been torn, or chewed off. In fact, it was hard for Daniel to imagine that he had been human at all.

One of the photographers working the scene turned pale and ran off somewhere behind Daniel and vomited just outside the taped off area. Apparently that spot had become the official site to relieve oneself of his breakfast, as another officer soon repeated the photographer's actions. After he was finished he walked over to them wiping his mouth and looking very pale himself. "What could have done something like this? I've seen animal attacks before but nothing like this, nothing this brutal," the officer asked.

"I really don't know," the wildlife manager said, "this isn't the behavior of any animal I've ever heard of around here, we can't find any tracks either." He looked over to Daniel for help, his face showing little hope of a positive answer. "You've lived here your entire life, right? You ever see anything like this?"

"Never," he said shaking his head, "not here and not up north either. Tell the truth I can't think of anyplace that something like this has happened, at least that I know of. I just don't see why someone would be ripped apart and left out like this instead of dragged off. Look at where we are, it almost feels like he was meant to be found." He gestured over to the hiking trail about fifty feet to their left.

"You're right about that, I was thinking the same thing. The problem is, who would possibly be strong enough to tear someone apart like that? It has to be a pack of wolves or maybe a bear gone rabid. I've never seen anything so brutal in my life," the officer admitted.

The three stood in silence for a few minutes looking at the scene. The only sounds were that of other officers softly talking quietly and cameras going off, mixed with the buzzing of the clouds of insects flying around the woods. With nothing more to do than look at the grisly mess, Daniel tried to think of some reason to get out of there, thankfully the wildlife manager spoke up for them both.

"Well, we're going to get out of here and get some people organized. No need for us to stay here and screw up your crime scene. We'll close the trails down and get some search parties out and try to find what did this so we can track it down and kill it. We'll let you know what's going on every step of the way. What are you going to tell the papers about this?"

"Animal attack under investigation I guess, but honestly I have no idea. That's above my pay grade. This is a first for me, and hopefully a last. I never want to see anything like this again. Makes some of the car accidents I've seen in my nightmares look tame." He shook his head and they shook hands, then the wildlife manager looked at Daniel and nodded. Both of them headed back to their trucks in silence, neither wanting to talk about what they just saw.

"I just don't know, never seen anything like it...." Daniel said to him just before getting into his own truck.

He turned to Daniel and shook his head. "All I know is it's going to be a long summer. And just between you and me, what I saw back there has me scared to death."

TWENTY

"So what the hell happened," Mark asked. He had gotten home late and as usual and was having his early morning cigar and coffee. Alex choked down a mouthful of charred pancake, holding up a finger up while he swallowed his food.

"A headache. A really, really bad one. I don't know if I passed out or if it happened while I was sleeping and woke me, I just know it hurt like hell and I ended up on the floor. I was worried something was finally showing up from the accident or something."

"Kinda late for things to start showing up I'd say. From what I was told, if anything was gonna come from it something should have happened by now, otherwise I'd still be taking you up there for tests every month."

"I know, I know," Alex said between bites, "it just scared the hell out of me and I wanted to be sure. Sorry if you got in trouble at work by the way."

Mark sipped his coffee and looked at Alex, amused. "For what? Getting a phone call from the hospital and signing a fax to release you. They're happy I'm there at all, as much as they've been driving me. I bet I could show up naked and they'd just smile and ask if I wanted to borrow some boots. They sure as hell won't say a thing about a medical emergency."

Alex rolled his eyes, "thanks for the visual while I'm eating, ass."

"You're welcome sweetie pie, now is that all it was, a headache? You're sure there was nothing else?" For the first time Mark had a genuinely serious look in his eyes when he asked the question, as if he was expecting more. Alex just shrugged.

"Yea, that's it. I won't be so panicky next time, I promise. Besides, that doctor's a real ass anyways, I'd rather not see him if I can help it."

"Yea but he knows you're case better than anyone, and I know he'd give it to me straight if something was really wrong. You'll just have to deal with him till you get your own insurance." Mark had a small smirk when he talked about Alex's doctor, and Alex was convinced the only reason Mark liked him so much was *because* of how much Alex didn't like him.

"Wonderful," Alex said sarcastically.

Mark grinned at him and put his cigar back in his mouth. They both sat in silence, looking out at the morning fog and watching fish jump in the lake. Alex jammed the last piece of pancake into his mouth and stood up. *May as well get to school early and catch up on some homework,* he thought. He'd go back to the library after school and look though whatever old newspapers Peggy may have dug up for him. Hopefully it wouldn't be too much so he could get out while it was still light and get down to the sand pit. He needed another trip out there to clear his head.

"So, when are you going to have enough time off work to get back out to the pit with me? Before the summer's over I hope, you'll need all the practice you can get before hunting season."

Mark sat back in his chair and sighed. "No idea, but it's not even summer yet so don't get your panties in a wad. I'll get out there eventually, but if one of those headaches comes back you'll let me know right? Or anything else for that matter..."

"Yea, yea I'll let you know. I'm taking off though, need to get some stuff done before the day starts. I'll catch ya later." He left Mark to his cigar and coffee and went inside to dump the dishes in the sink.

Maybe he was just stressed out, after all, and maybe that could cause the headache he had. He had been stressed out with the way Ethan's been, not to mention all the extra homework he'd let pile up. For now he'd just try to forget it and try to go on like everything was normal. Alex had no idea just how short lived his "normal" life would be.

TWENTY-ONE

S arah glanced down at the trail camera in her hand, then back up to the salesman behind the counter. They had left the city early that morning to make the long drive back up north. Jason was still sleeping in the car and she didn't have the heart to wake him when she pulled into the sporting goods store. Sarah left the car running and walked quickly inside, following the signs directly to the back to find the hunting section. She wanted to load up on game cameras and then pick up a few camping supplies they hadn't brought along.

"So all you have to do is hang this on a tree and it will do the rest, right? Do you know how good it is at taking pictures at night," Sarah inquired.

Sarah thought the clerk looked like the type to spend a lot of time hunting, a heavyset middle aged man with a wind burned face and a thick black beard spotted with grey, he looked to her like a real life mountain man that had been dragged kicking and screaming into civilization and forced to work in an alien world of fluorescent lights and pre-packaged food. She decided instantly she would trust any advice he gave her. He took the package from her with a calloused hand and flipped it over to show her the example pictures on the back. "Yep, this one's probably the best one you can buy for that. It has better night vision than some of the more expensive cameras and not enough bells and whistles to confuse you. If you want to make sure you get a good shot of whatever it is your looking for, I'd say get some bait and leave it about ten feet in front of the camera. With some food down the animals won't pay any attention to the camera, plus it don't make any noise when it's snapping pictures. Just make sure you check it every week and put new batteries in it every month. The best thing to do is leave the camera alone and only go there to download the pictures every few days. It'll take a day or two for your scent to go away depending on if it rains or not. If they smell ya they may not come around and you wasted your money."

Satisfied, Sarah took the camera back and pointed to the couple left on the shelves. "I think I can manage that. Are these all you have or are there any in the back? I'd like to buy as many as possible," Sarah told the clerk.

"Sorry that's all we have, you want me to order you some more? They'd probably come in in a day or two," he asked.

"No thanks, I'm in a hurry to get out there and start anyways. I'm sure this will be enough." Sarah handed her credit card over and waited for him to ring it through. The plan was to go into the woods off the main trails, and try to set up camp in as remote a location as they could find. Then put the cameras in a large circle around the camp with some piles of meat around them. With any luck, they could be out in the woods and getting things ready before dark.

"You know, it's kind of early to start scouting for deer. Hunting season ain't for months and by then they may not even be using the same trails. The big bucks tend to wander during the rut." The clerk said as he bagged the rest of the cameras.

"Oh, I'm not doing this for hunting, just doing some research on whatever else I can find out there," she said casually.

The big man shrugged his shoulders and handed her a receipt to sign. "Well good luck with whatever you're doing," he said

She signed her slip and glanced at her phone as he tied off the tops of the bags, stuffing her copy of the receipt inside. They didn't have much longer until they got to the trailhead and it was only about eight in the morning, and they still needed to get some more food for camp. They had only packed up a weeks worth of food and she didn't want Jason to have an excuse to make her leave any earlier than she wanted. She wasn't planning on coming out of the woods until she got her picture.

"Hey, do you have any freeze dried food here? Maybe some iodine tablets too," she asked.

"Yeah, a few isles down, do you want me to keep your bags here while you check," he offered.

"Yes, thank you, I won't be long," she said, eager to get back on the road.

She walked down a few isles and was happy to see they had a lot of choices for meals. She quickly picked out about a week and a half worth of freeze dried meals, stopping long enough to grab an empty cart to throw everything into. Scanning down the shelves further she found the iodine tablets and a small set of aluminum cookware. She grabbed two packets of the tablets and a set of the cookware, then threw in a pack of waterproof matches in case their lighters died or got lost.

They had been camping a lot before, so they had most of what they would need, but she knew from experience that it never hurt to be sure. She brought the rest of the supplies to the counter and handed her card over once more. Signing her second credit card slip of the day, she threw all the bags into her cart and made her way out of the store. Just before leaving she looked over at the stack of local newspapers and considered picking one up, but both her hands were full and she walked past them instead. *Probably nothing good in there anyways*, Sarah thought.

She had never been more wrong in her entire life.

TWENTY-TWO

Alex stood off to the side trying to stay out of the way while waiting for Peggy to finish putting a stack of books back on their shelves. She moved slowly, picking out books filed in the wrong places and moving them to their proper locations, all the while carefully taking books off her stack and placing them carefully where they belong. Alex could tell she took pride in how her books were arranged and didn't want to interrupt her, and Alex figured he had plenty of time anyways and was in no real hurry to get working. When she looked over and saw Alex waiting, he pointed at some chairs next to the computers and mouthed he'd be waiting there, she smiled at him and nodded before returning to what she was doing.

He stopped on the way to pick up a copy of the same newspaper Sarah Stowe had so casually ignored just a few miles away off of a small table next to the computer stations and plopped down onto one of the large chairs, sinking down halfway to the floor in the extra thick cushion. For once there was something besides high school sports on the front page, a currently unidentified body thought to be a college student from the area was found off one of the main hiking trails of Mt. Chocoura. The police refused to give many details except to say they thought it was an animal attack and are working closely with New Hampshire Fish and Game to determine what happened. The trails surrounding the area where the body was found would be closed off to the public until further notice, and police were asking the public to avoid going into the woods alone and to report any unusual animal behavior.

"Are you ready deah? I have the computer turned on and ready," Peggy said quietly. Alex jumped a little in his chair, he had been too involved in the story to notice her standing over him. He smiled at her and folded the paper in half, stuffing it into his backpack before pushing himself up out of the deep chair, "yeah sorry, got too involved in the story and didn't see you come over," Alex said with a hint of embarrassment.

She looked at the folded paper sticking out of his pack and shook her head with a frown. "Terrible thing that happened to that boy. I've always known that mountain was cursed. If you want my opinion, I don't think anybody should be up there at night alone, too many bad stories over the years."

"What do you mean," Alex asked, looking down at her curiously.

She looked up at him and gave him a serious look, "a lot of stories about that mountain, going all the way back to when they burned the top off to try to kill that Indian chief. Bad things happen up there at night. I don't think you'll find it in many of the newspapers, but I think I have a few books around here that tell the legends. I'll try to find them and bring them over. Do you know how to use the program deah?"

Alex looked down to the computer screen and shook his head. "I've never used it before, but I'm sure I can figure it out. Do I have to know the names of the newspapers I'm looking for," Alex asked.

Peggy shook her head, "all you have to do is type in a subject key-word and it'll bring up an articles close to what you typed in. It's like an internet search, but we had a young man from the historical society set this up so it only finds books and information we have around here." She had obvious pride in her voice as she spoke, and that pride was confirmed by the large smile on her face, "my grandson taught me all that, I've never liked those computers but I guess they're a necessary evil nowadays. Took him a week to get me to turn one on," she said with a chuckle.

Alex sat down in front of the computer, dropping his backpack down on the floor beside his seat. There was just enough room on the desk next to the computer to set his notebook down. He looked up at her and returned her smile, "thank you for your help. If you find any of those books, let me know, I could use all the help I can get."

"OK deah, good luck and let me know if you need any more help. I'll go find those books for you," she said as she walked off quietly, pausing to pick another book off a table, shaking her head at it as she carried it off.

Alex watched her walk away and laughed a little to himself. She seemed to be the only one in here who cared about things like that. He turned to the computer with a huff and tried to think of something to search for. Even after a few days to think it over Alex still had no idea what he should be looking for or how he should start looking. He glanced down at the newspaper in his bag and thought about what Peggy had said, and started to form half an idea. Maybe if he found an interesting event involving one family and the mountain he could use that for his paper. But how was he going to think of an event to use besides the one that just happened? On a whim, Alex typed in Mt. Chocorua and pressed enter.

The computer searched for a few seconds with the audible hum of an old and overworked machine before several links to articles appeared on the screen. Alex scanned the list of articles and sighed, not much stirred his interest, and no family names appeared. It was popular with day hikers, but he already knew that. Elevation under 3500 feet, not much to write about there. About the only thing remotely interesting was the fact that there used to be a three story hotel near the peak of the mountain. Alex clicked on a small picture of a three story building standing in what should have been an impossible location and scanned through the article. The building had blown off in 1915 and been replaced years later with a smaller cabin, that in turn had been destroyed in 1932 when a storm blew the roof off, then was rebuilt in 1934 with the cabin that stood there currently and held down with large chains for good measure. There was a picture at the bottom of the page showing the cabin Nadia loved so much, and to Alex's dismay the cabin where she had first met Ethan. Alex jotted down a few notes on it to tell her later.

Alex hit the back arrow key, clearing the screen for another search and sat for a moment trying to think of something else to search for. Starting to feel like he had just wasted another day, Alex could almost feel his eyelids getting heavy as the motivation to be there drained out of him. If he didn't think of something to at least keep himself awake, Alex knew he would end up giving up for the day. He leaned back in his chair, feeling his back crack a few times as he stretched his out, and looked around the library. People were busily walking around, picking out books or quietly sitting in chairs reading. He felt a bitter jealousy towards them. At least they knew what they were here to look for and what they wanted to do while he sat here without a clue, just trying to get started. Glancing down once more at the newspaper Alex got another idea, wanting to slap himself in the forehead for not thinking of it earlier. He turned back to the computer and typed in the word murder.

The computer hummed and searched once more before a long list of headlines from various local newspapers dating back decades appeared on the screen. *Plenty to choose from here*, he thought. His eyes scanned quickly down the list of articles, looking for any title that caught his eye. There were a surprising number of murders for such a small touristy town, but then again he figured any town is going to have its share of such things when you have as many people in and out as Conway does during its many tourist seasons.

Suddenly an article dated 1940 caught his eye and he felt his heart skip a beat. It was from an old newspaper called *The Reporter*. He clicked on the article and waited for the computer to load a scan from the paper itself up on the screen. The scan wasn't a very good one, and the picture at the top was blurred and splotchy, but the words were clear enough for him to read, and close enough to home to make his heart beat a little faster:

Tragedy strikes Roberts family once more as oldest daughter found killed.

Conway: Friends and family gather to mourn the death of Madeline Roberts, ten, found killed outside her family home in north Conway last weekend. Family claims she was last seen playing in the front lawn of the family home when Denise Roberts, the child's mother heard her scream and ran outside to find her missing. Hours later, members of the community found her body just inside the tree line of the property. Authorities have not released the cause of death but the investigation hints of foul play. This marks the third suspicious death in as many generations for the Roberts family, all the oldest daughters and all aged ten or younger, leaving some to believe the family is cursed. She is survived by her father Charles, her mother Denise, her younger brother Adam, and her younger sister Susanne. Services will be held at.....

Alex stopped reading at that point. He knew Nadia had a family history that she didn't know much about and wasn't supposed to ask. When they were younger, she and Alex had been looking through an old family album her mom kept hidden in her dresser. Nadia wasn't supposed to know about its existence growing up but had discovered it when she overheard her mother and grandfather talking about their sad family history, and mention the old photo album the family kept. She had snuck into her mother's room and found it while Alex kept watch for her mother. Alex didn't remember many details about the album, just that inside there were notes and old newspaper articles along with the faded pictures.

They didn't get past more than a couple pages when her mom walked in and ripped the album out of Nadia's hands. She sent Alex home and he didn't see her for the rest of the week. All she could say to him at school was that her mom said bad things happened in the past that she didn't like to think about, let alone talk about. That was the last time Nadia brought up her family and Alex never again dared to ask. Now here he was looking at an old article that may very well be part of what her mom was trying so hard to keep hidden. He sat looking at the words on the screen with conflicted feelings. Should he tell Nadia about this? Should he just let it go, or keep digging? Maybe this would be an invasion of her privacy, or at the very least her mom's. If she had spent so much time and effort keeping it from Nadia, Alex had no doubt that she wanted it to stay gone.

While he sat thinking he clicked on the small picture attached to the article to enlarge it. It had been scanned in separate from the rest of the page and wasn't as clear as the words. He could see what must have been the Robert's family gathered together in a small room. There were at least eight or more people in the picture, the immediate family sitting together on an old couch while people in the background either bent over to talk to them or held each other in their own moments of sorrow.

The mother and sister were wearing long black dresses, holding onto each other while the little girl cried against her mother. The mother was obviously still in shock, staring off into the distance while an older woman sat next to her holding her hand with a look of sympathy. The father and brother sat next to them, the brother in his father's lap with his head leaning against his shoulder. His father had one arm around the boy's shoulder but was paying him no other attention, instead leaning back slightly and talking to someone standing behind the couch.

All other thoughts ceased in Alex's mind as he looked at the picture. Although the faces were slightly blurred, and the picture old, the face that bent down to talk to the slain girl's father stood out to Alex like a spotlight, making his blood run cold. Right there in the middle of a picture taken in 1940, Ethan stood talking to Nadia's great-grandfather, looking exactly the same as he does today.

Alex spent the early part of the afternoon looking up as much as he could find about Nadia's family. The papers that were scanned into the library's program went as far back as 1880, a paper called *The New Hampshire Gazette*. There wasn't much from that old paper in the database, but he did manage to find one small article about a ten year old girl that was found killed in the middle of a field, the paper didn't mention the girl's name, but it did mention her father, John Roberts. He was listed as a farmer in the town records, but that's all that Alex could find on his life. He did come up one more time though, when Alex searched specifically for the Roberts family curse.

It doesn't take long for small towns to spread stories and rumors about anyone and anything that would be considered out of the ordinary, and Conway was no exception. Not long after the tragic death of his daughter, another paper, the *White Mountain Reporter*, printed a letter from an anonymous source about the Robert's family in its weekly gossip column. In the letter, someone who identified themselves as close to the family claimed that they had heard John Roberts admit in front of them that his family was cursed. The writer had a theory that John was guilty of adultery with a younger girl from a neighboring family, and that he had taken the child from her just after birth. The writer said that they believed his daughter had been murdered by the family of the child's real mother in a failed attempt to kidnap her when he refused to let them raise the girl after her birth mother had died. The writer's claim of proof to this story, how else would a family of dark haired farmers have a little girl with such bright red hair? And on top of that, John was always helping out strange people in town, *especially* strange women. They went on to tell a story about John getting involved with a strange women who had been in town, a strange *black* women, and what could be more suspicious of a man's character than *that?*

Alex sat back and thought for a moment. This was nothing more than an old gossip column, true. He could no more believe the adultery story than he could believe in alien abductions, but it was the mention of a red-headed girl in a dark haired family that got him thinking. As far back as he could tell from the articles he'd found her family had lost the oldest girl at least four generations in a row. Each time there were two or three kids with the oldest always being a girl, and it was always the oldest child that was found killed. The only problem was that there was no description of any of the girls except for one hard to believe letter from a gossip column. He had to know one thing in all this; was his friend in danger, was she going to fall victim to this "family curse?"

There were important differences between her and her ancestors though. First off she was an only child. Secondly, and more importantly, she was almost eighteen. Looking back through his notes, Alex saw it was always the first girl born to the family that was killed, but they had never made it past the age of ten. Somehow he was going to have to find out more about her family than her mother wanted even Nadia to know. She was his childhood friend and he loved her, so he felt an inherent need to protect her. At the same time, he didn't want to be cut off from her and her family for digging around in her families hidden past, or worse yet, opening an old wound in a family that had had more tragedies than they deserved. He couldn't let this go though, if her family was somehow cursed, she was next in line.

The next question he had to answer was what could be doing it? It seems strange that one family could lose so many specific people in such a long period of time, unless it was one person, or thing involved. That brought the picture from the funeral back to mind. There was no way to tell if the person in the picture truly was Ethan. True, he looked like Ethan's twin brother, but that picture was several decades old. There was no possible way someone could live that long and not age.

He printed out all the information he found on the family deaths, including the old picture. Taking out a piece of notebook paper, he quickly jotted down all the dates he could find on the murders, then cleared out the search of Nadia's family and typed in a new search for the dates he had jotted down. Was her family the only one struck with tragedy, or did other unexplained deaths happen around that time? Going all the way back to 1890, he started reading through old articles and gossip columns, and to his surprise, a pattern slowly emerged.

TWENTY-THREE

E ven though the path on Mt. Chocorua, the Liberty Trail, had been closed for two solid days, police and fish and game had found no other trace of what had really happened to the murdered college student. The search for evidence in the woods was scheduled to go on for the rest of the week, tomorrow two more groups of search dogs would be added to the already large groups of police officers, photographers, and Fish and Game officers slowly hiking up and down the mountain.

For the moment, one lone police cruiser sat idling at the entrance to the trail in an effort to keep curious kids and townsfolk away from the crime scene. The lone officer sat behind the wheel of the cruiser keeping watch while he willed himself to stay awake. He looked down at his dashboard clock and sighed, it was only three in the morning. His relief wouldn't be there until at least six.

Letting out an exaggerated yawn, he unscrewed the lid to his coffee thermos. It was already his fourth cup of the night, and the way things were going he had a feeling he would finish off the entire thermos long before the end of his shift. In the second it took to look down at his thermos to pour, a dark blur streaked past his front windshield and disappeared into the darkness of the forest. He looked back up, coffee cup in hand, and settled in for another three boring hours of nothing just as the bushes next to his car stopped waving. *This is the last time I volunteer for an extra shift overnight,* he thought.

Just off the trail, a lone figure ran at an inhuman speed into the forest, slowing down just before coming upon the black and yellow crime scene tape marking off the area. Coming to a sudden and silent stop, he quietly stepped under the tape and into the small patch of forest where the college student had been found torn to pieces, being careful not to step down too hard and leave footprints as he walked around. He was able to see everything clearly despite the dark, and it didn't take him long to discover the bloodstained patch of ground the body had been dropped on. Not that he needed to see, the smell of old blood was so overpowering that he could have found this place with his eyes closed. Bending down, he picked up a single stained leaf and put it to his nose, breathing deeply. It was definitely human. Suddenly, he was interrupted by the soft sound of crunching leaves as three large shapes slowly walked up to him, one in front, one on either side. The shape in front of him had made all the noise, and he knew it was on purpose. He knew they were more than capable of walking silently through the forest if they had wanted to sneak up on him. He looked up to see the shape of a very large pale white wolf slowly approaching. The wolf had its head down and ears back, deep growls came from its throat as it bared its teeth at the figure the moment he looked up. Its growls were joined by the growls of its two darker companions on either side, he ignored them. Instead he kept looking into the eyes of the creature that now stood in front of him. *"Tell me, was it you,"* the voice rang clearly in his head, like a sudden explosion of noise in a silent room. He continued looking the wolf in the eyes, and slowly stood up.

"No, I only feed, I don't kill. And even you know I would never leave this much evidence," he said, gesturing to the blood soaked ground around him. The growls subsided from the two wolves on his sides, but grew deeper and louder from the wolf in front of him. It took another step closer, a white ghost in a sea of darkness. It was much bigger than its two companions, its pale white fur unblemished by even a single spot of color. *A rare breed*, the figure thought to himself.

"How can I be sure? I will not risk my pack or my home!" The voice thundered in his head, sending the figure reeling while the wolf's eyes

burned into him, reflecting bright yellow in the faint moonlight between the trees, like a pair of headlights through a blanket of fog.

"Why would I have come here alone if it was me? The old hatreds are long in the past, and I have nothing to hide. There are others of my kind around, and I'll take no responsibility for them, except the one. Still, I don't believe it was one of them. I think the one whom I came for, the one I've been hunting for centuries, is back. This time, I mean to finish it." He held his ground against the white beast, even though he knew he would stand no chance if it was to attack. Very few alphas of this kind existed, one was born maybe every century or two, but the ones that lived had the strength of an entire pack, and the memories of all their ancestors. There was only one way to settle this, and that would be to make use of those memories.

"Did you bring it then? If the scent matches then we will help you, it is our enemy as well." The white wolf stood directly in front of him now, his head almost eye level with the figure standing before him.

"I have it." He said with relief. He reached into a hidden pocket sewn into the inside of his jacket and pulled out a small and battered metal box. He had carried it for a long time, never letting anyone else know of its existence or the secret it held. It was made of pure silver and about six inches long, held shut by a lock so complicated that it took the locksmith over a year to make. A modern day locksmith would have trouble getting into it without destroying it, and locking the box forever. He took a small and intricate silver key out of another pocket and inserted it into the small hole in the front. A series of small clicks came as he turned the key a full circle one way to release the first lock, then pushed the key in further to another hidden slot behind the first and turned it fully back to its original position. A final click and the top popped open for the first time in many years.

"Be careful..." he whispered, and held the open box out so the wolf could smell the old and very delicate object inside.

The white wolf took a small step forward and smelled, the great yellow eyes closing in concentration, digging for a memory over two hundred years old. The two wolves on either side let out a series of nervous whimpers, they didn't want to attack the figure that stood between them; but even more importantly they didn't want to face what he claimed to be here to kill.

After a moment that seemed to take a lifetime the wolf opened its eyes and stepped back. *"The scent matches, we will help you... But I will want to know more about it, soon."*

The figures eye's widened for a split second, half out of relief and half out of fear. He had been waiting for this for a long time, now that the moment seemed near his apprehension for facing his old enemy returned. Still, he would not turn back now. Too much had been lost, too much needed to be repaid. He closed the box, turning the key fully back once, then pulling it out slightly and turning it fully back the other way, locking the box once again. He placed the key into one pocket and the box back into its hidden pocket. He looked at the large white wolf that had now stepped back and relaxed slightly.

"It's going to take more than just us. Can you call on others when the time comes," he asked quietly.

"I can, though, I will not lead them here blindly to a slaughter. They will know the danger, and come of their own choosing. We'll see how many still hold to the old vow of our pack." This time the voice sounded ashamed, as it was forced to acknowledge the fact that the old ways of honor and promise faded away with the memories the younger ones no longer carried.

"I wouldn't ask anything else. I may be able to get others as well, but I can't be sure. My order will only come if things turn truly dire for all of us. Although, if things turn out like before, many could die."

The three wolves stood up and started walking together back into the darkness of the woods. The white wolf looked at the two smaller wolves in turn, telling them something the figure couldn't hear. They both nodded and ran off into the darkness. Just before the white wolf ran off to join them, he turned once more to the figure standing alone in the shadows of the trees.

"And the girl? What is your purpose with her?"

"I have my reasons, and they are my own. She can't know what I am, it may ruin everything. Do I have your help with that as well?"

The wolf nodded. *"The old agreement still stands. Don't kill and you have our help, kill and we will handle things, and you, differently."*

With those words still ringing in the figure's head, the wolf ran off into the darkness. He stood for a moment more, the smell of the wolves now overpowering the smell of old blood. Reaching into his coat, he touched the small silver box one more time. Although his and their bloodlines were traditionally enemies, he was in truth glad to have their help. This time he at least had an idea of what he was up against, and this time things would be planned accordingly. He just hoped they would come out of it alive.

TWENTY-FOUR

Kelly Johnson was a senior at the local high school and a top athlete on both the track and volleyball teams. Her morning routine included getting up early every day to run at least five to ten miles before school, and then got home late after practice to run another five to ten after school. She had slept through her alarm clock that morning and missed her early morning run, a slip that almost never happened and kept her mad at herself the entire day. Determined to make up for her lost miles that morning, she stopped on one of her favorite dirt roads after school, sending a text to her mom to let her know she'd be extra late for dinner. It was called Potter road, it ran alongside Conway Lake and was usually void of heavy traffic. The occasional breeze off the lake in a few spots made the end of the run pleasant, and the steep hills made the run challenging. Usually she reserved this run for pre-competition training, but the lost miles of the morning weighed heavily on her mind.

She parked her car at the entrance to an old logging road just off the main drag, then throwing her hair into a quick ponytail while she stretched and tied her running shoes. She paused just long enough to stuff the speakers of her music player into her ears before taking off, turning the music up on her player and jogging in near perfect step with the upbeat music. She only had a couple of hours of daylight left and no reflectors on her clothes, not wanting to get stuck running in the woods after dark she took off in a hurry and kept her pace fast. In her rush to get going she didn't notice the small and dirty car that slowly pulled off the road behind her and watched as she was getting ready.

The man sitting behind the wheel looked to be in his late teens, maybe early twenties. His eyes were hidden behind a pair of dark sunglasses that contrasted against the sharp features of his pale face. He kept his dark hair cropped short and wore plain clothes, doing his best to blend in so that no one who saw him would give him a second glance. Although his smile was disarming and his face young, he was in fact cruel and deadly, close to two hundred years old. He was a vampire, never staying in one town too long, and never for more than a couple meals. He came into town hungry, expecting to spend a day or two stalking the town in search for a meal. What a stroke of luck it was to have seen this girl pull off onto a lonely dirt road on his very first day in town! Even luckier, she was exactly his type. Young, athletic and beautiful, she was a girl who had a bright future ahead of her. A future he would take pleasure in denying her. He watched her run off with a smile on his face. He would wait just a little bit longer before taking her, following her just until it started getting dark before making his move. He hoped this road would remain empty of all but her for a few hours, but killing off a human witness or two wasn't really a big deal for him if worse came to worse. He turned off his car and watched as she rounded the first corner of the road, noting her long legs, white beneath her small red running shorts, and her blonde ponytail bouncing behind her as she ran. He would cut that off and take it as a trophy. He had hunted them young and athletic as long as he could remember. The blood tasted so much better that way.

He stepped out of his car and shut the door quietly behind him. He could still smell her in the air, could still hear her faint footsteps running down the road. The smell of her made him hungry, the sound of her footsteps made him eager for the chase. Unlike a lot of his kind that he knew and had met over his two centuries, he was very picky about his food. He was also one of the most sadistic. Like a cat plays with a mouse before delivering the fatal blow, he delighted in playing with his victims, often for hours, before finally ending their misery. Such weak little things deserved such torment, plus their screams and struggles amused him. It would be no different with this one. He would catch her, drag her off the road, and cut her open again and again, slowly drinking every precious drop of her blood to the music of her cries. Then he would carry her far into the woods and leave her to the animals. It's a game of death he's played countless times, in thousands of towns with thousands of girls over the course of his second lifetime. None of his victims had ever been found.

In a blur of motion, he took off running after the girl, moving through the woods with the ease of a deer. Sometimes he would stop a ways behind her on the road, watching her jog on, oblivious to the danger that followed. Only once did a car pass her on her way deeper into the woods. The driver slowed down to give a brief honk and wave as he passed her by, she waved back but otherwise never looked anywhere but the road ahead. He followed her silently, never far behind while the sun slowly started to sink. She stopped to look down at her watch after a while, jogging in place. When she turned around to make her way back to her car he slipped further into the woods and let her pass, his excitement growing. It was almost time to take her.

She passed when he was just a few feet off the road hiding behind a large tree, the smell of her so strong that he had to restrain himself from taking her right then and there. He was getting hungry. He was also ready to play.

Fifteen minutes later, shadows started making their way across the road as the sun settled below the surrounding hills. The smile on his face grew and he started shaking with anticipation. Taking off through the woods he passed his still unsuspecting victim and came to a stop just off the road ahead of her, hiding in the shadows between two large pines. She was running faster now, trying to beat the coming darkness and make it back to her car. He waited until she was almost past him before making his first move.

In a flash of movement too fast for her to see, he ran across the road behind her, running one finger along the back of her warm neck as she ran. She didn't slow down, just slapped one hand to the back of her neck thinking it was nothing more than a mosquito. A second later, she felt someone tap her on the shoulder as she ran. She skidded to a stop, almost tripping on the loose gravel on the road and looked around, taking her headphones out of her ears. "Hello," she called out between breaths.

She was greeted by nothing more than the sound of crickets in the woods and music playing softly from the tiny speakers that hung just below her neck. Suddenly she felt her ponytail being gently pulled as fingers ran through her hair and down the upper part of her back. Surprised, she whirled around quickly, but there was nothing there. She was starting to panic a little now; she was still almost a full mile from her car and even further from the nearest house. With a shaking hand, she reached down and turned her music player off, listening carefully.

Out of the corner of her eye she saw a hand come from behind, and felt cold fingers stroke her cheek. She let out a scream and whirled around a second time, once again there was nobody there.

"Where are you? Please just come out..." she called out, her voice barely more than a terrified whisper. Her heart was racing faster than it should have even after a run and she could feel her knees getting weak from fear. From somewhere behind her she felt a movement, and heard someone quietly chuckling.

She turned and ran, she couldn't take it anymore. All she wanted to do was get out of the woods and off this road. She had made it no more than half a dozen steps when something moving too fast to be real came out from the trees, the next thing she knew something caught her by the foot and tripped her. She felt gravel dig painfully into her arms as she landed hard on the dirt road. She let out another yell and pulled herself to her knees, trying to get back up and make another run for it. A cold hand suddenly grabbed hold of her ankle and pulled her back to the ground. Tears of fear were flowing freely now, blurring her vision, she let out a panicked scream and managed to look back but there was still no one there.

The woods fell quiet again, only the sounds of her own terrified whimpers and trees moving in the slight breeze breaking the silence. She stood up slowly, brushing sand and gravel off her arms and legs as she looked around. Blinking back tears she tried desperately to find whoever or whatever was tormenting her, but between the dark blacks and browns of the trees and the steadily darkening road she found no signs of her attacker.

"Who are you, what do you want?" she managed to call out into the darkness.

Suddenly, an arm clamped around her waist and a hand covered her mouth, she felt her body being pulled tightly against someone not much taller than herself. The hand around her mouth was ice cold, the arm around her waist felt like a steel clamp. She kicked and flailed as she was held tightly but it was no use, whoever had her was too strong. She felt the stubble on his cheek brush her face as his hand turned her head to the side, felt his lips brush her ear as he pulled her close. "Your death, your blood..." his voice was cruel, his breath cold enough to make her skin prickle.

Before she could react her feet left the ground and she was spun so fast the forest became nothing but a tangled mess of blacks and greens. The road vanished from sight as she was carried into the forest so fast that the air around her turned into a cold wind. She had no way of knowing how far he carried her, but it was only a few seconds before she was thrown to the ground hard enough to knock the breath out of her lungs. Then he was on top of her, pinning her body down with the weight of his own. She kicked and swung, screamed and twisted, trying desperately to do whatever she could to get away from the dark shape on top of her. It was all for nothing. He grabbed both her wrists with one hand like she was nothing more than a baby, pinning her arms painfully above her head. The bones in her wrist ground against themselves in his powerful grip. Then he clamped his other hand around her throat, gripping so tightly she almost couldn't breathe.

"Shhh..." he whispered into her hear, "there's no use for that out here, no one can hear you, you're mine..." His cold breath blew into her hot face, it smelled like death. He loosened his grip and let go of her throat, his hand sliding slowly up her neck to caress her face, he gripped it in his hand and turned her head one way then the other, looking her over. "You're a pretty one, much prettier than my last. I think I'm going to enjoy this town for a while if I can find more like you." He grinned down at her, his teeth reflecting what little light there was making a dull white slash across the dark shape of his face.

"Please let me go," she was crying too hard to speak, her voice little more than a whisper.

"Oh, I just don't see that happening, it's been far too long since my last meal..." his face came down against hers, the cold tip of his nose pressing against her cheek. She felt herself recoil in disgust when he opened his mouth and slowly licked the side of her face, "and you taste too good to pass up."

His cold hand continued to caress the side of her face as he smiled down at her before pulling it down slowly and lightly gripping the front of her shirt. Adrenaline surged through her as she struggled again to try to get free, trying to wiggle her body into a position to knee him in the groin. She felt his grip on her wrists tighten, heard a crack of her bones as one of her wrists broke. She screamed out in pain and struggled harder, his grip just tightened further.

"Now on to business..." he whispered, as the hand gripping the front of her shirt tightened and began to pull.

"Please no..." she begged. In horror, she looked up so see his grin widen, his white smile reminding her of the Cheshire cat. The sound of ripping fabric filled her ears as the front of her shirt was ripped off like wrapping paper. She cried harder, screamed out in disbelief, this just couldn't be happening.

"Don't worry," he whispered into her ear, "Its not what you think, it's much worse." He chuckled softly as he reached behind his back, her eyes widened as the bright gleam of a blade shone against the light of the moon. He put the blade close to her face, turning it back and forth slowly in front of her eyes. She screamed again and struggled harder than ever, the pain in her broken wrist red hot. He laughed out loud and pressed the blade against her chest just over her heart. Slowly he cut a deep gash into her skin, laughing sadistically at her screams. "I know, I know, it's not *traditional*," he said, sounding almost disappointed, "... but I like to take my time and I don't want you to turn." He bent his face down to the wound and began drinking the blood, she screamed out in agony when he pushed the tip of his tongue against her, licking along the length of the slash.

In her cries and struggles neither noticed another shadow suddenly appear over them. The vampire felt a powerful hand grab the back of his clothes and pull him off his victim. He was thrown backwards into a large pine tree hard enough for the wood to buckle and crack. With a yell of blind fury he focused on the figure that had interrupted his meal, briefly glancing at the girl lying on the ground looking back and forth between the newcomer and him. In a fit of rage he screamed and lunged at the newcomer, moving too fast for any human to see and track. Using only blind instinct to guide himself the vampire lunged forward, aiming to bite down on the newcomer's throat, wanting nothing more than to tear it open. In a movement faster than he could imagine possible the figure twisted and caught hold of both the vampire's throat and arm while he was still in the air, twisting again to slam him into a large boulder. The vampire felt the bones in his left arm shatter on the rock as the figure put everything he had into the attack.

The figure was on him at once, trying to pin the vampire's right arm down before the left arm had a chance to heal. Never in his almost two hundred years had he ever met anyone like this, all he could think was that this was another vampire here to take his well-earned meal from him. Before his right arm was pinned down, he struck the face of the attacker with all his might, knowing it should be enough to tear his head off his shoulders. There was a dull thud and the crack of a bone breaking when his blow landed, but the head remained in place. Slowly his attacker turned and looked down at the vampire under him. The vampire stared his attacker in the face and for the first time in his life felt fear. The attacker's eyes had begun to glow, two tiny points of yellow light shining out of the center of the figure's eyes like two suns in the darkness. The vampire had never seen anything like this before, *it must be some kind of trick*, he thought. He needed to attack now and not let this figure's mind games distract him.

He went in for another blow, putting all his rage and strength into the blow, wanting nothing more than to end the life of this demon with the glowing eyes. With seemingly no effort, his attacker caught his arm midair, and with one quick movement twisted it violently backwards, snapping the bones in the vampire's forearm like twigs. He screamed out in rage and pain and prepared to strike again, the bones in his left arm had almost healed, having every intention on striking up to claw those glowing eyes out of the figure's head. It was too late. Unable to break the iron death grip the shadowy figure had on his throat, the vampire felt himself being lifted off the ground, all his kicking and thrashing as useless to him as it was to Kelly not five minutes before. The figure's eyes glowed brighter as he slammed the vampire against another large pine, one of the dead lower branches pierced his back and stuck out of his ribcage just inches away from his dead heart.

"What do you want..." the vampire choked out. With the bright glow of those yellow eyes blinding him the vampire couldn't make out the face of his attacker, only a black shadow formed the shape of his head around those nightmarish and tiny suns. His ability to see in the dark did nothing for him now, adding to this unfamiliar sense of terror.

"Forgiveness..." the word was no more than whispered in the dark, the sound of a long blade being drawn almost drowning out the attacker's voice.

An instant later the vampire's headless body landed on the forest floor in a burst of blue flame, the forest illuminated with a sapphire glow. Both the body and head burned for a few moments before both turning black and fading into the re-emerging dark. The attacker looked down at the severed head briefly before crushing it under his foot. The head crumbled away to dust and the body collapsed in on itself leaving nothing but a pile of ash. A moment later the light that had been shining in his eyes faded away.

Looking through her tears and terror, Kelly had watched the brief battle with disbelief, unable to make out details of either figure. She tried to make herself small on the ground in hopes that she would be forgotten, that whoever won would walk away without her. Kelly tried sliding behind a tree sending a fresh wave of pain through the gash on her chest, a low whimper of pain escaping her lips. The newcomer turned slowly and looked at her lying on the ground, wrist broken and racked with pain and fear, Kelly knew escape was impossible. He slowly made his way over to her, a black figure coming towards her like a childhood nightmare. Her head began to spin as she felt her grip on consciousness slipping away as he stopped and stood over her. The last thing she saw was the figure bending down; the last thing she heard was her own terrified scream. Then her world turned to darkness.

TWENTY-FIVE

B y ten that morning Sarah and Jason had already hiked a few miles
into the woods, following a small game trail they found branching
off one of the secondary hiking trails leading to Mt. Chocorua. Sarah
insisted they branch off the hiking trail as soon as she saw a break in
the underbrush that the footsteps of countless animals had formed over
the years, much to Jason's dismay. All he wanted to do was get the week
over with, letting Sarah get whatever pictures she wanted before getting back to Boston as soon as possible. He loved camping with her, but
this was something different entirely. The truth was he had hoped to
never set foot in these woods again.

After a few hours of hiking along the tiny and winding path they
found a small clearing next to a stream that looked like as good a place
as any to setup camp for the week. Jason busied himself putting the tent
together and setting up the fire pit while Sarah slung her rifle over her
shoulder and took off along the trail; her cameras set to go and packed
away in her backpack. She had already set two of them out not far from
the camp as they made their way into the woods, and meant to set the
rest up in a large circle around the camp. She was determined to stay out
here until she got what she wanted, even if it took more than the week
Jason was hoping to get out of here by. She felt guilty about bringing
him back out here, she knew he wanted nothing to do with the wolves
again, but she felt like she had to make sure people knew what was out

there, and make sure somebody was trying to do something about it. She truly felt like she would be responsible if someone was to get killed by the wolves she saw and she had done nothing to stop it.

A sound of snapping branches just off the trail made her jump; she quickly swung the rifle off her back and pressed it to her shoulder, swinging it back and forth looking for the source of the sound. Another branched snapped just ahead of where she stood, letting out an unintentional yell she swung around and pointed the rifle at the sound, finger already starting to put pressure on the trigger. A doe and two fawns jumped lightly out of the bushes and onto the trail. The doe gave Sarah no more than a casual glace before stepping lightly off the trail, her two fawns following close behind. Cursing at herself, she took her finger off the trigger and slung the rifle back over her shoulder. If her father had been alive he would have yelled at her for being so careless with it. *"Never point a gun unless you know what you're shooting at and beyond, and keep your finger off the trigger until you've clearly identified your target."* The words her father had drilled into her head countless times rang through her and sent a wave of guilt through her gut. "Sorry dad," She muttered to herself, then adjusted the heavy bag of cameras and made her way down the path.

About ten minutes after the deer the smell of decay blew in, filling her nose strong enough to make her choke, she knew that whatever it was couldn't be too far off the path. Closing her eyes she forced herself to breathe deeply, turning her head back and forth until she found the direction of the smell. A light breeze blew another strong wave of the pungent odor to her, holding in a gag she turned her body towards it and opened her eyes. There was no trail leading off the path, but the underbrush was light enough, and she didn't think it would be too much trouble to push through.

Stepping off the path, she forced her way through some shoulder high brush, carefully avoiding a hanging wasp nest. After about fifty feet the forest opened up into a small field with a tiny babbling brook. It didn't take long to find the source of the smell, just off to one side of the field a dead black bear lay half scavenged and covered with flies. Rifle back in hand, she slowly walked over to the body and bent down.

The ground around the animal was too hard for any tracks, but like the moose that still haunted her dreams, the bear looked like something had torn the limbs off its body. She quickly took out her small digital camera and snapped a few pictures, getting as close to the bear as her stomach would allow. Wiping sweat off her brow Sarah looking around the edges of the field, seeking a good spot to setup her cameras. There were a few trees near the brook that would hold her trail cameras and still be in plain view of the carcass, but with enough low brush around them so it wouldn't be in plain view. "Perfect," she whispered to herself.

Dropping her backpack with a relieved groan Sarah pulled out a camera and made her way to what looked to her like the best of the spots and attached the trail camera to the tree, stopping long enough before walking away to make sure everything was working and turned on. Smiling to herself she stepped behind the tree and peeked around to make sure the camera would have enough view of the field to spot anything that came to finish eating the bear. Satisfied, she walked back and grabbed two more cameras from her bag, repeating the same process on two other sides of the field until she felt satisfied that she wouldn't miss anything that came anywhere near the carcass.

Satisfied with her work Sarah pushed her way back to the trail and started making her way back to camp, every now and then stopping to put another camera up along the side of the path. After about half an hour of walking she made it back, Jason had finished getting the tent set up and was busy making a late breakfast over the small fire he had managed to get going. The smell of eggs and bacon made Sarah's mouth water, she tossed the now empty pack next to the tent and sat down on a log next to him, letting out a tired sigh.

"Any luck" he asked.

"Yeah, I think so," she said, sticking a piece of bacon greedily into her mouth, "look at what I found out there." She pulled the camera out of her pocket and slid closer to him, leaning over so he could look at the little screen on the back. Shading it from the sun with her hand she pulled up the pictures she had taken of the bear. "I think they're around," she said between bites of bacon she was stealing off Jason's plate, "hopefully they'll be back to finish eating what's left." She looked over at him and grinned at the look on his face.

Looking at the pictures of the bear, Jason felt his appetite leave, he shot Sarah a look and sat the rest of his food onto her lap. "You could have shown that to me *after* I ate." He said, nudging her with his elbow. He pushed the camera away from his line of sight, his stomach giving a small lurch as he caught a glimpse the picture on the screen again.

"Sorry about that," she said laughing. She stuffed the camera back into her pocket and sat back looking around, stuffing some more food into her mouth, Jason could be such a wimp sometimes. She glanced up at the bright blue sky and back to Jason, a mischievous smile on her face. "You know, it's pretty hot, and that stream looks awful nice..." She put the plate on the log beside herself and stood up, brushing the back of his neck with her fingers as she stepped away and started making her way over to the stream. Jason sat back and watched her head off, smiling at the wink Sarah gave him over her shoulder.

"We didn't bring our suits..." he started to say, then grinned himself when she took her shirt off and threw it in his lap.

"I don't see anyone else here, do you" she called back, shedding clothes as she walked.

He jumped up and ran after her, his spirits suddenly lifted as all thoughts of the bear left his mind. Neither noticed the large white animal hidden in the thickets behind them. Its bright eyes watched the couple running towards the stream laughing for a few more seconds before turning and running off silently into the woods.

TWENTY-SIX

Alex sat brooding as he watched Nadia from across the cafeteria. He wanted to go over and talk to her about some of the information he had found on her family. Not all of course, just the cliff notes, he wanted to get a feel for how she would react before he told her too much. The problem was, she was sitting next to Ethan, who had suddenly changed lunches to be with her, and of course his two lapdogs were sitting across the table from them. He had no idea how both Ethan and the two brothers had managed to get their schedules changed, nobody else in the school seemed to be able to as far as Alex could tell. The more Alex watched them the more his irritation grew; this was the only period of the day he was able to hang out with Nadia without her jackass of a boyfriend hanging around and making things difficult. After almost an entire lunch of consideration Alex decided to leave them be and just go see her at the restaurant that weekend. He would try to broach the subject of her family's history then.

Turning his attention from Nadia and Ethan, Alex pulled the blue notebook out of his backpack and began looking down at the notes he had made at the library. The newspaper articles he was able to dig up didn't have as much information has he would have liked, but they did have enough for him to discover a pattern of killings and missing person cases as far back as the newspapers went. He had found repeating series of unexplained murders and events, all happening within a year to a year and a half, and all ending with the killing of one of Nadia's ancestors before the papers and town went back to normal. Alex wasn't surprised that the pattern had never been found before, after all it's not like it happened by any real pattern, like every ten or twenty years, it happened once a *generation,* and only once a generation *one family.*

In the oldest cases, things always started off with livestock being killed and drained of all their blood, or being taken away completely, leaving only pieces behind as evidence. Then there would be a period of strange attacks on people, illnesses where they would find strange bite marks and become pale and bedridden. All that would finally lead up to a few scattered disappearances, just not in every case. Alex found a few letters from victims in the gossip columns, all claiming to be the victim of a vampire, and all being dismissed as insane by local authorities. He didn't read through all of those columns, he was looking for real attacks or killings and not old folklore. Brushing the so-called vampire attacks off to the side, he had focused on the unexplained killings and disappearances.

Most of the killings were labeled as animal attacks; the few people that had been interviewed during these cases reported that the victims had been torn limb from limb. When Alex had read that, he had re-read the article about the college student being torn apart in the woods off one of the local trails. That had also been deemed an animal attack. Thinking about the attack on the college student, Alex worried that the pattern was starting up again, minus the livestock killings.

Irritably Alex pushed that train of thought to the side and picked up the half dried slice of lunchroom pizza sitting in front of him and took a bite, thoughtfully flipping through his notes until he found the old funeral picture he had printed off. He looked from the picture to Nadia's table. Ethan leaned over and whispered something into Nadia's ear, it must have been hilarious because she started laughing loud enough for Alex to hear from across the room. Alex snorted and rolled his eyes, looking back down at the picture. Did Ethan have family from this town too? He looked almost exactly like the person in the picture talking to Nadia's great-great grandfather. The person in the picture had a different haircut and clothes but otherwise identical; like a twin brother from a distant past. Alex just couldn't shake the feeling that that old picture was a major clue to the entire mystery.

Alex was watching them thoughtfully when Ethan noticed him looking and shot him the finger. Suddenly Ethan stood up and sat on the lunch table with a loud thud, blocking Alex's view of Nadia, stuffing his hands into his jacket pockets before turning away from Alex and back down to Nadia, Wes, and Dillon once more. Mr. Randall, a teacher from the art department walked over and started motioning for Ethan to sit back down, and although Alex couldn't hear the conversation, he could tell by Mr. Randall's gestures that he was getting more irritated with Ethan by the second. Wes and Dillon watched the exchange leaning back with grins on their faces. Ethan leaned over and got almost nose to nose with Mr. Randall, and for a moment Alex thought he was getting ready to spit in the teacher's face. Instead, Ethan said something Alex couldn't make out, and to Alex's surprise Mr. Randall simply nodded meekly and walked away, leaving Ethan to sit on the table as he pleased. Alex shook his head and looked back down at his food, it just didn't matter what it was, it seemed like Ethan got away with whatever he wanted.

A few minutes later the bell rang ending the period and causing the usual crowds of people streaming towards the trash cans on their way back to class. Alex sat and waited for the crowds to disperse, hoping to at least be able to say hi to Nadia without Ethan and find out if she would be at work that weekend. He turned his attention back to Nadia and Ethan, who was still sitting on the table with his hands in his pockets talking while Wes and Dillon wandered off. Nadia stood up from the table and leaned in for a kiss. To Alex's surprise, Ethan jerked away from her before their lips met, and for just a second Alex thought that Ethan looked genuinely angry she had tried. Nadia started to turn away, looking hurt when Ethan took his hands out of his pockets and cupped her face in his hands, turning her head to face him while stroking her cheeks with his thumbs as he did so. He said something to her quietly and she nodded, leaning her head harder against his right hand. Ethan lifted her face once more and looked into her eyes until she finally gave him a small smile. She leaned her face into his right hand one more time and kissed his palm, Ethen bending down to kiss the top of her head before letting her go.

Nadia walked slowly out of the cafeteria without noticing Alex, still looking slightly hurt. For the first time Alex understood what she was upset about that night on the beach. It was like Ethan really was repulsed by her and just stringing her along. Alex felt his irritation building up and stood as he watched as Ethan make his way to the gar-bage cans. Desperately trying to work up the nerve to walk over and confront Ethan, Alex stopped when he noticed Ethan looking around like he was afraid he was being watched. Alex backed off and hid him-self just outside the door to the cafeteria out of Ethan's sight, leaving his lunch tray sitting on the table.

Ethan looked over his shoulder at the few remaining people before walking over to the trash can and dropping his lunch in, then turned and gave the cafeteria one more nervous glance before quickly taking something out of his jacket pockets and dropping them quickly into the garbage can as well. Without acting like anything was wrong he turned and left the cafeteria, looking satisfied that nobody had seen him throw whatever he had in his pockets away. Alex waited until he was sure Ethan wasn't coming back before walking over himself, grabbing his tray as he went to the same garbage can Ethan had been at moments before. With his own glance around the room Alex peered into the can before dropping the contents of his own tray in on top. There were four disposable hand warmers sitting on top of the usual trash, still hot and melting through the remains of an ice cream bar. Slightly confused, Alex threw his own trash on top and left the room.

Seems kind of warm outside for those, he thought.

The last few classes of the day went by quickly. Alex heard very little of what any of his teachers said and took any opportunity he could to flip through his notebook again. He had considered trying to catch Nadia at the end of the day in the hallway but decided against it. All he really had were theories and he didn't want to upset her again, it looked like she had enough to be upset about after lunch. He'd wait until he got more information before talking to her, in the meantime he had to try to think of more places to look than the public library. He had spent enough time there already and figured he had everything he could get out of old newspapers, and as much as he had looked, he couldn't find anything in local history books that would help out. Lost in thought, he turned a corner too fast and ran into the yearbook table, knocking the money box and sign to the floor with a loud crash. "Sorry about that" he said, face turning red as he bent over to pick up the scattered contents of the table.

The two girls sitting behind the table broke down laughing as they bent over to pick up the sign and some fliers, making Alex's face turn an even deeper shade or red. "That's ok, as long as you buy a yearbook. Two if you really want to make it up to us." The girl closest to Alex said with a laugh. She was dark haired and slightly heavy set, Alex couldn't remember her name but recognized her face from student council elections and knew she was a year below him. Face still red, Alex handed her the money box and managed a small laugh.

"Maybe I will, but I seriously doubt I could afford more than one, just save one of the ones that don't sell and give it to me before they all go in the dumpster." Alex said as he helped pick the rest of the fliers off the floor.

She gave him a smirk before smiling and shaking her head, "nope we don't throw them away, school keeps them all in storage in the old building and a few always go to the library. I bet they have them all the way back to 1900 or something. Shows you how much the school hates to throw away money," she said laughing.

Alex smacked himself in the forehead and groaned, how could he have not thought of that before? He pulled out his cell phone and looked at the time, 3:30, the library would still be open for several hours, plenty of time to get there and see if they had what he wanted. The girl was looking up at him, obviously confused but at the same time had a buy-something-or-go-away look on her face. Alex grinned at her and slung his backpack over his shoulder. "Sorry, you just made me realize I've been both clumsy *and* an idiot. I'll come back and buy a yearbook, I promise."

"You better," She said only paying half attention. Knowing Alex was a lost cause she went back to helping her friend with ordering forms.

Alex walked quickly in the direction of the parking lot. He had no idea if the library would have what he wanted or not, but he wanted to make sure he had plenty of time to find out. He had just turned the corner that led past the locker rooms when something caught his foot, before Alex could react he found himself off balance and falling to the floor. Alex felt someone shove him from behind as he fell causing his head to slam into the metal lockers, white spots immediately filling his vision. Dazed, he tried to get up when large hands grabbed him under each arm and hauled him to his feet, spinning him around quickly and shoving him back so hard his back smashed into the lockers again hard enough to knock the breath out of his lungs. A padlock dug painfully into the small of his back, bringing tears to his eyes. With his head spinning and white spots still floating in his vision, he looked up to see who had attacked him. Alex groaned and looked up to see Wes and Dillon standing over him.

"I thought we had made it clear you were supposed to keep your distance," Wes said, shoving him again into the lockers.

Still dazed, Alex tried to move away from the lockers, but Dillon grabbed a handful of his hair and slammed his head into them hard enough for white spots to fill his vision once more. Alex let out a small yell and reached up to try and pry Dillon's hand out of his hair, but when he did Wes moved forward and punched him in the stomach with an upwards thrust, forcing all the wind out of his lungs once more. Dillon let go of his hair and Alex fell to his knees, tears soaking his face and gasping for breath.

"Next time we see you staring at us in lunch, or spying on Ethan, you're going to get worse than this," Wes whispered into his ear as Alex struggled to catch his breath, "don't think we're not watching you." Wes said as he stood up, slamming his knee into Alex's forehead so hard his head flew back and crashed into the lockers again, this time splitting his scalp and drawing blood. Alex slid down and sat on the floor, his head was spinning and he was having a hard time getting air. Wes and Dillon walked away laughing while Alex got painfully to his feet and made his way out of the building.

The library could wait till tomorrow.

TWENTY-SEVEN

Raymond Stewart pulled his cruiser to the side of Potter Road. At three thirty that morning, a local high school girl, Kelly Johnson, had been found unconscious outside the emergency room door of the hospital. Her wrists were nearly shattered and there was a deep laceration on her chest that took over twenty stitches to close, along with multiple scratches and bruises covering the rest of her body. Whoever had dropped her off failed to report in to the hospital, but *had* given her first aid. Her laceration had been covered, her wrists were in rough splints and she had been wrapped tightly in a blanket. The cameras outside the hospital were no help, apparently when the tapes were reviewed, the cameras showed an empty doorway, then cut off to just under a minute of static before coming back to life to reveal the girl lying alone and unconscious in the doorway. The desk attendant had stepped away to use the bathroom and came back to find the girl alone.

Things didn't get any less confusing after she had received treatment and was lucid enough to give a report. According to her story, she was running alone on Potter Road and heading back to her car when she was attacked. She reported that her assailant moved too fast for her to see, and by the time he had her on the forest floor, it was too dark to make out any details of his face. She said his hands felt like ice and his breath was cold and smelled awful. She said his grip was strong enough to fracture both her wrists with one hand while he cut her with the other, and although the assailant has ripped her shirt off there were no signs of sexual abuse. She reported he had torn her shirt for the sole purpose of cutting her, and that he had started drinking the blood from her laceration before he was attacked himself.

At that point, she didn't remember much of anything, saying everything had gone black. The decision was made to head out to the spot she had been attacked and search for whatever they could find.

Raymond stepped out of his cruiser and waited for a truck to pass before joining the other policemen and dogs that were getting ready to start searching the woods. He walked over and joined a small group of people who were busily looking over a map of the area trying to decide the best place to start looking. An officer Raymond didn't recognize leaned over the map and tried organizing people in an effort to setup a search grid. The man didn't look old enough to shave and yet here he was trying to tell people outside of his department how to do their jobs. Raymond rolled his eyes, he was glad to get help from other departments on cases like this, he just wished they wouldn't try to put themselves in charge just because they were helping out a smaller department, especially if they didn't look like they had any experience.

"I think if we walk ten feet apart in this direction we should be able to find whatever evidence is out there. If we do that, we'll be able to cover most of the ground within the hour, we'll go in one hundred yards before we come back out and search the next area."

Raymond only half listened to the officer leaning over the map and looked out into the woods behind the small group. As thick as the woods were around here he had little hope they would be able to find much of anything. Letting out a sigh, Raymond readied himself for a long hot day in the woods. He was too old for this.

According to the girl, this was the general location she had been initially attacked on the road, and she didn't think she was carried too far into the woods before the rest of the incident happened. If the girl was right, they should find a body or at the very least evidence of a fight before too long. And hopefully clues as to what happened.

More cars pulled up alongside the group, Raymond looked at the K-9 lettering on the sides of the cars and let out another sigh, this one of relief.

At least they were smart enough to get search dogs, he thought to himself. His thoughts were interrupted when another officer, Keith Bennett, walked up and stood beside him, gesturing to the hot and thick woods they were about to spend the day in. Keith was only two years out of the academy and still counted as a rookie in the department, but Raymond had trained him and knew he did good work. Plus he liked Keith, no small thing.

"Think we'll actually be able to find anything out there, gets awful thick the closer you get to the lake," Keith asked aloud.

"I really hope so, I don't want to be out here all day, I'm sure our self-proclaimed captain over there wouldn't mind though, looks like he's making himself right at home." Raymond replied irritably.

Keith looked over to the group of men surrounding the map and to the unknown officer trying to take the lead. Shaking his head he chuckled and leaned in close to Raymond. "Probably doesn't get any respect in his own department and wants to feel special here," he whispered.

"That's the way it always seems to work huh? You should head over to another department and try it yourself rookie, maybe they'll even let you carry a real gun," Raymond slapped Keith on the shoulder and laughed. Keith grinned, taking off his hat he dramatically used it to cover the gun in its holster, turning his head back and forth with his eyes wide pretending to look worried.

"Don't say that too loud, someone might notice my gun's not painted bright orange and take it away" he hissed.

The officer who had been talking to the group frowned and walked a few steps closer to them, "are you gentlemen going to join the search or stand here laughing all day," he demanded.

Still chuckling Raymond nodded his head, "just let us know when to move out Barney, we'll be ready to go when you are. And please tell me you have your bullet in your pocket, I wouldn't feel safe walking out there with you if you didn't." From behind him, Keith snorted trying to hold in a laugh.

The officer frowned and shook his head before throwing his hands in the air and turning around to join the others. A few minutes later the dogs were ready to go and the groups were making their way into the woods.

They walked slowly, the dogs sniffing around while the officers all kept their eyes to the ground. Raymond looked carefully at everything in front of him, the time for joking was over and he wanted to make sure he didn't miss anything. He'd been on the force long enough to know how subtle something extremely important to a case could be; a faint footprint in wet leaves, a drop of blood on a leaf, something that could easily be missed could mean the difference between a conviction and a lost case. Officers and dogs alike made their way in until the forest floor started turning marshy. The girl said she was attacked on hard ground, and she didn't have any mud or traces of mud on her body or clothes when she was found at the hospital. If she had been attacked this far in, no doubt she would have been covered in it.

They made their way carefully back to the road and started another search, putting the first person in line back to the spot the last person had been and moving the entire line down and made their way into the woods a second time. After they came back to the road for the third time they took a small break, carefully marking their places in line before the next search. A patrol car had pulled up with cases of bottled water and handed them out to the searchers, the woods were getting hotter by the minute and everyone's faces were turning red.

By the fourth trip in, Raymond was losing hope that there was anything to find and wondered just how accurate the girl's story was. If she was wrong in her details this case would be a lot more difficult to close, and worse, possibly send people into a panic thinking there was a lunatic on the loose. About fifty yards in the dog on Raymond's right started to act funny. Instead of sniffing the ground eagerly and pulling on his leash the dog slowed down and started letting out a series of low growls and whimpers. Suddenly the dog stopped in his tracks, his whimpering was now completely replaced by a series of vicious growls and his ears were plastered to the top of his head. Raymond and a few others had stopped moving and were looking over to the dog, he had never seen a search dog act like that before.

"What is it boy." his handler asked. When the officer started moving forward again, the dog backed up tight to the end of his leash growling, fighting to pull his head free of the leash.

The other officers had noticed the dog's behavior by then and had stopped to watch. The dog's growls were getting louder and his paws were digging into the ground as his handler tried to pull him forward. Raymond wiped sweat from his forehead and looked from the dog to the spot the dog was fighting to get away from. For a moment, he saw nothing out of the ordinary, just the usual coating of leaves and pine spills between the trees. Suddenly Raymond noticed some of the pine spills looked darker than others, as if they had been carried over and piled up, and hadn't yet had a chance to dry off completely. He walked over to the spot slowly, noticing the pine spills in that spot were just a tiny bit higher than the rest of the forest floor. The dog continued to fight its leash behind him and refused his handlers efforts to move forward. Raymond looked at the handler and motioned for him to stay back. When he got to the spot, he could see the pine spills were indeed fresh, and in a pile no more than half an inch high, but there was something else too. A small pile of grey and black ashes, almost in a splatter pattern, was sticking out of one side of the pile.

"I found something!" Raymond called. The rest of the line came to a stop just ahead and looked back. Keith walked over and kneeled down beside him.

"What do you got" he asked.

"No Idea, looks like ashes were buried here or something, hand me that stick right there." Keith picked up a small stick and handed it to Raymond. He gently removed part of the pile of pine spills, moving them to the side almost one at a time. More and more ashes were buried under them.

"What the hell are those from" Keith asked quietly.

"I don't know but let me try something" Raymond said. Taking out his pocket knife and a plastic bag, he scooped up a small pile with the blade and dumped them in the opening of the bag. Then standing up, he put his knife away and walked to the search dog with the bag closed. The dog looked past Raymond to the pile of pine spills whimpering, but otherwise didn't react. His handler started to say something and Raymond held up a hand to stop him, then slowly opened the plastic bag with the ashes and moved it to the dog's nose. Instantly the dog stopped looking at the spot and lunged, barking ferociously and snapping at the bag, his hair standing on end and his eyes wild. Raymond moved his hand back just in time to keep from getting bit, dropping the bag to the ground out of surprise. It took all the effort the handler could muster to force the dog back. When he finally managed to get the dog away from the scene, the animal pulled his handler in the other direction, tail between his legs and whimpering non-stop.

"What in the world could make that dog act like that? Those pups are so well trained you could teach them to drive the car" Keith exclaimed.

Raymond just shook his head, still a little shaken up from the dog's sudden lunge and took his time standing back up. With shaking hands Raymond picked up the plastic bag and stuffed it into his pocket. It took a moment longer than normal but he finally managed to pick himself up off the ground, allowing another officer who had made his way over during the commotion to steady him. He really was getting too old for all this. Other officers were taping off the area while others were slowly uncovering the ashes and taking pictures.

"I think this is above our pay grade," Raymond told no one in general, "see if you can't figure out where we can send this to get looked at, I'd like to know what the hell it is." Handing the bag over to Keith, he walked to the rest of the ash pile.

"What do you think it is?" The young officer who had put himself in charge was hovered over the pile looking confused. The pile, now mostly uncovered, looked to be in the shape of a body, a headless one.

"No idea, all I know is the more I look at it the stranger it gets, almost as if someone piled it up like this on purpose, look at that." The other officer pointed to a lower portion of the ash pile, then putting a glove on he used a pair of tweezers to pull something out of the pile. For a second no one could tell what is was; then using his other hand he brushed the ash off to reveal a charred and half-melted zipper.

"What's that right there" Raymond asked, pointing out a small piece of metal that was uncovered after the zipper was pulled out.

The officer put the zipper into a bag and carefully pushed some of the ashes out of the way to uncover the object. Then pulling it out of the pile it was obvious what it was. The handle had been burned off and the blade looked like it had started to melt, but there was no doubt it was the remains of a hunting knife.

TWENTY-EIGHT

The only thing that saved Alex from driving his car straight into the lake was that he felt the headache coming on. It had been a few weeks since he had had an episode, and he had truly hoped that they were over. When he left the school and drove home, his head only had a dull throb from where it had been smashed into the metal door of a locker so many times, but by the time he pulled onto the dirt road leading to his house, the dull throb was being replaced by a much sharper and more intense pain. Starting to panic, Alex pulled his car off the road before he even reached his driveway. He could see his house no more than a few hundred feet away, but he didn't want to risk passing out and driving straight past it and into the lake.

Alex managed to get the car turned off and door open as his vision filled with a blinding white light and his head fill with an even more intense pain. Barely getting his seatbelt undone Alex rolled out of the car and fell onto the dirt road. The last thing he remembered before he passed out was losing his lunch in the middle of the road as he tried to crawl to his house, then trying to pull himself up to walk using a wooden split rail fence that ran along the driveway. Alex let out a scream he more felt than heard, and fell once again to the ground as the world around him went black.

Memories within a dream. To Alex it was like watching a movie, and yet being involved at the same time. Things were less dreamlike than the last time he passed out, they were almost, well, solid was the best way he could describe it compared to the liquid feel things gave off the last few times. The memories from his previous episodes came back to him in a flood of images and feelings, still, he feared somehow he would forget everything again soon after he woke. He didn't know how he knew, he just knew.

He could see a young man running through an autumn forest, dressed in a strange green uniform that brought feelings of both pride and fear. The clothes were dirty, torn, the man looked both exhausted and scared, his pale face a mask of sweat and mud, his eyes wide as he continuously looked over his shoulders as he ran. The man running couldn't have been more than 18 or 19, with a similar height and build to Alex. The man's slight build enabled him to easily move through the thick trees and shrubs, ducking low hanging branches and jumping thick knots of roots and underbrush.

There was a strange sense of things as Alex watched, he could see the man running, see the whites in his wild eyes as he looked back every now and then like death itself chased him. Yet, although he could see this person running as if alongside him, Alex could also feel the man's movements, as if every pump of his legs and swerve of his body was not the man's, but Alex's own. Alex could feel the trees that brushed against him, feel the weight of his clothes, even the slap of the man's right boot as the soul, half torn off, sucked into the mud of the forest floor, slapping back up as he ran. The warm breeze had a frosty edge to it, and golden color shining through the leaves did nothing to tame the dread that rose in Alex's chest as he watched this deadly game play out in front of him.

The man was carrying a strange looking yet familiar rifle; it was very long, nearly as long as the man himself, and looked like nothing Alex had ever seen at the sand pit. The length of the gun made it difficult for the man to move when the forest finally closed in around him, getting caught on a mixture of branches and thick thorns, the man yelled out and nearly threw it to the ground. Alex watched the man's struggle, felt the burning in the man's arms as he switched the gun from hand to hand, his terror somehow intensifying beyond the almost unbelievable level it already was. With a quick pull, the man tore the gun free from a thick tangling of branches and thorns, not only snapping branches as he pulled but tearing the tree that held it half out of the ground.

The man turned suddenly, knowing that whatever it was that followed was now nearly on top of him. Alex felt a moment of panic when the man realized he could not get away, that his only options were to fight or die. The dizzying movements in front to Alex stopped as the man lifted his gun and took aim at whatever was pursuing him. The terror Alex felt instantly melted away to the familiar calm he felt when he shot his own gun in his own time at the sand pit. The same feelings of confident concentration swept over him as he watched the man look through a scope that was almost as long as the gun it was mounted on. Then, in the spit second before the runner pulled the trigger, things got stranger still.

Before Alex's eyes the world around the man switched from normal time to what seemed like slow-motion, leaving only the man with the gun immune. The trees and branches swinging in the wind moved slower and slower, the blowing leaves on the ground slowed their movements until they seemed to stand in place. The man's hands and head, however, continued to move at normal speed, unaffected by the change in time that surrounded him.

Suddenly the man's eyes changed, the dark brown coloring started to glow, a subtle change at first, getting brighter and brighter until it seemed like Alex was looking at the brilliant blue of a hot summer sky. His pupils lit up with a bright yellow light, getting brighter than the surrounding blue, making the man look like the sun itself was shining in his eyes, trying desperately to burn its way out, completing the illusion of looking into the sky. As Alex watched this transformation his own vision improved, every stitch on the runner's uniform stood out in perfect clarity, every branch and leaf on the ground and in the trees seemed to glow with their own energy, and the world around became more real and vibrant than Alex had ever seen in his waking life. Suddenly all movement around the man ceased, the branches stopped swinging in the breeze, the leaves on the ground held still, some standing on end or in impossible positions. There was an energy surrounding the man, a yellow mist that hung just above his skin. It seemed to be coming from his very limbs, slowly snaking itself down his arms and through his hands, until finally it flowed into the gun at the moment he pulled the trigger.

For half an instant Alex saw that yellow light shining out of the end of the barrel, like a flashlight beam shining through fog, until Alex heard the thunderclap of the gun going off. A familiar burst of fire erupted from the barrel and the space around the man filled with a thick blue smoke as the gun sent its deadly payload to its target. The lead ball that came out of the barrel glowed with the same yellow energy that had flowed from the man, and Alex saw the fire and smoke give way, as if the energy filling the ball pushed it off to the side and out of its own way.

An instant later time went back to normal. The leaves that had been standing in place fell to the ground, the branches that had stopped swinging began their subtle dance once more. The runner's eyes faded back to brown and the blinding glow left his pupils. As time returned to normal so did Alex's vision, the forest become dull once more, losing the vibrancy that had seemed both so out of place and completely normal not a moment before. The feeling of calm confidence was replaced by elation, Alex could see a small smile of victory appear on the runner's face; it didn't last.

Suddenly the terror returned, like a punch to the gut that would have knocked him down in real life, Alex's heart started to race once more, a relentless pounding that he somehow knew he shared with the man on the ground. As the man's eyes went wide he dropped the gun to the ground, springing to his feet and taking off without a second backward glance. Then Alex felt it, as the running man temporarily left his field of view Alex felt his terror build to a nearly paralyzing dread. That's when Alex heard, and felt, the evil that followed. Dark memories of pain and fire filled his mind, he heard the unearthly growls and snarls of the beasts, smelled death, tasted brimstone, and felt their hatred.

At their steady approach, Alex's mind became clear, full of foreboding. He began to finally sense what they were, and finally understand who the runner truly was. He started to understand his fear, started to remember why they were coming for him, and what they were capable of. They were creatures never meant to walk in this world, an abomination, an insult to life itself. They were monsters born of hatred and violence. They were the war hounds of hell.

The man was now moving through the forest faster than Alex had ever seen anyone run before, even so Alex knew the hounds were gaining ground, eager to tear the life out of the man running before Alex. Alex watched and felt the chase, trying to look back, to see what was chasing him, to confirm what he feared the most. He couldn't. He could only watch the fixed point of the runner, himself a helpless observer, being shown this terrible scene for some unknown reason.

Alex felt the man fall before he saw it happen. One second Alex was trying to look back at the steadily approaching nightmares, then the next he felt his foot slip on a wet and mossy outcrop of rock, sealing his fate. Alex felt the cold damp of the forest floor as the man landed, he felt a branch tear at the side of the man's face, a sharp pain that released a warm stream of blood, further exciting the monsters behind. Suddenly Alex no longer found himself a helpless observer, but actually inside the man himself. Remembering this later, Alex wouldn't be able to explain what happened, one second he was watching the man run, the next he felt himself being pulled into the runner, like a spirit being forcefully taken in by a body.

He looked up from the ground, face covered in mud and burning from the gash the branch had left across his cheek. The light of the forest disappeared, suddenly replaced with a terrible black smoke, thick and poisonous, covering him like a heavy wet blanket. There were two bright shapes circling Alex in the fire, the sounds of growls and hellish barks filled Alex's mind as the two bright forms emerged from the smoke. They were made of both flesh and fire, neither alive nor dead, existing both in this world and in the dead space between the next. As they circled, growling and snapping at Alex's face, the air around him heated to an unbearable level, singeing his hair and burning at his flesh. Alex's eyes watered and his vision became distorted in the heat, like trying to look through a mirage in the desert.

Pushing away the shock of suddenly seeing through the man's eyes and feeling his pain, Alex looked up in horror at the monsters surrounding him. Their teeth were the first thing to catch his eye, a mixture of bone and molten rock, they came within inches of his face as the hounds snapped at him while they circled. Their claws were long and sharp, as if someone cut the feet off a large cat and glued it onto the hounds, with each step they pierced both earth and stone, lighting tiny fires as they made contact with the forest floor. Their eyes seemed to pierce into Alex's soul, swirls of what looked like lava flowed around iris's that looked like burning charcoal. Their bodies were longer and thinner than a normal hound, like a stretched, emaciated mockery of what a hound should look like. They had no fur, instead their bodies were completely covered in a hellish fire that burned backwards, as if a vacuum was pulling the flames back down to hell itself. The smoke poured off their bodies in waves, thick, heavy clouds that clung to the ground the way dry ice creates a heavy fog, surrounding Alex and choking the very air he tried to breathe.

Alex realized his previous vision was repeating itself, this time he was seeing far more than he had before. Instead of coming in at the moment of death he had been forced to watch the events that unfolded before those terrible jaws came crashing down on his face. Alex heard the same horrible sounds the creatures made, once more felt the claws burn into his back, saw the bigger of the monsters approach...

Suddenly his vision faded once more, mercifully before the hound could make its way in for what Alex knew was the killing blow. The burning in his back faded as quickly as the stench of death and the feelings of being in a furnace. There was no sound, no pain. Alex felt like he was being moved through light and water, like his very spirit was being thrown across a vast distance, and maybe to a different time. For a few moments, his head swam and the world was a distorted mash of memories and feelings, that's when he felt the presence.

He didn't know who it was, a guide, or simply intuition, but he felt it all the same. It was leading him somewhere. He felt like the wind itself, blowing over trees and rivers that were slowly forming within the distorted sea of colors below. At once Alex felt himself being forced down, falling faster and faster, threatening to strike the ground like a meteor. Looking down Alex could see the tiny form of a dark figure below, silently stalking among a forest of white birch trees. Faster and faster Alex fell, unable to make out any more details of his surroundings, until finally falling into the figure and looking through his eyes. Once again Alex felt the sensation of being a spirit forced into a body, able to see what he saw and feel what he felt, but unable to control his actions or make his presence known. To his side Alex could still feel the presence that had led him here, like an unseen guide urging him on.

The figure blinked, bringing all of Alex's attention to what this man was seeing, and slowly starting to feel what the man felt. The man slowly continued to make his way amongst the white trunks of the trees, following the sound of laughing voices ahead. Alex felt the man's anger build each time those voices laughed, until finally he made his way close enough to see a couple sitting on the shore of a stream, both oblivious to the person watching them. The man's anger fell upon Alex like a tidal wave, threatening to pull him under and drown him in this man's misery, and amongst the anger a jealousy so dark it threatened poison anyone or anything that came too close to its source. Watching the couple Alex knew all of the hatred and jealousy was fueled by the couple's happiness, and most of all by their love for each other.

By the sounds of their voices Alex thought that they were a young couple, both sitting close to each other, their heads covered with the hoods of the white robes they wore, white silk rimmed with gold, pressing lightly against their bodies in the breeze. The man's anger darkened, and through his feelings Alex suddenly knew the true source of his hatred, knew where his jealousy came from. Although Alex could only see their backs through his host's eyes, he now knew what their happiness was about. He felt their love for each other burning strongly, but above that Alex felt their love for the infant child in the woman's arms.

Throughout all this, the presence remained, still invisible, sending as many feelings at Alex as the man he was currently residing in. Alex could sense feelings of deep sadness coming from it, along with a desire for Alex to understand what was happening. Alex could feel his head spinning with the weight of so many emotions, not only from himself and the man he had invaded, but also from the presence beside him. He worried he would burst from the strength of it all.

Unaware that his actions and emotions were being shared by another, the man moved a little closer to the couple, using the shadows of trees and large bushes to hide in, while the sounds of the stream and laughter of the couple masked his footfalls. The man whispered to himself in an unintelligible language, one Alex had never heard and was unable to make out. As the man's whispering became a steady rhythm of gibberish, Alex felt a sense of dread and imminent death fall upon his shoulders, so strong he could only hope the man he was within didn't notice it too. Instead the whispering became a repeating chant, the words remaining a mystery to Alex.

The couple continued to talk and laugh softly, both too involved in each other and their infant to sense anything happening behind them. Beside Alex the presence fought its own struggle, urges to both flee and fight filled Alex's senses. Alex knew it was forcing itself to watch whatever unfolded, painful as it might be.

Within his strange viewing room, Alex felt a familiar evil approaching from behind, the air seemed to grow colder and hotter at the same time, thick and poisonous. Even in his strange spirit form Alex felt a chill run down his spine; the hellish creatures that had killed him in his other visions were coming. A terrible realization hit Alex like a fist, the person watching the couple by the stream was summoning them.

In despair Alex tried to call out to the couple, tried to warn them to run, but he was helpless, an observer to a scene that had played itself out over a millennia ago. A greater sadness came from the presence next to him, so deep Alex thought his own heart would burst out of his chest. The hounds were just a short ways behind the man now, holding back and waiting for the man to call them to their dark deeds. Alex could feel their hunger to attack, their frustration as the man who had summoned them willed them to stay back. It was like feeling a powerful storm in a bottle, just waiting for the cork to be pulled so it could release its fury upon the world.

Still hidden within the trees, the man approached the couple slowly and deliberately, his anger and jealousy growing with each step. Alex watched the still oblivious couple, one of them threw their head back and laughed, the light hood came off his head and Alex could see him clearly for the first time. He was a young man, clean shaven with shoulder length brown hair. His face was lit by a smile more genuine than anyone Alex had ever met, there was no hint of reservation or maliciousness, just pure and unbridled joy. His laugh seemed to give off a life of its own, spreading joy to everything around him. Alex could feel love swell up from his wife, her happiness and love momentarily masking the darkness that approached them. When his eyes opened to look at her Alex felt a shock go through him, the man's eyes were bright blue, and in the center was the same light he had seen in the eyes of the man in the forest.

Suddenly with a laugh the man got to one knee and held out his hands for the infant. His wife handed the child over, a small bundle wrapped in white silk, eagerly and lovingly taken by its father. Alex heard the baby's happy laugh and squeals as its father took it into his arms. There was so much love and happiness in that one moment that Alex almost forgot everything that was happening, not even the presence he had felt next to him registered in his mind as he watched the three by the stream, just feelings of familiar peace. The man bent down and whispered something into his wife's ear and kissed her on the cheek before laughing and holding the baby up into the air. He stood up and walked down the stream, whispering and pointing things out to the infant. His wife watched him walk away with her head still tilted up slightly, looking like she had wished that kiss had never ended.

Until that moment the man had held his ground just out of sight, watching as the man walked away with his child, waiting for his moment. Alex once again was filled with his anger and jealously, coming back so powerfully it took over all other emotions. The sadness from the presence next to him came back three fold, mixed with the dread that comes moments before an expected yet unwanted event. Alex felt the man grin, an evil and malicious smile that would curdle the soul, and felt him slowly leave the forest and walk towards the woman. The hell hounds felt their moment approaching and moved in closer, their hate and desire to kill thick in the air that was showing the first signs of their black smoke.

The woman bent down over the stream, lifting her hands to gently push back the hood of her cloak, gazing at her reflection in the water. Spirit or no, Alex still felt his heart skip a beat when the hood fell back to reveal her face, horror rose in his chest and he tried to scream. When the light fabric fell back onto her shoulders Alex could see the familiar locks of bright red hair, the familiar curves that made up the profile of her pretty face, even her bright green eyes. It was Nadia.

Within the approaching man Alex tried to scream and thrash, tried to will the man back. All he wanted was for this to stop, to make the dream, or vision, or whatever the hell this was to end. He tried to turn his head away from what he knew was coming, tried to scream out to Nadia over and over as the man came up behind her. No words would come, and no actions he tried to take would work. The man now stood behind her, and throughout all the hated Alex felt there was something else, the elation of a predator that knew its prey was caught. His shadow came over her and Nadia jumped and turned, letting out a scream.

Inside Nadia's attacker Alex struggled to break free. He tried to scream, he thrashed and kicked, did everything he could think of to warn her of the approaching danger, all to no avail. There was nothing he could do, all he wanted now was to look away, to have nothing to do with what was about to happen in front of him, real or not. With an incredible effort his sight started to slowly turn away from what was happening. His head felt like it would burst, his heart felt like it was pumping faster than it was capable. Suddenly Alex screamed, out of the corner of his eye he caught a quick glimpse of the creatures that were waiting to lunge. They were holding back just far enough to keep their smoke from warning Nadia, but they were there. The grass under them had turned black and looked ready to burst into flame, a black scar across the pristine landscape. There were at least five, maybe more, all watching silently with their hellish swirling eyes. Alex screamed again when he felt hands on either side of his face, forcing him to look back through the man's eyes. Alex struggled to pull free of the grip, but the hands held him fast, forcing him to become the man once more.

"I'm sorry, we have no choice, I have to make you see."

The voice was a whisper in his mind from far away, but it was there none the less. By then Nadia had finally seen the man behind her, she was trying to get up off the ground, scrambling backwards in the grass trying to stay out of his reach. Before she had a chance to run the man bent down and grabbed ahold of the back of her robe, pulling her to her feet and turning her around. Alex felt the fabric in his own hands and heard the tearing sound it made as Nadia struggled to break free of his grasp. Nadia screamed out just as the man clamped a large hand around her throat, picking her up off her feet. There was still no sign of her husband or her child.

A mixture of elation and hatred filled the man as he held her above the ground, behind them Alex could feel the hound's excitement and desires to kill. The ground around them was now filled with thick smoke, the water in the stream started to steam and the grass at their feet blackened, in her struggles Nadia coughed at the stench of brimstone and death. The man pulled her in close, her face wet with tears and her eyes wide with terror, unable to cry out as he tightened his grip on her throat. Throughout it all Alex could feel another struggle within this man that made him sick to his stomach, an animal lust and excitement that grew with her terror. He wanted to do more than just kill her, but he also knew her husband would be back soon.

Alex could hear the hounds fighting each other to get closer, their snarling snaps and growls growing in anticipation. The man brought his other hand up and slowly slid it across Nadia's face until his fingers disappeared in the thick tangles of her hair. Her struggles becoming more frantic as she tried to breathe and fight her way out of this man's grasp.

"Shhhhh..." The man whispered to her as he grabbed hold of the side of her face.

Alex tried one more time to make it stop, he thrashed and kicked harder than ever, trying to make whatever he was tear the man apart from the inside, trying to will the man to put her down. He no longer felt any emotions from the man or his guide, his own terror and anguish masking the emotions that flowed into him. Sensing what was coming, Alex's heart raced faster, he could feel the walls of the man's mind as he threw himself against them. With a final sinister grin the man tightened his grasp on her head and throat and stroked her cheek with his thumb before twisting her head to one side with brutal strength.

Alex screamed inside the man's head as he felt the life leave Nadia's body and heard her neck snap. Her struggles instantly ended and her limbs went limp, and with a bitter laugh the man dropped her in a crumpled heap onto the ground. Alex wanted to throw up, unable to look away from the lifeless form laying on the ground. Finally the man seemed to remember the creatures behind him. The words he spoke may not have been English, but Alex knew exactly what they meant.

"Tear her body apart." He said, turning to leave.

Alex felt himself go limp with despair, all desires to fight were as lifeless as the girl on the ground. Suddenly he felt the presence grab hold of him and the sensation of moving through light and water as everything turned black once more.

Alex awoke to find himself back in his own driveway, the sky was starting to darken and the air was filled with the night's chill. The world was spinning and he was unable to stand, his few efforts bringing waves of nausea. Closing his eyes Alex sat still and waited for the feeling of vertigo to pass, something was clutched almost painfully in his hands, but he didn't trust himself to open his eyes and not throw up just yet. After what felt like an eternity the world stopped its constant spinning and held still once more. Alex opened his eyes slowly.

He was still lying just under the spit rail fence that ran along the property, he vaguely remembered using it to try to pull himself up. His car was still parked on the side of the dirt road that led to his driveway, thankfully he had managed to turn it off. Like before, the pain from his injuries were gone, there was no lump on his head and nothing on his face seemed swollen, he was once again healed. Unlike before, the memories weren't fading away, he remembered everything. The thought of Nadia's dead body and the feel of her neck breaking in his hands made his stomach lurch once more, and before he could stop himself he threw up in a coughing and gagging fit.

When the nausea had finally subsided Alex opened his eyes once more, still clutching tightly to whatever what in his hands. They were both filled with large chunks of splintered wood. Confused, he looked up to the fence he had tried to climb and felt his heart skip a beat. When he had passed out he had been holding the bottom rail, a large split log of wood at least eight inches thick. It was no longer attached to the fence; he had snapped it into three pieces.

TWENTY-NINE

After three days in the woods, Jason and Sarah's luck was going from bad to worse. Every camping trick they had learned throughout their lives just wasn't working, making life in the woods miserable. Sarah had made sure to tie all their food into a smell proof bag, hanging it high above the ground, yet the very first night some animal actually chewed through the rope she used to haul the food up, tore the bag open and ate their main supply of food. Jason tried to get Sarah to pack up that morning, but she pulled out the freeze dried food she had stored away and they had been living on that.

On her first trip out to check the cameras on the second day she leaned her rifle against the trunk of a tree for less than two minutes while she changed out the memory card in the first camera. When she turned around the rifle was gone. Thinking she had misplaced it or maybe it had fallen behind the tree she spent almost an hour looking for it, only to come up empty handed. Once again Jason urged her to leave the woods but her insistence, along with a certain form of adult bribery, changed his mind. Luckily they still had Jason's rifle.

That night there was a light rain. Normally that wouldn't mean much to them except that small tears had somehow appeared on all the walls of the tent and on the tarp that covered it. They woke up that night shivering, their sleeping bags soaking wet. Neither of them could figure out why a brand new tent would have so many small tears on its second trip into the woods. Jason was sure he had packed it up carefully the last time they had used it.

The next morning they were forced to pack up camp and move further upstream. As Sarah went to get water for their morning coffee, she discovered a dead and bloated deer, its throat torn out, had either fallen into or floated down to their little part of the stream. Jason almost got sick off the smell, and neither of them had the stomach to try and pull it out of the water. It took them the rest of the morning to find another camp site and get setup.

That afternoon was the straw that almost broke the camel's back. After getting the campsite setup for the second time, they dropped their supplies and reluctantly went back to the stream to cool off and cleanup. Jason's bad mood that had been forming the last two days faded away when Sarah insisted with a mischievous smile that they go skinny dipping in the stream again. Being a mile or two at least from the nearest trail they happily took advantage of the lack of people, and spent the next few hours laughing together in the stream. When they finally got out and back to camp they were greeted with yet another unwelcome surprise. Some animal had pushed the zipper open to their tent and made its way inside. Jason cautiously opened the flap of the door with the barrel of their remaining gun. When no animal jumped out at him he stuck his head inside, pulling it out a second later coughing and gagging.

"Whatever the hell got in there pissed all over our sleeping bags" he exclaimed.

"What do you mean" she replied, shocked.

"I mean, both our sleeping bags are covered in piss and the tent smells like crap" he yelled.

Sarah flinched, he had never snapped at her before. She knew the stress of the last few days was getting to him and she was feeling guilty for making him stay out here. Still, she wanted to see this through. The problem was with most of the food gone, holes in the tent, and now no sleeping bags, she knew it was going to be hard to keep him out here much longer.

"I'll tell you what," she said, "I'll pull the sleeping bags out and get rid of them somehow, maybe burn them, I don't know. We'll let the tent air out today, if it still smells we can use our spare blankets and sleep under the stars. Just give me tonight and tomorrow at the most, and we'll get out of here I promise, pictures or not."

"I don't think the tent is going to air out honey" he mumbled, a little ashamed of his outburst.

"Then we'll throw it out too, it's all torn up anyways. What do you say? Can you give me two more nights? It'll still be less than the week you promised me, and I'll make it worth your while." While she talked she ran her fingers through his hair, something that always calmed him down, and usually helped her get her way. Hoping he didn't catch the extra night she threw in, she brushed his cheek with her hand on the last part, knowing by the look on his face that he was about to give in. He finally relaxed and let out a long breath.

"Alright, just two more nights and then we're getting the hell out of here, and I'm not sleeping in that tent again!"

She leaned over and kissed him on the cheek, then brushing her hands off, she got ready to pull out the sleeping bags and try to figure out what to do with them. Jason carried his pack next to the small fire and got ready to make some coffee.

"I'm going to need this," he said to himself, "and something stronger when we get back home." Suddenly he realized something. "Wait, *two* more night? I thought you said tomorrow!"

Sarah just laughed quietly from inside the tent.

Just outside of earshot from the campsite, a large white wolf watched the couple move around their ruined camp. He had run too far away to make out the conversation and didn't want to risk coming in any closer and being seen. His fur was too bright to hide him effectively this time of year. From here he was downwind and able to smell them though.

Humans have different scents depending on their moods, with enough experience and practice, most of his kind could tell what they were feeling just by the scent in the air. He sniffed at the light breeze coming from their camp, making out enough of what was happening in the conversation by their scent and body movements to know that they were staying. For the past couple days he had done everything he could think of to chase them out of the woods short of scaring them out himself, and them seeing him was the last thing he wanted. With every trick he pulled he could smell frustration on them, especially the male. Today he could smell outright anger and watched closely for any signs of packing it in and moving out.

Things were getting dangerous in the woods around the mountain and he wanted them gone, and if the vampire was right about what they were hunting, he would have no time to babysit these two. When the male calmed down and began tending the fire again, he let out a quiet growl and barred his teeth at them.

"What is it going to take for these two?"

He had to restrain himself once more from charging into their camp and chasing them off himself, but to do that would be the opposite of what he was trying to accomplish. They had seen others from his pack already, they didn't need a second look at his kind to further their ambitions. Only one thing left to do then. If they were still insistent upon being out here he would have to leave them to their fate for a while. He had other business to attend to. With a final snarl at the couple he took off running, a white blur among a sea of greens and browns.

He made a loop away from the camp until he came to the small trail the woman had walked a few days prior. Following the faint scent she had left behind, he came to the first of her trail cameras. He stopped in front of it in time to hear the faint sound if a picture being taken. No matter. He stood with his front paws against the tree and bit down on the camera, then with a quick shake of his head he had it ripped off the tree. The sound of cracking plastic filled the air as he snapped the straps and loops that held it to the tree. When it came loose he swung his head and released the camera, throwing it against the tree with such force that the plastic front shattered like glass to reveal the insides. He took a half second to smell the inside pieces before he found the small memory card that stored the pictures, gripping it carefully in his front teeth he pulled it free, snapping it in half between his teeth. Hopefully when she found all her cameras ruined the woman would leave, and more importantly she would leave with no proof of his kind.

Satisfied with his work on the first camera, the wolf took off running down the trail to sniff out the rest, being careful not to run through any soft mud that would leave footprints. As he ran he swerved to avoid one muddy part of the path that came too close to the stream, missing the sound of another camera snapping a picture just off the path as he ran by.

THIRTY

Two to six weeks. That wasn't going to work for Raymond. The department had sent out the sample of ashes, or at least the "official" sample, down to some lab in Boston. They had promised to have it identified in two to six weeks. Already working on one unsolved case that seemed to be going nowhere, he didn't have the patience to wait that long. Raymond had quietly gone back to the site later that day and filled another bag with some of the ashes that had yet to be collected. Scribbling down a quick note about them on a sticky note in his car and taping it to the bag, he sent it off that day to a teacher at one of the state universities whose class he had failed a few years back.

His attempt at a second education hadn't gone very well.

Raymond had gone back to college wanting to end his career in the forensics side of law enforcement. More money, and a better retirement package. Unfortunately, he wasn't smart enough to make it through all the required courses, too many computers and too many complicated programs to learn to use. The worst part was that he had had to pay for the failed year of classes taken, the good part was that he had been on friendly enough terms with some of the professors, and that they allowed him to come back on occasion and use them as a resource for times like this.

Over the last couple of years, a few of his old professors had either retired of moved on, only a few were still in New Hampshire. Luckily for Raymond, Donald Harris was one of them. Donald was a professor of Biochemistry and considered a genius of his field. Meticulous in his work and obsessive almost to the point of insanity, most of his colleges considered him impossible to work with. Over the years Don hadn't changed much, he was short, skinny as a rail, and bald. Like a few others Raymond has met with well above average intelligence, Donald was very hard to get along with. Donald was also not shy about his general distaste for teaching, and considered most, if not all of his students incapable of learning Biochemistry to a level where they would be capable of making a contribution to the field in any meaningful way.

It was Donald's class, in fact, that had been the final straw in Raymond's decision to give up attempting college so late in his career. Raymond struggled with everything about the class, from the computer programs to the memorization of words he considered too big to be in the English language. After one particularly difficult assignment, with some overly snide comments from Donald, Raymond had had enough. He waited until class was over and confronted Donald at his desk. Raymond let loose with a strongly worded tirade about the treatment he had received from the professor throughout the class, and his declaration that he was quitting college and finishing out his career with some dignity. Donald had simply leaned back in his chair with a big smile on his face. The two had gotten along well ever since.

He pulled into the university and paid his parking, cursing under his breath as he handed over twenty dollars for the privilege. Raymond stepped out of his car and headed to his friend's office feeling like some cop in a crime novel. Part of that was the knowledge that what he was doing was illegal, and any information he received would not be able to be used in any court case that may come out of the investigation. Taking evidence from a crime scene and taking it without permission to a university was grounds for immediate dismissal. But at his age, Raymond didn't care about bending rules a little when he wanted to know something faster than typically came out of standard procedure, but mostly stuff like this kept him interested.

Raymond walked into Donald's office after a few unanswered knocks to find the man hunched over his desk marking papers with a red marker and frowning. From across the room Raymond could see a large "F" marked on the report on top of the pile he was grading. In his concentration, Donald didn't even notice Raymond walk in. Raymond had to laugh to himself a little, the man's face was so close to the paper that the tip of his nose had a red marker smudge across it.

"You know glasses would help you do that a lot better" Raymond said loudly from the door. Donald jumped in his seat, knocking a cup of coffee onto the floor and grabbing at his chest dramatically. Taking a second to catch his breath, he shot Raymond a quick finger. "I would if I could find them. I think one of my students walked off with them earlier this week."

"On purpose" Raymond asked.

"Yes, I think so, for some reason they think I grade them a little harshly" Donald mumbled as he picked up his coffee mug.

"You fail more than half of them if my memories right, myself included" Raymond laughed again.

"I wouldn't have to fail them if they would listen to instructions and do the work properly." Donald looked over at Raymond with a smirk, "and you deserved your F more than any student I've ever had. Anyways just because they are idiots doesn't mean they have to be thieves as well."

"I'd hate to tell you buddy, but most thieves are idiots. So you find anything on that package I sent you" Raymond asked before Donald could go on further about his students.

At that, Donald brightened up and sat a little straighter in his chair, a smile appearing on his face for the first time. Shaking his finger dramatically he motioned for Raymond to wait before nearly jumping out of his chair and running into another room. Raymond sighed to himself looking around the cluttered office and shook his head. The room was so cramped with papers and books that there wasn't an empty chair in sight. Instead, he settled for leaning against the top of a short bookshelf next to the door, being careful not to knock over the pile of papers scattered top.

Donald came back into the room a few minutes later holding a clipboard with a small stack of papers and the small bag Raymond had sent him attached. Seeing the excitement on his face Raymond held up a hand as Donald started to take a deep breath to talk. The last time Raymond had seen that look he had gotten an hour long speech full of words that would take up an entire page of a dictionary to spell.

"Give it to me in layman's terms buddy, this isn't official, I'm not even here. I just want the basic facts, not the chemical makeup or history of the procedures you used."

Donald let a breath out looking disappointed, he was indeed about to get into a long winded speech and was in fact looking forward to it. One of his favorite things to do was build suspense when he talked about interesting findings. Especially findings that interested *him*.

"Ok, if you insist on making it boring for me, so be it. But, I have to tell you even I was surprised at what I found. I ended up staying here for two nights in a row doing more tests to confirm. They were indeed human remains, but I think you knew that already."

"I did" Raymond said knowingly.

"Well, the strange part was not the fact that they were human, it was how old the remains are. When you first brought them to me I thought maybe the person had been cremated, the problem came when I took a closer look. You see, they're not ashes at all!"

"What do you mean? They look like ashes to me" Raymond exclaimed.

"Well, they're not. Let me explain, imagine taking a piece of chicken or steak and putting it down. If by some means the piece of meat doesn't go rotten or get eaten, eventually it would dry out. At first it would be hard like jerky, but after a long enough period of time you would be able to take it in your hand and crush it into powder. That's what you brought me, human powder."

Raymond stood quietly for a minute trying to let the information sink in, then shook his head. This is the second body found in the woods in a condition that makes no sense at all. "How..." he started, then stopped himself when he saw the look on his friends face. "Oh don't tell me there's more..."

Once again the short man gave a grin, "Yes there is, and it gets even stranger from there."

Raymond put his head in his hands, "Damnit... well go on then, I may as well hear the rest of it."

"I ran a DNA test on the remains, and before you ask me how I was able to do that so fast, remember you're not the only one with connections. The results were, well, multiple. In other words there were hundreds, if not thousands of individual samples of DNA in your sample alone."

"How is that even possible?" At this point Raymond was glad none of this was official, this was way above his pay grade, and he sure as hell didn't want to try to write the report.

"Honestly, I don't know. I can only give you a long shot guess. Either someone mixed countless samples of human remains up into one pile, which is highly unlikely considering how hard it would be to find human remains in this condition, or something else entirely."

Raymond motioned for him to go on, he wanted to get out of here and get a drink. "What else could it be?"

"Well, there are plenty of cultures around the world that believed if you consume the flesh of someone else that you could take in their strengths, that they would become part of you. This is partially true, as everything that you eat gets broken down and to some degree becomes part of your body. But if that were true, and you ignore the fact that the DNA would be broken down by the digestive process before being absorbed, then you would be dealing with the remains of a cannibal who had eaten hundreds, if not thousands, of people. And no, I'm not saying I believe that in the least, just a theory derived from old legends and the idiots that believe them."

At this point, Raymond had had enough, in fact, he was kind of wishing he had never sent the sample here in the first place. "Well, thanks for your help, I've got to get back and you need to finish grading those papers."

Looking disappointed again, Donald handed the small stack of papers over to Raymond but kept the bag of ashes, careful to take his clipboard back. "If you don't mind, I'd like to hang on to these for a while. I'll be able to get a better look at them when I get my good microscope back from maintenance, and I'd like to run the DNA test again.

Also, I'd like to show a copy of the findings to a friend of mine. He's an ex-student as well, and one of the most brilliant minds in the field that I have met besides myself; and that's saying something. He would be able to bring in a fresh perspective, he loved these sort of strange cases. It would be off the record of course."

"Do what you got to do, just make sure it stays off the record, the findings and where you got the samples, ok" Raymond said, lifting his eyebrows and lowering his voice to make sure he got his point across.

"That's not a problem at all, just call this curiosity on my part. It's not very often I find something I can't easily explain." He shook Raymond's hand then turned to get back to his grading. Just before Raymond got out the door Donald called to him, "You never asked me how old the sample was by the way." He called.

Raymond stopped and turned to look at him, he forgot about that, but to tell the truth he wasn't sure he even wanted to know at this point, "Ok you got me, how old" he asked.

A final, small smile spread over Donald's face as he looked up from his desk. "I'll have to double check the results of course, maybe run some more of the sample through again, but the results dated the remains to be at least one hundred and ninety to two hundred years old." And without another word he went back to his papers.

THIRTY-ONE

Chugging down the last of his third beer in twenty minutes, Lance Dalton sat alone at the corner of the bar watching the dance floor, glancing over at the entrance every few minutes. He was looking for strangers in the crowd, specifically good looking female strangers. So far it had been a hard night on him, too many of the women here knew him already, and that was a problem. Any woman that got to know him or make the mistake of dating him quickly got tired of him. Tired of his selfishness, tired of his possessiveness, and tired of him losing job after job due to failed drug tests.

The only thing he found that worked consistently was to find a girl who was either new to town and didn't know very many people, or better yet, a girl who was in a relationship of some kind that was going through a rough patch. He could swoop in and be the shoulder to cry on; effectively pulling off the good guy routine until he had gotten what he wanted.

"One more Cindy" he yelled to the bartender over the crowd noise, belching loudly as he slammed his empty bottle down.

Rolling her eyes, Cindy took another of his usual out of the cooler and handed it over, checking it into his tab while he took his first gulps. By the end of the night she knew his tab would be high, "You're not gonna be able to drive home if you keep that up, why don't you slow down for a change" she asked.

Ignoring her, Lance looked back to the dance floor, Cindy had made it clear long ago that she would never sleep with him, and that made her a waste of time and her opinions useless. Just as she shook her head and started to turn away Lance belched and grinned at her. "I'll call a cab if I have to, but I'm not going home tonight if you know what I mean, least not alone. Offers still open for you if you want."

He was leaning over the bar trying to get close enough to sneak in a kiss, even though he knew it would lead to him either getting slapped or punched. Cindy knew his tricks and stood back and out of his reach, rolling her eyes at his offers. "Never in your life, just take it easy tonight so I don't have to get you thrown out of here again." She said, walking away before he could reply.

Taking another long swallow of beer, Lance shot her the finger when he was sure her back was turned, turning his attention back to the door. A new group of people were making their way in and he wanted to make sure he didn't miss any good ones. The first two were a couple he didn't recognize, the girl kind of cute, he'll try for her later when her boyfriend goes to the bathroom. He didn't look big enough to make Lance nervous about hitting on his girlfriend anyways.

Suddenly another girl walked in, this one alone, and all thoughts of lance's previous target were forgotten. She walked in slowly, stopping to look around the small crowd in the steadily filling bar, and to Lance's dismay he saw that more than a few guys had taken immediate notice of her. She was slender, with an athletic build and long legs that stuck seductively out of her torn jean skirt. Her skin was light brown, her face framed perfectly by her long and straight jet black hair, but the thing that stood out the most were her eyes. Light grey, almost too bright to be real and outlined with a hint of dark makeup, in the low light of the bar her eyes stood out like gems. Even to what Lance considered his own high standards this girl was just plain gorgeous, but most of all she was alone.

Lance watched as she looked around the room, making her way quietly to the bar while blatantly ignoring every guy who approached her, sitting down alone at the opposite end. Cindy walked over and bent down, a few seconds later getting up to bring her a glass of red wine. The girl took it with a smile and handed over some cash, but put it down on the bar without a sip, watching the door. Lance waited until Cindy was looking his way then waved her over, shaking the empty bottle of beer to signal for another. She grabbed another out of the cooler without looking and plopped it down in front of him.

"What's the story with her" he asked, motioning to the girl who was still sitting alone and had yet to touch her glass of wine.

"Leave her alone, in case you didn't notice she's got a ring buddy." She said with a warning look. She really hated this guy, if he didn't spend so much at the bar every week she probably would have had him banned a long time ago.

Lance leaning over with a smile and a wink, he took her hand and whispered as low as he could into her ear, making sure she could still hear him over all the noise, "Don't really care about that, rings don't plug holes you know."

Cindy pulled her hand away and shot him a look, wishing she could just slap him across the face. She didn't look back as she walked away, ignoring another guy who was trying to get her attention. Maybe she shouldn't have become a bartender, she really hated all men at the moment.

Lance made a show of looking at her backside as she walked off, then turned his attention back to the girl. She was still watching the door and had yet to take a sip of her wine. He'd have to try to change that, sober girls weren't as easy to get.

Lance had just about finished off his beer when the seat next to her opened up. He jumped off his stool a bit too quickly, stumbling and having to catch himself on the bar to keep from falling. Taking down the last gulp of his beer, he walked around the bar and sat down heavily next to her. She gave a sideways glance and a small smile, then turned away looking around the room and giving occasional glances to the door, careful to avoid eye contact again. Lance leaned in close, to him that little smile meant she was going to sleep with him, he just needed to say the right things to make it happen.

"What's your name beautiful" he asked.

She didn't answer. Instead she looked straight ahead while she spun the still untouched glass of wine between her fingers. When he took another breath and begun to ask again she held up her hand to show off her ring.

"Delilah, not interested. I'm married honey." She spoke with a southern accent and Lance felt his determination rise. Now he *knew* she wasn't local, he decided he needed to work fast before someone else came and warned her off.

Cindy walked over and held out a fresh beer, Lance snatched it out of her hand without looking. Cindy shook her head and leaned over the bar, "everything ok over here" she asked Delilah.

Lance just shot her a warning look while taking a long drink of beer, "of course everything's ok" he said loudly, "go serve someone else, we're talking here." he waved his hand at her, ignoring her angry look.

Delilah smiled at Cindy and nodded her head, "Don't worry honey, I can take care of myself."

"See, I told you we're fine. Go pour someone else a beer" Lance said, cutting Cindy off when she started to open her mouth to speak. With a frustrated wave of her hand and a last glance at Delilah, Cindy turned and walked off.

"Don't push things honey, I'm waiting for my husband and you're getting awful close to pissing me off" Delilah said without looking over.

Lance ignored her and took a gulp from his beer, she was better looking up close than from across the bar. Yep, he was going to sleep with her. He looked around dramatically and leaned in closer to her.

"I don't see him around baby, and something tells me you're sick of him anyways and need to have a little fun."

Delilah's grip tightened on the stem of her wine glass, "trust me, you don't want anything to do with me... baby." Delilah quipped sarcastically. She shot Lance a warning look and slid over in her stool a little further.

He didn't hear a word she said. The only two things that had his attention at the moment was his beer and her chest. He slid himself to the edge of his stool and closer to her, moving slowly so he didn't fall off.

"You know Delilah, what your husband don't know won't hurt him. One little night of fun and you can go back to your boring little life with him, that is, if you can forget about me..." As he said the last few words he slid his hand onto her thigh, stopping just as the tips of his fingers brushed the bottom of her skirt. Instead of jerking back she turned her head to him slowly, rage filling her face.

"I'll tell you this once, take your hand off my leg..." her voice was low and her eyes were locked onto his.

He took his hand off and held both up in an I surrender pose, then finished off the last of the beer and leaned over to whisper in her ear, making sure his lips brushed her hair. "You know what I think," he whispered, "I think your husband doesn't do it for you, and you came here looking for a real man. Blow him off for the night and come home with me, I promise it'll be the best you've ever had."

As he was talking, he put his empty bottle down and reached up with his other hand, running his fingers through the long strands of her hair, brushing the tips of his fingers along the side of her neck. He was too drunk to notice her skin was cold to the touch. The rage on her face became more intense the second he touched her again, then she let it melt away and smiled. She leaned over and put her lips just above his ear, talking softly.

"You know what honey? You may be just what I need after all, if you think you're man enough to handle me that is..." she slid her own hand onto his thigh, "then why don't we get out of here and go someplace a little more private. A little walk in the woods maybe? What do you say?"

With a wink she stood up from the stool and pushed her glass to the middle of the bar. Giving Lance a seductive smile as she passed, Delilah ran her hand across his shoulders and headed for the door. Lance watched her walk out, taking a mental note of which way she turned when she got outside. He took a last look at his bottle, making sure he had finished off his beer before setting it down with a thud. He stumbled off the bar stool and quickly pulled his wallet out, hoping to get out of there before she made it too far.

"Ha! I told you I'd..." he started to say, but when he looked over Cindy was busy on the other side of the bar, and there was nobody sitting next to him to brag to.

Shrugging to himself, he threw the money carelessly down on the bar. Then, with one last glance at Cindy he turned and followed Delilah, the sound of country music fading behind him as Lance ran to catch up.

Stepping into the parking lot, Lance saw no sign of Delilah. He cursed loudly, thinking that she had left him behind. It wouldn't be the first time that happened. The story he'd tell his friends the next day would be the same regardless. He was just about to head back inside when he saw her walking around the back side of the building out of the corner of his eye. Smiling to himself, he took off after her again, following her into the shadows.

"I thought you'd left me behind baby" he called to her.

"And I thought you'd do the right thing and stay in the bar, but I guess we were both wrong" She said, walking further off and into the woods, away from the lights of the parking lot.

"Doing things wrong is how I like it baby." Lance said, following her into the darkness without a second thought.

She led him into the woods, taking him by the hand lightly before letting go and running ahead teasingly. In the dark it was hard for Lance to keep track of her, especially with the combination of her dark skin and his current lack of sobriety. She stopped before getting too far ahead, a strange smile still on her face.

With another small laugh she ran ahead just as Lance caught up with her. For a moment he lost sight of her, his eyes were adjusting to the night by then but he still wasn't seeing things clearly. Frustration was setting in as he tripped over rocks and scraped himself on branches, almost getting mad enough to turn back until he saw her standing next to a large pine tree, one strap of her shirt falling down past her shoulder. Lance grinned and ran to her, cussing again when she giggled and slipped behind the tree, deeper into the shadows.

"Over here honey, if you're not man enough to follow me out here, then maybe you're not man enough to have me" she called from the dark, tempting him further.

"Oh, I'm man enough baby" he said loudly, then listened for her laughter, following the sound through the woods.

She was getting further away and he had to move quicker to close the distance, several times he tripped over a root here or a rock there, unaware that the sounds of the people and cars in the town were getting fainter and fainter. She always stayed just out of his reach, but close enough for him to keep track of her.

At last, he came upon her, standing alone at the entrance to an old and forgotten cemetery hidden deep in the forest. She stood in the entrance of an overgrown stone wall smiling seductively. Lit up by the silver moonlight, her eyes shone like nothing Lance had ever seen, he wanted her badly and knew it was finally time to take her.

"Well it's time baby" Lance said when he caught up to her, slightly out of breath. He looked around at the cemetery, not his usual place. "You sure you want to be out here? Not that I'm complaining but we could go to your place or mine..." he said taking a couple steps closer to her. Her dress clung to her tightly and his eyes took in her curves greedily.

"Little girl's fantasy, my husband never would, you know." As she spoke, she unbuttoned the top of her skirt, tempting him to come closer. Although her smile was daring him to come and take her, he was too drunk to see the dangerous look in her eyes.

"Oh baby, I'll give you whatever you want" He said. They were close enough now so Lance could almost touch her. His eyes kept taking her in, not seeing the smile melt from her face, only to be replaced by a look of animal hunger that had nothing to do with Lance's desires.

"Even though I'm married you still would, you sure that doesn't bother you? Not even a little" she asked, her voice taking on a threatening tone Lance failed to catch. His mind was on one thing and one thing alone.

"Baby, marriage ain't nothin' but a ring and a piece of paper, if he ain't man enough for you then I will be" Lance boasted. He was getting tired of all this talking; he just wanted to get down to business!

Reaching out, he slid his hand onto her neck, working it up until he held the back of her head. He pulled her in close and kissed her, almost flinching away when she didn't kiss back. To make matters worse, her lips were ice cold. Suddenly, Lance got a bad feeling about things. He pulled back, shocked at the look of pure rage that met his gaze.

She looked up for just a second, tilting her head ever so slightly with the tiniest hint of a smile. Then her eyes narrowed and in a motion too fast for him to see her hand came up and grabbed his throat, her fingers digging painfully into his flesh. Lance yelled out and tried to pull away, but her grip was cold and strong, strong enough that for a second he wondered if this is what it felt like to have a pit bull clamp down on your neck. As he struggled he grabbed her wrist, trying to pry her off. Even though her wrist was tiny in his hand he couldn't budge it, it was like steel.

Her look of rage intensified and he felt his feet lift off the ground, then saw nothing but a blur of darkness as she threw him into the graveyard. He rolled over twice before the back of his head cracked against a gravestone, white spots filling his vision. Before he could get to his feet she was on top of him, knocking the wind out of his lungs before he could call out. In surprise he tried to push her off but she grabbed hold of both his wrists and jerked his arms downward, breaking both wrists and dislocating his shoulders. Finally able to get his breath, he let out a scream, she simply looked down at him, still smiling.

"I have friends, I..." his voice was cut off as she once again clamped her cold hand on his throat, cutting off his air.

"Honey..." she said, leaning in close to his ear, her breath cold, "men like you never have any real friends, and they're never missed long, that is if they're even missed at all."

She came down hard and sunk her fangs into his neck, feeding until the sounds of his screams died away and his struggles stopped. Then she sat up and grabbed hold of his head, twisting and pulling in one motion, ripping it off his shoulders. She stood up with it in her hands, looking down at the terrified and dead face in disgust.

"Trash, that's all you were, and that's all you were ever gonna be" she whispered to the head. With a final hiss, she threw it against a large headstone hard enough for it to crack in half as the head exploded in a shower of gore. She wiped her hands off on the grass before standing up and quietly buttoning up the top of her skirt. She walked calmly out of the graveyard and back to the club, wiping the blood off her chin with a torn piece of his shirt before casually walking out of the woods and back into the bar. She still had someone to meet and she intended to be there.

THIRTY-TWO

Alex woke just before the sound of his alarm filled the room. The memories of his blackout, clear and vivid as a bright blue sky just the night before, had started to fade, if only slightly. He still remembered all too much of the nightmarish visions, from being attacked in the woods to a girl's death, a girl identical to Nadia. Though the exact details felt more like a late night movie he had only been half awake for, enough of it stuck in Alex's memory to send shivers down his spine. The question he had now was what to make of the parts he did remember.

Jumping out of bed, he felt physically better than he had in months. Whatever it was that happened during the blackouts to heal his cuts and bruises seemed to be working overtime now. He felt lighter on his feet, more energetic, and when he looked in the mirror he got another seemingly impossible yet pleasant surprise. He looked thicker, more muscular. He certainly didn't look like a bodybuilder, but he didn't look like some 120lb weakling either. Curious, Alex stepped over to his dresser and grabbed hold of the top with one hand. He was able to lift one side off the ground easily, in fact it felt much lighter than he remembered it feeling the day he had to push all his furniture back into place following one of his earlier attacks.

Putting the dresser back down, Alex hopped into the shower, his mind buzzing. Something was obviously happening to him, something was changing him. But what? First all of his blackouts started off as headaches, making him worry that he had some sort of tumor or a late reaction to the car wreck he was in as a child. Now he didn't think that was the case. His recent scans at the hospital had shown nothing unusual, so the likelihood that it was something physical was almost zero.

Was he going insane? Maybe some sort of mental break down? Possibly, but once again he didn't see that as likely. Even though he didn't remember all of them, he knew he had dreams or visions every time he blacked out. He remembered enough from his last episode to scare away sleep for the next ten years or more if he thought about them too much before bed. The problem was they felt too much like memories, too real to be something his brain cooked up on its own. And finally, if it was just a mental break down then why did every black-out seem to co-inside with some sort of injury? An injury that always healed itself by the time he woke up.

Alex stepped out of the shower, his mind had gone from buzzing to spinning. It was all too much to think about at once, too many questions that he really had no answers to. Trying to clear his mind of the seemingly never ending onslaught of questions and thoughts running through his mind, Alex dried off and started getting dressed for the day. Maybe he was looking at this all wrong, overthinking things too much. Maybe it was a bit more straight forward than he thought. Maybe his mind, or something else he couldn't even start to guess at, was trying to make him see something he had forgotten, something he needed to know. Besides, the changes seemed to be helping him anyways.

Alex's mind ran through the remaining images from his visions as he dressed. The forest, the boy, the hounds, the... Halfway through putting his shirt on Alex stopped, Nadia! So far that morning Alex had managed to not think about the worst part of his vision, the one part that remained perfectly clear and the one part he desperately would like to forget. Somehow she had to be part of it. The history he found relating to her family, Ethan's strange behavior both towards Nadia as her boyfriend, and how he seemed hell bent on keeping her away from not only himself but all her other friends as well. Hell, Wes and Dillon even attacked him just for paying too much attention to Ethan in the lunchroom.

Suddenly another thought hit him; was Ethan getting ready to do something horrible? As much as Alex didn't like Ethan, it would be hard for him to imagine something like that happening except for one thing, the picture he had found in the library. It was strange that someone could look so much like Ethan so long ago; stranger still that he had been at the funeral of one of Nadia's ancestors. And in the lunchroom yesterday, Ethan dropping hand warmers in the trash when it was so warm out already...

A sick feeling crept into Alex's stomach; he must be going insane. He was getting ideas that couldn't possibly be true. Insane or not though, Alex knew what he needed to do next. He had to look at those old year-books, but most of all he had to find somebody who knew more about the town's hidden history than newspapers and yearbooks had to offer. Ludolf was right about one thing; this town's past was turning out to have more going for it than he had thought.

Feeling somewhat hopeful now that he had a sense of what he wanted to do Alex threw on the rest of his clothes and ran out the door, stopping just long enough to grab his backpack and wave a quick good-bye to Mark; who looked like he was in the middle of a battle with the fry pan anyways, cursing as he burned his hand and dropped the smoking remains of eggs into the wastebasket.

He was going to get to the bottom of whatever was going on, and he was going to learn the truth about Ethan one way or another, Wes and Dillon be damned. Alex smiled to himself at the thought of them trying to beat him up again, the way he was feeling today, he was really hoping they'd try.

THIRTY-THREE

For what could be the thousandth time, Donald checked the results of the third set of tests he had run on Raymond's sample of ashes. He had checked, double checked, and checked again. Then ran another sample through the series of machines and microscopes the various departments owned throughout the campus and started again. He may not have any friends on campus, but he was respected enough to get results from other departments when he needed things tested, and he got those results *fast*.

No matter how he looked at it, the sample came out the same way. Old, yes, but the sample didn't show signs of being burned, at least not by any normal fire if they had. They were also un-deteriorated, showing no signs of free-radical damage from life or even decay postmortem, they were perfectly preserved. DNA testing, something he was very proud to be able to get done and constantly bragged about, showed some sort of strange mutation that he had never seen. But the biggest shocker was when he looked at it through his most powerful microscopes to try to figure out what that mutation was and why the sample seemed so un-effected by age or decay.

What Raymond thought were ashes were actually tiny, microscopic pieces of dried human remains. They initially looked like beef jerky that had been ground down into a fine powder. When he looked closer at the pieces to see the individual cells themselves, he found that instead of the usual materials that made up the human body, each cell was made up of thousands, if not millions of microscopic crystals. Finally all the strange data, the mutation of the DNA, the preservation, even the way the sample seemed to have been turned into powder, was starting to make sense to Donald in an impossible way!

Somehow, whoever this sample came from was able to mutate their very cells from their usual frail state into something much more durable. If Donald could somehow find a way to replicate this mutation, he could potentially stop the aging process entirely! Lifespans could not only be extended indefinitely, but there was the potential for even more benefits that he could only guess at. This would change the world! His hands shaking in excitement, Donald fumbled through old papers and notes in his desk to find a phone number. As smart as he was, it was going to take at least two minds and several years to figure out the DNA mutation, how it works, and how to use it in regular people.

Finally, after a few minutes of cursing, he pulled out a small sticky pad with a name and cell phone number hastily written across it. Then putting it off to the side, Donald opened an old black phone book and flipped through until he found Raymond's number. Hands still shaking, he had a hard time punching the right numbers. Strumming his fingers on his desk, Donald impatiently waited for Raymond to answer.

"Hello" Raymond asked, sounding half asleep. It was nearly 3 in the morning.

"Ray! Its Don, I've just finished running more tests on that sample you brought me and, well, can you get me more? Is there any way possible you can get me more?"

"I'm not sure if I can," Raymond said mid-yawn, "it's from a crime scene and you're not supposed to have what I gave you in the first place, I could lose my job if it ever got out."

"Nobody has to know that you gave it to me Raymond, I'll be calling in a former student of mine to help me with this, I'll let him take the credit for the initial discovery. But you have no idea what you've stumbled on my friend, this is much bigger than any job. You may have found the fountain of youth!"

Raymond chuckled, in all the years that he'd known Donald he had never once referred to Raymond as "friend." Whatever was in those ashes sure had Don wound right up tight, and there was something in his voice that made Raymond want to at least try to help. Rubbing his eyes, he turned on his bedside light and wrote himself a note.

"Look, I can't promise you anything, but I'll head back out to the woods and see if there's anything left. It was a big pile and we didn't take it all. But Donald, you have to promise me where you got it from stays a secret, I don't care how big it is or what it is, I'm not involved. Got it?"

Donald let out another excited giggle, "Ok, Ok, Ok, just bring me what you can as soon as you can, I'll need to run a lot of tests and I'm not sure what I have is going to be enough. Raymond, this could be the biggest discovery in our lifetimes, I want you to know that."

"Wonderful" Raymond said before hanging up the phone. Donald hung up the phone and pulled the sticky pad over; this time he found it much easier to dial the numbers. It had been a couple of years since he had seen or heard from his former student, but he hoped the number was still good. If he was right, he was about to start a very long process of experiments and research, and for the first time in his life he knew he was going to need help. He just hoped his former pupil was up to the task.

A day later Donald could hardly keep himself from giggling with excitement as he watched his former student peer into the microscope. Throughout his entire career, Donald had been both blessed and cursed with one wonderfully annoying gift; he was too smart. He graduated high school when he was just fourteen, at the top of his class, completed not one but two master's degrees; one in biochemistry and one in mathematics by the age of 19. He completed his P.H.D. in biochemistry by the time he was 21. Answers came to him almost magically throughout his academic career, and he was offered several high level jobs in both medical labs and major universities straight out of college.

The problem was, he had terrible social skills and even less patience. He managed to not only get himself fired at an almost record pace at nearly every hospital and university he stepped foot in, but earned such a bad reputation that few other employers would give him much of a chance. That's how he found himself getting stuck at what he considered a subpar university; cursed to teach students he considered to be of such poor academic quality that they would find themselves lucky to get a job at a gas station, let alone make any real contributions to the world they lived in.

Raymond was one of the small number of students over the years that he found himself willing to interact with on more than just an academic basis. But that was mainly based on the fact that Raymond occasionally brought him things that could peak his interest for more than a few minutes; not on Raymond's intelligence. That he considered as sub-par as every other student that had no business attempting to take his class. This time Raymond had brought him nothing more than a small bag of what appeared at first to be ashes, but turned out to be the most exciting discovery Donald had ever seen.

Carbon dating had confirmed the sample to be anywhere between one hundred ninety to two hundred years old. It was as if Raymond had somehow brought him a ground up piece of a mummy, and from the woods of northern New Hampshire no less! Even ignoring where the sample came from and what it was, Donald still found something strange about it when looking under a microscope. The ashes just didn't look right. That was when he called the one person he genuinely respected as an intellectual equal. A former student from a few years back who breezed through both his regular and advanced class almost as easily as he himself had made it through his own education.

Donald knew the student as Owen White, and in all the years that Donald had taught at the university, Owen had stood out as both the most unusual and brightest student that he had ever met. Owen was a tall, well-built, good looking kid. He was a full head taller than Donald and looked as if he belonged on the football team rather than the chemistry lab. Like Donald, Owen kept to himself, always sitting in the back of the room and never raising his hand to ask questions. Other students, usually female, would sit by him for a class or two trying to get him to talk, blatantly flirting, but they would never stay by him long. Unable to distract him from the lecture or make him focus on anything other than his studies outside the classroom, they quickly moved on.

That focus and lack of social skills reminded Donald of himself and was the sole reason he didn't blow Owen off when he started approaching him outside of class to talk about his ideas on biochemistry. The two had spent many evenings and afternoons debating different experiments and methods, and Donald genuinely enjoyed the time rather than just trying to get through it and get back to his own work.

Regrettably, Owen never finished with his degree at the university. He left suddenly and without reasoning nearly two years ago. He did, however, leave his cell phone number with Donald along with a short note telling him to call him up if he ever found anything that would require two heads put together to figure out. Until now, Donald had never tried the number and was surprised it even still worked. All in all he was glad it did, this was too good to not have another opinion on.

"Well, what do you think? Is it incredible or what" Donald asked. As giddy as he was to share his discoveries, he was getting a little annoyed with the blank look on Owen's face while he peered into the microscope.

"What do you think it is? Looks like dried remains to me? Did you do a chemical analysis? Carbon dating? Maybe DNA testing to try to figure out what kind of animal it was?" Owen asked finally, standing up to look down at Donald.

Donald impatiently waved his hand, "yes, yes, yes... why do you think I called you out of the blue like this? The remains are human, eh well, humans. Carbon dating showed them to be almost two hundred years old. None of that is important though! Look closer and tell me what you see! Look around the edges of the pieces!" Donald was getting worked up now; surely as brilliant as Owen was he should be able to pick this out. In fact, Donald was still mad at himself for not seeing it straight away. With a slight shake of his head and a sigh, Owen bent down once more to peer into the microscope.

"What is it you think you see? It'd be a lot easier for me to look for whatever it is you want me to see if you'd tell me what to look for."

Frustrated, Donald looked up at Owen. He knew Owen saw what he had seen and was holding back, as if waiting for Donald himself to say the words. Then again, Donald had to admit to himself that he was hoping Owen would pick up on it by himself, proving that he wasn't seeing things that weren't there.

"You don't see it? The pieces were never burnt, they were shattered! They don't look like any dried remains I've ever seen. The pieces are crystalized! It's like the very cells that make up the sample were made up of microscopic crystals instead of flesh, and as old as they are, they show no real signs of decay or aging! Look at the data I've printed out, the DNA tests showed hundreds of individual samples from different people all thrown into one. Almost all the minor DNA samples are from females, but the bulk of the main structure shows only one individual male! I don't see how this is even possible but I don't see how the sample could be anything else. Have you ever seen anything like this? It would be the biggest break-through in the last hundred years, or more!"

By now Donald was near the point of shouting, his excitement magnified by flailing hands and non-stop pacing. All the while Owen stood quietly listening to him, a strange look that resembled a mix of fear and despair filling his face. Finally Donald stopped his pacing and shouting, looking up to Owen for some sign of acknowledgement of just how big a deal this was.

"I think you should check your results again, maybe run the sample through again before coming up with any conclusions..." Owen said quietly.

Donald stood in shock for a few seconds. He knew Owen could understand the results on the data sheets. He knew Owen could see the crystallization of the sample, he made sure the microscope was powerful enough and the crystals showed clearly before he even let Owen look at them. Why was he denying this? Didn't he know what this could mean? Confused, he tapped his finger on the stack of papers next to the microscope.

"I know it seems impossible, but I've run the tests through as many times as I could without destroying the entire sample. Every time I get the same results: crystalized DNA from hundreds of individual sources;

no signs of free radical damage in the cells or breakdown in the main DNA structure, other than the obvious shattered look of the crystals themselves. The age of the sample comes back the same every time, nearly two hundred years old. Somehow this individual was able to assimilate DNA from other humans into his own, the crystallization possibly being the by-product. If I am correct, he was able to stop the aging process by somehow using that mutated DNA to build onto his own!" Donald was getting excited again, his voice rising as fast as his hands were moving. He started pacing back and forth as he talked, not seeing the look of growing concern on Owen's face.

"Who knows what other changes his body went through, stronger, faster? I can only speculate. The important thing is if I can figure out how he did it and reproduce it, I may be able to extend human lifespans indefinitely! That's why I called you, I'm going to need help cracking the secret. I found some other unidentified chemical that seems to be what holds everything together, other than the fact that it's organic I can't tell what it is but it seems to have similar properties to that of the venom in some snakes. All I know is it's unlike anything I've ever seen and it will take two heads, not one to figure it out. You're the only person I've ever met that could match me in this kind of study, so I'm asking if you want it. Will you help me crack the code to immortality?"

He was out of breath after his ranting. Pulling a stool out from under the table, he haphazardly pushed some papers that were stacked up on it onto the floor and plopped down, leaning his arm against the table and knocking over even more papers. Owen stood for a moment, looking at the papers Donald had been pointing to, then quietly bent down so he could look into the microscope once more. Donald watched him impatiently, he thought Owen would jump at this opportunity. This kind of quiet and skeptical response was not what he had expected from the brilliant and passionate student he had known a few years ago. With a final sigh, Owen stood up and looked down at Donald. Dark eyes that looked almost black met Donald's, and when he spoke he spoke quietly, but the tone in which he spoke had a little more than a hint of a threat in it.

"I know you think what you found is important, that it can help a lot of people, but I need you to walk away from it."

Looking up at Owen, Donald couldn't believe what he was hearing. Possibly the biggest discovery of their time and he wanted him to walk away from it!? How could he possibly want that? What could possibly be the fountain of youth was sitting in a small bag on his table and documented on the pile of paperwork beside it, a puzzle waiting to be solved. Shocked, he asked, "how could you ask me to do that? I thought you would want to help me, not try to talk me out of the discovery that could define my career."

Owen took a step closer, holding his hands out with a pleading look on his face, "as a friend, I'm trying to tell you that you need to leave this alone. You're not the first to find this, and you won't be the last, but you have to trust me on this, it's dangerous. There are people out there that are sent out to keep these discoveries in the dark. It's getting harder to do, so their strategies are becoming more desperate. Burn what you've found and walk away, please."

The sincerity in his voice made Donald stand up and take a step back, even consider what Owen was saying. "How would you know about any of that, or this" he asked quietly, once again tapping the papers.

Owen glanced down at the papers and Donald picked them up, cradling them against his chest. The look that flashed across Owen's face when Donald picked up the papers sent chills up Donald's spine. He took another step back behind the table, trying to put some distance between himself and Owen. Owens's face went from pleading to irritated; he looked from the papers in Donald's hands to the door behind him.

"I can't let you leave with those, I'm sorry. You're one of the few people I've connected with over the years, so I'm asking you one more time, please just put them down and walk away. I'll even take care of all this for you. As a personal favor to me and yourself, put them down and walk away" Owen pleaded.

The look on Owen's face and the determination in his eyes put more fear into Donald than his size. Something in those dark eyes was dangerous. As Owen slowly walked around the table, Donald crept his hand into his pocket and pulled out a small revolver he carried whenever he worked late at the school. Owen didn't notice the small movement, keeping his eyes on the papers Donald kept clutched to his chest. There was no way that Donald could get to the microscope, but the remainder of the sample still sat in its small bag in the middle of the table.

"I'm sorry too..." Donald managed to get out, while he talked he quietly cocked the hammer back on his pistol. "I just can't leave this, it's too big and it will get me out of this sad little school." He pulled the gun out from under the table and pointed it at Owen.

Owen looked down at the gun and smiled. "Let's not play this game, you know you won't use that." He took another step around the table and held out his hand, "hand it over and..."

His words were cut off by the ear shattering crack of the gun as Donald shot his extended hand. In shock, Owen pulled his hand back and looked down at the wound. Donald took the opportunity to reach across the table and grab the small sample bag before turning and running for the door. He had taken no more than a couple of steps when Owen cut him off, standing between him and the door. Donald screamed in shock, Owen had moved so fast that he didn't look solid until he was already there, cutting off his escape. He had never seen anyone or anything move that impossibly fast.

Donald quickly lifted the gun and fired two more shots into Owen's chest. Owen didn't move, instead he just stood there looking down at Donald, all signs of friendship or pleading replaced by a look of animal rage. Owen lifted his shot hand to his head and pushed back some of the blonde hair that had fallen over his eyes. In horror, Donald watched the hole his bullet had made in Owen's hand finish healing itself in the few seconds that small movement took. The other two shots were hidden by Owens clothes, but by the way he was just standing there looking at him, Donald guessed that those wounds were closing themselves up as well. Finally, Owen broke the silence.

"When I first met you a few years back I figured out, pretty quickly, that you were one of the few people in the state smart enough to know too much if you ever somehow got a sample of us. I left you alone though, when I found that you weren't doing any research that could be related to us, until now. I'm sorry. I tried to warn you to stay away, but you're too smart and too persistent for your own good and you've left me no choice."

In another sudden movement too quick for Donald to see, Owen moved forward and bent down so that they were eye to eye, his dark eyes seemed to burn holes in Donald's head and he wanted nothing more than to run away screaming, or at the very least beg to be left alone. Paralyzed with fear all he could do was stand there and look back into Owen's now terrifying face.

THIRTY-FOUR

Alex couldn't help but feel both a little foolish and nervous when he walked into the library. It was Saturday so the school library was closed, but he figured what they had the public library would have as well. Peggy was working again and she smiled when she saw Alex walk in. Giving what he hoped wasn't too forced a smile in return he walked up to her and waited for a brief second while she answered a phone call.

"What can I do for you today deah? More old papers" She asked.

"Not today," Alex said, "I was wondering if you had any of the old yearbooks from the high school, and if you do how far back do they go?"

"I think we do deah, let me just check on the computah and I'll tell you what we got" Peggy replied.

She put on a small pair of glasses and started typing into her computer using her index fingers, grumbling to herself whenever she missed a key. Alex waited patiently while she fumbled with the keyboard, smiling at the comical look of concentration on her face, it reminded Alex of a child trying to keep his crayon marks in the lines of a coloring book.

"Ah, there they are," she said after a few minutes of typing, "we have them all the way back to when the school opened. What year do you want to look at?"

Alex considered the question for a moment, the picture was dated 1940, but for all Alex knew the boy in the picture could have graduated a year or two ahead of the picture, or maybe not even attended the school at all. He realized that the entire venture was just a shot in the dark and sighed, "I think I'll look at a few, can I have from 1935 to about 1940 or 41?"

"You can look at however many you want as long as you're the one that carries them" she said with a wink. "Go downstairs and past the children's wing, they're in the small reference room across from the bathroom. Section D will be on your far right as you walk in. Room's not used much so you should have it all to yourself."

"Thank you" Alex said, then quickly headed down the stairs.

At one point the bottom floor of the library was nothing more than a root cellar, a bare dirt floor and stone walls that held nothing more than junk collected over the years. Alex could almost feel the change in the air as he descended the stairwell, the subtle smell of damp earth couldn't be held back by the thin walls and concrete floor that were hastily put up during renovations about ten years prior. Alex could even see small stains in the carpet from where the floor was starting to crack underneath and water seep through. The small hallway had a feeling of lonely disrepair, almost making Alex want to turn back. Only the brightly colored nursery rhyme characters on the walls and the sounds of a small group of children laughing at some story kept the place from seeming unusable and abandoned.

Alex paused at the doorway to the children's room when a group of kids burst into laughter. There were about half a dozen small kids sitting in bean bag chairs around an elderly woman who had a book on her lap and a puppet shaped like a dog on her hand. Whatever story she was reading had the kid's complete attention, nobody noticed Alex standing in the doorway for that brief moment.

Moving on he came to the small room marked "local reference." In truth, the room was nothing more than small town politics. Alex could remember Mark complaining about his taxes going up when the library wanted to turn the "root cellar" into a fully useable wing using the children's room as an excuse just so the town hall could have "another place to store their crap," as Mark had put it.

Alex felt along the wall inside the doorway until he found the light switch and flipped it on. It took a few moments for the old lights to come to life, when they did one of the bulbs in the fixture kept flickering.

There was more than enough light to see, but Alex suspected he would have a headache by the end of the day from squinting at yearbooks in the flickering light.

The room was no more than a large closet, stuffed full of everything from old newspapers to thick binders filled with paperwork. There was barely enough room to move between the four bookcases that filled it, one on either wall and two in the middle marked from A to D. Curious, Alex walked around the shelves to see what the library considered local reference. A and B were mostly filled with old town reports and files of tax records, C had hundreds of maps and blueprints on one side, and dozens of binders on the other that were filled with newspaper clippings and pictures from local events over the years.

Uninterested, Alex turned to the shelf marked D, all the yearbooks donated to the library over the years were crammed into two neat rows on the top two shelves. They went all the way back to the early 20's. Having no idea what year to start, Alex grabbed the yearbooks from 1930 to 1933. Not wanting to carry them all the way upstairs just for the comfort of a table and chair, he sat down on the dull grey carpet and dropped two of the books beside himself. He doubted anyone would come in here anyways, considering the thin layer of dust on the bookcase and the flickering lights. He was willing to bet that he was the first person to really use this room in years.

Alex opened the first book, he could smell the age in the musty old pages, a mixture of mildew and dust filled the air as he started to make his way through the faces of the students. Looking through the old pictures, Alex couldn't help but laugh at himself a little. Here he was looking at faces of people who today would be anywhere from ninety six to one hundred years old or older, and hoping to find someone who was only a senior in high school amongst them. Maybe he had gone insane.

It didn't take long to get through the first book and move on to the next, classes were a lot smaller back then and Alex figured if he kept moving up through the years he should really only have to concentrate on the freshmen class before quickly scanning the upper classes in case of a new student. He spent the next hour slowly and carefully scanning each book, pausing every now and then to look twice at some of the more attractive girls or spend time reading the stories and remarks from students.

The cramped space and hard floor were starting to make his lower back hurt, and as predicted the constantly flashing light was giving him a headache by the time Alex pulled the 1939 yearbook off the shelf. He cracked his neck irritably, by then getting the impression that this was indeed on a wild goose chase. There had not been a new student in the yearbooks since 1932 and all the faces were starting to blur together.

Scanning through more freshmen faces, his stomach was rumbling loudly and he was getting more than a little frustrated with himself for even being here. He turned to the last page of freshmen pictures and saw nobody that even resembled Ethan. He stood up cursing and stretched the stiffness out of his back, feeling his spine pop in four or five places. It was time to get out of here and get something to eat.

Alex started to put the yearbook back on the shelf when he realized that he hadn't even gone past the freshmen class, he shrugged and opened the book back up. *May as well finish this one,* he thought. The sophomore and junior classes showed nothing but the same faces he had been looking at in the last few yearbooks; hell some of them even had the same hairstyle in every picture.

It was on the very first page of the senior class that Alex felt his heart skip a beat. There had been a new student transfer in that year, Charles Adams. He had a different hairstyle, but it was still blonde, and there was no mistaking those dark eyes. If it wasn't Ethan looking up at him from that old picture, it was his identical twin brother from 1939. Looking down at the page Alex's hands started to shake, and from somewhere inside he felt anger begin to build. The problem wasn't Ethan's picture looking up through the pages of time; he had almost expected that and was a little relieved if he was being honest with himself. The problem was another picture on the page, the picture of the teacher.

Alex had also seen her face in an old picture before. This time though, she was smiling instead of looking off and she was wearing a light colored dress instead of a black one. It was Denise Roberts, Nadia's ancestor and the mother to then nine year old Madeline Roberts, the girl who would be found dead less than a year later in her own back yard.

THIRTY-FIVE

G roggy and cranky, Raymond pulled onto the dirt road leading to the crime scene a few hours before he was due to arrive at work. He wanted to get into the woods and see if he could get Don what he wanted quickly, and hoped he didn't run into any co-workers along the way. It had been a long, sleepless night after Don had called and he wanted to get some coffee down before work. The girl who had been attacked out here was recovering well and given the ok to talk, and Raymond was determined to get there before the daily sun reporters crowded the room out and stressed the poor girl before he could talk to her. They had managed to keep the story quiet but Raymond knew that would end soon enough, especially with this being the second attack and possible homicide to happen in this small town in the last couple of weeks.

The forest was quiet, except for the sound of his own footsteps and the occasional chirping of birds there was nothing to distract Raymond from his task. It was only about six in the morning, there was still a chill in the air, and the early morning light peeking through the fog gave the crime scene a creepier feel than he would have liked. Raymond stepped over the crime scene tape with a groan and little hope that he would find what he was looking for, it had been almost a full week since the attack and although there had been no rain, he couldn't possibly see a pile of ashes staying in one place for very long. If they were indeed some sort of human remains like Don thought, the animals would probably have scattered what little remained after the forensics team had been there to the seven winds.

It turned out he was wrong. The ashes remained piled up on the forest floor like some sort of grotesque memorial, the only difference being the plastic sheet still covering them and the light covering of pine needles that had settled on top.

Standing there looking down at the outline of the pile under the clear sheet, Raymond thought he could see the shape of a body, a body missing its head. A chill worked up his spine and he shook it off, no use getting the jitters out here, not when where he wanted to be was sitting down drinking coffee in a warm building. He took a plastic bag and some gloves out of his pocket and bent down, carefully pulling small stakes out of the corners of the plastic sheet and peeling it back just enough to uncover a small portion of the pile. He put on the gloves and used the blade of his pocket knife to carefully scoop up some of the now damp ashes into the plastic bag until it was about half full, then sealing it back up and putting it into his coat pocket.

"Hope that's enough for you buddy, because I'm not coming back out here unless I absolutely have to" Raymond muttered under his breath.

The sound of a breaking twig startled him, and he almost fell over turning to see what made the noise. "Hello" he called.

The sound of something running caught his attention, Raymond managed to swing his head quickly enough to catch a glimpse of brown fur disappear behind a large rock. Still bending down Raymond kept still, listening for any other noise and looking for another sign of whatever was on the other side of the rock. Footsteps, so light he almost couldn't make them out crept around the far side of the rock, and the brown head of what looked to be a huge dog peeked around at Raymond.

Raymond's heart raced as he and the dog looked at each other for a few seconds, then with a quick growl the dog turned and raced off through the trees in the opposite direction, leaving Raymond alone once more.

"The hell with this" he whispered to himself. He recovered the ashes with the plastic sheet as quickly and carefully as he could, replacing the stakes with shaking hands. Finally he stood up with a groan and walked back to his cruiser as quickly as he could without running,   he jammed the keys in the ignition and sped out of the woods. He really needed his coffee.

☾

Raymond had no sooner sat down to his first sip of coffee when his phone vibrated in his pocket. It was still early and he really wasn't in the mood to talk anyways, so he waited until the vibrating stopped and went back to drinking. A few seconds later the vibrating started again.

Grumbling to himself, he took it out of his pocket and looked at the number on the small screen, it was Keith. Taking another sip of coffee, Raymond considered letting it go to voicemail but answered it anyways. Keith usually never called him unless it was something important.

"Hello" Raymond asked, unable to keep the irritation out of his voice.

"Ray! Where are you? I just tried calling you a second ago" Keith nearly shouted.

"I know, I was ignoring it hoping it would stop ringing. What's got you so huffy this morning?"

"You're going to want to come in here as soon as you can, there's been a break-in in the evidence room!"

Raymond sat back in his chair, genuinely surprised. This was just a small town with a small town police station yes, but he couldn't think of a way for someone to break into the evidence room without getting caught. "How'd they get in and what did they take" Raymond asked.

"That's the strange thing, you'll have to come in and see for yourself how they got in. It's not how they got in that's strange, it's what they took that'll really make you scratch your head." Raymond had never heard Keith sound this serious, he certainly had Raymond's curiosity peaked.

"Alright you got me, what did they take? And did you get their pictures printed up off the security cameras? We could have them to the sun before noon."

There was silence on the line for few seconds, Raymond heard Keith sigh before he started talking again. "No pictures from the cameras buddy, not this time. Just come in and help us make sense of all this, I sure as hell have no idea what to think of it all. And Ray, the only thing they took were those ashes from the crime scene last week, and we're not the only ones that were robbed. The sample we sent off to the lab were stolen as well."

Raymond reached into his pocket and felt the bag he had filled up that morning, at least there was more at the scene that could be picked up. In reality he was more concerned about somebody getting in and out of the evidence room than what was stolen out of it.

"Ok" he said finally, "I'm on my way in. Find out if someone is going back out to the scene to see if there is more or if the animals have torn them all up. I'll meet you in the security room when I get there, that is if they'll let us in. I'd like to have a look at the video tapes from last night."

"Got ya," Keith said, "but Ray, it's called digital now, we stopped using video tapes years ago."

Raymond smiled a little; at least some of the humor was back in Keith's voice. "Whatever, I'll be in there soon. Just stay out of the real cop's ways till I get there, rookie."

"Screw you too buddy," Keith said with a laugh, "I'll be here anyways." And with that he hung up.

THIRTY-SIX

A lex looked at the photocopy of the yearbook page and scribbled down some notes in his notebook. After he had put the yearbook back on the shelf, he had turned to the binders with all the event pictures and clippings. Comparing his notes from the newspaper clippings to the years marked on the binders, he had searched in vain for more pictures or clues to either Nadia's ancestors or signs of strange killings or happenings in the town. There was nothing to be found except small town gatherings and events since the early 1900's. No talk of the Robert's family, no more pictures of the boy who looked like Ethan. It seemed that they had both kept a low profile.

Alex had left the library feeling a small sense of accomplishment, but also a feeling of dread. Everything he had experienced and found in his research was coming together a little too neatly to be just coincidence. So far his digging had confirmed at least four of Nadia's direct female ancestors in four consecutive generations had been killed. Even though they all died much younger than Nadia is now, they were all the firstborn daughters and all in the direct family line sharing the same last name. The town records he searched had shown that the first little girl had been killed back in 1895, then another in 1914. There was nothing else he could find about the first two except the record of death scribbled down for both, and the mention of them when the next little girl died in 1940. That was the only death he knew much of anything about, including a description of the little girl. There was still one more death he had to find more information on, one Alex felt would tie the rest together, Nadia's aunt.

He had found that she had been killed in 1965, but the only record to be found in the library were basic town records and obituaries. Everything else was removed with a small typed note scanned into the computer that said the information had been removed per family's request. It didn't matter anyways, he knew where to get the information he needed. Alex just didn't know how he was going to get it.

It was tucked away in the old family album Nadia's mother had gotten so upset about all those years back. Somehow he was going to have to convince Nadia's mother to not only let him see it, but also tell him what she knew of a family history she seemed so intent on wanting to bury. He also didn't want Nadia to know about it, at least not yet. If his visions were some kind of warning, and if he was right about Ethan, he was going to have to know exactly what he was up against if he had any real hope of stopping anything from happening to her.

THIRTY-SEVEN

When Raymond pulled into the police station, he had no idea what to expect. The parking lot was as full as he'd ever seen and he had trouble finding a place to park. The night shift people who were usually gone long before Raymond started his shift were all still around, either getting questioned or filling out reports. Trying to avoid running into any of his superiors, Raymond looked around the crowded room for Keith, he wanted to find out what Keith knew about the break in before the chief sent him up to the hospital to talk to the girl. Raymond finally found him walking out to the parking lot looking discouraged.

"Keith" he said, motioning for him to come over. Keith nodded and walked quickly to meet him, grabbing Raymond's arm and pulling him off to the side.

"This is just messed up" Keith whispered, "chief's blowing a gasket over this. Nobody saw anything, nobody heard anything. I managed to peek at the screens when they were reviewing the footage from the parking lot. Man, all I can say is that whatever it was looked like a person, but moved too fast for the camera to get a good shot."

"What do you mean moved too fast? I thought those cameras could pick up anything. How the hell did he even get in? There's no door that goes into the evidence room from the parking lot" Raymond exclaimed in a hushed tone.

Keith just shrugged, "I don't know how to explain it really, I guess it was like watching someone running in a movie with the fast-forward going full speed. You could see the person on camera and make out they were wearing all black and a mask, but man, I've never seen anyone move like that in my life. Seemed impossible really. And they got in through the window buddy."

Now Raymond was really confused. "The window" he asked, Keith just shrugged again. "There's no way, don't we have that window fenced up or something?"

"Yep, re-enforced metal mesh bolted right to the concrete. Go out back and take a look, I think it's still on the ground out there. You'll see what I mean."

Before Raymond could ask what he meant by on the ground the chief walked up. Keith nodded to him and patted Raymond on the shoulder, walking off before the chief could ask him what he was still doing here. Raymond looked to him and gave a quick wave before turning back to the chief.

The chief's name was Chris Peterson, he had been in charge for almost two years now and, all in all, Raymond thought he did a good job at it. He had a medium build and was by no means the biggest guy on the police force, but he was the one nobody wanted to piss off. After graduating high school he joined the police force, making it through the academy at the top of his class and spending almost a year on the force before enlisting in the marines. He then spent nearly ten years in the service before getting wounded in Afghanistan when a roadside bomb went off, taking him out of combat and leaving him with a permanent limp in his left leg. He received an honorable discharge and returned home where he won the spot of police chief by a voter landslide. He still kept his hair cut short and had the constant demeanor of a soldier, running the police station as much like the armed forces as he could without being too overbearing. He was the first police chief Raymond had worked for that he genuinely respected as more than just a politician.

"What happened" Raymond asked. Chris's jaw clenched and he shook his head. Raymond could tell he was furious and had no idea where to start, or whose head to put on a platter for it.

"I'm sure by now you know there was a break in in the evidence room. Whoever it was took that bag of dirt we got from the crime scene in the woods. The sample we sent to the lab was stolen too not long after, same person as far as we can tell. Moved too fast for the cameras to make a positive ID and ripped the fencing over the window right off the concrete wall."

Chris cursed and shook his head again, Raymond couldn't tell if it was in disgust or aggravation, probably a bit of both. "I know you're probably going to want to stay here with us and try to figure out what happened, I know it was your evidence that was stolen, but I need you to head up to the hospital and talk to the girl, have her re-tell the story now that she's lucid. Parts of it sounded off the wall before, now I'm not so sure."

Raymond just nodded, he'd been expecting this anyways and really didn't want to sit around looking at camera screens or filling out paper-work all day. "I'll head up there now, call me if anything changes or if you find anything ok" Raymond requested.

"I'll try to remember, I think a few heads are going to roll for this. Never in my life..." Chris cut himself off and shook his head again. Raymond could see he was getting himself worked up thinking about the break in, and he sure didn't want to be around when the inevitable blow up happened. Chris was too serious about things running smoothly and people doing their jobs right to take this quietly. Raymond decided it was time to head up to the hospital.

"Good luck sir, I hope this gets sorted out quickly."

"Me too. Let me know what the girl says" and with that he walked off towards the security room where certain members of the night crew waited nervously. Taking the opportunity, Raymond left the station and got into his cruiser. It was going to be a long day.

"I'm here to talk to the attack victim, Kelly Johnson. We were told that she was able to talk and I'd like to get a statement" Raymond told the secretary sitting behind the check in counter. She peeked curiously at his badge before nodding and typing Kelly's name into the computer. Raymond stood drinking his second cup of coffee as he waited for her to pull up the information, lack of sleep was setting in and he could feel his irritation rising when she paused to answer the phone. When she finally looked up at him and gave the room number Raymond had to force himself to remain polite. With a forced thank you, Raymond groggily sipped his coffee and headed through the automatic doors towards the recovery and observation wing. He was met at her door by a short bald doctor who looked even more irritated than Raymond felt. Meeting the doctor's eyes, Raymond got the impression that the man was genuinely sorry to be forced to acknowledge the existence of another person in the same room.

"Can I help you" the doctor asked curtly. Raymond looked down and read his name badge. The picture on it showing a mirror image of the bitter expression that the good doctor now had plastered on his face.

"Yes, Dr. Richardson," Raymond said pulling out his badge, "I'm here to get a statement from the attack victim, but since I've caught you here can you tell me anything I should know about her?"

The doctor rolled his eyes, "I'm not at liberty to talk about my patient or her condition, whatever you need to know you can get from her." And without another word he started to walk away, Raymond side stepped in front of him and held up a hand.

"The girl is eighteen, not a minor, and she is the only witness to her attack. I need to know what you know in order to help her case. Now, I can either get a court order for her records and be forced to call you down to the station to tell me about them, or you can make this quicker for both of us and tell me about them here and now."

The smaller man's face got red, and for a second Raymond thought the man wanted to hit him, but instead the doctor let out a grunt and opened up his laptop, quickly typing in Kelly's name and pulling up her file.

"The girl was attacked. She suffered multiple scrapes and bruises. She had two broken wrists. She had a deep laceration on the left side of her chest. She lost enough blood to require a transfusion. She was found unconscious outside of the emergency room alone six nights ago. No signs of sexual assault. Anything else?" He asked curtly before starting to walk away again.

Raymond once again stepped in his way, feeling an urge to throw his coffee in the doctor's face, but he didn't want to waste a good cup and kept his composure. Making himself take a deep breath, Raymond took a gulp of coffee before asking the next question, "can you tell me why she's still here at the hospital, seems to me six days is a long time for broken wrists and a cut."

Rolling his eyes again the doctor sighed and looked back up from his computer. "Well, it's a good thing you're not a doctor then. She suffered from some sort of poisoning yet to be identified. It was a very tiny amount but it almost killed her, seemed to be causing some changes in her body on a chemical level, but there either wasn't enough of it, or it worked its way out of her system after four days. She'll be under observation until we're sure she's clear of whatever it was" the doctor explained.

"How did she get poisoned in the attack? A needle? What do you mean changed her on a chemical level" Raymond asked almost to himself.

The doctor's grip on the laptop tightened, looking more irritated then ever he rubbed his eyes and shook his head at the ground, "I don't have time to get into all that, and I doubt you'd understand anyways. The poisoning seemed to be in her blood and it seemed to emanate from the laceration on her chest. Like I said, it almost killed her, but at the same time it seemed to increase the healing process on both her wrists and her laceration. It also appeared to make her physically stronger for a short period." The doctor held up his hand when Raymond started to talk, "we don't know why so don't ask. Now is there anything else or can I get back to my patients before they check themselves out?"

This time Raymond rolled his eyes, he was tired of talking to this irritating doctor and anxious to talk to the girl. "One last thing, what can you tell me about when she was found? Did the cameras show her arrive or who may have brought her here?"

The doctor snapped the laptop shut. "Do you see hair on top of my head? Oversized ears perhaps?"

"What do you...?" Raymond started.

The doctor cut Raymond off mid-sentence, "do you see a furry tale growing out of my ass or a small red jacket with little gold bells on my shoulders? No? Then obviously I'm not one of the trained circus monkeys that works security here. I suggest if you want to know anything about the cameras or what was shown on them, you should go to the security room and talk to your fellow community college graduates and leave the grownups to do our jobs. I have patients to attend to, and none left for you. Talk to your victim, get your statement, and let me get to work." With that he took off in the opposite direction before Raymond could respond.

Muttering a few choice phrases under his breath, Raymond walked up to the room and knocked on the door.

"Come in" a small voice called from inside.

Raymond walked in, eager to talk to anyone other than the short man that just walked away from him.

THIRTY-EIGHT

Alex decided the rumbling in his stomach was too much to ignore, and as it was still reasonably early in the day, he stopped off to get a quick bite to eat and see how long he would have to talk to Nadia's mom before she went home from work that day. The small dirt parking lot of the diner was almost full, not unusual for a late Saturday morning. He took a quick glance around the parking lot and didn't see Ethan's car, and with a sigh of relief he parked and went inside.

The small restaurant was full of people and the sounds of conversation. It took the cashier a couple of minutes to even notice Alex had come in while she tried to sort out a large families' bill. Finally, she looked to the door and saw Alex waiting to get a seat.

"Sorry Alex, busy this morning. You want a table in Nadia's section" she asked.

"If she can handle another customer" Alex said with a grin.

"I'm sure she can handle having you there, she's training a new girl so she'll have some help anyways." She marked a spot off on the seating chart and led him to the smaller room behind the main dining room. Alex thanked her and waited quietly for Nadia to show up, listening to a couple next to him argue about where to buy a new TV.

"Kind of late for breakfast isn't it" Nadia asked from behind Alex, making him jump. He looked up at her and grinned.

"Kind of rude to be sneaking up on customers isn't it" he asked playfully.

She grinned down at him and rolled her eyes, "Well, you don't count, I know you'll be back no matter what I do" She said laughing.

As she was talking, another girl walked up behind her holding a pot of coffee and Alex felt his heart skip a beat. She had long black hair tied up into a neat ponytail that hung down to the middle of her back, light brown skin and light grey eyes that felt like they could look straight into his soul. He had never seen a girl that beautiful in his life. For a moment all he could do was stare until Nadia stepped between them and smacked Alex lightly upside the head.

"Alex, this is Delilah, she just started working here and we're hoping she stays past the summer. Delilah, this is my friend Alex, we grew up together just up the road from here."

Delilah smiled down at him and held the pot of coffee out, "nice to meet you, coffee?" she asked, her southern accent making her even more attractive to Alex.

"Umm, yea... sure..." he managed to get out.

Nadia rolled her eyes again and stepped to the side while she poured Alex some coffee, then motioned to the rest of the tables in the room. "Could you see if anyone needs a refill while you have the pot out here, then we'll head back and carry some orders out."

"Sure thing" Delilah said, giving Alex a wink before walking off.

"Umm bye... nice to meet you..." Alex murmured as she walked away. When her back was turned, Nadia lightly hit him on the side of his head again.

"Don't stare like that, it's just her first day and I don't want her scared off. It took me too long to finally get some help in here" she said quietly. Alex felt his face get hot.

"Sorry, just the usual" he said quietly.

Nadia looked quickly around, then bent down close to his ear, "I'll try to find out if she's single." She whispered. Then with a wink, she stood up and wrote his order down. "That gonna be all for now Alex?"

"Yea, that's all," he said, "I need to get back home and get working on my project anyways, I've been slacking off. What are you up to the rest of the day? Meeting up with Ethan or something?"

"Nah, he's gone for the weekend" she said, waving off the question, "I have a feeling I'll be here most of the day, boss likes to stay open till the place empties, then we have to do inventory. I swear I feel like I never get to see the outdoors during the summer anymore."

"Well, at least you have a job. If you feel like it, you should stop over after work, been too long since we've hung out." Alex said, unable to keep the bitterness out of his voice, Nadia didn't seem to notice.

It had been a long time, they hadn't spent more than an hour together since she started dating Ethan. Alex had always been annoyed with how Ethan kept her to himself all the time, but now that he thought it may have more to do than him just being a jealous boyfriend, Alex was going to have to try harder than ever to separate her from Ethan. At least until he found out what was going on.

"I'll try, it has been too long. In the meantime, try not to scare my help off, ok" she joked quietly before heading off to take orders.

Alex watched her go, resolved to eat as fast as he could and get out of here. If he was going to have a chance to talk to her mom, today may be his best oppertunity. At least he knew Nadia wouldn't be home for a while. Now he just hoped her mom wouldn't throw him out of her house when he came asking questions she didn't want to answer.

Nadia lived with her mom in a small, year round cabin next to the lake. In fact, Alex could have driven home and walked to her house, but he was afraid of losing his nerve if he stopped anywhere else. He pulled up to her house slowly, the sound of gravel crunching under his car tires marking his approach. Still, that subtle sound was enough to bring Nadia's mother to the door, smiling and giving Alex a friendly wave as he drove up. *I May as well get this over with*, he thought to himself.

Her name was Margret Roberts, the middle child of three, her older sister, Nadia's aunt, had been killed when she was too young to remember, and her younger brother, Steve, hardly ever came around. Unlike Nadia, both Margret and Steve had straight dark hair and brown eyes, and for the longest time the joke around the town was that Nadia wasn't really Margret's daughter, a joke that made Nadia furious every time somebody brought it up. Nadia was an only child and she and her mom were very close, her mother had never married and since her uncle never really visited, they were the only family each other had. Alex had always liked her and she had always treated him like a son, and the smile on her face as she waited for him to walk up to the door made Alex second guess if he wanted to have the conversation he was about to with her. She was the closest thing he could remember to having a mother.

Alex got to the door and nervously clutched the blue notebook with all the notes and photocopies he had found in his research. She pulled him in the door and gave him a hug, then led him into the small kitchen and sat him down.

"Alex, sweetie, it's been too long, I've missed you! You want some tea? Maybe some coffee? I was about to pour myself a cup, I can get one out for you too dear," she didn't wait for Alex to respond, instead getting out a second cup and pouring coffee into it, then sitting down across from him with a smile.

"So how have you been" she asked, "I never get to see you anymore and Nadia's off with Ethan all the time, makes things a little too quiet around here for me."

Alex sipped his coffee and gathered his thoughts, he didn't want to jump right into this, but at the same time he didn't want to get too distracted with small talk either. For all he knew, Nadia could come home at any time, and if she overheard any of what he was thinking she probably wouldn't talk to him for a long time. Or ever again if Alex was right about Ethan.

"He's kind of the reason I'm here, I need to talk to you but I'm kind of afraid you'll throw me out and not let me come back" Alex said nervously.

Margret smiled over her cup at him and gave a wink, a habit she and Nadia shared. "I don't think you have to worry too much about that sweetie, you know I'm not overly fond of him either. Just between you and me, I kind of wish she would have broke it off a long time ago" she said the last part quietly, as if afraid Nadia would walk in and overhear her say it.

"It's not about him just dating her, I've been doing some research for a big project at school, I've had to look up some local history and, well, I've found some things and I think, well I…"

She held out her hand and put it on top of his, giving it a small pat, "go ahead sweetie; you know you can always talk to me."

Alex took a deep breath, may as well just say it and hope for the best. "I think Ethan has something to do with the deaths in your family, and I think he's back for Nadia."

Margret jerked her hand back quickly, the smile instantly fell off her face and she gave Alex a look that made him cringe in his chair, "Alex, that's not funny. Why on earth would you say something like that?"

Alex knew he had to be careful with what he said, he knew this all sounded crazy enough even with the evidence he had gathered. But also, he knew he needed to know what Margret knew just to confirm his theories. If he didn't say things just right, Alex knew she would shut down on him and he would never find out what he needed to know.

"Please, just hear me out for a minute, I know it sounds crazy but I, well I found a picture…" he managed to stammer out. With shaking hands, he slid his notebook onto the table and opened it just enough to pull out the copy of the funeral picture and the article it was attached to. Slowly, Alex pushed the papers across the table in front of her. Margret was about to say something when she looked down at the picture, her eyes instantly widened and her face went pale.

"Where did you…" she started to say, then looked at the face of the boy talking to her great grandfather from all those years back, "Oh my god…" she whispered.

"Please," Alex said quietly, "let me tell you what I've found and what I think. You know I would never bring anything like this up if I didn't think it was real and I didn't think Nadia was in danger. You know me…"

209

Margret's eyes never left the picture, tears dropped onto the photograph that neither bothered to wipe away. "I've see this before, why didn't I..." she whispered almost to herself. She slid the picture back across the table and looked at Alex, this time with a hint of belief in her eyes.

"Ok," she said, "tell me what you've found."

With a sigh of relief, Alex started at the beginning when Ludolf had handed out the assignment and Alex had started his research. He told her about Ethan's strange behavior with Nadia, how he had been keeping her away from both him and her other friends, all the while not getting too close to her himself. Alex even told her about the incident with the hand warmers in the lunchroom, and Wes and Dillon's attack in the hallway. The entire time she sat and listened, occasionally sipping her coffee or wiping her eyes, but it wasn't until Alex brought out the yearbook picture he had found that he got the reaction he was waiting for.

THIRTY-NINE

Kelly looked up at Raymond as he entered her hospital room and the first thing he noticed was how pale her face was and the dark circles around her eyes. It gave her the look of a skeleton, so much that Raymond had to hold back a shudder. With a weak smile she motioned for him to sit down on the chair next to her bed, pushing away a table holding a tray of untouched hospital food while he sat down and pulled out a small notebook.

"I look worse than I feel, doctor says he thinks I'll make a full recovery in a couple more days" she said.

Raymond felt a small pang of guilt for his reaction when he walked in, he'd never had a problem with bodies at a crime scene or the brutal wounds he sometimes had to photograph on victims, but the sight of someone who looked so close to death always unnerved him.

"I'm glad to hear that," he said finally, "I hope your doctor treats you a little better than he did me just a second ago." He tried to make the joke light-hearted and ease the poor girl into his questions, but the only reaction he got was her rolling her eyes.

"Yea, he's just awful. I don't think he could say anything nice if he tried. My parents said he's very good though and that I should just put up with it. Personally, I think I'd rather have someone not so good if he's always gonna be like that." She motioned to the small notepad in his hand and finally smiled. "I thought all you guys were using laptops and tablets now, what's with the paper?"

Raymond chuckled and sat back in his chair, it felt like he was sitting on a rock but he made himself look as comfortable as he could. "I guess I'm just old-fashioned, never did like those computers. If you think you're up to it, I'd like to ask you some questions about the attack."

"Go ahead," she said, "I can't get it out of my head anyways. I even dreamed about it when I was knocked out from whatever poison they said I had in me."

"OK," Raymond said gently, "start from the beginning and tell me what you remember."

She took a deep breath and pulled a small silver cross on a gold chain out from under her hospital gown, wrapping the chain around her fingers she looked back to Raymond. "Sorry," she said, "it keeps me calm when I think about it. My dad gave it to me after I was baptized years ago. He told me my faith could protect me from whatever evil's out there, I just wish I had it on when I was running, maybe it would have stopped him." Tears were starting to form in the corners of her eyes as she fumbled with the cross, all Raymond could think to do was give her an encouraging nod.

"That's ok" Raymond said, motioning for her to go on.

"Well I stopped off on Potter Road to take my afternoon jog. I've been going there for years ever since I read the Harry Potter series," she laughed to herself softly, "silly, I know, but it always seemed to bring me luck at the track meets. Anyways, I was trying to make it a fast jog because I started late and wanted to get done before it got too dark. I was on my way back to my car when someone tapped me on the shoulder. I turned around but no one was there, so I just kept going. I thought it was just my imagination since I was still running, but then I felt someone run their fingers through my hair. I remember taking my headphones out and calling, but nobody answered. That's when I felt cold fingers touching my face. I looked around again and didn't see anybody, but I heard him laughing at me. I remember panicking and running away, but then he grabbed my ankle and I fell. Then I...."

At that point Kelly started to cry, she held up the hand holding the cross for him to wait just a second. Raymond didn't say anything, he let her cry. A few minutes later she managed to stop, then she tapped the cross on the side of the cast on her other hand like she was using it to knock on a door. With a final sniffle she looked back to Raymond.

"Sorry, it's just hard to think about it" she said with a weak smile.

"Do you need a break? I can get you a soda or something" Raymond offered. Kelly just shook her head no and kept going.

"No, I need to get this done. After I fell, I yelled out and asked what he wanted. Then he put his hand, his cold dirty hand, over my mouth and told me he wanted my blood." Stopping for a moment, Kelly shivered and gripped the cross tight against her chest, covering the right cast with fingers sticking out of her left cast.

"That was when he picked me up and carried me into the woods. I swear we were moving so fast I thought I was on a roller coaster. I didn't know anything could move that fast in real life..."

Raymond thought about what Keith had told him earlier about the thief moving too fast to be real. This case was turning out to be too much.

"Do you need a break" Kelly asked, noticing Raymond looking off. He shook his head at her and smiled.

"Sorry about that, us old guys do that from time to time, keep going, I promise I'm listening."

"It's ok, I know I sound crazy" she said with a small, unsure laugh.

Raymond was about to tell her she didn't but just as he opened his mouth to say it she held up one finger and kept talking.

"When he brought me into the woods, that's when things got really bad. I was fighting and screaming, I don't even remember when he broke my wrists, I just know I screamed louder when he did. Then he ripped off my shirt and I thought he wanted to... well, you know. That seemed worse to me than anything else, until he brought out that knife. He said he didn't want to turn me, whatever that meant, that he wanted to go slow... that's when he cut me." While she talked, her eyes started to get wide as she stared off at the wall, remembering that awful night.

"His breath was cold," she said still looking at the wall, "but when he put his mouth on me, when he licked me, it burned. I think that was the poison the doctors told me about, something on his tongue, all I know is it felt like fire. He was sucking the blood out of my cut when the other showed up and pulled him off."

"The other" Raymond asked, interrupting her.

She looked over to him, confused.

"You didn't know? He's the one who brought me here."

"Who was he? What did he look like?" Raymond asked. Kelly just shrugged.

"Don't know, it was too dark. He was bigger than the other, he threw the smaller one around like a doll. I think I was losing it by then because I swear he pulled a glowing sword out from nowhere and stabbed the smaller one. They said something to each other before he did, but I couldn't hear it. The last thing I remember was the smaller one that attacked me looked like he caught fire for a split second, a bright blue fire, then fell down and burst into dust. I was screaming when the bigger one walked over to me and, and I swear his eyes were glowing yellow in the middle. Anyways, that's all I saw before I passed out and woke up in the hospital."

"Is there anything you can tell me about the bigger one? Any features you remember? Hair long or short? Stuff like that."

She shook her head. Still holding her cross, Kelly settled further into her bed and shivered. Raymond could see she was getting too tired to talk much more, and he wanted to check out the security footage before he left. "No, just that he was bigger than the one that attacked me and his eyes..."

"You said they were yellow? I thought it was too dark by then to tell that."

"No," she said quietly, "they were *glowing* yellow. They looked like the reflection you see when a cat looks at you sometimes, but they weren't reflecting anything, they had their own light."

Raymond breathed in heavily. *Poor girl must have been out of it pretty bad by then*, he thought. A buzzing in his pocket distracted him, frowning, he reached in and took his cell phone out. Keith had sent him a text message. He fumbled with the phone for a second, muttering to himself, he was never any good with these things. Kelly looked over and giggled softly, then held her hand out for the phone.

"Let me see it, don't worry, I won't read it, just pull it up for you" she assured him.

Raymond really didn't want to hand it over to the girl, but then again, it may be important and he didn't want to wait till he saw Keith again to figure out what he wanted. He really hated cell phones. Embarrassed, he handed it over. Kelly took it from his hand and touched a couple of buttons before handing it back over, "just hit the big one in the middle, it'll pull up the message."

"Thanks," Raymond said, hitting the button she pointed out.

"Sorry buddy, nothing left at the crime scene, looks like the animals tore it up just before we got there."

"Damn," he muttered to himself. Donald may not get what he wanted after all, it may have to go into evidence.

"What did you say" Kelly asked. Raymond looked over to her and shook his head.

"Sorry about that, just talking to myself. I'll let you get some sleep."

She smiled at him tiredly from the bed, "thank you, I am getting tired. Feel a little funny too, guess I need some sleep."

Raymond stood up to leave, then a thought occurred to him, he turned back to Kelly. "What was it you told your parents you thought attacked you anyways? I promise I won't think you're crazy."

She looked up at him from the bed, Raymond thought the circles around her eyes had gotten darker in the short time since he had walked in. Finally, she answered him in an almost matter of fact tone.

"Isn't it obvious? It was a vampire."

Walking down the white hallways, Raymond felt sorry for the poor girl once more. She had been through a lot in the last week and now he was afraid it was going to take her years to get past it, if ever. There was no way he could believe she was anything but delusional.

Vampires didn't exist outside of horror movies and folk tales, and they certainly didn't exist in the small town of Conway, New Hampshire. This was going to make the case harder to solve, and even if they did find the sick SOB who attacked her, no jury or judge in the world was going to believe her story.

Another thing was bothering Raymond as well. With the evidence stolen from both the station and the lab part of the sample was sent to, he was going to have to use the ashes that currently sat in his pocket to try to solve this case. It may be the only thing that will link the attacker to the girl in terms of physical evidence, the clothing that she had worn the day of the attack were still at the lab and he had little confidence that they would find the same ashes on them.

When he reached the small security room, the door was slightly ajar. Peeking in, Raymond saw a young man staring at several screens that were running through various parts of the hospital. He gave a knock on the door and the young man turned around quickly, startled by the appearance of someone at the door. Raymond held out his badge.

"I'm Raymond Steward, Conway police department. I'm here to ask about the night Kelly Johnson was found outside of the emergency room." He put the badge away and held out his hand, the young man stood up and gave it a quick shake.

"Name's Doug Harrison. Sorry, I wasn't working here that night but I'm happy to help you out any way I can."

Raymond stepped into the small room and pulled a chair out from under the set of TV screens. He raised his eyebrows to Doug in a silent question and Doug motioned for him to have a seat. "I'd like to see the tapes of that night if you have them, specifically the ones from the emergency room doorway where she was found. Also, do you have the name of the nurse on duty that night?"

Doug shrugged and gave Raymond a regretful look. "I can show you the tape, I just don't think it's going to do you any good. The screens may show different parts of the hospital, but every camera has a 24 hour memory. We saved the tapes from the emergency room that night but they don't show anything except an empty entrance way, then they shut off and when they come back on the girl is laying alone just inside the doorway. The nurse on duty that night was away from the desk at that time and didn't see how she arrived."

Raymond raised his eyebrows again, "What do you mean they shut off? I've never heard of a camera just shutting off."

"Neither have I. Here, have a look," Doug replied, sliding his chair over to a blank television screen. He turned it on and pulled an old VHS tape off the shelf. It was blank eccept for a piece of masking tape with question marks hastily scribbled with a marker. "Don't laugh at my tape," he told Raymond with half a grin, "it's all we can afford in the budget."

He pushed the tape in and pressed play before Raymond could respond. The quality of the tape wasn't all that great, but Raymond didn't have any trouble seeing what was going on. The doorway to the emergency room was lit bright enough for the camera to see clearly through the glass and into the drive up lane just past the sidewalk. Doug pointed to a corner of the screen. "Pay attention to the time, notice it's just past 9:25 pm here, then..."

The screen started to flicker, then at 9:26 the screen filled with static. It stayed that way for about half a second before coming back to life once more, first flickering static, then a shot of Kelly laying in the entrance-way alone. When Kelly's image came up, Doug tapped the corner of the screen. It showed 9:28 pm. "It may not look like much of a difference, but it is. My supervisor blew it off but I couldn't, that's why I made an extra copy of the tape. I've never once seen an almost two minute lapse in footage. The strangest part is that the camera still had power running to it, otherwise it wouldn't have kept track of the time. Having to reset the timers on the security system after power failures is part of my job."

While Doug was talking, Raymond watched the screen, it took nearly five minutes for the nurse to come back and find the girl on the floor. Whoever dropped her off must have brought her in at almost the same moment she had left her desk. He jotted some notes down in his notebook and stood up to leave. "Can I get a copy of the tape for my records" he asked Doug.

"Sure thing, I'll have one sent to the station today. I hope you catch the bastard." He stood up and shook Raymond's hand. Raymond thanked him and left the room, then a thought occurred to him.

He looked back down at the notes of his interview with Kelly and something didn't make sense. If she got attacked just at dark, then why did it take more than an hour for the girl to be brought to a hospital that was just over twenty minutes away?

He decided to stop at her room one more time to see if she was awake. Maybe she could remember something about that time, maybe not, but he at least wanted her to think of it in case something came back to her later. He was just about to her door when he heard her begin to scream horribly inside. Without knocking, he opened the door and rushed in.

Kelly was screaming at a pitch that almost seemed inhuman. Her back was arched to the point that only the top of her head and feet were still touching the bed. Her eyes were rolled up into her head, and to Raymond's horror it looked as if the whites of her eyes were full of blood.

Before he could call for help a nurse ran into the room and rushed to Kelly's side. She tried to get a needle out when Kelly grabbed hold of her arm, and still screaming, began to thrash around. The nurse dropped the needle to the floor and started to scream, her eyes wide with pain. Raymond felt his stomach lurch as he heard the bones in her arm break.

Now, it was the nurses turn to thrash around. She tried to pull her arm free of the smaller girl's grip without success, her hand was turning blue and hanging at a strange angle. Raymond ran over and tried to help pry Kelly's hand free of the broken arm, her fingers felt like steel cords and he was unable to budge them.

In his panic, Raymond didn't notice other nurses and doctors running into the room to help. The next thing he knew Kelly threw both him and the nurse she was holding across the room, he landed on top of the nurse's shattered arm and heard her scream out loud enough to make his ears ring. Still panicking, Raymond jumped up and pulled the nurse to her feet with her good arm. In his old age he didn't know he could still lift someone like that.

By then there were too many people in the room to have a clear view of Kelly but he could still hear her screaming, although by now her screams were getting quieter, turning into inhuman moans and sickening gurgles. For a moment, he was tempted to force himself back to her bedside, the desire to help someone in trouble was still strong after all his years on the force. When he looked at the doctors and nurses crowded around her bed, he decided against it, he'd just get in the way.

Raymond led the crying nurse out around the crowd of people trying without success to hold Kelly down. The few words he picked up from their shouting at each other didn't sound good for the girl. With effort, Raymond got the nurse to the emergency desk where she was quickly led away by another team of nurses, her arm had swollen to at least twice its size and had turned a horrible mixture of blacks, blues, and reds.

Heart beating out of his chest, Raymond flopped down onto a chair behind him, closing his eyes and trying to calm his breathing down. After a few minutes he felt a tap on his shoulder. One of the nurses who had come into the room after they had been thrown was standing over him with a look of concern on her face.

"Sir, are you alright? Do you need attention" she asked hastily.

Raymond shook his head, his heart had calmed down and his breathing was almost back to normal. "No, no, I'll be ok. How's the nurse doing?"

"Both bones in her upper arm were shattered. She'll be ok eventually though."

"And the girl?"

The nurse gave him a sorry expression and shook her head, "I'm sorry, the poor girl died just after you got out of the room." And with that she walked away.

Raymond bent over and put his head in his hands. He was going to have to get to the station and fill out a report. He was also going to have to turn in the ashes he had picked up this morning and fill out some kind of report to explain why he had them in the first place. In the meantime, he had a phone call to make, not like the day could get much worse anyways.

When he got out of the hospital, he pulled his cell out and dialed the number to Donald's office. After a few rings a woman answered. "Hello, how can I help you" she demanded.

"Oh, sorry, I was trying to reach Donald Harris, did he move to a different office?"

"No sir, I'm sorry. This is his office, I'm Cheryl Cunningham, I work for the university. Did you have and appointment with Donald?"

"Not today, he's expecting me this week though and I was trying to call about that. Can you leave a message for me" Raymond asked urgently.

"I'm so sorry to inform you sir, but Donald Harris was found dead this morning by one of the custodians. He hung himself."

FORTY

Alex did all the talking for the first hour or so, trying his best to explain what he had found, leaving out the changes to himself and strange dreams he had during his episodes. Margret sat quietly, every now and then pulling out an article or looking at a picture from his notes. She looked at the yearbook photo the most, always side by side with the picture from the funeral. She didn't comment until Alex pulled out the copy of the gossip letter.

"Why would you have a letter from a gossip column in all this? You have to know that wouldn't be true" Margret asked.

"I know," Alex said, "it was the description of the little girl that made me copy it, that's why I need to talk to you, I need to know if there are any more pictures of the girls that were killed in that album you have."

Margret let out a little gasp. "How do you know about that? I've kept that locked up for years."

"Nadia and I found it playing years ago, remember? Your reaction when you found us looking through it stayed in my mind and it made me remember it. I need to know if they all looked alike. All the family pictures you have around here show dark haired people, in the picture from the funeral everyone had dark hair, heck even you have dark hair. It looks to me like all the victims from your family shared Nadia's red hair and green eyes. They are always the oldest girl, and it's always once a generation. The only difference I see now is that Nadia is older, but

I'm worried that something still may happen, and I think Ethan will have something to do with it."

Margret shook her head, "I still don't think so Alex, I just don't see how it's possible. You may be right about one thing though, hold on one second."

She stood up and walked into her bedroom, a few minutes later coming back out holding the album that Alex had seen briefly years before. She held it like it was something to be feared, like she didn't want to touch it. "Our family has been keeping this since the second time one of the girls were killed. I don't like to pull it out, or even think about it. I've always hoped that it wasn't real, or at the very least over..."

She turned the album over and opened to the back cover, flipping past a few dozen blank pages until she came to the last collection of clippings and pictures. She turned the album so Alex could see the page, several pictures were taped on forming a collage, all of the same little girl. Margret smiled and pointed to one picture in particular. The picture showed a girl with curly red hair weighed down with mud and leaves, hanging down around the girl's shoulders and soaking her shirt. A smear of mud ran across her cheek and up to the bottom of her left eye, the same shade of green as Nadia. She also shared Nadia's mischievous grin as she held a bullfrog up against her face with the same childlike pride Alex could remember in Nadia the day they met. The picture was dated 1965.

"I was too young to remember Annie," Margret said quietly, "she was seven when they found her, not long after this picture was taken. My mom told me she was out in the front yard catching fireflies when she disappeared. They found her two days later, in the woods. She was only seven." She wiped a tear from her eye and took a sip of coffee before going on.

"Every time I see this picture I think of Nadia, I never let her leave my sight when she was little, even when she met you I was watching."

Alex smiled at her and pulled the album closer, Margret didn't stop him, instead taking his cup and pouring the last of the coffee into it from the pot. Alex was about to tell her no thank you when something in one of the pictures caught his eye. "Do you have a magnifying glass or something" he asked.

"I think dad had one for reading, hold on, I'll check the study." She walked into the next room and rummaged through drawers until she brought out an old magnifying glass with a wooden handle. She handed it to Alex, looking at the album from over his shoulder.

One of the pictures in the corner dated 1964 had a large gathering of people around the family house. It looked like they were standing for a family reunion photo, but Alex knew that was just speculation and didn't ask.

Annie and her family were gathered together near the middle of the group, Annie herself leaning up against her mom who was busy trying to hold a squirming little girl who could only be Margret in her arms. Alex moved the glass away from them and towards the back right hand side of the group. The person who caught his attention was standing in the last row, all the way at the back as if he was trying to hide from the camera. Even though the picture was small and old, it was pretty obvious by his expression that he didn't want to be part of it.

Alex would have never noticed him except for his blonde hair, and when he pulled the magnifying glass closer, his dark eyes. It was the man who looked like Ethan. Standing behind him, Margret gasped and dropped the mug, sending hot coffee all over the kitchen floor. Neither noticed.

"It can't be..." Margret said quietly, then pushed Alex to the side and took the magnifying glass for herself. She stared quietly at the picture, comparing it to the yearbook photo and the photo from the funeral.

"This is what I needed to know," Alex said quietly behind her, making her jump a little. "We have pictures of Ethan, or someone that looks an awful lot like him, dating all the way back to 1935, and always near the girls. Not only that but, it's always the first born girls who turn out to have red hair and green eyes. I don't know about you, but I think it has to be a little more than just a coincidence."

"But why now? Why after so long? She's not a little girl anymore, she's almost a woman. I thought she was safe..." Margret said trailing off.

"I promise you I plan to find out, one way or another. I don't know what's going on or why, but I'm going to stop it" Alex assured her.

Margret nodded, wiping more tears from her eyes. Then with a sudden jerk she looked up at Alex in a panic, "what about Ethan!? I have to get her away from him! It can't happen again it just can't."

She ran to the counter and pulled her cell phone out of her purse, hands shaking she fumbled to open it. Alex quickly ran over to her, putting his hand over the phone.

"What are you doing" Alex asked her.

"I have to call her, I have to tell her she can't see him again, I have to..." She was cut off when Alex took the phone from her hands, closing it before she could finish dialing Nadia's number.

"You can't!" he said, "if this is real, if it's happening, then Ethan can't know we're on to him, and she can't know anything either. You know her, she'll either stop talking to us and cling to him, or she'll act different in front of him and force him to make his move. I have to find out what's going on first, then we can figure out what to do."

Slowly, Margret began to relax, a little at least. Still shaking, Margret shook her head in agreement. "Ok, ok. I don't like it though. If he starts acting strange, or if she acts any different, I'm putting an end to it. But I'm not giving it long, a week at the most..." her words faded off slowly, like she was trying to come up with how to solve an impossible riddle.

Alex nodded, then looked her in the eyes, "a week then. I'll follow him around and see if I can't figure out what to do, or if I'm even right about him. I may not like the guy, but if I'm wrong about this I don't want to make her think she's dating a monster for no reason. I'll come back here next weekend and let you know what I've found."

"Ok, but let me give you something that will help us both out if we have to confront Nadia..." She took one more trip out of the room and came back with a black backpack. She handed it to Alex. He gave her a questioning look as she unzipped the top of the bag.

"It's all my camera equipment," she said, "keep it on you and if you can, get proof of whatever he is, or whatever's happening."

"I'll do what I can," he said. Alex helped her clean up the coffee spill and pieces of the mug that had scattered about the kitchen, then after a quick agreement not to tell Nadia that Alex was there, he left. This was going to be hard and he knew it. He had no idea what he would be looking for, and he certainly didn't know anything about following people.

One week. As Alex drove the short way home, he started to worry if it would be enough time, but at the same time Alex worried that waiting a full week may be too long.

FORTY-ONE

Chris Sproles, the nighttime officer at the Conway Police Station, popped a second batch of headache killers into his mouth. It had been a long day for him. He monitored the security cameras throughout the department and it was his responsibility overnight to make sure nothing happened, and call for help if something did. The night before, he failed at that task, and one trip to the bathroom was all it took. He was gone no more than five minutes, and in that small amount of time someone, some seemingly inhuman freak of nature, had managed to rip steel fencing off a concrete wall, break into the evidence room, and make off with evidence for an ongoing investigation.

Needless to say he spent most of that day filling out paperwork and answering very loud, and sometimes angry, questions from his superiors. Now, here he was less than eight hours after he had left the longest shift of his life working the same job he had almost lost over a bathroom break. In his mind he ran through the checklist he had made himself to avoid that happening again.

Coffee pot was moved out of his room, he would only allow himself one cup a night. Bathroom break was already taken care of, and if need be he would call one of the girls away from the front desk to take over. It was also going to be a very long time before he brought a magazine in to read on the job. If this happened once, it could happen again, and there was no way he was going to get caught with his pants down, again.

It was just after one in the morning. Chris picked up his now cold cup of coffee and took a small sip, looking from one screen to the next. So far the night had been quiet, a drunk or two brought in, normal shift changes, but all in all not much activity around the building.

A flickering screen caught the corner of his eye, he looked over to notice the entryway cameras were showing nothing but static, suddenly they went black. A second later the cameras in the hallways started to show static, and as they went black the cameras in the entryway came back to life. Curious, he tapped in a few commands to try to bring the cameras back, nothing happened. He tapped the button for the intercom at the front desk.

"Hello? Jess" He called out, there was no answer.

The next set of cameras in the hallway just outside of the security room started to show nothing but static while the cameras at the front desk came back to life. He looked at the screens and got a shock, Jessica, the nighttime girl, was unconscious and half hanging out of her chair. In a panic, he picked up the phone to call for help, but when he put it to his ear there was no dial tone, the phone was dead. Footsteps were coming closer to the security room, echoing loudly on the tiled floors. His heart racing, Chris jumped out of his chair, reaching for his sidearm just as the lights in the room and all the screens went black. Breathing heavy in the darkness, he heard the sound of the door handle being turned, then the slow creak of the hinges as the door swung open. He took a stand in front of the sound and held his gun out in front of him, using the slow sound of the door opening as an aiming point.

"Who's there!? I have a weapon drawn" he yelled. The door creaked open slowly until it came to a stop, gently tapping against the wall.

The room was dark enough so that the tiny bit of light still in the hallways silhouetted the figure standing in the doorway. He was taller than Chris but not by much, and it stood in the middle of the doorway not moving.

"I said I have a weapon drawn! Put your hands in the air and get down to your knees!"

The figure took a step forward, Chris could feel his hands start to shake. He had never been in a situation like this before. He was starting to panic.

"This is your last warning! Put your hands in the air and get down to your knees! I *will* open fire" as he yelled, the figure stepped forward again, only this time two tiny points of yellow light started to glow where it's eyes would be. In the faint light Chris could see the figure's arm start to move. He pulled the trigger.

Click.

Chris's heart almost stopped. Panicked, he pulled the trigger again several more times.

Click, click, click...

"Shhhhh..." was the only sound the figure made. Chris's eyes rolled into the back of his head and his knees buckled.

As he fell to the floor, the figure bent down quickly and grabbed hold of the front of his shirt, lowering him to the floor slowly. In the dark, the figure looked down at Chris, his form slightly lit by the two yellow lights in his eyes. He stepped over Chris and to the video screens.

He quietly spoke a few unintelligible words and the screen in front of him came to life. Controls moved on their own and buttons pushed themselves until the video of the previous night's robbery appeared. In the dark, the figure's eyes narrowed as he watched the footage, waiting for the thief to appear on camera. It didn't take long.

The police and technicians who had spent a frustrating day slowing down the footage to get a clear shot were unsuccessful, only able to make out a blurry human form. The man now looking at the footage needed no help to see, he'd had a lot of time to practice. He knew exactly what he was looking at.

Having found what he was looking for, the figure stood upright. The yellow light fading from his eyes while the screen turned black once more. Stepping over the still unconscious guard on the floor, he closed the door quietly behind himself. As he walked out of the building, the lights and cameras sprang back to life behind him. Like at the hospital, nothing had been recorded to identify the man who had been there.

Across town at the hospital, the body of Kelly Johnson was scheduled to be sent off for autopsy to a bigger hospital and better labs than
Conway could provide. The poison that had killed her was deemed to
be too dangerous and too unknown for the lab there to handle, and at
the moment, her body was being held in a plastic bag in cold storage.
Her parents had already come and collected her personal belongings,
leaving only the silver cross with her body. Her father requested it stay
with her until she could be returned home for burial.

The room was cold, full of stainless steel doors that lined the walls
to store the bodies. A large stainless steel table used for autopsies sat
bolted to the floor in the middle of the room, waiting for its next occu-
pant. The only sounds in the room were the light vibrations coming
from the air conditioning in the ceiling and the plastic tick of an old
clock on the wall. The quiet in the room was suddenly broken by the
muffled sound of tearing plastic coming from one of the storage cubbies
on the wall. The plastic stopped tearing, and was soon replaced by a
panicked shuffling around.

Thud!

One of the steel doors buckled slightly, the flat surface now had an
outward facing dent in its middle.

Thud! Thud, crack!

With every hit the door buckled outwards a bit more, the metal
hinges that held it on bending with every blow, the concrete around the
door cracking. Finally, with one huge blow, the door broke off its hinges
and fell to the floor. For a moment there was silence in the room again;
then a pair of small hands felt their way out of the black hole in the wall.
They were quickly followed by the rest of Kelly Johnson, she crawled,
naked and trembling from the hole and fell to the floor, landing on top
of the door she had just beaten off the wall.

She stood up and looked around, confused and slightly disoriented.
Something was wrong with her, she could feel a change within herself
but at the moment couldn't put her finger on it. The room was dark, the
few lights that were on were either the tiny LED lights blinking on some

of the equipment in the room, or the exit sign above the door. Even with the extremely low light, she could still see everything as clear as day. She could hear every sound as well, the low vibrations sounded like drums, and from across the room she could hear a fly buzzing against the tiny window up near the ceiling. She could also smell everything around as well, from the dizzying smells of various chemicals, to a smell that sent painful pangs of hunger throughout her body.

In the corner of the room she found the source of that smell, a large steel refrigerator sat vibrating alone, padlocked shut and marked with a large biohazard sticker. The smell coming out of it sent an animal hunger through her so intensely it threatened to knock her to her knees. She slowly walked over, and without realizing what she was doing snapped the padlock off the door like it was no more than a piece of brittle plastic. The flood of light that came from inside when she opened the door made her blink in surprise. When her eyes adjusted, she saw containers labeled with different blood types lining the shelves.

The smell and hunger grew more intense as she peered into the refrigerator, the smells coming from the containers more tempting than any meal she had smelled in her entire life. Pulling the nearest container out, she ripped the top off and looked inside, it was filled with bags of blood. Blind instinct took over and without thinking she grabbed one of the bags and tore the top of what looked like a nozzle off with her teeth and sucked the bag dry. She had never tasted anything so good in her life, it was like a drug. Before she knew it she had drank all the bags in the "AB" container and was moving on to the next.

When she finally stood up again, she had finished off all the blood bags in the fridge. Wiping her mouth she could feel a surge of strength filling her body. A drop of blood landed on her chest and she looked down, noticing for the first time that she was naked. She searched around the room for clothes but came up empty. The only thing she found was a small brown envelope on a desk with her name written across the top. She tore it opened and dumped the contents onto the floor. A few papers fell out, as well as a small plastic bag that held the cross her father had given her. She scooped the bag up and took the cross out, playing with it in her hand as she picked up the papers. It was some sort of medical form ordering her autopsy. She flipped through the papers and found one line that caught her attention. Time of death: 10:37 am.

She sat on the floor in shock, then looked around and for the first time realized where she was. A morgue. Feeling like she had been punched in the gut, Kelly put her head in her hands and screamed into them, then in a blind rage jumped up and pushed the steel autopsy table. The metal buckled under her hands and the bolts that held the table down ripped out of the floor. The table slid across the room leaving deep scratches in the tile before slamming into the opposite wall with a crash.

She heard footsteps coming quickly down the hall, she could tell they were still a ways away but she knew where they were heading. In a panic, she looked around for a way out of the room. All she saw was the small window that the fly was still bumping against in an effort to escape to the outdoors. The footsteps were almost there, Kelly looked from the closed door to the window, then once again following blind instinct she ran and jumped at it. To her surprise she jumped high enough to effortlessly grab hold of the window ledge and pull herself up. The window was not made to open so she put the fist that was still holding the cross through it, shattering the glass and climbing out, she felt the shards cut deeply into her body.

She fell out the other side and landed on a concrete walkway. From the corner of her eye she saw a deep gash on her upper arm and watched in horror as it healed itself before her eyes. The other cuts on her body were healing just as fast, the pain of them leaving even faster.

She quickly hung the cross around her neck and took off running, moving faster than she ever thought was possible. Not used to the speed she was moving, she barely managed to dodge trees and cars as she flew between buildings and parking lots. A car suddenly pulled off the road and into a parking lot just as she ran through it, cutting her off. Surprised, she moved too far off to the right in her panic and found herself running across a street where another car nearly hit her, its headlights blinding her temporarily. To avoid the collision, she cut too hard to her left and found herself tripping over railroad tracks and rolling down a hill. She came to a rough landing against a boulder at the bottom and lay there crying.

"Well, well, well, what do we have here?"

She jumped up at the sound of the voice, turning to see a large, rough looking man in dirty clothes walking over to her from a small camp fire. Kelly held her hand up against the fire's bright glare, barely able to make out the form of the man staggering over to her. He smelled like cheap whiskey and urine, and in his drunkenness nearly tripped before he could make it over to her. Kelly heard his heart beating through his clothes, speeding up in his chest as his bloodshot eyes moved up and down her body, taking her in greedily. Somehow she could feel his drunken desires for her as he stumbled over, his emotions almost overshadowing her own.

"Please... I just... please just leave me alone" she said in a small voice that was still choked with sobs. The smell of whiskey and urine became more intense as he staggered closer to her. The sound of his heart beating was like a drum.

His breathing became heavier as his eyes continued moving up and down her body, she got to her feet just as he stepped within reaching distance, her back against the boulder.

"Don't worry, I won't hurt ya..." he muttered drunkenly, all the while reaching into his coat pocket. "You just be a good little girl and everything will be all right..." he staggered forward again and put his left hand against the boulder, leaning his face in close to her. His teeth were almost rotted away, the few that remained poked through bleeding gums like gravestones.

"Please..." she said again, her words were cut off when she felt something cold and sharp against her throat. Her eyes looked down and saw the handle of an old kitchen knife in his hand, her eyes went wide.

"I said you just be a good little girl," the hand not holding the knife slid down the rock. He stroked her hair and ran his fingers along her arm. She shuttered and recoiled from his touch, the man hissed and pressed the knife harder.

Fear suddenly turned to a strange mixture of anger and hunger. The faster his heart beat in his chest, the more she felt the same animal instinct from the hospital take over. She felt his hand touch the side of her breast as his face came closer to hers, and the second she felt his lips brush her cheek she grabbed hold of his left wrist and twisted.

The man screamed as the bones in his upper arm broke with two quick snaps, then she tightened her grip on his wrist and crushed the smaller bones, the fingers in his hand instantly going limp. He screamed louder and tried to get away, but Kelly pulled him closer and bit into his neck. Still screaming, he stabbed her repeatedly with the knife while she sucked the blood from his neck. Lost in her frenzy, Kelly was oblivious to the knife that continued to stab her.

After a few minutes, the man stopped struggling and dropped the knife to the ground, little more than a moan escaped his lips. She held him up and drank until there was nothing left in him, dropping him to the ground like a piece of garbage. She looked down at the body and stepped on his chest, feeling his rib cage give way under her foot.

"Bastard" she whispered.

Flipping him over like a rag doll, she tore the coat from his body and put it on, more to cover herself than as protection against the chill of the night. The stab wounds from the knife had already closed by the time she stood up to get her bearings.

No longer in a confused panic, she walked up the hill and over the train tracks she had tripped on. She knew where she was. There was an outlet mall about a mile down the road, she could make her way there to get some better clothes.

Reaching under the filthy coat she had taken from the drunk, she touched the cross hanging around her neck, taking comfort from the tiny item. Then, careful to stay in the shadows, she walked off towards the outlet mall, unsure of what she was going to do after that.

FORTY-TWO

Jason was starting to get worried. Sarah had been gone since late afternoon to retrieve her trail cameras. He had opted to stay at camp and make sure nothing else went wrong and to pack up what he could. Most of what they brought was going into the first garbage container he saw on his way out of this miserable forest. The tent, the sleeping bags, even their clothes. They could stop on the way home and buy more. This was the last night they were going to be here, one more night sleeping wrapped up in a blanket and then it was back to the real world. Jason couldn't wait to get out of here.

He stoked up the fire and started pacing around the camp. He should have never let her walk off on her own. She had promised to be back before dark and had taken the rifle along, so he had reluctantly agreed to let her go. Throwing another log onto the fire, Jason continued to impatiently pace around the camp. It was at least a full hour after dark when he finally heard footsteps coming towards camp and saw the bobbing of a flashlight.

"Sarah, is that you" he called.

"Yea, it's me" she called back. Jason almost collapsed with relief.

He walked back to the fire and sat down on a log, trying to look like he hadn't just been pacing like a worried father on his daughter's prom night. When she stepped into the clearing, she headed straight for the fire, the expression on her face told Jason her day had not gone as planned.

"What took so long" he asked.

She gave him an irritated look and unzipped her backpack, opening it up fully and dumping the contents onto the ground. A large pile of plastic pieces fell out of the bag, forming a jagged pyramid on the ground.

"That's how it went," she said angrily, "almost every camera I brought was destroyed, and the worst part is whatever did it took all the memory cards out of the cameras and took off with them! What the hell does that?" She gave the pile of plastic pieces a kick, sending some of them into the fire. Jason was tempted to comment on how bad it was to burn plastic but wisely kept his mouth shut. Instead, he quietly slid next to her and put his arm around her shoulders.

"I'm sorry we came and got nothing babe" he said softly.

She looked at him from the corner of her eye and gave a tiny smile. "Not nothing I hope. I said *most* of my cameras, not *all* of them. It missed one." She said happily. Sarah pulled her only untouched camera out of the pocket on the front of her backpack and handed it to Jason with a grin.

"I'll go put the card into the laptop, you sit here and have some coffee, you definitely look like you need it." Jason told Sarah, he bent down and kissed the top of her head, then went to their remaining supplies to get the laptop and plug the card in. Sarah had just finished making her cup when Jason came back, laptop in hand.

"It's still downloading, but it looks like you have plenty of pictures to go through."

"How's the battery" she asked between sips.

"Full, I used the solar charger while you were gone."

She smiled at him and rubbed his leg, "you're too good to me" she said, then put her head on his shoulder while she waited for the computer to finish.

"Only because I love you" he told her.

A few minutes later the computer gave a small beep, it had finished downloading all the images. Sarah took the laptop and sat upright, looking like a kid on Christmas morning. Jason watched her as she started clicking through pictures, thinking of how cute she looked when she was concentrating.

"Bird, bear, deer, deer, another deer, another bird..." listing off all the animals in the pictures, Jason could tell she was losing hope. He took a sip from her coffee when she let out a gasp. Her eyes went wide and she looked up at Jason excitedly.

"Jason, look at this! I got it" She exclaimed with excitement, turning the computer so he could see.

The image showed a huge white dog, if it wasn't for its size, Jason would have thought it was a husky, but he had never seen one that big in his life. The camera had caught it running, and even as fast as the camera took the picture, the animal still looked slightly burry. The thing Jason noticed about the animal the most was its eye, bright yellow, almost glowing.

"Kinda looks like a big husky doesn't it" Jason asked.

"That's no husky. It looks exactly like what attacked us, just a different color" Sarah remarked.

"So what do you want to do" Jason asked. Sarah looked at him and smiled.

"I'm going to take this picture to the police station and shove it down that grey haired bastard's throat. I saw the look on that old cop's face when we told him what happened, he thought I was crazy. Well, this time he won't be able to tell me there's no wolves around here, they'll have to do something."

"And you think one picture of a dog is going to make them come out here? I think we should just show the picture to Fish and Game and let them handle it. They got to have trappers or something, I'm sure of it."

"If Fish and Game want part of this, then the police can get them involved. I'm going to go back into that station and prove to them I'm not an idiot before someone comes out here and gets killed. And it's not a dog, it's a wolf."

"Actually, he's a *werewolf*" A voice said loudly behind them, making them both jump.

Sarah almost dropped the computer and Jason fell sideways off the log. A tall man stepped into the light of the fire. He was thin, dark haired and looked to be middle age. But it was his smile that set Jason on edge, like the man was trying to hide something dark.

"Where did you come from" Jason asked. Sarah slid closer to Jason, closing the laptop and putting it lightly on the ground behind the log.

"Oh, now *that* is a good question that would require a *long* answer. To keep things simple, I'll just say I was walking the woods when I came across your lovely little campfire and came over hoping to warm up. I walk around these woods a lot, as well as the mountain you're camping at the base of. It's a powerful place that brings back a lot of memories for me."

As he was talking, he stepped lightly over the log and sat down on the ground next to the fire. Jason thought he almost looked like a daddy long legs spider trying to sit like a human when he crossed his long legs and held his hands out to the fire. After he made himself comfortable, he looked down at the pile of broken cameras and picked up a large piece.

"My *my*, he certainly made a mess of your cameras didn't he? Well, it's not a surprise really. I sincerely doubt he wanted you to get a picture of him."

"Look buddy, I'd hate to break it to you, but werewolves don't exist. What we got a pic of on that computer is nothing but a big dog or a plane old wolf. I'm not trying to sound rude, but that's all it is. Now what did you say your name was" Jason inquired, glancing over at the rifle out of the corner of his eye as he spoke. Jason was sure if this guy turned out to be crazy he could get to it, but he still pushed Sarah a little bit further down the log and away from the man that had just appeared out of the woods.

The man took one of their empty cups and helped himself to some of their coffee. Jason wanted to say something but the feeling he was getting from the guy made him think otherwise. Sarah nervously looked up to Jason from the log and he gave her a reassuring smile and squeezed her hand. The man took a large gulp of coffee Jason would have considered too hot to sip and brought his attention back to the couple.

"If only you little humans knew what walked amongst you every day. You sit content thinking you own this little planet; that you live at the top of the food chain. Well I hate to break it to *you*, but you don't. Werewolves, witches, even vampires; they all exist. Everything from your childhood nightmares lives amongst you quietly going about their lives. But don't worry, yours is not the only ignorance in the grand scheme of things. They themselves don't know about *us*. You see, *we* created *them*. As for my name, don't worry, you won't be around me long enough for it to matter. My time with you isn't about names or stories of the things that go bump in the night. All you have to worry about is why I'm here."

Jason knew it, this guy is insane. He glanced back at the rifle then back to the man sitting next to the fire. The man followed Jason's line of sight and grinned.

"Please my friend, if it makes you feel better by all means go pick up your gun and bring it over. I can wait." He took another gulp of coffee and watched Jason expectantly.

Unsure, Jason slowly stood up and brought the rifle over, then making sure it was loaded, he sat back down next to Sarah, setting the gun across his lap with the barrel pointed slightly at the man on the ground. "Feel better now?" the man asked.

"No, not really. To tell the truth, you're kind of giving me the creeps, sorry. Now, if you're not going to give me your name, at least tell us why you're here" Jason demanded. Sarah reached over and gripped Jason's hand tightly, he gave her another squeeze and waited for the man to answer.

The man grinned darkly and stood up, spreading his arms out as elaborately as a magician. "Well, we come down to it at last. Think of me as a game planner. The werewolf you took a picture of, the vampires, and eventually even the witches I was talking about, they are all pawns. Pieces I intend to use to get what I want. My purpose for being here tonight is twofold. I need to perform a couple spells..."

Jason gave him a look and Sarah was about to comment when he said the word spells, but he quickly held up his hand to stop them.

"Please, don't look at me like that, I'm no witch. The spells I intend to use are well beyond the skills of even the most powerful witches. The first spell will give power to a key I'll use to activate a beacon on the mountain. That one is easy and I only need one of you for that. The other spell... well let's just say every general needs his elite soldiers, someone to do the really *dirty* work. That is the hard one, and requires an act so dark that it puts a permanent mark on the spot where it was performed, allowing a doorway to open just enough to let my... pets... through."

"What kind of act" Sarah asked, her voice shaking a little. He looked at her darkly; an expression of giddy anticipation filling his thin face.

"The only act dark enough to truly curse a place, the murder of an innocent."

While he spoke Jason and Sarah saw his eyes change. The whites of his eyes started to fade, a darkness, like black smoke spread out from the center of his eyes, filling the whites until they were completely black. As his eyes darkened the centers started to glow with a red and yellow flickering light, like fire through a keyhole. The man loomed over them like a monster from a fairy tale, reaching into his pocket and pulling out a shiny black piece of wood. A blade that looked like black glass grew out of the dark handle, its jagged edges glimmering in the fire-light. Blood dripped from between his fingers, as if the growing blade was cutting his hand as it grew, each drop sizzling in the dirt as they fell to the ground at his feet. Sarah screamed and Jason fired the gun, a thunderous boom filled the air as he shot the man in the chest, making his ears ring. The man just looked down at them and laughed.

"Sarah, run" Jason yelled.

Jason grabbed the barrel of the rifle and swung it at the man laughing down at them. The man caught the back of the rifle with one hand and held it, his grip splintering the wood. Jason tried to pull the rifle away, but the man's grip was too strong, he twisted the gun out of Jason's hand and held it above his head; the wooden stock caught on fire and the metal started to glow red. He swung the gun at Jason and hit him across the side of his face, the red-hot metal both burning and tearing a deep gash into his flesh. Jason grabbed his cheek and fell over scream-ing just as the man turned to see Sarah running out of the clearing. He threw the hideous dagger, and suddenly Sarah screamed and fell as it sunk deep into her calf. She reached back, trying to pull the long blade out of her leg. She screamed and pulled her hand away from the black handle. It was white hot and burned her hand, leaving a large piece of skin from her palm on the handle.

"Sarah" Jason screamed, he tried to crawl to her but was stopped when something heavy came down on his back. He looked back to see the man bent over him, holding Jason to the ground with one hand. The man bent down so that his lips were just barely above Jason's ear.

"Stay" the man whispered, in one sudden motion the man clenched his fist and twisted his hand, Jason screamed, filled with an indescribable pain as he heard the sickening *crack* of his spine breaking just below his shoulder blades. All feeling from the waist down left him and he suddenly couldn't move his legs. The man stood back up and walked over to Sarah, humming to himself and smiling pleasantly, blood dripping off the hand he had used to break Jason's spine.

"Please..." she whispered, holding out the hand that had not been burned. Still humming, he bent down and ripped the dagger from her leg, the fiery glow in his eyes becoming more intense at the sound of her screams. With his free hand, he grabbed hold of her neck and lifted her up until her feet dangled almost a foot above the ground.

"Shhh..." he whispered, wiping the tears from one side of her face with the back of the bloody hand holding the knife. She could feel the smeared blood from Jason's back on her cheek and tried to scream out again in pain and fear. His hand clamped down harder and cut off her air supply, he leaned in close and smelled her.

"I can smell it on you, on you both. You're both bathed in blood. Your deaths shall be more powerful than you can imagine as the sin I commit will be that much greater. The beacon I bring to life shall be seen by the offspring of my kind for hundreds of miles, the body count in this pitiful little town will soar. You should feel honored. But first, I must bring my pets back, but it will not be your death, or his that brings them. Oh no, the act must be much darker. It will be the death of your unborn child that summons them."

Jason tried to crawl to her, pulling himself on aross the ground with his arms. He watched in horror as the man picked her up by her neck and held her above the ground like a rag doll. Digging his hands into the dirt, he continued to pull himself towards them, desperately trying to get there before anything else happened to Sarah. He saw the man whisper something to her, then saw her eyes go wide as he slid the knife down and press the tip against the exposed skin of her midriff. He reached to her and screamed.

"Sarah, no" Jason screamed in horror as the man plunged the knife in, letting enough pressure off her throat so she could scream, his smile going wide. He twisted the knife once before pulling it out, the blade making a sickening suction sound as he pulled.

The man let go of her throat and Sarah fell to the ground, her eyes were wide, but she no longer screamed. Now she only let out a pitiful moan, holding both hands against the knife wound. Jason looked into her eyes, and as he desperately crawled to her he saw a single tear fall from her eye, she looked at him and mouthed the words "I'm sorry."

The man held the knife up and examined the blade, it was now pulsing with a dull red light, "perfect," he whispered to himself, bending down and plunging the blade into the ground next to Sarah. He stood over the knife and held his hand out, then closing his eyes he whispered a silent incantation and stepped back, eyes glowing brighter than ever.

Still crawling, Jason felt the ground under him shake ever so slightly. The earth under Jason getting hotter as he pulled himself along, burning the palms of his hands and tips of his fingers. Jason never felt the heat, the only thing he could think of was getting to Sarah. She was only about six feet in front of him now, and for the first time since she had been stabbed she made an attempt to move. Digging her right hand into the steadily heating earth, she tried to pull herself closer to Jason.

Suddenly the ground around the knife gave out and a fissure just a few feet across opened up. Black smoke and flames poured from the opening as the smell of rotting flesh and fire filled the air. The ground close to the fissure began to glow red from the heat, suddenly the shirt Jason was wearing burst into flames, and out of the corner of his eye Jason looked back to see the clothes on back of his lifeless leg catch fire, the soul of his hiking boot melting onto the now glowing ground. Still he crawled; he was only a few feet from Sarah, whose clothes and hair were catching fire as well.

Ignoring the pain and blood, they both crawled to each other. The demonic man had stepped back, ignoring them and watching the fissure, his eyes flickering like the fire pouring out of the ground before him. They had almost reached each other when Jason heard the sounds. Snarling and growling, clawing and scraping. Then the first pair of claws emerged out of the fire, climbing out of the hole like a monster from a dungeon, followed by the most horrifying creature Jason had ever seen.

It came out of the smoke, large and terrifying. It had the shape of a dog, but that's where comparison to any dog Jason had ever seen ended. Its eyes were black holes in a head with no fur, only bits of bloody and dripping gore clinging to a skull. The body was the same, a skeleton held together by more scraps of rotting flesh, its beating heart and organs visible between its ribs. Blood poured off its teeth as it snapped at the air, falling to the ground in steaming puddles. When the first hound pulled itself out of the hole two more of the rotting creatures followed. The first hound snapped at the other two as they emerged, both bowed down avoiding its jaws before snapping back, growls coming from the back of their rotted necks.

Finally, burned and filled with pain, Jason and Sarah met. He grabbed hold of her outstretched hand. Tears of pain and sorrow filled her eyes when they looked at each other. "I'm sorry..." she whispered above the terrifying sounds of the creatures.

"I love you..." Jason said as they both started to choke in the heat and poison of the fire. She gave a weak smile and squeezed his hand with the little strength she had left.

"Jason, he killed our..." she started to say, her words were cut off by cracking and exploding sounds around them.

The three creatures in the middle had come together in a circle, howling into the night. The sounds of thousands of human screams came together to form three distinct and horrifying howls. As they howled, everything more than five or six feet away from them started to freeze, almost instantly. Rocks split and trees exploded as the heat was drained from them, flowing in waves to the creatures. The longer they howled the bigger the frozen circle grew, heat flowing out of everything and attaching to the hounds. Their bones began to glow, their rotted flesh began to smoke. The blood dripping off them boiled till it glowed like molten rock. Suddenly, the three creatures erupted into flame and smoke as the frozen circle around them grew. On the edge of Jason's vision he saw what looked like burning wings spread from the dark figure who had summoned these monsters.

Sarah and Jason pulled themselves closer to each other, using the last bit of strength they would ever have. The last thing Jason saw before the ground around him erupted into flames were the creatures transforming from beings of rotted flesh and bone into creatures of flame and smoke. Then the world turned into fire and pain, leaving nothing behind but two charred corpses, arms stretched out and hands clasped in one final act of love for each other.

FORTY-THREE

It had been far too long a day for Raymond. Into work early, only to end up staying late and filling out endless piles of paperwork and reports from the hospital incident. That poor girl, first she had to experience a horrific attack, then die painfully just when she thought she was getting better. Her parents had arrived not long after she passed, and Raymond had done what he could to try to tell them what had happened. Even though he felt no responsibility for the girl's fate, it weighed on him just the same.

Now he was driving to another death, this one hitting closer to home. The woman he had spoken to on the phone told him he was free to come up and check Donald's office for some personal belongings Raymond had claimed to have left behind. Since his death was ruled a suicide, no investigation would take place and he was free to take back what was his. Raymond knew she had only agreed because he was a cop, and that worked out just fine for him.

When Raymond had informed her he wouldn't be able to make it up until later that night, she arranged to leave a note for the night-time security guard to let him in to pick up his items. That was fine with Raymond, he didn't believe that Donald's death was a suicide and wanted to have a look around his office. The fact was he was afraid it had something to do with the sample of ashes that he had brought him.

That's the real reason he came, to find out if Donald's death was really suicide, and if not, was he somehow responsible. Raymond hoped not.

The parking lot was empty and he was able to park next to the main doors to the science building without paying the usual fee. He pressed the call button next to the door and waited for the security guard to finally make his way over. Raymond flashed his badge as the man walked up. A buzz from inside, a click of the door, and the guard waved him inside.

"Names Raymond Steward, I talked to a Cheryl earlier today about picking a few things up from Donald Harris's office" he said, holding out his hand. The guard shook it and nodded.

"Yea, she told me. Thought you'd be a little earlier than this. I'll have to lead you up there, the doors have all been locked up 'till we can find family to come and pick up his belongings."

"I'm afraid that won't happen," Raymond said, "as far as I know he didn't have any family left, and he wasn't exactly the marrying type."

The guard nodded, "Yea, I kind of figured that. He was kind of a loner and not really good with people, no offense, I know he was your friend."

"None taken, I know the truth about him, known it for years. Where was he found?"

The guard pointed to the top of the staircase they were walking up. The building was only five stories tall so the elevator was seldom used, so if he had been hanging from the top of the stairs, it was a sure thing he would have been found fast.

"Found by the nighttime janitor early yesterday morning. They said they think he did it sometime around one or two, but that's only rumor, I can't tell you anything for sure."

"Can I talk to the janitor" Raymond asked.

"Not for a couple days, he took some time off to calm his nerves. I can't blame him really, I think I would have too" he replied.

"Any cameras?"

"Not in this building, all the expensive equipment was moved to the new wing a few years back, and the university wasn't about to put the money into a system for the old wing."

By that time they had reached Donald's office, the guard snapped a large ring of keys off of his belt and opened the door for Raymond, stepping aside so he could get in. "You want me to stick around? Normally I'd have to, but I doubt a cop really needs a security guard babysitting him."

"No, thank you, this place is such a mess it may take me a while." Raymond gestured to the cramped and messy room, the guard nodded and clipped the keys back onto his belt.

"Ok, I'll be back in a bit to check up on you, holler if you need anything."

The guard started to walk away when Raymond thought of something, "Who was on duty last night when it happened? Besides the janitor that is. Was it you?"

The guard nodded, "Yea, it was, wasn't in the building though. Someone set an alarm off in the girl's dorms and I had to check on that. Skeleton crew is all we have after the budget cuts."

"Yea, kind of figured something like that. Thanks anyways" Raymond said.

"No problem, I'll be back soon," and with that, the guard headed back towards the staircase.

Raymond turned to the cluttered office and sighed. He had no idea where to start or even what he was looking for. He walked over to Donald's desk and started rummaging through drawers. As excited as Donald had been when he was on the phone, Raymond thought finding any papers about his findings or the ashes themselves wouldn't be all that difficult. He remembered from his days attending Donald's classes that he always kept his favorite projects and papers out where he could find them and have quick access. He had no such luck going through the desk.

Raymond spent the next hour going through the frustrating piles of student papers and research Donald had randomly strewn around his office, not one paper talked about the ashes and no sample remained. After a while he turned to the large microscope Donald kept on a cluttered table by the door. Looking carefully around the bottom edges, Raymond searched for any signs of the ashes, there was none to be found on the table, but something flashed in the light as he moved around, catching his eye. There was a small piece of broken glass sticking out of the small space between the microscope and table.

Using a pen from his pocket, Raymond flicked the glass out and picked it up. Raymond recognized it as a broken edge from a sample plate that would hold whatever someone was trying to look at through the microscope. Curious, Raymond tried to lift the heavy microscope up onto its edge, but the device was heavy and he slipped on the floor. Cussing, Raymond barely stopped himself from cracking his head on the side of the metal table. As he fell his foot slipped a small ways under the table, kicking something small and heavy out the other side.

Muttering under his breath, Raymond pulled himself up and walked around the table, a small revolver sat against one of the metal legs, its barrel pointing into the darkness. Using his pen, he picked it up to take a closer look. It was a snub nosed .38spl, and as close as Raymond held it from his face, Raymond could smell burnt gunpowder. No doubt it had been fired recently. He stood up and set it down on the table, pulling a pair of gloves out of his coat pocket. He picked it back up and carefully opened the cylinder, three shots out of the six had been used. Footsteps coming down the hall startled him, Raymond quickly wrapped the gun in a handkerchief and tucked it into his coat pocket as the guard walked into the room.

"Any luck finding what you needed" he asked.

"Sadly, no. I've been through all the papers sitting around and I can't find a thing. I don't know how he got along in all this mess." Raymond took a scrap of paper off the table and wrote down his number, "if the university doesn't have any luck finding family, give me a call and I'll come pick up whatever needs to be taken out of here."

The guard took the paper and stuffed it into his pocket, "will do, what was it you were looking for anyways? I can have them check through everything and send whatever it was when they find it."

"Oh, nothing too important," Raymond said, "Just a folder with some paperwork I had left here last time I came to visit. I would have come at a better hour but it's been too busy at work during the days and this was my only chance."

They walked downstairs in silence, Raymond gave the guard one last handshake on his way out and stepped into the parking lot. He felt the revolver in his pocket and cussed himself. He should have given it to the guard, but that would have meant having to eventually tell the department his reasoning for being here in the first place and what he was after. Handing over crime scene evidence to a university professor because he was too impatient to wait on a lab would not be looked at too well by the department, especially after the last few days. Just before Raymond opened his car door his thoughts were interrupted by voices coming from around the corner.

"Look, I'm telling you that's where I saw him. I've never seen any-one run that fast, it had to have been a ghost or something."

Laughter followed, "you've been smoking up again haven't you" a girl asked.

"Dude, I'm telling you I saw it, maybe he offed that guy last night or something." the first voice insisted.

Raymond stepped away from his car and followed the voices around the corner. Four college students were standing around with cans of beer in their hands and an open box at their feet. When they saw Raymond come around the corner, they quickly tried to hide the cans behind their backs, Raymond held up his hand and shook his head.

"I don't care about that, who said they saw someone out here last night?"

Three of them pointed to the one closest to Raymond. He was the smallest of the group, wearing a university hoodie and pants that must have been two sizes too big. When his buddies pointed him out he rolled his eyes and took a gulp from his beer, turning away from Raymond.

"Don't push it," Raymond said, irritably stepping in front of him and pulling out his badge, "Just tell me what you saw."

The kid's eyes widened and he dropped his beer to the side, "sorry," he said holding up his hands, "I was heading back to my dorm from a party when this big dude came running out of the building there. He looked kinda pissed off so I hung back. He just kinda stood there for a sec looking around before he took off running. When he did he just, like, disappeared."

"And what did the big guy look like? And what do you mean by disappeared?"

"Big dude, I don't know. I didn't see much of him except that he was built like a football player and had blonde hair. Didn't get close enough to see more than that, I didn't exactly try see his whole face. And I don't know man, it was like he started to run, then just went off at light speed. He was standing there one second, then he was gone the next... and no, I wasn't smoking anything" he said loudly, looking back at his friends who were all trying to hold in their laughter. Raymond could tell they were all drunk, but he was off duty and out of his jurisdiction. That, and he really didn't have the patience to deal with them.

"Well, thanks anyways, and get rid of those beers before someone on duty finds you with them. I'm willing to bet not one of you are old enough to be drinking in the first place."

A few of the kids snickered and the group wandered off. Laughing to himself a little, Raymond got into his car and spent the entire ride back thinking about what he had found, or not found in the office. All the evidence was gone, as well as any paperwork and research that Donald had on the matter. Something else still bothered him, although Donald was certainly eccentric, Raymond would never think he would be capable of suicide, especially when he was as excited about a project as he was when he called Raymond the night before. Also there was the gun, three shots fired, probably the night he died, and all this happening on the same night that his evidence was stolen from the station a few hours away. What the hell was going on?

FORTY-FOUR

A lone figure stood on the top of Mt. Chocorua, backlit by a sunrise that was just starting to peek over the hills in the distance. Strange markings had been scratched into a basketball sized rock at his feet, obvious from the trail. He didn't bother to try to hide his handiwork, knowing passing hikers would just assume it was the work of some teenagers who had been drinking, or not notice them at all.

The man bent down and pulled out a strange looking knife, the jet black wooden handle worn smooth from centuries of use. The blade looked like black glass, humming lightly and pulsing with a dull red light. Whispering a few unintelligible words, he slashed his other hand open and covered the blade with his own blood before plunging it into the rock. The blade piercing into the hard granite like a hot knife into butter. A quick turn of the man's wrist and the handle broke off, leaving the glowing blade stuck deep into the rock. Putting the handle into his pocket, he held his hand over the rock and whispered a few last words.

The ground under his feet shuttered slightly and the rock started to sink into the mountain. Unseen to any human eye, tiny whiffs of smoke started to seep from the cracks formed in the earth and stone by the burrowing rock. As the stone settled itself halfway into the ground, the smoke slowly started pouring out from further and further away, as if a fire was spreading through the ground around the stone and pushing itself out of the mountain. No human would see or feel the flames, they would never sense the smoke. The spectral fire would spread over the exposed rocks and dirt that made up the top of the mountain, a giant torch that would call his pawns, like a moth to a flame.

Smiling, the man stood and walked slowly down the trail that would take him off the mountain, every now and then turning to admire his handiwork before the top of the mountain disappeared when he walked below the tree line. His work was done for now, soon the entire mountain would burn, calling every vampire for hundreds of miles to this tiny tourist town. The body count will rise as the mountain's influence on them got stronger, it will make them hunger, it will make them feed. Then he would use them. All that came within the mountain's influence would be his slaves, and this new army would be used to overpower those he really wanted. They will come to him, bow to him, and if necessary, die for him. The board was now set, all he had to do was wait for his pieces to arrive.

The white wolf raced through the forest, dodging trees and brush instinctively as he moved faster than any wildlife biologist would think remotely possible. He was closely followed by two others, one grey, one dark brown. He raced towards a campsite that he hoped would be empty even though what he saw, and sensed, said differently.

He had been sound asleep in his human form when the alarm went off in his head, a sixth sense that was completely in tune with the world around him. Something had happened, something bad. His suspicions were confirmed when he looked out his window to see smoke rising in the distance. Normally this wouldn't put him in the state of alarm he was in now, but this was no ordinary smoke. The supernatural knows the supernatural, no human would react to the smoke, in fact, no human would even know it was there. At the moment it was faint, even to him, but as the minutes ticked on it gained in strength and potency, and it was evil.

Werewolves had gained a bad reputation over the centuries, the few people to know of their existence knew only that they were short tempered and prone to change and attack if provoked. In truth, they instinctively watched over both humans and each other, one of the few creatures on earth with the ability to take down vampires when they got too careless with their feeding.

This, however, was not the work of vampires, this was something different. The creature that had set this spectral fire had already killed once this summer, his scent was all over the mountain, though he had yet to discover it hiding places. Now he was afraid the creature had struck again and killed off the couple he had been trying to scare out of the woods.

With his two pack mates following, he couldn't move as fast as he wanted, still, they arrived at the base of the mountain in less than fifteen minutes. They walked slowly down the game trail, smelling traces of not only the couple, but also something supernatural, something that sent chills up even his spine. Sensing something dark, the white wolf sent a mental signal for the other two to back off while he went on alone. If the couple were still alive, he didn't need to risk having three of them circling the camp. If they weren't, and the creature was still there, he wanted to be able to get away quick if things turned ugly.

The smell of burned flesh hit him before he was within sight of the camp, it was a thick smell that clung to the inside of his mouth, making his stomach turn. Then he was there. Throughout his life he had fought several wandering vampires and seen the horrible ways they tried to cover their tracks from humans. This was something entirely different. This was impossible.

The camp was surrounded by a ring of melting frost and ice. Trees had burst and fallen over, there blackened leaves hanging limply from shattered branches, rocks had cracked and crumbled to pieces, instantly frozen. The circle of frozen destruction must have gone on for fifty or sixty feet, everything caught in its path had been killed and destroyed. In the center of the frozen waste lay a charred smoldering patch, everything within a blackened ruin.

The burned patch was roughly twenty feet wide, the ground still hot and smoking. The pads on his feet burned, the sand in the center of the patch had melted into glass, the ground had a strange sunken look to it. Not far from that were the remains of the couple, their bodies charred black.

"*Damnit...*" the wolf sat back and let out a howl, a few seconds later he was joined by the others. They both let out a small yip when they got to the smoldering ground, surprised by the heat.

"*What could cause this*" the grey wolf sent the question straight to the white wolf's mind.

"*I don't know, the scent is the same from where we found the boy's body, and it matches what was in the silver box.*"

"*Is it a vampire? Can they do this*" the brown wolf asked.

"*No, whatever did this is different, the vampires fear it. I think it's time he explained what it is we're hunting. I think it caused whatever is happening on the mountain, I just wish I knew why.*"

The grey wolf stepped forward, nervously glancing at the top of the mountain. "*I don't like that. He'll be back today, we'll talk to him. Are you going to call on the others? Is it time?*"

"*Not yet, soon. I want to know what's happening first, and what that is.*"

He motioned his nose up to the mountaintop. The strange smoke was still small but getting bigger, and he could now see black flames rising in the smoke.

"*What about them? Do we bury them or will you tell the police?*" The brown wolf asked.

The white wolf pondered for a moment, then growled in anger at the scene. "*Bury them when it's cool enough to get them. We need to keep this quiet, I think it is going to be too dangerous for humans to be involved.*"

"*Dangerous for us too...*" the grey said.

The white wolf stood over him and growled, the grey wolf whimpered and hung his head. "*It's our job to protect the humans, do you think you were born into our pack just for the hunt? We exist for a reason, and this is it.*"

The white wolf snapped at the two smaller wolves, with a yip they both ran off into the woods. The wolf looked from the scene before him to the mountaintop. He only knew one thing to make of all this; it was going to be bad, very bad.

FORTY-FIVE

Alex woke the next morning with a pit in his stomach. His plan was to start following Ethan after school that day; he just had no idea how to do it without being seen. After a quick shower, he pulled out the bag of camera equipment and dumped it out on his bed. The last thing he wanted to do was fumble with a bag of stuff he knew nothing about while he was trying to concentrate on staying out of sight. It was a digital camera, and by no means a point and shoot. Three extra lenses fell onto the bed next to the camera itself, and luckily for Alex, and instruction manual. He flipped through the manual with impatient frustration. It was at least an inch thick and may as well have been written in Latin. Alex knew nothing about photography and didn't have the time to learn all of the technical lingo that filled the overabundance of pages in the book.

After almost a half hour, Alex was finally able to at least figure out how to get the camera on all automatic settings, and even managed to figure out how to put the biggest lens she had on the thing. He pointed the camera out the window and took a couple pictures of the furthest thing he could get it to focus on. Feeling satisfied when he saw the pictures come out alright on the tiny screen on the back of the camera, Alex carefully found a place in his backpack to store it where it hopefully wouldn't get destroyed. A quick glance at the clock told him he didn't have much time to get going, leaving the rest of the camera stuff scattered on his bed, Alex went into the kitchen for a quick breakfast.

Mark was burning food between puffs on his morning cigar. Alex rolled his eyes and sat down opposite him at the counter.

"What you burning today" Alex asked.

"Your breakfast, black eggs and toast sound good to ya" Mark responded. He took a long puff off his cigar and tapped the ash out into a cereal bowl next to the stove, then filled a plate with half charred food and slid it in front of Alex.

"Well I guess it's about time anyways." Alex said.

"'Bout time for what?"

He gave Mark a grin, "about time I threw something up, I was starting to get worried I may be getting fat off all that real food I've been eating lately."

"Smart ass," Mark said, "by the way, I got you something as an early graduation present. Wasn't going to get you anything but a buddy of mine had it and it was too good a deal to pass up. Course, if you're going to make fun of my cooking again, I may just keep it after all."

Alex took a bite of eggs and did almost throw up, it had been too long since he'd had Marks cooking. "What is it" he asked after choking down the bite.

Mark took a puff off the cigar and grinned at Alex, "first finish your breakfast, then I'll decide if you're going to get it or not."

It took nearly ten minutes of gagging while Mark laughed at him, but Alex managed to finish off the entire plate. Feeling like he just ate something bad for a dollar, he looked back to Mark with a sour expression and wiped the tears from his eyes. Mark laughed at him again, gagging himself on some coffee that went down the wrong tube.

"Serves you right, now where is it" Alex asked, grinning at Marks coughing fit.

"Alright, alright. Go into the living room, it's on the couch." He said.

Alex got up and took a few steps into the living room to find a long cardboard box sitting on the couch. Fumbling with the tape he knew Mark had overdone for his benefit, he finally got the box open. There was a rifle inside, it looked just like the .22 he had, but it was much bigger, and when he picked it up it was much heavier. It was a lever gun just like his, same gold color and everything, but this one had elaborate engraving covering the brass. Alex looked at the barrel, it was labeled .44mag instead of .22lr. There was a box of ammo tucked into the corner of the box the gun had been sitting in.

"It's a little bigger than you're used to, but I think you can handle it." Mark said standing behind him, "I figured it'd suit you as a graduation present, and you needed more of a man's gun anyways. Buddy at work had it and offered it to me cheap, said he'd never even used it, liked his .308 too much. So there you go, happy graduation and all that crap."

"Thanks," Alex said, grinning broadly while looking over the gun, "I'll give it a tryout this weekend. You want to come with me?"

"If I can I will, but no promises, works getting pretty busy again. You better get off to school before you're late; I'm going to go hit the hay." Mark left the room while Alex put the gun away, leaving behind a cloud of cigar smoke.

Looking at the clock, Alex saw just how close he was to not making it to school on time. He grabbed his backpack and ran out the door. It was going to be a busy day, and Alex didn't want to be late starting it.

The day started off with Alex getting to school just in time to really notice Ethan's behavior towards Nadia for the first time. Ethan had his arm firmly around Nadia's waist, pulling her in a little closer when anyone walked by them and swerving her away from friends she used to stop and talk to nearly every day. The more Alex thought about it, the more he was surprised he hadn't noticed Ethan's behavior before. Then again, Nadia didn't seem to notice either. Ethan's voice dropped to a whisper as Alex got closer to them, making it impossible to hear what he was telling her. Nadia did, however, say hi to Alex, earning an angry look from Ethan. Wes and Dillon were following behind them, when they saw Alex they gave him a second, then third look, whispering to each other.

At first Alex wondered what they could be going on about, were they planning another try at beating him up? Then Alex realized, he didn't have any marks from their attack the other day. No doubt that would be strange to them, they knew how hard they had gone at him and knew he should at least have a black eye and a few scrapes, yet Alex knew he looked healthier than ever and even winked at them when they walked by. Although he didn't turn around, Alex knew they were both glaring at him as he walked by.

At lunch Alex made sure to sit close enough to hear at least part of the conversation, but kept himself behind a pillar so that they couldn't see him listening. They spent most of the lunch period talking the usual gossip, homework, tests, college plans, and so on. Alex was about to give up and rethink his plan when Nadia excused herself early to meet with a teacher about a college essay.

Suddenly the conversation went quiet, the three boys whispering in hushed voices Alex was unable to make out above the chatter in the room. Alex tried leaning as far around the pillar as he could without them seeing him, but the sound of the other hundred or so kids in the room continued to drown out their whispers. He concentrated on their voices, trying to force out the chatter and laughter of his other class-mates. As he concentrated, a small pain started to form in the back of his head, becoming more intense as he concentrated on the whispers. As the pain grew, so did their voices, until it was like he was sitting with them at the table.

"I'm telling you Ethan, I think you're right about him, we damn well made sure he knew to leave you alone, but I'm telling you he doesn't have a mark on him. No bruises, no black eyes, no nothin'," Wes said quietly.

"We beat the hell out of him man, I didn't think he'd even show up today. Did you see how the little ass winked at us? I want to have at him again, this time really teach him a lesson," Dillon hissed.

Alex heard Ethan sigh, "Look, we need to hold back for now. I need you two to just follow him today. Keep an eye on him as long as you can and tell me what he does, how he acts. I need to keep him and every-body else I can away from Nadia."

Alex could feel his face turning red with anger, still, he forced him-self to keep listening.

"Really? Man, why are you even bothering with her anymore? If you're right about Alex then you don't need her in the way. Besides, you know you don't care a thing about her, and it looks like real trouble is coming anyways. Did you look at the damned mountain this morning? What the hell is that" Dillon asked.

"What is it you're not telling us? We're not like you; we didn't go after this thing hundreds of years ago," Wes said.

Alex suddenly felt like someone punched him in the stomach, what did Ethan think he knew that Alex didn't know about himself? Not to mention, *hundreds* of years ago? If that was true then the pictures *have to* be of him... Alex shook the thoughts from his head and forced himself to keep listening.

"Look, Dan says if you want our help you need to start talking, he wants to know what you know or he's not going to call the rest of the pack." Dillon added.

"Look," Ethan said, Alex could tell he was getting angry and holding back from yelling at the brothers, and what was Dillon talking about when he said the rest of the pack? Alex wondered before Ethan started talking again, interrupting his thoughts. "I don't know what the hell that is up there, it didn't happen last time. And I don't know what the hell it is we're after. I only saw it once, and only for a split second, in the *dark*, I didn't get a good look. Just tell Dan that the last time this thing was here it nearly killed off your entire pack, and I'm all that's left of my family. Just do me this favor and follow Alex, it's just like the last time... As for Nadia, I've told you all once and I'll tell you again, my reasons are my own. That's it, end of story" Ethan snapped.

"Ok, Ok, Just take it easy, we don't need to start yelling here. We'll tell Dan what you said, what do you want us to do about Alex" Wes asked.

Ethan let out a breath, Alex could tell he was calming himself down. "Just wait for him after school, follow him home or wherever else he goes, but stay back. I'll head up to the mountain after school and check out whatever is going on up there, the Liberty trail's the most popular one so I'll head up that one and see if it's affecting any of the people there. We'll meet up after dark."

The bell rang, signaling the end of the period, the sound of lunch trays banging and people getting up drowned out the conversation.

Alex waited behind the pillar for them to leave, the pain in the back of his head was slowly fading away, but he was feeling a burst of energy in its place. Alex felt like he could run a marathon without breaking a sweat. Suddenly he got an idea. Wes and Dillon would be waiting for him outside in the parking lot after school, but he wouldn't be there. He now had other plans.

Alex waited until the cafeteria was empty before getting up to leave. Quietly, he ducked out the side door and walked around the far side of the building to his car. There was still a couple hours of school left to go, plenty of time for him to get up the Liberty Trail and find a nice place to hide with the camera. Hopefully he'll get something good, he wasn't sure he'd get a chance like this again. Alex drove around the back side of the building to keep as many eyes off his car as possible, then headed down the long driveway of the school. Twenty minutes later, Alex had parked his car in a nice hidden spot by the trail and was on his way up the mountain.

FORTY-SIX

North of Conway was the small town of Berlin New Hampshire. Just off a seldom used logging road in the middle of nowhere, there was a small log cabin where a man named Dale Briars lived with his wife Chloe. They were both vampires, he was getting close to the one hundred fifty year mark while his wife was only ninety two. Neither looked older than forty. Dale had been taught by the vampire that made him that if he wished to stay in one place and avoid a lifetime of running then he needed to keep his head down and kill as few people as possible.

Taking that lesson to heart, Dale hadn't drained a human for over ninety years, instead living off the blood of animals. It was an acquired taste as far as he was concerned; animals left a bitter taste in his mouth and didn't hold him off nearly as long, but human blood was like a drug. Even a little taste would leave him craving more, and Dale had found it was much easier to stay at a permanent residence for long periods of time if he wasn't killing off the local population. Chloe had never tasted human blood, something he had made sure of from the day he made her. Together they lived a quiet life outside of the small town, only keeping each other's company and avoiding as many of their own kind as they could.

That morning he was sitting out on his porch looking off into the forest. He could hear deer moving around and smell every squirrel and raccoon that came within a hundred feet of the small cabin. Chloe was inside getting breakfast ready for them both, quietly humming a tune

Dale didn't recognize. Even though neither of them slept, they still liked to keep up the tradition of three meals a day as a reminder of the lives they both left behind. Just beyond the tree line of his yard he heard a large deer slowly munching its way through the low brush. By the size and smell of it he knew it was a big buck, one that could be drained and feed the both of them for the next week or so. As he stood up to chase it down a stern voice behind him made him stop.

"Leave him alone Dale, I don't want you running off and getting filthy before we eat."

He sat back down in a huff and waited for Chloe to put the tray down in front of them. a large tray of jellied bear blood with a hot tea kettle of water and a small dish filled with a white powder. The powder was dried blood plasma from cows that Chloe ordered somewhere online and liked to have as tea. She sat down and spooned a small pile into a cup, then poured hot water on top and handed it to Dale.

"He's a big one you know, keep us fed for a while" Dale said.

He took a spoon and stirred the plasma into the hot water while Chloe spooned some of the jellied blood onto his plate. He had to admit as much as he missed human blood, Chloe did a fine job making the animal stuff at least edible.

"You can get him later, sit down and relax for once." She said smiling at him.

He took a sip of the tea and started to dig into his jelly. He had just taken his first bite when he noticed hot water spilling all over the table around his plate. He looked up to see Chloe staring off in a daze, all the while pouring hot water into her overflowing cup.

"Chloe? Are you alright?" he asked. She kept pouring water into the cup and staring off into the woods. The look on her face concerned him, it was the look of a hungry newborn.

"Can you feel him? He's calling us..." she said quietly, "we need to go south, we need to feed..."

"Feed on what? We have breakfast right here" Dale said, confused.

"Human blood..." Chloe whispered.

As she spoke a light flickered in her eyes. No, not just light, for a second Dale thought he saw flames. Then he felt it too, a tiny yet powerful urge to go with her. It was like someone was calling to him, a tiny voice impossible to resist. And the hunger, it was faint, but it was the same hunger he had felt himself as a newborn. And only one thing could satisfy it...

Then as suddenly as it came the urges left him and the tiny voice fell silent. He looked up to see Chloe shaking her head and blinking her eyes.

"What just happened" she asked, "I think I blacked out. Do we black out?"

"No," he said, "I have no idea what that was. We better not go back into town for a while, I don't want it to hit us again around people. Are you ok? You look strange."

Chloe held her hand up and rubbed the side of her head, giving Dale a weak smile. "Yes I'm alright, just a little dizzy. I think you're right, let's stay away from town for a few days. I'll go get something to clean this up, finish your breakfast." And with that she stood up and kissed the top of his head before going back inside.

Dale put a spoonful of jelly into his mouth and thought about what might have happened. He hadn't felt that kind of urge since he was first turned; it was like he was starting to lose control of himself. He took another sip of his tea and sat back in his chair.

"Strange," he whispered to himself, then went back to concentrating on trying to find the deer again.

Unseen by human eyes, the top of Mt. Chocorua was slowly but steadily catching fire. The spectral flames and smoke were spreading to every crack in the rock face of the summit. The rock with the strange markings and broken blade was slowly digging itself deeper into the mountain, spreading its poison. The markings were now glowing red, and a substance that looked like blood was dripping out from around the edges of the broken blade. A hiker walked right through the fire and smoke, right past the glowing rock, and didn't see or sense a thing.

As the fire spread, so did the spell's influence. The younger the vampire, the quicker it would take them, but as the fire spread and the spell became more powerful, older and stronger vampires would be enslaved as well. Then finally, when it was strong enough, the fire would start to take the werewolves into its power as well. From a distance, the man who had started the fire watched silently, smiling to himself. A week, maybe two, then the fire should be strong enough to enslave even the oldest of vampires.

He whispered a few quiet words into the air and a thick, black smoke started to spread behind him. The smoke was heavy, clinging to the ground like tar, it rose no more than a foot or so above his feet. He felt an intense heat on his back and heard the approach of snarls and growling. His smile grew to a menacing grin.

"Are you hungry my pets" he asked quietly, not looking back at what he knew approached.

"Because I have a chore for you..."

FORTY-SEVEN

A lex stood by the small cabin impressed with himself. The Liberty Trail was by no means the hardest hike in the state, but he had always had to take a few rests on his way up. Today he had ran the length of the trail strait up to the Liberty cabin without so much as a deep breath, in fact he wasn't even sweating. Whatever had been happening to him was doing him wonders, even if it came at the price of a headache or passing out.

He looked down at his cell phone, he still had over an hour before school ended, and no telling how much time before Ethan made his way up here. He looked around the cabin for a good hiding spot. The cabin stood in a small clearing surrounded by stunted trees and small pines, but there were not enough of them to give adequate cover unless he went back downhill, and that was out of the question. Alex wanted to see everything Ethan did when he was up here without having his view blocked by boulders and branches. Looking around, his only real option was to keep going up the mountain and hide behind a boulder off the trail where he would have a good view of the cabin.

It took him nearly half an hour to find a spot he was happy with. Nearly halfway up the remainder of the trail and over about fifty feet or so, Alex found a crevice between two boulders wide enough to hide between. His efforts to make it to his spot drew more than a few looks from curious hikers. Alex just waved and held his up camera, but in

265

truth he really didn't think they would put much thought into what he was doing. Satisfied with his spot, he leaned against the bigger of the two boulders and pulled out the camera, snapping a few test shots of the cabin. The long lens he put on the camera was able to zoom in close enough to see the rust on the large chains that held the cabin down against high winds.

Looking at the cabin, Alex though about the fact that there had once been a three story hotel where the current cabin now stood and that it had been blown off the side of the mountain. He sat for a few minutes wondering what it would have taken to get a multiple story hotel built on the side of a mountain when his thoughts were interrupted by a couple of laughing hikers on their way down the mountain.

Alex watched them make their way down the path, weaving and disappearing between rocks and trees until they finally reached the cabin and stepped inside. Then a large boy with blonde hair came out of the woods and stood in front of the cabin, it was Ethan.

Quickly, Alex picked up the camera and used the long lens to watch. Ethan was standing still and looking up past Alex to the mountain's summit, seemingly unable to look away. Alex focused on his face, every few seconds it looked like Ethan entered some kind of a trance, his jaw would relax and his eyes seemed to lose focus. After a moment of looking off into space Ethan would shake his head and blink a few times before looking back up to the top of the mountain.

Alex snapped a few pictures while Ethan was in his trance, then a few more when he would snap himself out of it. The longer he looked up at the mountain the more worried Ethan appeared. Alex couldn't be sure, but it looked as if Ethan was trying to fight off some sort of powerful urge, he had seen the same look on Mark's face when he lost a bet on a football game and he had to give up cigars and coffee for two weeks.

Movement caught Alex's eye when the two hikers walked out of the cabin laughing. Alex focused on Ethan's face as they came out, a strange expression, like an animal hunger, filled his face as he looked at the two girls walking over to him. When they started talking to Ethan, Alex couldn't tell what they were saying but he was guessing at least one of them was flirting with Ethan. *All girls flirt with him*, Alex thought bitterly. It seemed for a moment like Ethan would go into his strange trance again and focus on the mountain, but one of the girls waved her hand in front of his face and snapped him out of it. Alex could tell by the way the other girl's shoulders moved that she was giggling.

The second Ethan snapped out of his trance he looked at both girls smiling, then leaned in close to them one at a time, whispering something Alex couldn't make out. For a second they held onto their flirty smiles, then just like Ethan they fell into a trance. As Ethan spoke whispering into their ears, their shoulders went limp and their smiles faded. Both girls looked up at Ethan blankly, Alex kept snapping pictures.

Ethan smiled and walked a small circle around both girls, inspecting them like a judge looking at livestock at a fair, occasionally stroking one of the girl's hair or turning their head to look at their faces. Then once again standing in front of them, Ethan took one girl's face in his hands and slowly turned it to the side, tilting her head away from himself. Then, pulling her hair back from her neck, Ethan moved at a speed Alex didn't think possible and bit into her neck.

Alex's heart was racing and his hands were shaking, it was hard to hold the camera still enough to take pictures, but somehow he managed to keep pressing the button. After what seemed like an eternity, Ethan stood up from the first girl and stepped back, she was still in a daze and didn't react to any of Ethan's actions. He wiped her blood from his mouth and tilted her head back up, fixing her hair as he did so. He then moved onto the next girl and repeated the gruesome process, moving her head and hair, latching onto her neck and drinking her blood. As Alex continued to take pictures, he could see a terrible look on Ethan's face. I was like looking at the blind greed of a dog that refused to let go of his bone. Alex could see an almost physical effort on Ethan's part to stop and stand back up.

When he was finally finished, he bent down and looked them in the eyes, whispering once more and snapping them out of their trance. Both girls looked confused, staring from Ethan to the cabin, all hints of flirtation replaced by trepidation. Ethan smiled warmly and said something to them Alex couldn't hear, instantly both girls seemed to relax. Finally, all three of them walked back down the trail together. The girls moved slowly, occasionally stumbling on the trail. Ethan had to put his arms around their wastes to help them regain their balance a few times before they were finally out of sight. Alex sat behind the boulder shaking and sweating, closing his eyes to get the image of Ethan drinking their blood out of his head. He couldn't.

Alex sat there the rest of the day, waiting for dark. Every now and then more hikers would pass by, laughing and talking, he ignored them all. Finally, the air started to cool off and the sun started to set. Alex slowly got to his feet, stretching the stiffness out of his limbs. Even with all the changes he had gone through, sitting jammed between rocks for half a day didn't feel good to him at all. The tingling in his legs didn't go away until he was in front of the cabin itself. Alex took a minute to look for traces of Ethan's attack on the girls but came up empty handed. The sun started to sink below the horizon, turning the sky a disturbing shade of red. Alex walked back down the trail to his car, clinging onto the camera for dear life.

Darkness had settled in long before Alex made it back to his car. By then he had managed to calm himself down a little, but not much. Fumbling with his keys, Alex opened the driver's door with shaking hands and dropped himself into the seat heavily. Dropping his forehead onto the steering wheel, he closed his eyes and waited until his heart rate dropped and his breathing slowed.

"What the hell is he?" Alex said aloud to the empty car. He picked the camera up off his lap and carefully put it back inside his backpack, dropping the bag to the floor in front of the passenger seat almost carelessly.

Alex knew what he was though, in fact, it all made sense. The old pictures Ethan looked too young to be in but was, the strange feeling Alex got when Ethan looked into his eyes that day in the parking lot. Hell, even the hand warmers Ethan had stuffed into his pockets that day in the cafeteria just before touching Nadia. Alex had thought that hand warmers in the early summer were strange, but Ethan was using them to warm his cold hands before he touched Nadia. Impossible as it was for Alex to accept, he knew he had to. Ethan was a Vampire.

Alex looked at himself in the rearview mirror and shook his head, this was all crazy. Vampires didn't exist, they were something out of old horror movies and stories. They were myths, legends, make believe. The problem with that train of thought is that Alex now knew otherwise, and he had the pictures to prove it. The pictures! He had to get them to Margret.

Alex started his car, rolling down his windows to get some fresh air. He had to get to Nadia's house and tell her mother what he had seen before Ethan could do anything to Nadia. What did he want from her? Did he want her for a snack? Dinner? If so, why stick around so long, was he putting her in a trance like he did those girls on the mountain? Slowly draining her until she died? Is that what he did to her ancestors? Drain them and kill them to cover his tracks? It had to be.

Alex put the car into drive and started to slowly pull out of his hidden parking space. Suddenly, a deep growling started in the bushes just outside his open window. Alex turned his head just in time to see a huge wolf coming from the bushes, its teeth bared and its ears down, slowly moving in for the kill.

FORTY-EIGHT

Raymond took the next day off siting personal reasons after the suicide of his friend. That morning, he called Keith and arranged to meet up after his shift that day. They were good enough friends for Raymond to trust, and he needed to tell someone what had been going on. Keith was also young enough to get involved without thinking things over too much, which helped as well. He pulled his car up in front of Keith's house and honked the horn, Keith came out and tried to wave him inside. Raymond honked the horn again and waved his hand out the window, motioning for Keith to come out. Keith gave a shrug and held up a hand, then went back inside and came out a minute later with a thermos of coffee and a couple cups.

"Really buddy, we gonna do this conspiracy style? I thought you were coming in for some beers" Keith said with a laugh.

"Driving helps me think is all. At least you brought the coffee. What happened at the station last night? When I called this morning it sounded like it did the morning before. Another break in?"

Keith shook his head and sighed, "you really don't pay attention to work if you're not there do ya? Yea, another break in. This time some guy walked in and knocked everyone out cold. Didn't take a thing, just looks like he watched security footage from the first break in."

"What does he look like? If he just walked in he'd be shown on the tapes, do they have him yet?"

"Nope, sorry there buddy, the cameras all shut off. Tech guys can't explain it and boss man is furious, again."

Raymond did a double take, "cameras shut off? What do you mean?" he asked.

Keith just shrugged again and poured some of the coffee into a mug, setting it down in the cup holder next to Raymond before pouring himself a cup and taking a sip. "Don't know old man, I saw it myself. One minute they were showing the entrance and front desk, the next they went black and didn't come back on till the guy was past them. Don't know how, but the guy managed to only shut off the cameras he was in front of, and only long enough to walk by. Everybody that got knocked out can't remember a thing, and none of them have any marks. The only thing they can remember was everything going black, then waking up on the floor."

"Kind of like the hospital" Raymond whispered quietly.

"What was that" Keith asked over his coffee.

Raymond glanced at Keith sideways, "this all stays between you and me, got it? No reports, all off the record."

"Ok grandpa, whatever you say." Keith jested.

Raymond told Keith everything, starting from when they found the strange ashes in the woods to Donald's suicide. He told Keith about giving the ashes to Donald and the late night phone call begging for more. He told Keith about the kid that claimed to see someone there the night Donald died and how he moved too fast to see, just like the security tape showed, and how all the samples were stolen within twelve hours of each other that same night. The entire time Keith kept quiet, only nodding every now and then while he drank his coffee.

"I found this in his office when I went there to look for the first bag of ashes," Raymond said pulling out the revolver and handing it to Keith, "don't worry, rookie, it's unloaded now."

Keith shot him the finger and smelled the barrel, "yep, it's been fired recently," he said, looking over at Raymond, "you don't think he killed himself do you?"

"No I don't, I think whoever broke into the evidence room killed Donald and then came for our sample. He must have used our paperwork to find the lab we sent a sample to and took that one as well. I just don't get the cameras though. Why didn't they turn off for the first break in? Why only the second break in and the hospital" Raymond wondered.

"What about the hospital?"

"The night the girl was found after the attack. The cameras over the emergency room doors went black by themselves. When they turned on again she was lying in the doorway by herself, I saw the tape myself when I went to question the girl."

Keith slurped down some coffee and stared out the window quietly. "You'd almost think it was two different people after the same thing, feels like two different people to me. What do you think" Keith asked.

Raymond shook his head, "a little more than just coincidence, other than that I don't know."

"What did the girl say attacked her again?"

"Poor girl was out of it, said she was attacked by a vampire."

Keith choked on his coffee as he held in a laugh, "sorry buddy, didn't mean to laugh at that" he said when he saw the expression on Raymond's face, "it's just a little hard to believe that..."

He was cut off when something flew out of the woods and came to a stop just in front of the car. Raymond yelled and slammed on the breaks, but it was too late. Something slammed onto the hood and crashed into the windshield with a sickening crunch, rolling over the car and landing in the middle of the road. The car came to a sudden stop, the smell of burned rubber and the sound of squealing tires barely registering to Raymond as burning coffee filled his lap.

"What the hell was that" Raymond yelled.

"I don't know, turn around. Maybe you hit a deer or something."

Raymond did a U-turn in the road, one of the headlights was broken and he had to put the brights on to see much past the shattered windshield.

"My god Ray, I think that's a girl in the road" Keith said quietly.

They both jumped out of the car and ran to the girl, she was sprawled across the yellow lines lying face down, blonde hair covering the side of her face. Keith bent down and put two fingers on her neck, feeling for a pulse. The girl lay silent and unmoving, her clothes torn to shreds from rolling on the pavement.

"No blood, but no pulse either," Keith said, "I think she's dead."

Raymond bent down and looked at the side of her face, it was too covered with hair for him to make out her face. With shaking hands Raymond gently moved her hair back to look at her face, he only pushed it back a few inches before he felt his heart skip a beat. "What the..."

"Ray, you need to call this in, it was an accident. She just ran in front of us. Where the hell did she come from" Keith yelled. His face had turned white in panic and he was pacing back and forth in the road.

Raymond looked up, his face was whiter than Keith's, "I know this girl, but it can't be her, she died in the hospital."

Keith stopped pacing and looked at Raymond in shock, "that Kelly girl? Ray are you ok? We need to call this in now! We don't have time for..."

Suddenly, the girl in the road opened her eyes, Raymond jumped back and yelled, falling almost all the way onto his back. With blinding speed, she jumped up off the ground and turned to Keith, a look of animal hunger and blind rage spread across her face. Raymond felt a scream catch in his throat as a gash that went all the way down to her cheek bone healed itself and saw the girl reset the bone in her upper arm with a sickening snap. Then, before either man could react she jumped at Keith, picking him up off the ground and pushing him back against the car. Raymond couldn't even get himself to his knees before she went for Keith's throat.

FORTY-NINE

Alex stared in horror at the growling monster that approached, too shocked to move or react. Never in his life had he ever seen a dog that big. Its eyes reflected the red lights from Alex's car, giving the creature a hellish look. Its dark brown fur was standing on end along its neck and back, its snarl revealing huge white fangs. As its deep growling got louder Alex felt his teeth rattle, slowly Alex reached over and turned the key. When the engine roared to life the wolf took a few steps closer to the car, angling itself back to cut off Alex's escape. In a blind panic, Alex threw the car into reverse and hit the gas pedal as hard as he could.

The small car lurched into gear and tore out of his hidden space, spitting gravel and dirt into the wolf's eyes as Alex backed off. Snapping at the flying gravel, the wolf shook its huge head and with an angry bark lowered its head and took off after the car just as Alex spun around and tore out of the parking lot. Alex had just hit the main road when the wolf appeared in his rearview mirror, chasing him down with impossible speed, and gaining fast.

Alex hit the gas harder and felt the small car lunge forward, watching the speedometer as it slowly climbed; 45, 55, 65... Alex looked into the rearview mirror and cursed, the wolf was still gaining. Alex turned away from the mirror and pressed the gas to the floor, knuckles turning white as he gripped the wheel, barely keeping the speeding car steady as he raced through turns and over hills. He could hear the wolf barking and snapping through his open window but he didn't dare look back to see where it was.

Then, in mid stride the wolf reared back and jumped, a flash of brown fur flew over the car and landed in the road in front of Alex, turning around quickly to face him down. Alex yelled and slammed the breaks, the car swerved and fishtailed between the lanes, tires screamed as they tried to cling to the road. The wolf lunged at the car as Alex struggled to maintain control, slamming the gas back down the second the car passed by, its teeth snapping just inches from the passenger side window. The car lunged forward once more and gained a little distance from the wolf as Alex straightened it out in the correct lane.

The wolf was once again almost on top of Alex by the time he saw the lights of Conway ahead. Gripping the steering wheel as hard as he could, Alex kept his foot firmly on the gas until he passed by the first set of shops. He heard the wolf howling in frustration just as Alex looked back to see the wolf force itself to a stop just before it could follow Alex into the lights of the town. Before losing sight of the wolf Alex saw it sit back and howl before running off and disappearing into the woods.

With his heart racing, Alex made himself slow the car down to the speed limit, carefully making his way down Main Street. He needed to get to Nadia's house and show Margret what he had, and now there was a new sense of urgency. Alex had no doubt somehow the wolf had something to do with Ethan. Had he been seen anyways? Did he not wait long enough before coming off the mountain?

With these questions in his mind, he turned down the road that would take him back to Nadia's house. He had wanted to drive on the main roads, it was a longer drive going the back route and there were less people along the way, not to mention more woods to drive through. Unfortunately, Alex knew he had no choice after being chased off the main drag, going back would risk running into the wolf once again. He had to take the back way through the woods. Taking a deep breath, Alex drove into the darkness of the forest.

Alex scanned the forest relentlessly for the first few miles, terrified that the wolf would jump back out of the woods and land in front of the car. After a few nervous minutes, Alex finally started to relax and loosened his grip on the steering wheel. Suddenly, a grey shape burst out of the woods and slammed violently into the side of the car. Alex heard the sound of crunching metal and breaking glass as the car was driven into the other lane. Holding on for dear life, Alex struggled to regain control of the car before it was spun completely around. The grey wolf was spinning around for another attack when Alex hit the gas once more, barely keeping the car from driving off the road. He looked in the mirror just in time to see the grey wolf bracing itself to lunge after him.

"Where the hell did you come from" Alex yelled at the mirror. The wolf was gaining faster than the last one and Alex worried if it had done enough damage to his car to slow him down.

Panic once again setting in, Alex willed the car to go faster, pressing the gas as hard as he could with the sounds of barking and the snapping of teeth coming closer and closer to his open window. The wolf ran alongside of the back of his car, slamming its body against the back corner and nearly forcing Alex to drive off the road once more. Alex screamed and kept his foot on the gas, all the while concentrating in his efforts to keep the car on the road. The wolf let out a series of barks that seemed to pierce into Alex's skull, causing him to close his eyes just long enough to lose sight of the road ahead. As suddenly as he appeared, the wolf jumped off the road and disappeared into the woods just before Alex saw the sharp turn in the road ahead.

Still gripping the steering wheel tightly, Alex wasn't able to slow down enough to keep the car crashing off the road. Slamming his breaks and turning the wheel in panic, the car squealed and slid sideways into the turn. Alex felt his stomach lurch as the entire driver's side of the car left the ground. Alex saw the remaining glass on the side of his car shatter as the car rolled violently onto its side, then heard the loud *thud* as the car came to a sudden stop just before rolling all the way over. Alex opened his eyes and looked up to see two large dents in the roof and felt his stomach lurch again as the car was almost thrown right side up. A crashing thud and squeal of metal, then suddenly the car was still. Before Alex could recover or even know what was happening, Alex felt a hand reach in and tear his seatbelt off with a quick snap of metal and tear of webbing. The door was violently pulled open and Alex found himself being dragged out and pushed against the ground. He looked up into Ethan's angry face.

"What were you doing up there?! What did you see" Ethan yelled into his face.

"I don't know what you're talking about" Alex said, terrified.

The look of rage on Ethan's face intensified as he picked Alex up with one hand and slammed his back into the car, looking into his eyes so that they were almost nose to nose. Ethan's dark eyes stared straight into Alex's, his breathing became steady and his voice dropped down to an almost soothing tone.

"You know what I'm talking about, you were up there weren't you? Tell me what you saw Alex, I need to know what you saw…"

As Ethan talked, Alex felt the familiar beginnings of a headache in the back of his head. Suddenly, all the fear started to melt away, and in its place, anger.

"Get off me." Alex said quietly. Then he saw it, a faint reflection of white light in Ethan's eyes. As the anger grew inside Alex, he felt a kind of electricity run throughout his body, his muscles tensed up, seeming to vibrate with stored energy. Suddenly, without thinking Alex grabbed Ethan by the throat, and in the split second before throwing Ethan across the road, Alex saw fear in his eyes.

Ethan flew back and landed in the grass on the other side of the road, digging a deep gouge in the earth where he landed. With blinding speed he stood up, pure rage filled his face. That's when Alex heard growling from either side of him, he turned to see that both the brown and grey wolf had crept in on either side, between the car, wolves, and Ethan, Alex was surrounded. The anger Alex felt melted away, replaced by fear as the two wolves slowly approached, heads down and teeth bared. Ethan looked at Alex from across the road and smiled, all hints of mercy gone.

"I've had it with you," Ethan said quietly.

Suddenly, Ethan seemed to vanish, with blinding speed he ran across the road after Alex. One second he was standing fifteen feet away, the next he once again had Alex pinned against the car. Ethan balled his hand up into a fist, rearing back to hit him, the look in Ethan's eyes wild,

Alex knew he meant to kill him. Closing his eyes in anticipation for the blow, Alex didn't hear the light footfalls and low growling. He only felt himself being dropped and Ethan being jerked back, the killing blow stopped as Ethan's arm was pulled back inches from his face.

Alex opened his eyes to see a white wolf, this one much bigger than the other two, take Ethan's arm into its mouth, and with a quick jerk of its head and body throw him further across the road than Alex had. The white wolf turned and faced down the other two wolves, deep growls coming from the back of its throat. Both the brown and grey wolf lowered their heads and whimpered before running off into the woods.

"What are you doing" Ethan yelled from across the road.

The wolf stood its ground between Ethan and Alex, head lowered and teeth barred it continued to growl at Ethan. The two stared each other down, as if they were having their own private conversation Alex couldn't hear. After what seemed like an eternity, Ethan stood upright and pointed at Alex.

"Fine" he yelled at the wolf, "but if you're wrong, I promise you'll regret it! He'll kill us all" and with that, Ethan disappeared into the darkness of the road.

"Thank you" Alex whispered to the wolf, falling to his knees as his legs turned to jelly. It turned around to face him, its yellow eyes staring into his before it jumped over both Alex and the car, vanishing into the woods in the same direction as the other wolves.

Breathing a sigh of relief, Alex tried his car, it started.

Alex slowly pulled into the driveway to find Margret running out to meet him. She took one look at his car and her face went pale, "Alex, what happened?"

"Ethan, and he has pets. Come on, I have to show you something" Alex said. He grabbed the backpack with the camera and led her inside.

"Is Nadia here?" he asked

"No, she'll be home soon. Now what happened to you? You look like death."

As they were walking into the house, Alex pulled the camera out of the bag and handed it to her, hoping it wasn't damaged in the attack. "Just look on there, I'd tell you everything will make sense but I'd be lying if I did." As she took it he plopped down at the kitchen table feeling suddenly dizzy. Margret looked at him concerned.

"Are you sure you're alright? Do you need to go to the hospital?"

Alex shook his head, "just stress, I promise I actually feel fine. Please, just look at the pictures."

Margret flipped the camera on, not hearing Alex sigh with relief when it came to life, and started looking at the pictures. When she got to the pictures of Ethan drinking the girl's blood her eyes went wide and she let out a little scream. When she finished looking at the pictures, Margret put the camera down on the table and shuttered.

"What is he" she asked finally.

"Honestly, I think he's a vampire," Alex said, trying to ignore the look on her face, "I know it sounds crazy, hell, I'm not sure I believe it even after everything I've seen. It's just, it would explain everything. Take the old pictures for example, how could it possibly be Ethan if he's *not* a vampire, aren't they supposed to live forever or something? The only thing I do know for sure is that he's dangerous, look what he did to those two girls in the pictures! There was blood dripping off his chin!"

"OK, calm down Alex," she said, his breathing was getting heavy again and he was getting dizzy. Alex had to force himself to calm down, the more worked up he got the worse his dizziness got.

"What happened to you" she asked.

Alex told her everything, from the conversation he overheard at lunch to hiding on the mountain, then being chased down by the giant wolves, and finally Ethan's attack when he nearly flipped the car over. Margret sat at the table looking more anxious by the second. Finally, when Alex had finished, she looked at him, her face pale and terrified.

"What are we going to tell her? I mean she's..."

They both jumped when her cell phone rang, holding up a finger she ran over and looked at the screen, "It's Nadia, hold on one sec dear" she said, Alex nodded.

"Honey, where are you" she asked. Alex heard Nadia's voice but couldn't make out what she was saying, not that he had to, the sudden look of panic on Margret's face told him enough. "No, I'd rather you came home, don't worry why, I'll tell you when you get here..."

Alex concentrated, this time hearing Nadia telling Margret to stop being silly before laughing and hanging up. Margret looked at Alex, her face was paler than before and her eyes were wide.

"She said Ethan called her, she's on her way to meet him for dinner..." Margret sank into a kitchen chair and started crying. Alex walked over and gave her a quick hug and kiss on the forehead.

"I'm on my way to get her now. I'll bring her back, I promise," he said.

"What are you going to do about Ethan? Look at your car, what's he going to do to you" she asked.

"Don't worry, I picked something up from home on my way here. Where did she say they were meeting?"

"Up at the high school" She replied softly. Margret was staring straight ahead and shaking. As Alex walked past her to the door, she grabbed his arm and looked up at him desperately.

"Bring her back. Please" then she broke down crying.

Alex gave her one final kiss on the top of her head and walked out the door. He ran to his car and tore out of the driveway. He had to get to her before Ethan found her, or those wolves.

The family curse had to end.

FIFTY

Nadia hung up the phone and shook her head laughing. Her mother could be so panicky about things. She was excited about dinner with Ethan, it was the first time *he* had called *her* to do something in months. Ethan had been even more distant than usual the last week or two, but when he called her at work, he had sounded genuinely excited about seeing her and taking her out to a nice dinner. *Maybe things are turning around for us,* she thought to herself.

Nadia drove up the long driveway of the school slowly, they still had yet to put lights along the road leaving it shrouded in darkness, and she was afraid of hitting one of the many students who walked along its length to the stores at the bottom of the hill. Luckily, there were no students on the road that night and the parking lot was empty. She pulled up to the front of the building and waited, Ethan said he'd meet her out here after he finished up filling out some college applications online in the library. She had just parked her car when her cell phone buzzed in her purse.

"Ethan? Where are you" she asked.

"Out back by the football field, helped one of the janitors carry something to the storage sheds. Meet me here" he asked.

"Be right there babe" Nadia said.

The parking lot out back was just as empty as the front, and to her surprise there were no lights on around the football field or adjoining buildings. She pulled the car over next to the field and tried to peer out into the darkness, wondering why he would be carrying anything without any light to see by. When she didn't see Ethan she parked the car and stepped outside. The night was clear, and up here away from the main town the stars blanketed the sky, Nadia looked up and caught a glimpse of a shooting star lighting a path across the sky. Smiling to herself, she closed her eyes and made a wish before walking between the gates and out onto the field.

"Ethan" she called out.

There was no answer. She walked a little further out and looked around. The stars gave off plenty of light now that her eyes had adjusted, but there was still no sign of Ethan.

"Hello" she yelled out, "Ethan?"

"Back here" Ethan finally answered.

She turned, smiling to the sound of his voice; it was coming from the bleachers. She let out a schoolgirl giggle and ran over. Ethan was standing in front of the dark space beneath the bleachers. Laughing, she shook her head at him while she walked over.

"Under the bleachers? A little cliché don't you think" her voice trailed off and laughing faded as she walked closer and saw the look on Ethan's face. He looked angry.

"Ethan, what's wrong" she asked.

Ethan shook his head at her, then from behind him Nadia heard the sound of something growling, something big.

"Ethan..." she began to say when first one large form emerged from the darkness behind Ethan, then another. Two monstrous wolves appeared on either side of Ethan, starlight reflecting from their eyes, and from their teeth. Ethan took a step forward.

"I'm sorry Nadia..." he said quietly, the two wolves matched him step for step as he approached.

Fear set in as she watched them approach. Fumbling in her pocket, Nadia brought out a can of pepper spray and pointed it at them.

"What do you want" she asked, the hand holding the spray was shaking in front of her. She took a few steps back as Ethan kept coming closer, the look on his face scaring her more than the two animals following him.

"Look, I'm just gonna go" she said backing up. Whatever he was up to, she didn't like it.

Ethan shook his head at her slowly, "I can't let you go anywhere, I'm sorry."

Nadia couldn't take it anymore; she pressed the button on the pepper spray and shot back and forth, trying to hit both Ethan and the wolves in the eyes. One of the wolves ducked, but she managed to get both the other wolf and Ethan in the eyes, the beast dropped its head with a yelp and Ethan jerked back. Using the distraction, Nadia turned and ran as fast as she could to get to the car before they knew what was happening.

Instantly, the first wolf started to chase her down, but Ethan held out his arm and stopped it. The wolf gave Ethan a quick bark and snapped at his hand but stayed in place. Nadia ran past the gate and slammed into her car, dropping the pepper spray onto the ground. She opened the car door and fumbled with her keys just long enough for Ethan to appear at the back of her car.

The two wolves suddenly appeared on either side of the car, blocking her escape. Finally, she managed to get the key in the ignition and start the car. One of the wolves jumped in front of the car just as she hit the gas but Nadia refused to slow down, forcing the wolf to jump over the car at the last second as the she tore off. Nadia looked into the rearview to see Ethan and the two wolves watching her drive away, feeling a momentary relief until she turned back to see a girl suddenly appeared less than twenty feet in front of the car. Nadia screamed and slammed the breaks, stopping just inches before hitting her.

"Delilah" Nadia said quietly.

Delilah smiled into the car as she walked over before standing in front of the hood and casually bending down. Nadia screamed as Delilah lifted the front end of the car off the ground as easily as a child picking up a toy. In a blind panic, Nadia hit the gas again, but the front tires spun a foot off the ground as Delilah held the car up in the air. Suddenly Ethan seemed to materialize outside the driver side door. He looked in at Nadia and casually opened the door before she had a chance to reach over and lock it.

"Take your foot off the gas Nadia, you're not going anywhere with the tires off the ground" Ethan said.

In her shock, she didn't realize that she was still pressing the gas down. Breathing heavily and trying not to cry, Nadia slowly let go of the gas. Ethan looked in and nodded at the keys, then reached in and shut the car off, taking the keys out and putting them in his own pocket.

"Get out of the car" he said quietly.

Delilah set the car onto the ground and Nadia slowly climbed out, falling to the ground between sobs. Ethan bent down in front of her, picking her chin up with one hand until she looked into his face. His hand was ice cold.

"Shhh..." he said, "get up, we have a lot to talk about."

Ethan lifted her off the ground like a parent picking up a baby and set her down on her feet. The two wolves closed in on either side and Delilah walked up and stood beside Ethan, putting her arm around his waist before leaning up to give him a kiss on the cheek.

"What, wha..." Nadia said, then broke down into sobs again.

She couldn't believe what was going on, everything seemed so impossible. Ethan once again put his cold hand under her chin and lifted her face to look at him. Nadia turned her eyes to Delilah and back to Ethan. He nodded, understanding the question without her having to ask.

"I believe you've already met my wife Delilah. Now like I said, it's time we had a serious talk."

FIFTY-ONE

Margret sat at her kitchen table looking through the pictures Alex had taken while sipping a cup of coffee with shaking hands. Throughout her life, she had heard stories from her parents and grand-parents while she listened unseen from the next room. It wasn't until she had become pregnant with Nadia that her parents finally gave her the family album and told their sad family history. They told her they thought it was something supernatural, that was killing the girls but they didn't dare to guess what or why. As a result Margret had kept a constant eye and near death grip on Nadia for the first eleven or so years of her life, hoping against hope that Nadia would pass the age and the family curse would fade away into memory. Now here she was, possibly looking at the very monster that had been after her family for over a century.

"Damn you" She whispered to the image in the camera.

Her thoughts were interrupted by a knock at the door. She looked at the clock, Alex had only been gone about ten minutes. Did he find Nadia on the way and stop her from going? *Probably not,* she thought to herself, *Alex wouldn't bother knocking.* Wiping the tears from her eyes, she went to the door and peeked out the window. There was a man standing there she had never met before, but he seemed familiar to her some-how. Margret cracked open the door, he smiled down at her warmly but didn't say anything.

"Can I help you" she asked after a moment's silence.

"Yes, thank you. I'm here to talk to your daughter, is she home" he asked, continuing to smile down at her.

"No, she's not home right now. Can I ask who you are and what this is about?"

"You must be her mother, Margret right," he asked. His smile remained warm and his voice was cheerful, but there was something in his eyes that made Margret nervous. She braced her foot against the bottom of the door in case he tried to push it open. "Well, it's so nice to meet you finally. I've been watching you both for quite some time now and I thought that this would be the perfect opportunity to introduce myself. My name is Sam, and I'm here to kill you and burn your house to the ground."

As he spoke, the whites of his eyes faded to black, as if they were being filled with a dark smoke, while a red flickering light started to form in the pupils of his eyes. His smile turned into a menacing grin, and before Margret could react he slammed his left hand into the door. The door shattered inward, sending Margret flying backwards into the kitchen. Her head slammed onto the edge of the table sending a blinding white pain throughout her body, and her eyes filled with blood from a large gash a flying piece of the door had opened across her forehead. The man walked through the ruined shards of the doorway and into the kitchen, reaching her in two large steps. He bent down and grabbed the back of her shirt, flipping her over and around on the floor. He took a handful of her hair and pulled her screaming to her knees.

"I'm going to ask again, where is your daughter?"

Margret tried to pull his hand out of her hair, but his grip was like iron. Margret looked at him with tear and blood soaked eyes and spit in his face, "Leave her alone" she screamed.

Still holding Margret up by the hair, he reached down and tore a strip of fabric from the front of her shirt, using it to slowly wipe the blood from his face. "Now, is that any way to treat a guest in your house" he asked darkly.

Margret struggled to break free of his grip, kicking her feet and hitting with her hands, trying to claw at his horrible eyes. He ducked back avoiding her attacks, then hit her across the face with the back of his hand. She felt the bones in her nose and jaw break, then everything went black. The man stood, dropping her to the floor and looking around. He saw the camera on the counter and picked it up, turning it over and quickly flipping through the pictures with a smile on his face.

"Now that's something interesting." He said to himself.

Eyes still flickering brighter than ever, he looked back to Margret's unconscious body sprawled on the floor. "Tsk, tsk, tsk, now that won't do." He picked her up and set her on the table face down, then snapping his fingers in front of her face and she instantly came to, no longer able to pass out from pain as his spell took over her consciousness.

"...Hut do yu ant," the words came out a jumbled mess as Margret tried to talk with a broken jaw.

He put his hand on her back, digging his fingers into her flesh as easily as someone reaching into jelly. With a quick twist of his hand, the man snapped her spine, paralyzing her from the waist down. Ignoring her screams, he casually turned and walked out the door with the camera in his hand.

"Finish it" he said as he left the house.

Through her tears, Margret saw an orange flickering light approach the house. A thick, black smoke drifted into the kitchen, rising no more than a foot off the door, it filled the room with the smell of death. Suddenly, the sounds of snarling and snapping of jaws filled the air. That's when she saw them.

The creature came through the doorway, growling and snarling at her. It was a horrifying monstrosity, made up of fire and smoke. The fire fell from its body in waves of heat, cascading to the floor like an unholy waterfall, the thick smoke covering the floor like a deadly blanket. It was as if the fire were trying to burn its way back down to hell. Drops of molten liquid dripped off its teeth and out of its mouth, falling to the floor like lava. Margret could hear sizzling as each drop hit, starting its own tiny fire and causing small glowing spots of orange and red to show through the thick smoke that refused to rise. Every sound it made, every snarl, every growl, and every bark was made from the sounds of agonized screams, the tortured cries of thousands of damned souls, all echoing from the bowls of hell with every sound the creature made.

Then it reared back and howled. Thousands of screams and cries of agony mixed together, creating its cry. Windows cracked and shattered and furniture grew frost and splintered as the temperature in the room instantly dropped. The coffee she had been drinking froze and the cup cracked while frost and ice formed as the heat was sucked out of everything the demonic howl touched. Margret could feel the heat of her body being sucked out, flowing in waves and streams, merging with the hound and intensifying its flames. She screamed as her face and hands blackened, cracking as frostbite set in instantly, but the creature didn't take enough to kill her. Suddenly, its howls stopped and the temperature in the room rose quickly as the monster started walking towards her, its feet charring black paw prints into the wooden floor of the kitchen. It looked at Margret, its eyes were a swirling mixture of reds and blacks and yellows, water from the lake of fire.

Two more creatures walked in, snapping at each other and suffocating the air with their heat. Margret tried to crawl off the table but her frostbitten hands wouldn't work and the weight of her dead legs held her in place, her body wracked with pain and helplessness. She just wanted to pass out, to be taken into the blissful mercy of unconsciousness, but the man's spell made it impossible, forcing her to witness her own gruesome death. The creatures approached, circling the table, the putrid smoke filling the room enough to rise like water filling a bowl.

She screamed for the last time as the creatures pounced, lying helpless on the table as they tore her apart piece by piece, devouring her while the house around her started to burn.

Not far from the house a figure watched helplessly from the darkness of the woods, as his frustration grew, so did the yellow light coming from his eyes. The woman was done for; there was no way around that. As much as he wanted to help, there was no way for him to defeat the three hellhounds that he knew to be there.

"Beautiful, aren't they" a quiet voice asked from behind him.

He didn't bother to turn around, he knew who it was. He heard the other man's footsteps in the leaves as he walked closer.

"Abominations," he answered in a whisper.

"Oh, now don't be like that, they serve a purpose." The other man walked up just behind the first, red light still flickering in his eyes.

"What do you want" the yellow eyed man asked.

"You know what I want" the other whispered.

"You have my answer. It hasn't changed."

"I can wait. You will need me soon enough. Your spell is breaking on him, soon you may have another enemy and need my help."

"He won't remember everything. I'll have time to influence him, bring him back to my side once more."

The red eyed man chuckled, "not this time my friend, your spell didn't just bind him and *his* memories, it bound your instincts as well. She's back again, and in front of you for years. Take that fire you see as a gesture of friendship, I can help you brother."

The yellow eyed man felt something on his shoulder, he reached up and took it. It was a camera.

As he took the camera, the red eyed man vanished, and with him the sounds of the hellhounds vanished as well. The yellow eyed man cursed into the darkness, the other was right. When they cast the binding spell, it bound some of his own instincts and abilities as well, letting her soul return undetected. He felt her now though, and that meant the binding was weakening, soon to break. He had to act fast, he would only have a couple of days of confusion, maybe a week, once the spell broke for Alex to know what he was. Once that happened, there was the chance that his true purpose could be awakened, but not without her. She was the only one who could awaken him fully.

He looked at the pictures on the camera, he could use this. In one fell swoop he would remove the threat that could awaken Alex, and bring Alex back to his side once more. He didn't like it, but it had to be done. Nadia had to die, and it had to look like she was killed by a vampire.

With the solution to his problems figured out, he relaxed. The yellow light fading from his eyes once more. He dropped the camera to the ground and crushed it under his foot before slowly walking through the woods back home, a lone figure in the darkness, lit only by the glowing ember of the cigar in his mouth.

FIFTY-TWO

Alex drove as fast as he could, the wind blowing at his face from the broken windows helped to relieve the strange dizziness that had been getting steadily worse since Nadia's. With the road occasionally blurring out when the dizziness got bad, Alex was forced to pull over twice to throw up. The only thing that kept him going was fear for Nadia, he had to get to her.

Alex pulled over a third time with his head spinning out of control. He ran a couple of steps to a small pond and ducked his head into the cold water. His anxiety for having to stop and his fear for Nadia's life were growing by the second. Alex lifted his head out of the water and screamed in frustration, slamming his fist into the cold water. Why does this have to be happening now? He stood up and took a couple of unsteady steps back to his car, tearing off down the winding road.

The water must have helped, suddenly the world stopped its spinning and Alex was able to drive through the sharp turns of the road without feeling the need to throw up. With the dizziness subsiding, he gained a little more confidence and pushed down harder on the gas. He had no idea what he was going to do when he found Nadia. He had no illusions about being able to beat both Ethan and the two wolves on his own, but he would be damned if he let anything happen to her. If he just gave her enough time to get away while they killed him he'd be happy.

Suddenly, Alex's head filled with a blinding white pain, more intense than anything he had ever experienced before. His hands gripped the wheel like he was being electrocuted, his entire body suddenly stiffened out, forcing his foot even harder down on the gas while he screamed out helplessly. The car tore forward, its wheels screeching nearly as loud as Alex's screams. He had no control over either himself or the car and the pain was too great for him to force his eyes open.

Alex never felt the split second sensation of weightlessness when his car drove off the road and dropped into a pond. With his foot still on the gas, the tires found enough purchase at the bottom of the shallow water to drive out and sink in the deeper water before the engine was drowned out. The last thing Alex felt besides the pain in his head before he blacked out was cold water rushing into the car as it quickly sank.

Finally, the car was swallowed by the pond and the night went quiet except for the last remaining air bubbles floating to the surface of the pond. Just as the last air bubble broke on the surface of the water, a bright, white light illuminated the pond from within. Suddenly, the submerged car exploded underwater with enough force to send pieces of metal and glass flying ten feet in the air above the pond's surface while everything around the pond was soaked with the water that flew fifty feet in the air in every direction.

For just a few minutes the twisted remains of the car door hung above the road in an old pine tree until the limbs could no longer support the weight. It fell onto the road with a metal clang before coming to rest on the pavement, the last unnatural sound before the night became silent once more.

End of book one

EPILOGUE

Mark pulled his old truck off the road just in front of the twisted remains of the car door. It lay across the double yellow lines of the road, that one twisted piece of metal telling him all he needed to know. The binding spell had broken.

He had known the moment it happened, his own senses, dull for the last seventy two years, were now as sharp as they had ever been. He could hear more, feel more, but most importantly, his strength was back. All of it.

The binding spell he was forced to place on his brother all those years ago had bound a large part of the abilities he had come to rely on since the beginning of the exile. True, he had done alright for himself since then, but the second the binding broke, he felt everything return in a flood of strength and sensations. He picked up the car door with one hand, the metal buckled and twisted easily in his grip. With one effortless swing of his arm, he sent it skipping across the pond like a stone, hearing it clang against a tree on the other side before bouncing back into the pond with a large splash. He smiled to himself as he took a cigar out of his pocket and lit it.

Suddenly, he heard what he had come here for. The small sound of air bubbles breaking the surface of the pond made him smile. He inhaled on the cigar as he waited, the red ash lit his face with a dull red glow with every breath. He watched as the bubbles braking the surface of the water came closer to the shore, the pupils of his eyes glowing yellow with anticipation.

Finally, a head broke the surface of the water, and in the darkness Alex walked out of the pond as easily as if he was walking up a small hill. From the center of his eyes, a white light pulsed, and in his hand he carried the lever gun Mark had given him as a graduation present. Mark took another puff of his cigar as Alex approached, seemingly oblivious to the cold water pouring off his clothes.

"What happened to me" he asked.

Mark smiled at the question, Alex didn't remember everything, and if things went right, he never would. He had to be careful though, if the memories came back, things would not go well.

"A spell brother, you were caught in a spell. It's taken me a long time but I've finally found you. You're going to need my help."

Alex closed his eyes, the white light momentarily cut off.

"I can feel her, she's returned," he opened his eyes and looked up at Mark, the white light more intense than ever, "where is she?"

Mark looked down at him, the yellow light in his own eyes suddenly matching the intensity of the white light in Alex's.

"Vampires have her. They took her to get to us, to trap you."

The light in Alex's eyes grew to a blinding intensity, lighting both Mark and the road in front of Alex up like two flashlights. He gripped the gun hard in his hand, a white light started to glow from the barrel. Then, with an enraged yell he turned and swung his other fist at a large tree, the impact shattering the wood like a stick of dynamite and sending shards flying. With a series of cracks and a loud splash, the tree hit the water and sunk, Mark looked at the shattered remains of the tree, smiling broadly before turning back to Alex.

When Alex looked back at Mark, two enormous wings had appeared on his back, seemingly out of thin air. Alex stretched them out, filling the road, every feather glowing with its own light. When Alex spoke next, Mark couldn't see his face. All he could see were the lights glowing in his eyes and wings, everything else a sea of darkness.

"Then I will kill them all."